DOUBLE
TAP

DOUBLE TAP

HANIA ALLEN

**FREIGHT
BOOKS**

First published 2015

Freight Books
49-53 Virginia Street
Glasgow, G1 1TS
www.freightbooks.co.uk

A CIP catalogue reference for this book is available from the British Library

ISBN 978-1-910449-00-4
eISBN 978-1-910449-01-1

Typeset by Freight in Garamond
Printed and bound by Bell and Bain, Glasgow

the publisher acknowledges investment from
Creative Scotland toward the publication of this book

Hania Allen was born in Liverpool, and has worked as a researcher, a maths teacher, an IT support officer and finally in information management at the University of St Andrews. Her first novel, *Jack in the Box,* was published by Freight in 2014. *Double Tap* is the second in the Von Valenti series.

She lives in a fishing village in Fife.

Chapter 1
Tuesday, June 5th, 2001

He dropped the weapon and slumped against the rail. God, his body ached; even sucking air into his lungs made his chest burn. The soft June wind set up a murmuring in the trees, urging him to close his eyes and let the sound lull him to sleep, but this was no time to stop. When you reached the bridge, you didn't have far to go and, anyway, he'd promised the others he'd make it.

It hadn't been such a good idea, though, running through the woods on an empty stomach: there was lightness in his head and the stitch in his side was growing worse. He stumbled forward, but tripped on a loose board and fell sprawling. The sound disturbed a squirrel, which shot out from the bushes in a rush of indignation and ran up along the branches towards a sky threaded with white. The effort of keeping his head back to follow the bobbing grey tail made him dizzy and, disregarding what he'd learnt in training, he loosened the neck straps and removed the face guard. The air smelt of earth and grass, and he inhaled deeply, ignoring the pain in his lungs. There was a sudden buzzing in his ears, but he couldn't tell if it was real or the sound of insects skating over the water.

It was then that he heard it, a noise both unfamiliar and unexpected. A flock of crows burst into the air, wheeling and cawing before reforming to fly east. He staggered to his feet. And he heard it again. Closer now. Close enough that there was no mistaking the sound. His heart lurched with shock.

He ran a trembling hand over his mouth, and looked

around desperately. If he hadn't glanced back along the bridge, he'd never have seen the man, never have seen what he had in his hands.

The ground seemed to rush away, so strong was his fear. He bolted into the wood, searching frantically for the path. On the other side of the field, there was the farmhouse, with an entrance into the tunnels. But that meant breaking cover. A quick calculation told him the man would be at the boundary fence long before he reached the farm. It wasn't worth the risk.

The bushes were thick in this part of the wood and might deter a pursuer. He dropped into a crouch and rolled into the shrubs. Ignoring the gorse scratching at his face, he crawled on his belly until he found a small clearing. Then, lying on his back, the damp leaf-rot smell filling his nostrils, he paddled furiously with his hands and covered himself with soil and leaves.

Seconds later, he heard the pained creak of wood as someone stepped onto the bridge.

He stared into the clouds, praying that whoever it was would keep to the path and pass him by. Maybe the man would cross the field, giving him a chance to steal back through the trees and reach the safety of the road. He listened, his heart galloping. The footsteps were coming closer. Then they stopped. For one delirious moment, he thought he heard them recede. He counted to twenty and raised his head. The man was standing a short distance away, scanning the landscape, his back turned.

He fell back, his mind unravelling. Had the man heard him move?

There was a tentative rustling, and then a crashing as something thundered through the undergrowth. Another second and it would be over. He tried to scream out his name, shout to the world that everything was wrong, that this shouldn't be happening, but his throat closed in on the words. Reason told him he had a chance if he crept further into the thicket.

Instinct told him he'd never make it. Panic overwhelmed him. He sprang to his feet and charged into the field, windmilling his arms furiously.

The first shot struck him between the shoulder blades. Strangely, there was no pain, just a sharp blow as though someone had clapped him on the back. Numbness spread through his body, his legs buckled, and the sky tilted wildly around him.

A large shape blotted out the light.

Sweet Jesus, it couldn't end like this, it was a mistake, he had to tell him that, had to make him understand. He gazed into the pitiless eyes, moving his lips, but the words refused to come. In desperation, he turned onto his belly and, clawing at the earth, tried to drag his body along the ground.

With the second shot, a light exploded in his brain, flooding his world with an unremitting, beating agony. And then there was nothing, and more nothing, and all he'd ever known was that unbounded shimmering blackness.

Chapter 2

Von Valenti glanced at her watch. Her client was late. Or perhaps it was she who was early. It was a habit of hers to come well in advance when meeting clients for the first time, especially in a public place. It gave her the opportunity to observe their approach. How they held themselves, their facial expression (or lack of it), and what they'd chosen to wear told her more about their state of mind than anything else. Once they met, the guard came down like a visor, and she had to work hard to prise it open to discover what they were hiding.

She let her clients choose the locations of their meetings. That, too, told her something. On the grassy mound behind her was the façade of the Greek temple known as 'Edinburgh's Disgrace', all that had been built by architect William Playfair before funds ran dry. Below it was the jumble of buildings making up the Observatory and, opposite, the sooty circular tower of Nelson's Monument. Calton Hill was a public place but it was clear why the client had requested they meet here: although it was lunchtime, there wasn't a living soul about.

She stifled a yawn. The baby had kept them both awake last night with her incessant crying. This couldn't go on much longer. She was sleeping through her work and people had started to notice. And her anxiety attacks, which she thought she'd left behind in London, had returned.

She'd chosen to wait at the Dugald Stewart Monument, a huge stone urn imprisoned in a cage of fluted columns, because it afforded a view of the steps from Waterloo Place, steps which the client would climb as the quickest route to Calton Hill. Across Regent Road, the gravestones of Old Calton Burial Ground clung to the grassy slope. Any steeper, and the grimy stones would come tumbling into the street. Behind the cemetery, the dull blue and white arches of North Bridge flashed suddenly as the sun emerged from behind the clouds.

She saw the woman long before the woman saw her. Shoulders slumped, she was trudging up Regent Walk, stopping now and again to catch her breath. Her grey hair was scraped back into a wispy ponytail and a sudden fierce gust lifted it and blew it about her head. Seeing Von, she raised a hand, setting her face into a tired smile.

Von smiled back, waving a hand in acknowledgment, her smile fading as the woman reached her. The softened jawline suggested she was in her mid-to-late fifties, although her complexion was that of someone half her age, and she carried with her the reek of a lifetime spent putting others first.

She was panting from the climb. 'Miss Valenti?' she said, dropping her large tote bag. The wind blasted her denim jacket open, giving Von a view of the pink cotton cardigan.

'You must be Mrs Pattullo,' she said gently, taking in the red-rimmed eyes.

Relief flooded the woman's face. 'I wasn't sure you'd be here. It's me own fault, like, I couldn't remember what time we'd agreed.' Her voice was shrill, the accent, Liverpudlian. 'I knew we'd get a bit of privacy here. It's quite a way, though, going the long way round, but I couldn't make it up them steps, not with me asthma. I'm sorry I suggested this spot now.'

'I can give you a lift back to work if you like.'

'Oh, there's no problem going down steps. It's going up them that I can't do.' Her eyes drifted to Princes Street. The city centre was heaving with local shoppers and the ever-present

5

tourists and, from Calton Hill, it was impossible to distinguish which was which.

'Where do you work?' Von said lightly, wanting to keep the conversation on safe ground for a little longer. Once they moved to the reason for the meeting, there'd be no going back.

'The Balmoral. You probably know it, that big hotel by Waverley station.' She stared hollow-eyed at the ornate grey stone building, its saltire flapping wildly on the clock tower. 'I'm a chef, Miss Valenti,' she added, her voice quivering.

'Is it interesting work?'

'Yes, but it's manic most of the time. Hotel kitchens always are.' The woman glanced around. 'I need to sit down. I'm feeling a bit faint.'

Von was on the point of suggesting they go to a café on Princes Street, but her boss at Swankie and Vale Professional Investigators had made it clear that this client needed special handling, and Calton Hill had been her choice. 'How about over there?' she said, indicating the benches in front of the Observatory.

Mrs Pattullo picked up her bag, and they took the path beside the flowering broom bushes and up past the Portuguese cannon. The strengthening wind plucked at their clothes.

The woman turned her clear-eyed gaze on Von. 'You're not from round here, Miss Valenti. That's a London accent.'

Von smiled to herself. She was being checked out. But she'd be doing the same if the situation were reversed. 'I grew up in the east end.'

'I lived in London for many years. Moved from Knotty Ash to make me fortune. I didn't, as things turned out. But I loved the place. What made you leave?'

'My daughter. She had her first child three months ago. Up here.' She hesitated, unsure how much to probe. The wrong question and the case would fold like a house of cards. 'So what made you leave, Mrs Pattullo?'

'I got married.' The light vanished from the woman's eyes. 'To a Scotsman who likes his drink.'

Von glanced at the bruises on Mrs Pattullo's neck. No wonder the woman hadn't wanted them meeting at her house. Silently, she reached across and covered Mrs Pattullo's hand with hers, imagining the inebriated husband sneering at his wife, losing it and lashing out in front of a stranger.

'I haven't long, Miss Valenti. I think your agency's told you what this is about.' She played with her hands. 'Me son's gone missing.'

Von was relieved she hadn't had to broach the subject. It was one of the first things she'd learnt: don't rush it, make small talk and wait for the client to raise the issue. 'When did you see him last?'

'Ten days ago. May 24th. I keep a diary of when me and Phil meet. It helps me keep track, like.'

Von looked hard at her. Why would a woman keep a diary of her son's visits? 'Tell me about Phil,' she said, injecting a note of encouragement into her voice. 'What's he like?' She was careful to use the present tense: if she was going to learn anything useful, his mother would have to believe her son was alive.

The transformation was immediate. Mrs Pattullo's face glowed with maternal pride. 'Oh, he's such a love. When he was little, he was a bit of a scamp, but they all are at that age, aren't they? Used to play football indoors. Dead good, he was, but he drove me round the twist. You'll like him when you meet him, Miss Valenti, you really will.'

It no longer surprised Von how few people could describe their children in a way that was helpful. 'And you see each other often?'

'Every couple of days. Always in the same place, like. Which is why, when he wasn't there, I became worried.'

'And where is this place?'

'Princes Street Gardens. By the bandstand. Easy for me to get there in me lunch hour.'

'So how old is he?'

'Twenty-five next month.' A note of excitement crept into her voice. 'I'm planning something special for his birthday. A big party with a fancy cake. He can invite them friends of his.'

The way she was talking, Phil could have been five, not twenty-five. 'Does he have many friends?'

'Oh, dozens. They live with him.'

Dozens? And they *lived* with him? 'Where?' Von said slowly.

'Everywhere. They move around. Didn't I tell you? He's homeless.'

Von drew in her breath. A homeless person who moved around Edinburgh, missing for ten days. If it were up to her, she'd have made her gentle excuses by now. But it wasn't up to her: Swankie and Vale never turned down cases, however hopeless they might seem. She kept her tone matter-of-fact. 'And his friends are . . . ?'

'Homeless too.' The woman said it as if it were the most natural thing.

Von didn't ask why Phil Pattullo wasn't living with his parents: now the dam had burst, his mother seemed incapable of stopping.

'He has lots of places where he sleeps. Goes all over Edinburgh. Can't think of an area he hasn't been to. He needs to move around, you see. Says it's safer that way. Not everyone takes kindly to having the homeless on their doorstep. Sometimes he's in hostels or B&Bs. But lately, he's been sleeping in Princes Street Gardens.'

'Any particular reason?'

'To be with his friends. Some of them have dogs, like, and they can't get a room if they have animals. Just as well it's warm now summer's here.'

Von ran a hand through her hair. Princes Street Gardens. That was something at least, a place to start. Phil Pattullo's friends might provide her with a solid lead. But surely his mother had thought of this? 'Mrs Pattullo, when he didn't show, did you talk to his friends? See if they knew where he was?'

The woman played with the buttons of her jacket. 'No-one could tell me anything.'

'Do you know the names of any of these friends?'

'He talks about a judy called Mhairi.' She gazed at Von without blinking. 'I bring him food every couple of days, but he gives most of it away. He's like that, you see. Has a heart as big as Buckingham Palace. I scold him about it, and he denies it, but I can tell. And he's losing weight.' She fished in her bag. 'This is what he looked like a year ago.'

The photograph, taken from the waist up, was of a young man in his late twenties. He had silky blond hair, combed back from his forehead and hanging over his shoulders. His face was blurred, as though he'd moved his head at the last minute.

'He's not like that now,' Mrs Pattullo was saying. 'That stomach's gone. He's thin as a rake. And he wouldn't be if he ate what I brought him. The Balmoral does a good cuisine. You ever eaten there, Miss Valenti?'

'Once or twice. Is this the most recent photo you have of him?'

'The only other ones are of him as a child. He didn't like being photographed.'

'Because he was overweight?'

'He wasn't overweight,' Mrs Pattullo snapped.

Brilliant. Now she'd antagonised the woman. 'I just meant that he doesn't look like a rake in this picture.'

'When he lived with us, I always gave him second helpings.'

It was the perfect segue. 'And that was a year ago, you said?'

Mrs Pattullo nodded silently.

'So what made him leave home?'

'Well, first he jacked in his job. Said it was turning his brain to mince. He worked in a solicitor's office. Wasn't a solicitor himself, like, I think he helped prepare papers or something.' Her expression hardened. 'He was earning more than Duncan.'

'Your husband?'

'And that was what caused the problems between Duncan and me.' She shrugged as though domestic abuse were to be expected in marriage. 'Anyway, Phil legged it a few weeks later.'

'Because of what was happening between you and your husband?'

Her eyes grew vacant. 'He told me he saw angels.'

'Angels?'

'The minute he opened his eyes in the morning. They were everywhere. In his room, in the house, in the garden. When he went out, they were on the streets and in shop doorways.' Her breathing grew shallow. 'He was terrified of them. I asked him what they looked like but he couldn't describe them. He painted them instead. Did hundreds of paintings. He destroyed most of them before he left home, but I managed to save one or two.' She delved into her bag and produced a sheaf of papers. But instead of handing them to Von, she rolled them up and laid them on her lap. 'In order to survive, like, he had to develop a system. He'd walk past them without looking into their faces.' Her voice became detached. 'Then, one day, they spoke to him.'

Von stared straight ahead, her throat tightening.

'They told him to live simply. So he walked out of the house. He tried to come back once, but' – the colour leached from her face – 'it was too terrible. The way he kept slapping his head. And, oh God, the screaming. The neighbours were all for calling the bizzies. As long as he lived rough, he said he didn't see them.' Her head drooped. 'You understand now why

I can't have him live at home, Miss Valenti. I'm not a bad mam, like. The best I can do for him is bring him his food. He's quite happy now. That's what counts, isn't it?'

'Have you thought of taking him to a doctor?'

'Whatever for? There's nothing wrong with him.'

The woman was in denial.

'Does Phil have any defining features such as tattoos or piercings? Or scars?' Von said,

'Nothing like that.'

'Birthmarks?'

'No birthmarks.'

'And there was nothing different about him when you saw him the last time, on May 24th? He wasn't worried about anything?'

'He was happier than I've seen him for ages.' She clutched the roll of paintings to her chest.

'May I keep the photo?'

The woman's eyes were full. 'It's me only one . . .'

'I'll return it to you once I've found him.' She hesitated. 'Is there anything you'd like to ask me, Mrs Pattullo? You know our rates?' This was the part she hated, having to talk money with a grieving client.

'I went through them figures with your firm. They explained everything.'

'Your husband doesn't know you've engaged a professional investigator, does he?'

'He's washed his hands of his son. It's a terrible thing, Miss Valenti, when parents turn their backs on their children.'

Von looked away before the woman could see the expression in her eyes. She wondered what Mrs Pattullo would think if she knew that she herself had left her baby daughter to be brought up by grandparents, while she forged a career as a detective in the Metropolitan Police.

'I need to get back,' Mrs Pattullo said. 'We've a big do on tonight. A thousand vol-au-vents don't prepare themselves.' She got to her feet. 'So what happens next? Do you get in touch, like, or should I phone you?'

Von stood up. 'Contact me if you think of anything that'll help. It doesn't matter how small. Otherwise, I'll be in touch when I have something.' Seeing the raw grief on the woman's face, she added quickly, 'I hope it won't be too long. One last thing, Mrs Pattullo. When you discovered that Phil was missing, did you go to the police?'

'The bizzies weren't interested. They took a note of his details but that was all.' She held out her hand. The nails were bitten to the quick. 'Thank you, Miss Valenti.'

Von took the hand and squeezed it, wondering not for the first time what had possessed her to take a job as a professional investigator. There were other ways to make a living.

The woman turned away, hunching her shoulders against the wind. Von watched her go, imagining the inevitable meeting in the not-too-distant future when she would have to tell her that her son had vanished without trace. As a former police officer who once ran murder cases, she was used to breaking bad news to hysterical relatives. But telling a mother that her son was dead was one thing. Telling her they'd been unable to find him was another.

She picked up her shoulder bag, seeing only then that the woman had slipped the bundle of paintings through the handles. She unrolled them slowly.

They were watercolours and, as far as she could tell, not badly executed. But if this was what Phil Pattullo was seeing, she could understand why his life had turned to ash. If she half closed her eyes, the angels seemed benevolent enough, their wings extended, their hands folded in prayer. But a closer look belied their attitude of holiness. Their faces were like Phil's in the photograph, blurred beyond recognition. Except for the eyes. They stared out remorselessly, searing themselves into her consciousness. She felt a cold hand touch her heart. What had happened to Phil that such horror had entered his life? She flicked through the paintings, studying them for clues as to what could be going on in his head. With a sigh of frustration, she rolled them up and stuffed them into her bag.

She took the long way back to Regent Road, following the winding path down the hill. The knot in her stomach tightened as she thought of Mrs Pattullo, a woman who had a husband handy with his fists. And a son who had abandoned her to live on the streets. A son, missing in a vast crowded city. If she'd been a betting woman, she knew where she'd have put her money. She leant against the railing for a moment, pulling her jacket tight against the chill breeze. A sense of helplessness descended like a cage. What was the likelihood she'd find Phil, let alone find him alive?

Chapter 3

DI Steve English had the radio to his ear and was trying to listen through the crackle. He could see his colleague watching him in the rear-view mirror. DS Fergus Harry, a dark-haired man with high cheekbones and a boyish smile that drove women crazy, would guess what the call meant: a diversion to a crime scene.

'Change of plan,' Steve said, replacing the handset. 'We're going to Bonnington. Know it?' The question was unnecessary. Fergus, recently recruited to Lothian and Borders, and young enough not to have developed a cynicism for police work, had a knowledge of Edinburgh and its surroundings that was close to encyclopedic.

'Quickest way is to head out on the A71 towards Livingston, sir. Where in Bonnington in particular?'

'Ever heard of The Paradise World of Paintballing?' He caught the raised eyebrow. 'Aye, well, neither have I. You'll see it before we get to the town.'

'Righto, sir.'

As they drove along Dalry Road, Steve stared out of the window, wondering what had made him accept the secondment from Strathclyde Police to Lothian and Borders. His mates at Glasgow's Pitt Street headquarters had crowed with laughter when they learnt he was moving to Edinburgh. Itchy feet was the official reason, and one he'd been quick to promote, yet that wasn't it. Despite his best efforts, he'd been unable to fit back into police work in Glasgow. He'd thought, after his time with the sassenachs in London, that it would be the easiest thing in the world to return home. He'd given Pitt Street his best shot, taken the dirt thrown at him without complaining, but he'd rapidly come to sense an unevenness in the way he was treated. His DCI had made him feel as welcome as bum boils, giving him a hard time along with the hard cases. As Steve soon discovered, the man had tried for a job at the Metropolitan Police and had been turned down. He knew that Steve had had a successful career there. Aye, sour grapes simply wasn't in it.

He'd made the right decision, though, Edinburgh would be good for him. And there were more lassies in the nicks here. He'd seen them gawping at him, and caught the phrase, 'looks like a young Mel Gibson'. He snorted. Young. He was in his early forties. Was that young these days? He caught Fergus watching him and realised he'd been mumbling to himself. That was a habit he had to break. He resumed his examination of the city's buildings.

The houses thinned as Gorgie Road gave way to Calder Road, and they crossed the Edinburgh bypass, the buildings yielding to quilted fields turning brown in the drought. The car sped down a road edged with high bushes that drooped in the hot afternoon. Steve wound down the window and stared into the immense sky. Och, you could say what you liked about the weather but, on a day like this, there was no better place than the Edinburgh countryside. Except perhaps Glasgow. He smiled to himself. He might be living in Auld Reekie, but he was, and always would be, a Weegie.

'Nearly there,' Fergus said, turning off at the Bonnington sign. 'So what's the job, sir? A paintballing accident?'

Steve dragged his eyes from the landscape. 'The owner thinks so. We'll find out soon enough.'

Minutes later, they saw the billboard with The Paradise World of Paintballing in large blue letters. A high gate led onto a well-maintained road and, after several hundred yards, they pulled up at a squat concrete building. There were two cars outside, a silver two-door Maserati, and a light-blue Ascari. Fergus cut the engine. Protocol demanded he open the door for a senior officer, but Steve was already out of the car.

He winced as he put his weight on his right leg. The gunshot wound, sustained on duty a few months earlier, hadn't healed properly, and he walked with a pronounced limp.

He instructed Fergus to stay outside and watch for visitors, and pulled open the glass door.

The entrance gave onto a small room, unfurnished except for a chair on which lay a neatly folded copy of The Scotsman. To left and right were closed doors. Directly ahead was a door that was ajar, giving a glimpse into the corridor beyond.

His first thought was that Fergus had missed a turning: the place was deserted and there was no indication that this was a club's reception. There must be another building somewhere. He was about to place a call to the police station when the door on the right opened. A well-built man in his twenties, wearing a combat-style camouflage jumpsuit and yellow kerchief round his neck, stood staring at him.

Steve's initial reaction was one of shock. The man's clothes were covered in blood. There was even blood in his hair. But then he realised his mistake: the acrid odour of fresh paint reached his nostrils as the man came towards him.

'Mr Ranald McCrea?'

'Yes.' The man's brow furrowed. 'Who the hell are you?'

Steve drew out his warrant card. 'Detective Inspector Steve English. Lothian and Borders Police.'

'I expected several officers.'

He didn't like the colour of the lad's face. The complexion was like cheese. 'I was in the neighbourhood, Mr McCrea. I got the call.'

'Well, thank God you came quickly, Inspector.'

'Can you tell me what this is about?'

'There's been an accident. Although . . . ' He seemed reluctant to continue.

Steve looked into the clear blue eyes. 'Mr McCrea, you put in a 999 call.'

'He's out near the woodland.'

'You were the one who found him?'

'Yes. He's Jamie Dyer, a friend of mine.' Beads of sweat stood on his brow. 'His eyes are open. He looks dead. I suppose it must have been a heart attack . . . '

'You didn't disturb the scene, did you? Or move him?'

High spots of colour appeared on McCrea's cheeks. The effect against the paleness of his skin was grotesque. 'I'm not a fool, Inspector,' he said through clenched teeth. 'I know about contaminated crime scenes. And I've not changed out of my clothes or taken a shower.'

Steve's eyes moved over McCrea's face. Interesting how the lad was quick to say it was a crime scene when, a second earlier, he'd been talking about a heart attack. 'You'll need to show me where he is, Mr McCrea.' They had to hurry. If there'd indeed been a crime, the first sixty minutes were crucial.

'It's not far, I can point it out on the map.'

Steve took in the lad's paint-spattered brown hair and the frown lines in his jutting forehead. And the desperation in his eyes. Aye, he didn't want to go out again. 'By all means show me the spot on the map, Mr McCrea, but I'll need you to come at least part of the way with me.'

The man's shoulders drooped. He gestured to Steve to follow him.

McCrea's office was a model of tidiness: no papers on the large desk, just an Apple Mac, a printer, and a silver-framed photograph of an elderly man. On the wall opposite the window, there was a large map. Steve recognised the Bonnington road on the left.

'This fence marks the club's boundary,' McCrea said. He indicated a point on the bottom left-hand corner. 'This is the gate you came in by.'

'And where did you find Mr Dyer?'

'He's lying in this field here. He'd nearly made it. He was heading for the building behind the one we're in. We call it the farmhouse, although it's nothing more than a dilapidated barn. Once you reach the farmhouse, that's the end of the game.'

Steve had seen the terrain from the Bonnington road. The landscape was mostly trees and bushes, with little open country, ideal for playing hide-and-seek. 'What's the quickest way there?'

'There aren't any roads, just a few paths, so you can't drive.'

He had no protective footgear with him and would have to be careful where he trod. But this year's unprecedented drought should work in his favour, and the ground would at least be dry. 'Let's go, Mr McCrea.'

They exited by the front door. McCrea turned sharp right and led Steve to the back of the building. A few yards away was a large wooden construction. 'That's the farmhouse, Inspector. Behind it is the field. You can't miss Jamie. He's right at the end, as you reach those bushes.'

'And you're sure it's Jamie Dyer?'

'Absolutely.'

He considered the lad's glazed eyes, the face coated with perspiration, and felt suddenly ashamed he'd made him come out. Without a word, he flicked open his mobile.

Fergus arrived quickly, stopping short as he caught sight of McCrea.

'It's okay, Fergus, it's paint. Can you stay here with Mr McCrea? I won't be long.' He set off in the direction of the farmhouse.

The wooden A-framed building was solid enough, although one or two planks were missing from the front wall, and the huge door was secured with a rusty padlock. McCrea was right. It was more of an outhouse than a dwelling.

Behind the building was a large field, the brown-wilted grass giving way to clover. In the distance, a mass of flowering shrubs smeared the field's edge with yellow. Further still, there was a wood.

He hurried across the field, taking care where he put his feet. The uneven ground and thick grass made the going difficult, and he soon found himself sweating into his clothes. He tried to imagine running across this terrain, and failed. His leg injury had made him give up football, a passion of his since childhood and, to keep fit, he'd tried weightlifting but hadn't taken to it. He was out of condition, he didn't need his shortness of breath to tell him that. Aye well, it was his own fault for letting his gym membership lapse.

The body was so well camouflaged that he nearly tripped over it. He fumbled for his gloves, taking in the scene, automatically making mental notes.

A young man in his early thirties was lying on his back. His hair was cropped close so it was impossible to tell the colour, but Steve guessed fair to light brown given the shade of the eyebrows and lashes. The eyes were open and stared in a frenzy of terror out of a startlingly white face. The jumpsuit was identical to Ranald McCrea's but was almost unmarked. He knelt and brought his face close to the body. The same pungent paint smell, although much fainter than on McCrea. He placed two fingers under the man's chin. The skin was clammy but not cold. There was no pulse.

A sharp noise from the wood made him look up. He felt his skin prickle. 'Who's there?' he shouted into the trees, his voice suddenly hoarse. There was no reply. He stood up slowly.

Were there foxes in the wood? Aye, probably. Foxes were taking over the country. Just what they needed, a carnivorous animal in the vicinity of a corpse. He scanned the bushes, his breathing soft. Nothing moved within the mass of broom. Nothing was audible but the humming of the bees above the yellow.

He crouched over the body. It was clear what had happened: Ranald McCrea and Jamie Dyer had been out having a game of paintball and, now, Jamie Dyer was dead. But how? Could a well-aimed paintball kill? He doubted it. Something else had ended Jamie Dyer's life, yet there were no obvious marks, no bruises, no evidence of knifing. He examined the body for bullet wounds but found none. Could Jamie Dyer have died of natural causes, as Ranald McCrea suspected? He looked at the face. No, this wasn't a heart attack, he'd seen faces of heart-attack victims. That look of horror came from somewhere else.

He was tempted to turn the body over, but knew better. He'd have to wait until the Senior Investigating Officer arrived.

Something caught his eye, a darkening of the ground beneath the body. Darker than a mere shadow. Taking care not to disturb the corpse, he lay on his front and put his head at the level of Jamie Dyer's. He stared for several seconds. Then, wriggling slowly, he worked his way down the body, flattening the grass around the corpse with his fingers. Comprehension finally dawned.

Jamie Dyer had not died of natural causes – the ground beneath his shoulders was slick with blood. The stench, masking the sweet scent of clover, filled his nostrils.

Despite his years as a police officer, he could still be surprised at how much blood leaks from a body after the heart stops pumping.

Chapter 4

'Can you tell me precisely what happened, Mr McCrea?' Steve said, keeping his eye attentively on the other man. 'Start from the beginning, please.'

They were back in McCrea's office. Fergus had been sent to direct the Scenes Of Crime Officers to the field where Jamie Dyer's body lay.

McCrea had changed into a dark-brown suit. It was a long moment before he spoke. When he did, he tripped over the words, as though he had something he needed to get off his chest. 'The three of us were testing new equipment from a specialist American firm.'

Steve's head shot up from his writing. '*Three* of you?'

'Myself, Jamie, and Jamie's sister, Lexie. Lexie Dyer.'

'And where is Miss Dyer now?'

'Gone back to work.'

He felt his anger rising. 'You let her leave what you yourself said may be a crime scene?'

McCrea raised his arms and let them drop. 'Lexie couldn't stay for more than half an hour. She had some meeting or other. She left before the game finished.' He swallowed noisily. 'I didn't realise anything had happened to Jamie till after she'd gone.'

'I'll need Miss Dyer's details.'

'She works at Bayne Pharmaceuticals. In Livingston.'

Steve's eyes drilled into McCrea's. 'So the three of you were having a knockabout? Is that it?'

'We were giving the new markers a try. There's a tournament a week on Saturday.'

'So, what did you do? Exactly.'

'How much do you know about paintballing, Inspector?'

'Next to nothing.'

'There are different ways you can play. What we were playing is called woodland paintball, the Americans call it woodsball. You play outside in natural landscape. It's our preferred game.'

'And where were you playing today?' He nodded at the wall. 'Can you show me?'

McCrea got to his feet. 'When we're just having a knockabout, we use this area here.' He tapped at the map. 'We go out one at a time, in five-minute intervals, from the back door of the main building.'

'This building we're in?'

He nodded. 'We play in the woods usually for about an hour, then we go over this bridge and through the bushes, across the field to the farmhouse, and finish at the back door.'

The route they took was a large circle, starting and ending at the main building. 'What time did the game begin?'

'We got here at twelve-thirty. We were ready to start about fifteen minutes later.'

'And you were definitely the only people playing?'

'Yes. I went first, then Lexie, and finally Jamie.'

'So Miss Dyer left the game after half an hour, you and Jamie continued to play, then you returned.'

'That's right.'

Steve raised an eyebrow. 'But without Jamie.'

'You've seen the extent of our woodland. He could have been anywhere. He's a good player,' McCrea added with a cold smile. 'He keeps himself well hidden when he wants to.'

'When did you realise something might have happened to him?'

'When he didn't come back. I checked his locker. It was still locked. I waited a bit, then I became worried.'

'So you went looking for him?'

McCrea's lips twisted. 'Christ, poor Jamie.' He ran a hand over his eyes. 'Was it natural causes, Inspector? Can you tell?'

'The pathologists are examining him now, but his death looks suspicious. It's why we took your clothes and swabbed your hands. It's just as well you didn't wash. A firearm discharge residue test has to be done quickly.'

'So that's what the test was.' He seemed to appreciate the significance of Steve's words. 'You're saying Jamie was shot?'

'He may have been.'

'And the fact that you tested me for residue means I'm a suspect?' he said nervously.

'You need to see this from our point of view, Mr McCrea. You were the last person to see Jamie Dyer alive. I'll need your contact details as well as the name and address of the club's owner.'

'I'm the owner.' He removed a card from his pocket. 'This has my address and my numbers.'

The lad seemed young for an entrepreneur. Steve glanced at the card. 'You work at Bayne Pharmaceuticals too, I see.'

'Most of Bayne's are members of my club.' He smiled faintly. 'It's a private club, really. I decide who joins.'

'I couldn't help noticing security is a bit on the lax side here.'

'How do you mean?'

'No-one on reception.'

He shrugged. 'If members want to play, they arrange matches between themselves and they book them on the club's database. Everyone has a key to the front and back doors. They come and go as they please.' The corners of his mouth lifted. 'You look surprised.'

'Is that how it's usually done?'

'Not in most paintballing clubs. But, as I said, I run this club for my own convenience.'

'So, how does it work, once players arrive?'

'They change in the locker rooms.'

The locker rooms, the showers, and the equipment room led off the main corridor. Steve had accompanied McCrea to the men's locker room when he changed out of his clothes. The man had pointed out Jamie's locker, still secured, the key missing.

'I notice the lockers are coin-operated, Mr McCrea.'

'Yes, you wear the key round your wrist, like in swimming clubs.'

'I take it there's no master key?'

'I'm afraid not.' He seemed distracted. 'If someone loses a key, and it does happen from time to time, we have to take the hinges off.'

'And after you change, what happens?'

'You pick up your gear as you go out. There's a door at the back that takes you outside.' He chewed his lip. 'Inspector, Lexie won't know that her brother ... '

'That's all right, Mr McCrea. One of my officers will handle all that.' Steve watched the passage of emotions on the man's face. Aye, the lad had had a shock, and no mistake. He was bearing up well, all things considered. 'Do you happen to know who Jamie Dyer's next of kin is?'

'Their parents have passed on,' McCrea said vaguely. 'Lexie can tell you.'

'And did Jamie also work at Bayne Pharmaceuticals?'

'He works in Bayne's Glasgow branch. In the manufacturing plant.'

'Bit of a long way to come for paintballing? There are clubs in Glasgow.'

'As I said, Inspector, we're having a tournament soon and we needed to test new equipment from a specialist American firm.

Jamie was playing in that tournament. He was very competitive. He wouldn't pass up the chance to try out new kit if he thought it could give him the edge in a match.'

'Can you think of anyone who'd want to kill him?'

'No, Inspector. And that's the truth.'

Interesting comment. As though the rest were lies. 'One last question, Mr McCrea. Apart from yourself and Miss Dyer, who else knew that Jamie would be here today?'

A look of understanding crossed the other man's face. 'I really don't know. Jamie may have told any number of people, work colleagues, club members at Bayne's. He must have informed them at Glasgow that he'd be away.'

Steve closed his notebook. 'Well, I think that's all for the moment. We'll need you to come down to the police station and give a formal statement.'

'Now?'

'It's best. While it's fresh in your mind. I'll make sure someone brings you back to fetch your car. I take it the Maserati's yours?'

'It belongs to Jamie. Mine's the Ascari.' He sighed in irritation. 'Can I at least ring Bayne's and tell them I won't be at work this afternoon?'

'We'll do that, Mr McCrea.'

Steve watched a constable take McCrea out to the police car. He drummed his fingers on his lips. The man had had a shock right enough, but his answers didn't ring true. He was lying about something or, at best, was not telling the police everything.

Steve pulled on his gloves, and took the door to the corridor.

He paused. Something felt wrong. Something about the crime scene. And a crime it definitely was now. There was no doubt that Jamie Dyer had been murdered. That look in his eyes. And that blood. The murder weapon was missing, although that wasn't unusual; murder weapons were rarely abandoned at crime scenes. Yet there was something else. Something he couldn't put his finger on. He let it go. Experience told him it would come to him if he didn't keep thinking about it.

The equipment room was at the end of the corridor, past the locker rooms.

He'd been paintballing only once. The Chief Super at Pitt Street had organised a game, thinking his staff needed team-building, and haring around shooting each other with paint-filled balls would do it. His colleagues, the women in particular, had run around like demented creatures, splattering each other as though they were in a video game. Having recently been shot, he found he couldn't bring himself to play. After a decent interval, making sure he got himself marked with paint (honour was at stake here), he limped off the field. Now, in this place, he was reminded of the game and its aftermath: the drubbing he got from the Chief Super, a man not known for his sensitivity.

Serious money had been pumped into this club. The equipment room, which ran the width of the building, contained several racks of the same type of camouflage jumpsuits with integrated ammunition belts worn by both Ranald McCrea and Jamie Dyer. Steve fingered a suit, not surprised to find it padded; he could still remember the sting of a paintball striking at close range. Next to the racks, there was a large container for the masks. These had built-in fog-free goggles and were the type that cover the face from hairline to chin, leaving the top and most of the back of the head exposed. On the walls were the shelves for the guns, which he knew were called markers and, at the far end of the room, hundreds of paintball cylinder containers were stacked in cardboard boxes next to a metal stand holding the small compressed air tanks. The strong smell of paint was everywhere, despite the open back door. He glanced out, seeing the farmhouse only yards away.

The niggling feeling he'd pushed from his mind had

returned. Until he discovered what was behind it, he wasn't leaving the site. Von would have known immediately, of course: she had a knack for detail, and the bulldog tenacity to use it to her advantage. But Von wasn't here.

He looked at the open door, then at the equipment. What had McCrea said? You change, then pick up your gear on the way out. Of course. It was staring him in the face.

Jamie Dyer wasn't wearing a mask. Nor did he have a marker. So where were they?

Chapter 5

Princes Street in the early afternoon on a June day was not somewhere Von would have been from choice. Far too many people pushing their way as though the sale of the century had been announced. Yet, in all the months she'd spent in this city, she'd never known a day when Princes Street was quiet.

When she was a girl, her Dad had taken them to Edinburgh on holiday. She remembered trudging up and down the hills, much steeper for a child than for an adult. But what had struck her most was the way people talked, using strange expressions and pronouncing words differently. Even now, after living here all these months, she still had difficulty understanding what people said.

Since leaving Mrs Pattullo, she'd wandered through the Gardens, chatting with the homeless gathered around the fountain, looking for anyone who could help her find Phil Pattullo. She'd drawn a blank. Only the name 'Mhairi' had elicited a response, and she'd been directed to the east end of Princes Street.

A boy with bleached-blond hair and a grubby face was sitting leaning against the wall outside the Carphone Warehouse shop, a floppy-eared black-and-white puppy in his arms. He was staring at the ground and trying to keep the wriggling dog from making a break for freedom. In front of him was a paper cup containing silver coins.

'Hi there,' Von said cheerfully. She took a ten-pound note

from her purse. 'I'm looking for Mhairi.'

The boy lifted his head. Seeing the note, interest blazed on his face. Without taking his eyes off the money, he blurted, 'She's over there.' He moved the puppy onto his shoulder, holding it with one hand as it tried to lick his neck, and waved down Princes Street. 'That's her. Outside Disney's.'

Von peered through the crowd of hurrying shoppers. Further along, a woman was sitting on the pavement, legs stretched out over a blanket, watching people going in and out of the Disney Store.

The boy licked his lips and made to grab the ten-pound note, but Von held it out of reach. 'You sure that's her?' she said.

He looked puzzled. 'Course. Everyone knows Mhairi.'

'It's just that, if you're mistaken, I'll come back and take this off you.' She tried to say it as though she meant it, but without menace in her voice.

'I'm not a liar,' the boy said, flushing.

'I didn't say you were. I said you might be mistaken.' She offered him the money.

He snatched at the note and stuffed it inside his jeans, then returned to hugging the dog.

Outside the Disney Store, Von squatted in front of the person identified as Mhairi. The woman was middle-aged, with a frizz of brown hair, and was dressed in a checked flannel shirt and an orange-patterned skirt down to her ankles. Her face wore traces of having once been attractive, but time on the streets had coarsened her skin. Despite this, there was an expression in her dark eyes that suggested she knew what her situation was, and didn't give a damn.

'Mhairi?' Von said.

The voice was deep and throaty. 'Who wants to know?'

'My name's Von Valenti. I'm looking for someone.'

The woman hooted with laughter. 'Aren't we all, old darling.'

She studied Von openly. 'I think you're looking for a man, Von Valenti.'

'I am, as a matter of fact, but not in the way you mean.'

There was a sudden frantic yelping from down the street. Von straightened quickly, and pushed her way back through the crowd to the Carphone Warehouse. Two youths in hooded sweatshirts were showing an unhealthy interest in the boy with the puppy. The taller wore a Burberry baseball cap and was tossing the dog into the air and catching it just before it hit the pavement. The other, whose trousers were falling down and exposing the top of his Union-Jack underwear, had pulled the boy to his feet, and was holding a knife to his throat.

Von cursed herself for a fool. They'd have seen her hand over the tenner.

The knife-wielding youth was leaning into the boy, too preoccupied with saying something into his ear to notice her. She gripped the youth's arm and pulled it back. With her hand balled, she landed a blow on his wrist that made him drop the weapon with an agonised cry.

'Piss off,' she said, spitting the words, 'before I do something you'll regret, and I won't.'

He wheeled round.

She looked squarely at him. 'Do I need to say it again?'

His fury turned to amazement, and then to hilarity. Burberry Cap had dropped the puppy and was staring open-mouthed. She didn't give him a second glance; it was the youth rubbing his wrist who needed her immediate attention.

Without warning, he lashed out. The punch would have been good if it had landed, but she hadn't forgotten her police training. She blocked the movement, grabbed the youth's hand and twisted it until the pain made him sink to the ground. Then she kicked him onto his back and placed her foot on his neck, making it impossible for him to move without choking.

Burberry Cap legged it.

A knot of people had gathered. She was hauling the youth to his feet when a policeman, one of the Princes Street regulars, came forward. He took in the scene and, sighing heavily, dragged the hoodie up and led him away. He must have seen the knife on the pavement and the hoodie holding it to the boy's throat, but it was obvious he didn't intend to do anything other than move the youth on. From the warning look he threw Von, she suspected he thought she'd been meddling. She felt her colour rising. She'd never have allowed this on her patch in London. But she was no longer a DCI. She had no jurisdiction here.

The blond boy was cradling the whimpering puppy and staring at the flick knife, his eyes wide with fright. She picked it up, folded the blade in, and slipped it into her trousers pocket.

'Might be an idea to take yourself off somewhere,' she said, crouching and stroking the puppy. 'His pal could come back.' She gestured towards the Gardens. 'He won't try anything in there. There are some people I think you know by the fountain.'

The boy got to his feet and backed away, his eyes on hers. She was tempted to follow him, to see he got to safety, but he disappeared into the crowd crossing the street.

She returned to the Disney Store, finding Mhairi standing with her hands on her hips. The woman was tall, head and shoulders above Von.

'I saw all that,' Mhairi said. She eyed Von appreciatively, and then lowered herself onto the ground. 'You handle yourself like a pro, Von Valenti. Where'd you learn?'

'Here and there.' When it was clear this answer wouldn't satisfy her, Von added, 'I was brought up in east London.' If that didn't satisfy her, nothing would.

'You were pretty quick to keep out of that copper's way,' Mhairi said, studying her.

She dropped her gaze. Mhairi seemed like a woman who

could tell a person's life history by looking into their eyes. 'You know how it is, Mhairi. We all have things we'd rather keep from the plods.' Hinting she had a past would give her street cred. 'So, can we talk? I'm betting you could use a cup of tea.'

'Amen to that, old darling.' The woman made to get up, then sat back against the wall. 'When were you born, Von? What day and month?'

'March 16th.'

'Ah, Pisces. I can trust a Pisces.' She gestured at Von's trousers. 'And anyone who wears embroidered bell-bottoms that went out of style with the Ark is worth the time of day.'

'They were the only clean ones I could find.'

Mhairi got to her feet, and rolled up the blanket.

'Where'd you like to go, Mhairi?'

'Jenners, of course.'

Von forced herself not to smile. How often did a member of the homeless club have the money to eat there?

The rich aroma of coffee, mingled with the smell of buttered toast, greeted them as they entered the second-floor café. They took a table by the window. The Scott Monument was directly opposite, its Gothic spires, darkened by the soot of Victorian Edinburgh, towering above Princes Street.

Von gave their order to a waitress.

Mhairi watched the girl leave, then took the bread rolls and sugar packets from the table and stuffed them into her bag. Her hands were dirty, the fingers stained yellow. 'Rumour has it that this place will soon become self-service so I'm making the most of my opportunities.' She looked at Von with steady eyes. 'You said you're looking for a man, Von Valenti. I'd give up that idea and stay single.'

'Sounds like you've had your heart broken.'

'Who hasn't? Been married twice and they both ended in disaster.'

Her tone suggested she wanted to talk about herself. This didn't surprise Von. People had always opened up to her, it had been part of her success as a detective. And instinct told her the woman could be an invaluable ally in the hunt for Phil Pattullo.

'So what happened, Mhairi?'

'I did something I used to sneer at. Put an ad in the lonely-hearts column. "Genuine seeker of fun, friendship, and sexual congress." You know the sort of thing.'

She did. She'd been tempted herself.

'Anyway, it worked. Prospect Number One came along. After some great sex, we were married. I didn't expect it to last more than a few years. But something unexpected happened. I fell in love with him.' Her eyes took on a faraway look. 'He ticked all the boxes. Didn't even snore.'

'But he left you?'

'By the time I fell in love with him, he'd fallen out of love with me.' She shrugged. 'My bad luck. You ever been married?'

Von shook her head.

'Bet you've had plenty of laddies after you, though. With that lovely face and dark hair.'

'Hardly plenty,' Von said, feeling herself blushing. 'And they all ended disastrously.'

The waitress arrived and set down tea things and a three-tiered plate of sandwiches and cakes. After she left, Von poured for herself and Mhairi. She wrapped her hands round her cup and sipped at the black liquid. It was just as she liked it: strong without tasting bitter.

Mhairi stuffed the sandwiches into her bag. 'Aren't you eating?' she smiled.

'I'm trying to give it up.'

'Men don't like women who rattle. Husband Number Two told me that.'

'So what made you marry again?'

'Simple. I was lonely.' Her smile faded. 'Nobody ever lies about being lonely. Oh, I could have gone on for years on my own but I decided I needed to live with a man again. Husbands aren't so bad. They eventually do what you want although you have to take a lot of nonsense from them first.'

'Who was he, then?'

'A stand-up comedian.' Her eyes grew wistful. 'Dark hair, green eyes, and a GSOH. Good Sense Of Humour,' she added, seeing Von's face. 'A man like that could laugh me into bed. Took me a while to find him, mind. You have to kiss a lot of frogs before you find a prince.' She looked sourly at Von. 'Turned out I married a frog.'

'You married a Frenchman?'

'No, I married an English frog.' She picked the cherry off the top of a bun. 'Shortly after we came back from our honeymoon, I discovered he had habits I couldn't stand.'

'Such as?'

'Cutting his toenails into the sink. Totally unbearable in my book, right up there with slaters and lentil soup.'

'Let me guess. *You* left *him* this time?'

'Tried to. But when he saw me packing my case, he walloped me. Twice on the head and once, really hard, in the stomach. The neighbours found me lying in my own sick.' She shook her head. 'I called the coppers. Thought it'd be a cut-and-dried case and he'd end up in the slammer, but the powers-that-be were on his side.'

'How so?'

'Dunno. Somehow he made it sound as though it was all my fault. Got off with a caution.' There was bitterness in her voice. 'The divorce went no better. He got the house, the building society savings. Everything.'

'How the hell did they decide that?'

'I don't know, with a ouija board? Anyway, never trust a man with hair on his back. He's the reason I'm on the streets. But I manage. And I do it with a smile glued to my face. It's what the grown-ups do.' She took an Eccles cake from the stand. 'So where in east London you from, Von Valenti?'

'Whitechapel.'

'No kidding? I went on a tour there, once. The Jack the Ripper Tour. It was great. We finished with a gin and tonic at The Ten Bells.'

Von smiled to herself. When Whitechapel was mentioned, it was always Jack the Ripper that sprang into people's minds.

Mhairi's tone became businesslike. 'So who's this person you're looking for, then?'

'Phil Pattullo.'

At the mention of the name, the woman's expression softened. 'A really sad case. Lovely boy.' She tapped her head. 'But no-one home upstairs.'

'His mother told me about the angels.'

'Nice lady. Comes and feeds us. How come you know her?'

Von hesitated. What she did for a living was one rung up from being a copper in the minds of the public. Yet somehow she didn't think it would bother Mhairi. She decided on the truth. 'I'm a professional investigator. I used to be a detective.'

'I did wonder. You saw those lowlifes off pretty sharpish. Not everyone would tackle a lad with a knife.'

She knew what Mhairi would be thinking: she'd be wondering why she gave up police work.

'So you're working for the mother?' Mhairi said.

'She contacted my firm because she hasn't seen her son for ten days.' Von leant forward. 'Look, Mhairi, you know what's going on around here. The people in the Gardens haven't seen him. They said you may have. They speak highly of you and I know you look out for them.'

There was an edge to the voice. 'Someone has to, old darling.'

'Can you remember the last time you saw Phil?'

'Time stops when you're living on the street. One day is like another and you lose track.'

Von struggled to conceal her irritation. 'You may not remember the day, but do you remember what frame of mind he was in? What he spoke about?'

Mhairi's expression cleared. 'Hold on. Yes. It's coming back to me like a song.'

She waited, resisting the urge to fire questions.

'I remember now. He wasn't like himself, not like himself at all. He was much happier. He boasted he'd made some posh new friends. City types, he said they were. Young.'

Von felt the blood sing in her ears. This could be the lead she was after. But why would a group of young professionals make friends with the homeless?

The woman had guessed her thoughts. 'Phil can be great company when he doesn't see the angels. Sometimes they take the day off and go back to wherever they come from.' Her face broke into a grin. 'He cracks these unbelievably rude jokes. I roll around on the pavement when he does that. He makes a fortune those days. Tells the punters he'll either make them laugh or give them their money back. You know, if I could do that, I'd be so rich that people would have to pay to talk to me. No, Phil isn't like the others, like the saddos you get on the streets. You see, he's chosen the life. And that makes all the difference.' The light died behind her eyes. 'I know, because I didn't.'

'Did Phil say anything about these friends? Who they were? Did you get their names?'

'I honestly don't remember.'

'Did you see them together?' Von said, feeling the desperation rising. If she couldn't get names, descriptions were better than nothing.

'He said he meets them down in the Grassmarket. It's one

of his places. He parks himself on a bench near that blue police box. I'm thinking they work near there. But I've never seen them.'

It was a start. She could ask around the Grassmarket. But who would remember a group of young professionals? The place was heaving with them; they crowded out the bars. Yet perhaps someone would remember a group of young professionals hanging out with a homeless person.

Mhairi's brow furrowed. 'These friends of his. They take him places.'

'Like cafés? Or restaurants?'

'Not just there. Places like the Odeon on Lothian Road. One thing stuck in my mind, though, because it was a bit odd. He said they promised to take him paintballing. Some big club over Livingston way.'

Von sat back, stunned. 'Don't you think it's strange, people like that befriending him?'

'I befriended him and so did the others who sleep rough.' Mhairi smiled sadly. 'You haven't met Phil, have you? When the demons aren't with him, he can be a real charmer.'

'So did he go paintballing?'

'Dunno. Last time I saw him was when he told us about it. He was fair excited.'

Von played with her teaspoon. 'Tell me honestly, Mhairi, what do you think's happened to him?'

'He's found a new patch somewhere, everyone moves around. The churches give us the odd hot meal and some blankets, though they do that mostly in winter. And there are the night shelters.' She stroked the tablecloth. 'He always comes back to the Gardens, though. To see his Mum. Not for the food – he gives us most of that – but to see her. That's why I think . . . ' A look of pain crossed her face. 'Well, you've seen what can happen on the streets.'

Von pushed the cup and saucer away. Perhaps it was time to visit the mortuaries.

Mhairi gripped her sleeve. 'I like him, Von, I really do. If you hear anything, come back and tell me.' She smiled wryly. 'You've got my address.'

'Will you keep asking around? Help me find him?'

'Amen to that.'

Von pulled a twenty-pound note from her purse. 'This is for your time, Mhairi.'

'Thank you, old darling.' The woman pocketed the money quickly. She looked dreamily into Von's eyes. 'You're my new best friend.'

Chapter 6

The large tent had been erected at the far end of the field. It sat squarely inside a much larger area that was taped off, a row of yellow markers indicating where it was safe to walk. Approximately twenty uniformed policemen, supervised by Fergus, were systematically searching the field, moving in slow lines.

Steve trudged purposefully towards the tent, having received a call from the DCI informing him that he was officially on the murder squad. And advising him to get his finger out. The DCI was not a man who minced words.

Steve showed his warrant card to the duty officer, signed the log sheet, and ducked under the tape.

The photographer, a tall slim girl with a helmet of blue-black hair, had finished her work and was standing outside the tent, watching him approach. He knew her slightly, having worked with her on his first Edinburgh murder case, that of an elderly woman who'd killed her husband by lacing his faggots with paraquat. It had all been downhill from then on, with murders that were much less imaginative. After the case, he'd toyed with asking the girl out for a drink but the look of indifference in her eyes had made him think better of it.

'Everything inside's been photographed, Inspector. I'm waiting for further instructions.'

'Has anyone been down there?' he said, nodding towards the bushes.

'Not yet, and it'll be ages before the uniforms get anywhere near it.'

'So, who's the forensic medical examiner?'

'Not someone I know.'

'Pleasant?'

'Delightful, Inspector. But with a big dollop of scary.'

'Aye, I've met a few of those,' he said, grinning. He put on a gown, mask, and overslippers, and stepped into the tent.

At this time of day, it was bright enough for only a single arc light. Over the hum of the portable generator, he heard the voices of the Senior SOCO and her staff. He recognised the big bear of a man with her as the new Procurator Fiscal.

The body of Jamie Dyer lay on the ground, turned over so he was face down. His arms were stretched out, the tips black where he'd been fingerprinted. A portion of the jumpsuit had been cut away, exposing, between his shoulder blades, a large dark wound ringed with purple bruises. But it was his head that drew Steve's gaze, and held it. The depression in the back of the skull was like a small crater. Shards of bone, sheened with red, were scattered across the grass.

A square-faced man, gowned and masked, was kneeling over the body. He glanced up and spoke to his assistant. They turned as Steve approached.

'I'm DI Steve English.'

The man got to his feet and peered at Steve over tortoiseshell glasses. 'We've been waiting for you,' he said, pulling the mask down.

'So what can you tell me?'

'He was shot twice from behind. One in the torso and one in the head. A professional hit.'

Steve had seen this type of shooting before. A double tap – first shot to get the victim on the ground, a second in the head to finish him off. 'I take it it's too early to tell what he was shot with?'

The pathologist frowned at the body. 'That will have to wait for the post mortem. There's huge damage at the bullet entrances, as you can see, but no exit wounds.'

'He was shot in the back, but was found face up,' Steve said thoughtfully.

'That's right, Inspector. Someone turned him over.'

'You don't think he could have turned himself onto his back?'

'He'd have been able to move after the first shot – it missed the heart – but the second bullet killed him instantly. Why anyone needed to satisfy himself that the poor sod was dead is beyond me. Half the head's missing. You think the killer turned him over?'

'Or somebody else. I take it there were no cartridge casings near the body?'

'Nothing, I'm afraid. And I understand the murder weapon hasn't been found either. Having seen the landscape, I don't envy you.'

Aye, the place was being thoroughly searched but he doubted they'd find either the cartridge casings or the weapon. The absence of spent casings suggested the killer hadn't used an automatic or a semi, or if he had, he'd taken the casings away to prevent identification. Not only could the head stamps on a casing's base identify the manufacturer and the weapon's calibre, the casings themselves could be matched to the firearm by both the ejector and firing-pin marks on the metal. Without casings, they would have to rely on the bullets, and they would be recovered at the autopsy – the absence of exit wounds meant they were still inside the body. All things considered, it could have been worse.

'I take it he wasn't killed elsewhere and his body moved,' he said.

'Not judging by the quantity of blood we found in the soil.'

'Do you have a time of death?'

'Rigor hasn't set in yet, Inspector. Swelling of the eyelids suggests he was killed between half past twelve and half past one.'

It tied in with what Ranald McCrea had said about their lunchtime knockabout. And Jamie's body had been cool, but not cold, an hour earlier. 'Did you find a key round his wrist?' he said suddenly.

'The Senior SOCO has it.'

He glanced at the woman, whom he knew only as Gloria. Her surname was unpronounceable, which was why he couldn't remember it. She caught the glance and came over.

'We've dusted it for prints, sir,' she said, handing him a labelled bag. Inside was a small fat key.

'I'll be back with it.' He signed the sheet and left the tent.

The photographer was still waiting outside. 'Do you need me for anything more, sir?'

'We may do.' He saw irritation flare in her eyes. He couldn't blame her. After the initial flurry of activity, a police photographer's job involved hanging around in expectation of tasks that usually didn't materialise. She turned away and watched the uniforms combing the field.

He glanced at the key in his hand, then at the bushes behind him. The bushes won. To get a leg-up in this case, he needed a clear picture of Jamie Dyer's last hour.

'I'll be over there if anyone wants me,' he said to the girl.

She dragged her eyes from the uniforms and nodded reluctantly.

The sun was high and the air thick with the scent of pollen. The only sound was birdsong. He waded into the mass of yellow shrubs, taking care where he put his feet. But the ground was dry, covered in old leaves and seed pods, and there were no discernible footprints. As he pushed through the bushes, they tugged at his clothes, snagging the material of his dark-blue suit.

Minutes later, he found what could have been a path. He crouched to examine the ground. Was this the route Jamie Dyer had taken? Had his killer pursued him here? Or had he been lying in wait? What had Ranald said? *Once you reach the farmhouse, it's the end of the game.* Aye, the players would have had to take this path. And the killer could have been hiding in these bushes, waiting for Jamie. It was an ideal place for murder, remote from habitation, remote from prying eyes.

The photographer was at the edge of the field, watching him. He took the path in the opposite direction. The bushes, which grew ever more sparsely, gave way to woodland. It was damp underfoot here, and he was seriously considering abandoning his mission, when he saw them.

Footprints.

His pulse quickened. He squatted beside the path, taking in the size and complexity of the pattern. Definitely trainers. And not Jamie Dyer's; he'd been wearing smooth-soled leather shoes, slightly worn at the heel. The prints seemed identical, a mix of circles and lines enclosed in a figure-of-eight, and were mostly in good condition. From the spacings, the wearer had been walking, not running. If this was the killer, it suggested he was in control. He'd get Forensics down here to spray the ground to bring up the detail. A couple of the prints were deep enough to have plaster casts taken, and the forensic database of trainer treads might throw up a match. Cartridge casings would have been better, but at least this was something solid to take back to the DCI.

Taking care where he put his feet, he skirted the treads and followed the path further into the woodland.

He heard it before he saw it.

A few yards ahead was a shallow burn. Drooping willows fringed the bank, and a thick haze hung over the water, reflecting the sunlight streaming through the trees. He peered through the wood. The trees shrank into the distance, huddling together, crowding out the light. It would take an army to search that wood. He wondered how far on the uniforms were. Probably still in the field.

He turned back to the stream, only then seeing the bridge. The railings were solid enough but the foot-boards were rickety, the wood weathered to a light grey. There was a bright red splodge on the slats. It could be paint, or . . . He took a hesitant step forward. It took a second to register what he was seeing.

He hurried back to the edge of the field and shouted to the photographer. She arrived running.

'Get Forensics over here. And Gloria too. There are footprints along the path. That's not all,' he added, as she began to turn away. 'There's a bridge further on. You'll find Jamie Dyer's face mask and paintball marker there.' There was nothing further he could do here. 'If anyone wants me, I'll be in the main building.'

A short while later, he was in the men's locker room, opening Jamie Dyer's locker.

First to come out were the black suit and cream shirt, which he placed on a plastic sheet. Next, was the dark-green woollen tie. The final item was a red Nike duffel bag containing a pair of black Hugo Boss boxer shorts, a large white John Lewis towel, and a tube of Carolina Herrera For Men shower gel. He sat on the bench and considered the items. So what was missing? Socks and shoes. Jamie Dyer had worn them while paintballing.

He wandered into the shower area, taking care not to slide about in his overslippers. The floor was bone dry. But then, Ranald McCrea hadn't showered after the game. In the corner, there was a large plastic basket, presumably for the paint-splattered clothes. He glanced inside. It was empty. He wondered what the laundry bill was for the club's jumpsuits.

The women's locker room was warm and musky. The basket

in the damp shower room contained a single jumpsuit. He pulled it aside, seeing a paint-spattered yellow kerchief. The last time he'd seen one like it was round Ranald McCrea's neck. So Lexie Dyer wore one the same. Maybe all the club members did.

Back in the men's locker room, he searched through the pockets of Jamie Dyer's suit, noting where the items were. Nothing unusual: a fine lawn handkerchief (folded and unused), a mobile phone, house keys, car keys, and a wallet containing credit cards and one hundred and fifty pounds in notes. He replaced everything as he'd found it in the locker and relocked it; time to return the key to Gloria, who would see to the bagging and tagging of Jamie's effects.

After a final glance around, he made for the door. There was a row of lockers at the exit. The doors gaped open, waiting for someone to place their clothes inside, insert a coin, and remove the key.

All but one. Its door was closed. And the key was missing. The breath left his body. Someone else had joined in the paintballing game.

Someone who was still out there.

Chapter 7

'I'm going as fast as I can sir,' the red-faced constable was saying. 'The hinges are a bit stiff.' He had flinty eyes, and was running to fat, with rolls of flesh swelling over his collar.

Steve rubbed his forehead. 'Sorry. It's just that I'm in a hurry.'

'Everyone's in a hurry, sir,' the man said, his tone even.

Steve kept his attention on the screwdriver, trying to reign in his impatience. Ach, he knew fine well the man could be doing this more quickly. He was tempted to wrest the tool from the chubby hands and do it himself.

'Nearly there, sir.' With a sudden wrench, the metal door came off its hinges and fell to the floor with a clatter. Inside the locker, there was a bundle of clothes and a pair of shoes.

'That'll be all, constable.'

He waited until the man had gone, then spread out the plastic sheet and removed the linen suit and leather shoes. He patted the suit pockets and drew out a thick wallet. Unlike Jamie Dyer's, which contained mainly money, this was crammed full of cards. Barclays credit and debit cards and several store cards bore the name Bruce Lassiter. As did the membership card for a boxing gym in Glasgow. He studied the card's photo, taking in the wide smile, blue eyes and light-brown hair. On the back of a dog-eared flyer for the gym, there was a scribbled phone number.

He sat on the bench, his thoughts in a whirl. As soon as he'd seen the secured locker, he'd sent the searchers into the woods. And now he had a name: Bruce Lassiter. So had Bruce

Lassiter killed Jamie Dyer and scarpered, still in his paintballing clothes? He'd be pretty conspicuous wearing a paint-smeared camouflage suit in the streets of Edinburgh, even in a car. Perhaps he'd hoped to get back here and change, and was hiding in the woods, waiting for the police to leave.

Steve's mobile rang.

'You need to come down here, sir,' came Gloria's voice. 'We've found someone.'

'Bruce Lassiter,' he said matter-of-factly. 'Where was he hiding?'

'In the woods.'

'Did he put up any resistance?' He thought of the weapon that had killed Jamie Dyer and his stomach turned over.

'No, sir. He's dead.'

His voice sounded strange to his ears. 'Where are you?'

'Over the bridge. You can't miss us. We'll have the tent up by the time you arrive.'

'How did he die, Gloria?' he said, knowing the answer.

'Exactly the same as the other poor bugger.' A pause. 'Will you be long, sir?'

'I'm on my way.'

He continued to sit on the bench, struggling with his thoughts.

A second double tap. Two paintballers killed in a professional hit. What the hell was going on? He went through the contents of the wallet more carefully. In a small pouch, he found half a dozen business cards. When he saw the name of the company that Bruce Lassiter worked for, he remembered why he'd become a detective. It was what every investigator hoped to find in a multiple-murder case – something that linked the victims.

And he had it in his hands: Bruce Lassiter was also an employee of Bayne Pharmaceuticals and he worked in the

Glasgow branch, the same branch in which Jamie Dyer worked. He felt like laughing.

A short while later, he was following the path across the field and through the broom bushes. He reached the footprints, which now glowed with the purple chemical used to bring up their treads, and paused for a closer look. Whoever wore the trainers had large feet.

At the bridge, he saw that the paintballing mask and marker had been removed. Gloria was nothing if not efficient. The items would be with Forensics, where he was sure that fingerprint and DNA tests would confirm they'd been used by Jamie Dyer.

The tent was on the other side of the burn, on the edge of the wood. If he'd continued over the bridge, he'd have found Bruce Lassiter's body himself.

'You'll need to put on a fresh gown and slippers, sir,' the duty policeman said. Steve knew the protocol: he had been back in the main building and cross-contamination was a possibility.

He stripped off the protective clothing and took a new set from the basket.

The tableau inside the tent was eerily the same: a single arc light, Gloria talking to the Fiscal, and the pathologist and his assistant kneeling beside a corpse lying face down and dressed in a paintballing jumpsuit. The fingers were being printed, each digit pressed lightly into a black pad. Yet there was a subtle difference. If this was Bruce Lassiter, his face mask was on and his paintball marker was lying beside him.

Steve approached cautiously, conscious of the heavy treacly stench. The tent was tiny, wedged between the stream and the trees, and the stink of blood made him retch.

'Same MO?' he said, swallowing back the bile.

'Shot twice from behind,' the pathologist said, peeling back a section of the jumpsuit and indicating the star-shaped hole in the torso.

'Time of death?'

'About the same as the other.' The man inserted a finger into the wound. 'Before you ask, it's not possible to say who went first.'

So, both men had been shot from behind, about a hundred yards from one another. Ranald McCrea's words came back to him: *We go out one at a time, in five-minute intervals, from the back door of the main building. I went first, then Lexie, and finally Jamie.*

Yet Ranald had made no mention of Bruce Lassiter. Something he'd have to ask the gentleman.

He pictured the scene – a killer, biding his time, waiting for two men to come past, picking them off systematically. He'd have hidden in the dense woodland where the high interlacing branches reduce the level of light. Yet Jamie Dyer had been shot in a field. The killer would have had to break cover and follow him past the jungle of hedges onto open ground, where he'd be exposed. It made no sense.

'Spent casings?' he said.

'Alas, none, Inspector.' The pathologist threw him a doubtful look. 'You didn't really think we'd find them, did you?'

'I see his mask's still on.'

'I was about to turn him over when you came in.'

'Hold on. You mean you found him face down?'

'Unlike the first victim. Significant?'

'Everything's significant until proven otherwise.' He was conscious he'd stolen a quote from Von.

The pathologist was watching him over the rim of his spectacles. 'It's quite possible he was turned over, Inspector, then turned back. There's a way you can tell, of course. When you first turn a corpse over, it sighs as air is expelled from the lungs.'

He felt sweat trickle down his back. He'd experienced that once before when he turned over the body of a woman who'd been buried alive.

'Shall we?' the pathologist said.

At Steve's nod, the man and his assistant turned the body onto its back. He winced as he heard the faint exhalation. There was a sudden glint of metal from the key round the victim's wrist.

When the photographer had finished, Gloria pulled the key over the corpse's hand and fingers. She lifted the head gently, reached round the back to undo the clasp, and pulled off the protective mask.

The man had light-brown hair, cut short in military style. He looked in his late twenties. As far as Steve could tell, this was the person in the gym-card photo.

The pathologist was peering at the man's face. 'That pinkish hue is the onset of livor mortis. It was absent in the first corpse. It's another indicator that this one's been lying on his front.'

Steve knelt to get a better look at the feet. Bruce Lassiter was wearing green trainers with gold markings. But they weren't like the trainers people wear to the gym. They were built up round the ankle and shin, like army boots, with the bottoms of the jumpsuit pushed inside. He'd seen that green-gold colour before. He sat back on his heels, wondering where.

The figure-of-eight pattern on the soles was identical to that of the footprints on the path. But those prints couldn't belong to Bruce Lassiter: they were on a part of the trail he hadn't reached. Nor did they belong to Jamie Dyer, who'd worn leather shoes. Could they have been made by the killer?

If that was the case, the killer had worn the same make of trainer as one of his victims. And then Steve remembered where he'd seen green-gold trainers before – a pair had been taken away with Ranald McCrea's paintballing clothes. So Ranald McCrea wore trainers like Bruce Lassiter's. And like the ones that had made the prints on the path. Significant? Aye, most certainly. He got to his feet. There was nothing more he could do here. Time to get back to the office.

A short while later, he and Fergus were driving through the main gates.

'The bush telegraph's been busy sir,' the sergeant said, nodding at the clutch of waiting reporters. 'They've seen the police traffic.'

There was a sudden squeal of brakes as the car narrowly missed a Ford Fiesta.

'Jesus,' muttered Steve, 'the driving here's worse than in Glasgow.' He stared out of the window. Aye, some mincy heid who shouldn't be behind the wheel. He had a sudden glimpse of large brown eyes in a face fringed with dark hair. His heart somersaulted in his chest. 'Stop the car, Fergus. Now!'

The Fiesta had pulled over and the driver was opening her door. Steve limped out of the car and gazed, unbelieving. He saw the smile in her eyes, the familiar way she lolled with her weight on one leg.

'Hello, stranger,' she said.

'Von,' he murmured. The blood sang in his ears. He was conscious that Fergus had stepped out of the car and was watching them. After what seemed like an eternity, Steve said, 'What are you doing here?'

She nodded at the blue-lettered sign. 'I came to see the owner of The Paradise World of Paintballing.'

He heard his words as though they were spoken by someone else. 'He's not here. We took him to the station.'

'Ah.'

'Fancy a drink?' he blurted when the silence had gone on too long.

She chewed the inside of her lip. 'I can't, Steve.'

An hour later, they were in a wine bar on George Street.

'Okay,' Von said, climbing onto one of the high stools, 'one drink and then you're on your own.'

'Still drinking vodka tonics?' he said, smiling.

'Always.'

He gave the barman their order. 'I heard you were in Edinburgh,' he said, meeting her gaze before looking away.

'I moved up to be with Georgie. She's had the baby. I'm a grandmother now.'

'A boy?'

'Girl.' She paused. 'So how come you're not working in Glasgow? And how did that happen?' she said, touching his leg.

'I was shot in the line.' The accident had been his fault and, although he and Von had worked together for years and she knew everything one detective knows about another, he still needed her to think he was one-hundred-percent competent. But he could see the question forming on her lips. 'Look, Von, I'd rather not talk about it, if you don't mind.'

'Okay,' she said quietly.

'I requested a transfer from Strathclyde Police. I'm working out of Livingston. They opened a new station there earlier this year.'

'So what's your DCI like?'

'He goes into a tailspin whenever I say anything sensible.'

Her laughter filled the room. Heads turned admiringly and he felt a throb of pride seeing the men's envious looks.

'Well, he's missing a trick, Steve. You were the best copper I ever worked with.'

'Now you're making me blush. And, anyway, I happen to know that's not true. So what are you doing these days?'

'Living quietly.'

'I meant, what job?'

'I'm a professional investigator.' She ran a hand through her hair. 'I know what you're going to say. Oh, God, not another one of those.'

'I wasn't going to say that, no.'

'I work for Swankie and Vale. They're the largest in Edinburgh.'

'I've heard of them.' He took a sip of his malt. 'What made you become an investigator?'

'I tried being a store detective but I fell over in a dead faint from sheer tedium. Being an investigator is better although the hours are murder. It isn't so much twenty-four seven, as twenty-five eight.'

He smiled. 'And what's it like roaming Edinburgh's mean streets?'

'Actually, there's less of that than you might think. I usually get assigned matrimonials. I sit in my car with a camera, freezing my tits off, trying to catch blokes with their pants down. Right now, though, I'm looking for a homeless person. Name of Phil Pattullo. The single lead I have is that he was going paintballing in some place near Livingston. The Paradise World of Paintballing is the only club in the area. I was hoping to catch the owner.' She hesitated. 'I gather from the police presence there that something's happened. Just tell me you didn't find Phil Pattullo's body.'

'As far as we know, we didn't.'

She put her hand over his. 'I'm not fishing for information you can't give me.'

He stared at her hand. No ring.

'I wouldn't mind talking it over with you, Von.'

'You know you're not supposed to,' she said sternly.

'But I'd like to.'

They exchanged smiles. He took it as a signal to continue. Briefly, he told her about the two corpses, how they'd been found lying, and that they'd been killed with a double tap. 'It was a pro job, boss, no question.'

She punched him lightly on the arm. 'I'm no longer your

boss, Steve.'

'Sorry, force of habit.'

'When were they killed?'

'They've been dead since lunchtime.'

'Me too.' She turned the glass in her hand. 'So no cartridge casings. It could be a revolver. But it's more likely to be an automatic, or semi, and the casings have been lifted.'

'There are any number of weapons a pro could use.'

'Not in this country now that firearms have been all but banned.'

'What would you use?'

'To kill someone professionally?' A smile crept onto her lips. 'I like to think I've grown out of that. Seriously, I'd go for a sawn-off shotgun. Easy to steal. Easy to conceal. With a shoulder harness, I could walk around the streets of Edinburgh and no-one would know.' She tilted her head. 'But as it was a double tap, we're not talking a shotgun. What did the entry wounds look like?'

'Huge damage.'

'I'm guessing no exit wounds?'

'You got that right. I think the bullets were jacketed hollowpoints.'

'I'm inclined to agree.'

It would account for the nature of the wounds, right enough. Jacketed hollowpoints release the energy on impact and cause tremendous damage at the point of entry. Ball ammunition does it the other way round: minimal damage at entrance, and a large exit wound. They'd find out for sure when the bullets were extracted. With luck, they'd get the make and model of the firearm.

'How would you proceed on this case?' he said.

She gulped down the remains of her drink. 'Two men were murdered professionally at the same time and in the same way.

Find out what links them.'

He hadn't told her he'd found the link, that they both worked in the Glasgow branch of Bayne Pharmaceuticals. 'We've still to get them formally identified but the club owner, Ranald McCrea, told me that one of them's Jamie Dyer. We found clothes and a wallet belonging to a Bruce Lassiter.'

'Then turn over the rock on Jamie Dyer and Bruce Lassiter.'

'Find the motive and you find the murderer, eh?' It was the maxim she'd lived by at the Met. His eyes held hers. 'I've learnt from the best, boss.'

She seemed amused. 'Von. It's Von now, not boss.' She shifted on the stool, her face catching the light from the window.

'You're looking grand, you know. That pixie-cut suits you.'

'The barnet? The baby was always being sick into my hair.'

'So what's your next move on the homeless lad case?'

'I need to talk to Ranald McCrea. You've told me his paintballing club's now a crime scene so I can't reach him there. I'm hoping he's in the book.' She looked at Steve without blinking.

He took the hint and fished McCrea's business card from his pocket. She copied down the information.

Watching her write, he had a sudden thought. 'Look, Von, we should keep in touch over this. You might find out something relevant to my murder case and I might hear something about your Phil Pattullo.' He swallowed the rest of the malt, feeling her eyes on his.

'Okay.' She pulled out her phone. 'Give me your mobile number.'

'I'd better go,' he said, after they'd exchanged contact details. 'I need to get back to the station. If I don't show up soon, the DCI will have my balls for breakfast.'

She climbed down from the stool. He could see she didn't want to leave abruptly. He moved towards her and they exchanged an awkward hug.

'I'll be seeing you,' he said.

Her expression softened. 'In all the old familiar places.'

With a backward wave of the hand, she was gone.

The barman rang up the bill.

'Keep the change,' Steve said, handing him a twenty-pound note.

The man held the note to the light. 'There is no change.'

'Keep it anyway,' Steve said irritably.

Chapter 8

Ranald McCrea lived in a part of Edinburgh which Von rarely visited, her cases taking her mainly to the city's north and east. She was cruising down the Queensferry Road, trying simultaneously to keep her eyes on the traffic and look for the turn-off to Ranald McCrea's street. A pair of hand-holding teenagers sauntered across the road. She swerved violently to avoid them, mounting the pavement. Jesus, she'd nearly hit them. The girl stared, her mouth open, and the boy gave her the finger. It was times like these that Von missed being a DCI. Rank has its privileges, and one of them was having someone else do the driving.

She turned off into an area honeycombed with private roads. When she finally found the house, she realised why it had taken her so long. She stared in surprise at the warm stone façade. But this had to be it, the numbers on either side were right. Little wonder she'd missed it: Ranald McCrea lived in a church.

Hoping she was right and she wasn't disturbing a congregation in the middle of a service, she tugged at a contraption that looked like it should ring a bell. An age later, a woman in a nurse's uniform pulled open the heavy-hinged door. Her putty-like skin and the hard lines on her forehead and around her mouth suggested she was in her fifties. Eyes like a weasel's took in Von's bell-bottoms and black quilted jacket.

'My name's Von Valenti. I'm looking for Mr Ranald McCrea. Is he in?'

'You've come at a good time,' the woman said. 'Today's one of his good days. He's been out in the garden, but he's settled in now.' She heaved the door open. As Von passed her, she noticed the woman's giant bun. The starched cap perched in front of it looked faintly ridiculous.

The church had been converted tastefully, with many of the original features left intact. A jet of brightly-coloured flowers cascaded from the stone baptismal font to the right of the door. At the back of the room, a hi-fi system was stacked on the high altar, the over-large speakers sitting like sentinels on either side. There were two doors behind the altar, probably leading to an extension added to provide bedrooms and bathrooms. The pews had been removed to make room for the plump chairs and overstuffed sofas, and a strange blend of ancient incense and modern leather filled the room. The sun, which wouldn't set for a couple of hours, was streaming through the panes of stained glass, stamping vibrant colours onto the furniture.

'Just go straight on,' the nurse said, motioning towards the round walnut table.

Von took a few steps. She caught her feet on the overlapping rugs but managed to stay upright.

A man in his sixties was sitting stiffly in a damask-covered chair, his hand covering the newspaper on his lap. Although it was warm inside, he was wearing an overcoat which fell to below his knees. Seeing Von, his expression brightened and he held out a veined hand in greeting.

'It's all right,' the nurse said under her breath, 'he's house-trained.' She raised her voice. 'Isn't that right, Mr McCrea?' Not waiting for a reply, she continued loudly, 'It's your lucky day. You've got a visitor.'

A look of bewilderment shadowed the man's pale-grey eyes and, for a second, Von thought he was going to weep. She leant over and grasped his trembling hand. Her mind was in a whirl.

This was Ranald McCrea? The owner of The Paradise World of Paintballing?

The man released her suddenly and laid the palm of his hand against her face. 'Daphne?' he said, his mouth quivering.

'Daphne's not here today,' she smiled, glancing at the nurse. 'I'm Von.'

'Von, Von,' he muttered as though trying to remember. He looked around the room, confusion in his eyes. 'Where are we, my dear? In what town?'

The nurse was bringing over a chair. She shot Von a warning look.

'We're in Edinburgh,' Von said, sitting.

'Really? I thought we were in Stamford Bridge.'

'I'll bring the tea, Mr McCrea,' the nurse said cheerfully. Von made to stop her but she disappeared behind the altar.

She studied the man's lean face with its greying stubble. He hadn't shaved for days. Was this the Ranald McCrea who worked as a research biochemist at Bayne Pharmaceuticals? No, she'd got the wrong Ranald McCrea.

The man was patting the newspaper. A glance at the date told her it was over a week old. 'Anything interesting there?' she said encouragingly.

'Anthony Eden has resigned as prime minister.'

'Oh, has he?' She took a quick peek at the door. There was no sign of the nurse.

Voices filtered in from outside. Someone young and insistent was giving orders. *Those low branches have to be lopped off. Can you do that tomorrow?'*

The man perked up at the sound. 'Daphne? Where are you?' He grew agitated, struggling to catch his breath.

She gripped his hand. 'I'm here,' she said, unable to think of anything more appropriate.

He turned moist eyes in her direction. 'Where have you

been?' His head bobbed as he spoke.

She dragged her gaze to the door. Where the hell was the nurse? And who was Daphne? What was she supposed to say? She had to think quickly. Tears were gathering at the corners of his eyes. 'I've been out shopping.' It was a safe reply.

'Where are we, Daphne?'

'Where do you think we are, Ranald?' she replied, smiling.

'We're in Stamford Bridge, my dear.' He seemed unsure. 'Aren't we?'

'No, we're in Edinburgh.'

'Edinburgh? I thought we were in Stamford Bridge.' He gave his head a small shake.

She squeezed his hand, wondering what the significance of Stamford Bridge was. Had he been happy there in his youth? With Daphne?

A door behind the altar opened and a broad-shouldered man with brown wavy hair walked in. He was wearing a ribbed navy sweater and olive-coloured moleskin trousers. Seeing her, he stopped short, his face set in anger.

'Who are you?' he said, his voice barely under control.

'I'm Von Valenti. I'm looking for a Ranald McCrea. The nurse thought I came to see this gentleman.' She smiled at the older man, who kept his grip on her hand.

'And haven't you?'

She looked into the cool blue eyes. 'I've come to see the Ranald McCrea who owns The Paradise World of Paintballing.'

'That would be me. This gentleman's my father.'

'Also called Ranald McCrea?'

'Most people come to see me at my place of work,' he said with a cold smile. 'My father's the one who has visitors here so it was an honest mistake on the part of Mrs Lillie.' He turned to his father. 'We're going to leave you for a while, Dad,' he said in a friendly tone. 'We're going to be next door. And Mrs Lillie is coming along with the tea.'

'Who are you?' the man said, looking up at him with huge eyes. He started to rock gently back and forth.

'I'm Ranald. Your son.'

Von turned away, unable to bear the look of hopelessness on the younger man's face.

He straightened. 'Best if you come through to the back,' he said to her.

She stood up to follow him but his father wouldn't release her. Embarrassed, his son took the man's hand and prised his grasp from hers. In the slight tussle, the newspaper fell to the floor.

'Did you know that Anthony Eden has resigned?' the older man said in a voice edged with anxiety.

She picked up the newspaper and set it down on his lap. 'Yes, I've heard.'

'It's this way,' the younger man said brusquely.

He led her out of the room into a small super-tidy office. Other than a desk and chairs, the only item of furniture was a free-standing printer-copier machine. Sunlight poured through the leaded casement windows, making soft yellow pools on the floor.

Through the open window, she glimpsed a large garden with diamond-shaped beds, the flowers running wild, and a ragged lawn losing the fight for existence to the congregation of bushes and cypress trees. Tucked into the right angle formed by the walls of the church and the extension was a statue, stained green by the weather. It was an angel, wings folded, head bent. Ranald had inherited a cemetery when he bought the church. With a jolt, she realised there would be ancient graves out there.

McCrea gestured to her to sit at the desk. 'Sorry about that,' he said, taking the chair opposite.

'Mr McCrea, please, there's no need to apologise.' She smiled. 'Your father thought I was someone called Daphne.'

'Daphne was my mother. She died when I was a small boy.'

'It must be very difficult for you.'

'We've got Mrs Lillie. And I've managed to negotiate some days working from home.' He brushed the hair off his brow, and his voice became businesslike. 'I'm assuming you're here about Jamie Dyer, Inspector. So can you tell me anything? Was he shot?'

He thought she was a detective. If she didn't put him straight, she was, technically, impersonating a member of the police, an offence liable to imprisonment or a fine. 'I'm not police,' she said quickly. 'I'm an investigator. I'm on a missing persons case.'

He nodded, a frown forming.

'His name's Phil Pattullo.'

For an instant, she saw the flame of recognition flare in his eyes, but he was quick to dampen it.

'I know that Phil was going paintballing, Mr McCrea. My source tells me it was to a place near Livingston. Your club is the only one anywhere near there.'

He played with a paper clip, picking it up and letting it drop. 'Your source is mistaken. We've no-one by that name registered as a member.'

'You know the names of all your members?'

'Of course. It's a private club. I'd remember a name like Pattullo.' He slid his arm onto a manila folder next to the Apple Mac. The movement was defensive, and not lost on her. She recognised the involuntary gesture, had seen it many times in her years as a detective: whatever was in the folder was something he didn't want her to see.

'Can your members bring guests?' she said.

'They're allowed to sign people in, yes.'

'So it's possible Phil Pattullo came with someone.'

'If he did, then his name will be on our system. The rules

state that everyone who plays has to enter their name, whether they're a member or a guest.' He gestured to the Mac. 'I can access the system from here.' He tapped at the keyboard. 'How far back do you want me to go?'

Phil had been missing for ten days. 'A couple of weeks. Perhaps three.'

'And how do you spell Pattullo? One "t"?'

She spelt the surname.

A few seconds later, he swivelled the screen to face her. The pop-up window displayed the message: Search Key Not Found.

It proved nothing. She hadn't seen the search term; it could have been Mickey Mouse.

She pulled Mrs Pattullo's photograph from her bag. 'This is an early photo of Phil. It's not a terribly good one. Do you recognise him? Have you seen him at your club?'

He looked at the photograph for longer than seemed necessary. 'Maybe he's yet to approach me.'

'If he does, or if anyone wants to sign him in as a guest, will you please get in touch?' She scribbled her phone number on a scrap of paper and handed it to him.

'Of course.' He smiled suddenly. 'Is there anything else I can do for you?'

'You've been very helpful, Mr McCrea. I'll see myself out.'

'I'll come with you, I'm going out myself.'

In the church, Mr McCrea Senior had moved to an armchair under the glowing stained glass. A shaft of crimson fell onto his head, reddening the thinning hair. His eyes followed Von as she passed, their expression suggesting he was struggling to remember who she was.

She paused outside. 'Thank you for your time, Mr McCrea.'

He nodded curtly, and waited for her to leave first.

She sat in the Ford, watching in the rear-view mirror. As he settled himself behind the wheel of the light-blue Ascari, she started the ignition and moved away. She drove onto the Queensferry Road, then turned at the next roundabout and returned to McCrea's street. A minute later, she was again parked a little way from the church. Ranald McCrea's car was gone.

She left the Ford and sneaked through the front gate.

The path at the side of the church was covered in pink gravel, which would crunch as she walked. She slipped into the bushes and crept towards the cracked stone urn under the office window. After a furtive glance around, she stepped onto the path, trying not to make too much noise on the small stones, and climbed onto the urn. She squeezed through the window and dropped noiselessly to the floor.

She paused to listen. Nothing. Either Mr McCrea and the nurse were sitting quietly, or he was alone and she was in the kitchen. It was unlikely they'd come into the office but anything was possible. There was no time to lose.

She pressed a key on the Apple Mac. The screen sprang to life and a box invited her to enter a password. Damn. She'd hoped the club's system would still be up and running, but it must have been the type of application that shut down automatically when there was no activity. That left the manila folder. Inside were two completed application forms for The Paradise World of Paintballing. Could these be Phil Pattullo's new friends, requesting membership? With one eye on the door, she scanned the pages. But the dates of birth were wrong. Mhairi had referred to young professionals, yet both of these applicants were in their sixties. Probably men who were retiring and wanted to relive their youth by running around splattering everything that moved.

She was closing the folder when she spotted another sheet under the forms. It was a letter. Seeing the crest, she felt a sudden tingling in her blood. She read the text through twice, then stood staring straight ahead. She was so engrossed in her thoughts that she didn't hear the door opening.

'Daphne?' came the wavering voice.

Her gaze flew to the door. Mr McCrea had come into the office, and was standing watching her. She could see, behind him in the church, the nurse's back, just feet away.

Without turning, the woman said in a raised voice, 'Daphne's not here, Mr McCrea. But she'll be back soon.' The weariness in her tone suggested this wasn't the first time she'd had this conversation.

Von's eyes skimmed the room, her heart galloping. The only possible hiding place was behind the door. But the man would surely give her away. She was considering making a dash for it through the window when the nurse moved out of her line of vision. A second later, she heard a distant door open and close. She leant against the wall, the tension draining away.

'Daphne,' the man said again, his voice a whisper. 'Where are we? What town, my dear?'

She looked at the troubled eyes and trembling mouth. Then she walked over to him, took his face in her hands, and kissed him gently on the lips. 'We're in Stamford Bridge, Ranald.'

His expression cleared, and tears of gratitude coursed down his face. 'Oh, Daphne,' he murmured. 'Daphne, my love.'

She released him slowly and, with a sad wave, climbed out of the window.

Chapter 9

In Edinburgh's Old Town lies a street known as the Cowgate, so called because cows were once herded along it towards the city's markets. Students of history will know that the Irish revolutionary, James Connolly, leader of the Easter Rebellion and martyr for the cause of Irish Independence, was born there. Guide books include descriptions of the Magdalen Chapel and St. Patrick's Roman Catholic Church, buildings on the Cowgate concerned with the welfare of living souls. What the books don't always tell their readers is that there's another building on the Cowgate, one concerned not with the living but with the dead. This building sits behind a row of bushes and is entered from the side. If you don't know its function, you'll be forgiven for thinking it's a newly built nursery school. But Edinburgh City Mortuary, a two-storeyed construction, was erected in the sixties.

It was early evening and Steve was waiting outside with the Procurator Fiscal. This necessary ritual should have been undertaken by the Senior Investigating Officer but, by the time the police had tracked down Lexie Dyer, the SIO had been called to a meeting, and instructed Steve to deputise. Steve shifted his weight off his right leg. Just his luck he'd been conscientious about staying late and getting his report done. And his reward? Accompanying Lexie Dyer while she identified her brother.

A car pulled into the parking area and two women stepped out. He recognised the slim-hipped lassie with the dark floppy hair as the Family Liaison Officer; the tall blonde with her would be Lexie Dyer. He let out a breath. Thank God they could get on with it. The sooner it was done, the sooner they could all go home.

'Are you Miss Alexandra Dyer?' he said to the blonde.

The woman nodded without looking at him. It was clear she was as anxious as he to get this over with. She lifted her head then, and he saw an attractive face with intelligent eyes almost hidden by her fringe. Too much makeup, though. She pushed back her hair and he caught a trace of musky perfume, heavy for her age, which he guessed was early thirties.

'I'm Detective Inspector English,' he said. He turned to the Procurator Fiscal and made the introductions.

There was an awkward pause. 'Well, are we doing this thing or aren't we?' Lexie Dyer said. Her voice was low-pitched and not Scottish. Steve guessed Home Counties.

He was used to such behaviour, which masked the nervousness felt at having to identify a corpse. He caught the Fiscal's eye. The man turned and led the way inside. As they followed him down the white-walled corridor, Steve listened to the man's feet tapping on the hard lino and wondered if he could get through this without disgracing himself.

The small room holding Jamie Dyer was as spotless as the rest of the building, and Steve was reminded of the biblical phrase, 'whited sepulchres'. In the centre, on a silver trolley, lay the sheet-covered body. The pathologist who'd attended at the crime scene was standing silently with his assistant, a short middle-aged man with sunken cheeks.

The assistant glanced at the Liaison Officer, who took up position behind and a little way to the left of Lexie Dyer. Steve braced himself on her right. Aye, right enough, they'd all seen too many people faint onto the corpse.

At a signal from the Fiscal, the sheet was drawn back to

expose the head. Steve forced himself to look at the dead man's face, expecting the same look of horror he'd seen when he found the body. Mercifully, the pathologist had closed the eyes, and the waxy face was almost serene. It was just as well that Jamie Dyer's mortal wounds weren't visible from the front.

There was a sharp cry and Lexie Dyer's hands flew to her mouth. She turned away, groaning. This sudden display of emotion made Steve uncomfortable. He hesitated, and then stepped forward, but it was the Liaison Officer who slipped her arms round Lexie.

Protocol required him to ask the question. 'Is that your brother, Miss Dyer?'

She nodded, her eyes closed, her hands over her mouth.

'You have to say it.'

She let her hands drop. 'Yes.'

'You're sure?'

She looked up at Steve. 'I'd recognise my own twin, wouldn't I?'

Twin? Not something Ranald McCrea had mentioned. He glanced at the corpse, seeing only a slight family resemblance.

Lexie bent her head and the Liaison Officer led her away. The Fiscal seemed unsure as to how to proceed. After a muttered exchange with the pathologist, he nodded at Steve and strode out of the room.

The attendant replaced the sheet and wheeled the trolley away. Steve knew where it was headed: the lift down to the cold store, to await the post mortem. He leant against the wall and closed his eyes. Being with the dead brought on his nausea. In fact, being in this building was enough. He loosened his tie and, ignoring the watching pathologist, almost ran from the room.

The two women hadn't yet left the building. Lexie Dyer's colour had returned and she was thanking the Liaison Officer but making it clear she no longer needed her help.

Steve paused, a hand on the door. 'I'll take Miss Dyer home,' he said.

'Very well, Inspector.' The Liaison Officer smiled at Lexie, and left.

'I'm not going home,' Lexie said firmly. There was a challenge in her eyes, as though she were daring him to contradict her. 'Well, are we going for a drink, or what?'

He was taken aback, both by the question and the brash tone in which it was delivered. Before he could reply, she added, 'I'm sure you've got a lot of things you want to ask me, Inspector. We might as well do it over a drink.'

He smiled encouragingly. 'Where would you like to go, Miss Dyer?'

'How about the Grassmarket? You know Federico's? It's a cocktail bar. Does awfully good drinks. It's not that far and I could do with some air.'

She seemed to want to take charge, and he let her, relieved she'd recovered from seeing her brother laid out on a slab. He'd never been good with grieving relatives. Not like Von. He found himself wishing she were here, running the case, like the old days.

Five minutes later, they were sitting in the sort of drinking place he usually avoided. He preferred quiet pubs to noisy bars full of the young and successful. Surprising for this time of day, the room was almost empty. He ordered a rum and Coke for Lexie and a glass of Glenmorangie for himself.

Seeing the malt, she raised a perfectly plucked eyebrow. 'Drinking on duty? I thought you'd be having coffee.'

'As it happens, Miss Dyer, I'm no longer on duty.'

She threw her head back and let out a full-throated laugh. Had the place not been empty, people would have turned to stare. She reached behind her head and pulled something from her hair, causing her thick mane to fall over her shoulders.

'That's better,' she said, shaking out her curls. 'See? I'm not on duty, either. So you'd better interrogate me before I get too blootered. I don't intend to see this day out sober.'

Her behaviour caught him off guard. He was tempted to suggest they do this another time but he had a full glass of whisky in front of him. He'd either have to sip it and make small talk (which he was crap at), or down it in one (which would be a crime against single malts).

'Can you tell me about this morning, Miss Dyer?' He pulled out his notebook. 'The paintballing game?'

She pushed the fringe out of her eyes. 'We were testing new equipment from a specialist American firm,' she said, her words escaping in a rush. 'We have our big annual match on the sixteenth and we decided to have a game and try the markers. Our team is holding the annual cup, so it's terribly important we win and all that.' She tasted her drink. 'I left before the end. I'm the Human Resources Director at Bayne Pharmaceuticals. My life is meetings, meetings, meetings.'

'What time did you leave the club?'

'Lord, now you're asking. About one o'clock. My first meeting was at two-thirty.'

He sat back, studying her. 'Tell me about your brother, Miss Dyer. What sort of a person was he?'

'I didn't know him terribly well.'

'Really? I thought twins are meant to be close.'

'We were close enough but, you know, we led separate lives. I saw him at paintballing but hardly at all, otherwise.' She kept her eyes on her drink. 'I saw more of him at college. We both went to Edinburgh Uni. Great place.' She lifted her head, smiling faintly. 'Bet you're going to say it's not as great as Glasgow. That's where you're from, isn't it?'

'That obvious?'

'Fraid so. Those vowels are unmistakable.'

'And what did Jamie study?'

'Business studies and marketing, but he took other subjects too. He really was a whiz at nearly everything. He was going to be a millionaire before he was thirty-five.'

'Did your brother have any enemies?' Steve took a sip of whisky. 'That you know of?'

'Well, he and Ranald were always at each other's throats. But that's Ranald for you. He can be a real prick sometimes.'

'In what way?'

'Don't get me wrong, Ranald wouldn't harm a fly.' Her eyes widened. 'Oh golly, I'm saying all the wrong things, aren't I?'

'Are you?'

'They got on really well. They were just different people when they were paintballing. All that testosterone, you know? Each had to win at all costs.'

'And who usually won?'

'Oh, Jamie. Every time. He was brilliant.' She made a face. 'Ranald took it badly. He and Jamie were rivals at Uni too.'

'Ranald went to Edinburgh?' Steve said in surprise.

'That's where Jamie and I met him. Ranald was great fun in those days before we all had to grow up.'

'And what form did Ranald's fun take?'

She threw him a crooked smile. 'He once took someone's Mini Cooper apart and reassembled it on the roof of a high-rise. Dreadfully puerile, and rotten for the poor student, but it was a hoot and a half, don't you think?'

Steve cast his mind back to his meeting with Ranald McCrea. The man hadn't struck him as having much of a sense of humour but, then, he'd just discovered the body of his friend. Lexie, on the other hand, was trying to act as though Jamie would be joining them any minute and they'd all have a few laughs. But he'd seen this type of bravado before in the newly bereaved. Although the poor lass was doing her best to put a brave face on it, he couldn't help but notice the slight tremor in her hands.

'Then there was that time at Uni when Ranald got Jamie drunk,' she went on. 'When Jamie woke up the next morning, he had a tattoo.'

'A tattoo? Dare I ask where?'

'On his arm. Forget which one. It was cherries. On a stalk thing.' She tried a smile. 'Jamie wasn't best pleased. Like me, he wasn't a great fan of the whole marking-the-skin thing, but what could he do? His girlfriend quite liked it. That was unusual, having a girlfriend. Jamie wasn't one for commitment. He mostly picked up girls at bars for the odd, you know, one-night stands.'

Steve watched her gulp the rum and Coke, and decided on a gamble. 'Jamie's wasn't the only body we found in the woods, Miss Dyer.'

She choked loudly and spilt the drink down the front of her blouse.

'We found a second body.'

'A second body?' she whispered. 'Where?'

'Not far from the bridge, at the edge of the wood. It was Bruce Lassiter.'

He watched the emotions follow each other. 'Bruce?' she gasped. 'My God. What the hell was he doing out there? He wasn't supposed to be playing. Are you sure it was him?'

Lassiter's mother had identified the body that afternoon. And his partner had come through from Glasgow. They'd had no difficulty tracking the man down: his was the phone number on the back of the boxing-club flyer in Bruce Lassiter's locker.

Lexie's face had bled white. Aye, she'd had a shock, and no mistake. 'I'd better take you home, Miss Dyer.'

She clutched at his arm. 'How was he killed? The same way?'

'The same way. You said he wasn't supposed to be playing. So why do you think he was out there?'

She made a gesture to indicate that, whatever his reasons, she found them incomprehensible. 'He was mad on paintballing, as much as Jamie and the rest of us. But we told everyone we'd be testing the markers today and so not to come. He can't have got the message, can he?'

'Or chose to ignore it. Maybe he wanted a crack at those new markers too.'

'He wasn't always brilliant about using the database, he had a reputation for just turning up. It caused problems sometimes.' She ran a shaking hand over her eyes. 'He was such an awfully nice person. Really genuine. I can't believe this.' She lowered her voice. 'Does Ranald know?'

'I suspect someone has told him by now.' Steve swilled the whisky round his glass. 'Jamie and Bruce both worked for Bayne's Glasgow branch, I understand.'

'They did.' Her gaze widened. 'And? What are you implying?'

'At the moment, nothing. I'm trying to find what links them. The fact that they worked in the same place is something I can't ignore.' He waited but she seemed disinclined to engage further in the conversation. 'What type of work did they do in Glasgow?' he said finally.

'The usual things you do in manufacturing plants. Jamie was the import/export manager. He headed up a team that sourced the chemicals for the medications, then made sure the finished products got to their destination. That sort of thing.'

'Lots of travel, then?'

She nodded. 'He had a flair for languages.'

'And Bruce did the same job?'

'He checked the quality of the finished product before it was packaged for export. He reported to Jamie.'

Jamie and Bruce worked in the same team, then. They had

been killed professionally so it was likely to be a contract. Taken out by whom, though? And why dispatch them so far from Glasgow? There were plenty of dark corners in that city where a killer could work quickly and silently. He'd lived in streets where people were killed for the coins in their pockets.

'How do you think Bruce got to the club today, Miss Dyer? We only found two cars, your brother's and Mr McCrea's.'

'Bruce wasn't allowed to drive,' she said tonelessly. 'He had a form of epilepsy prohibiting him, poor boy. Terribly inconvenient, but there you are.'

'So how did he get to the club? It's off the beaten track.'

'Jamie used to bring him. He must have brought him today.'

'But don't the players congregate at the back before going out?' Steve said, watching her. 'You'd all have seen him, surely.'

She seemed flustered. 'Yes, of course we would. Silly of me. No, Bruce must have come on his own, after the game started. He sometimes worked out of the Livingston branch, you see, where the scientists are. He'd discuss with them things like whether a drug needs to be packaged in a certain way, or stored at a specific temperature. When he was in Livingston, he'd take a cab to the club.' She seemed suddenly keen to leave. 'Is there anything else, Inspector, or can I go now?'

'Of course.' He closed his notebook. 'I'll take you home.'

'There's really no need.' She pulled her jacket around her, ignoring the Coke stain on her blouse. 'Thanks so much for the drink.'

He watched her leave. She'd be going to see McCrea. They could console each other. He wondered idly whether Ranald and Lexie were in a relationship. More likely she held a torch for Bruce Lassiter, given her reaction to his death. What puzzled him was her relationship with her brother. *I didn't know him terribly well.* Strange comment from someone who confessed to paintballing with him at every opportunity.

No, something wasn't right. He downed the rest of the whisky. Ranald and Lexie had some sort of agenda. It wasn't what connected Jamie and Bruce that would help him solve the case, he realised suddenly. It was what connected Jamie and Bruce to Ranald and Lexie.

Chapter 10

It was quiet when Von got home. Home was a top-floor flat in Gardner's Crescent, south-west of the city centre. She shared it with her daughter, Georgie, and her granddaughter, Kylie, although she could never think of the baby as that. (What in heaven had possessed Georgie to pick that name?) The flat wouldn't have been Von's first choice, and something on the ground floor would have been easier for her daughter and the buggy, but it was all she could afford.

She stood in the hall, breathing in deeply. The first time she caught Georgie smoking in the same room as the baby, she pulled the fag from the girl's mouth and threw it down the lavatory. From then on, to keep the peace, Georgie had taken the cigarettes into the corridor. It was less than ideal, but what could she do? She was out working all the days and most of the nights. She exhaled slowly. No trace of smoke. That was something, at least, a minor triumph. But she knew what it meant: Georgie wanted something.

She dropped her bag, took off her jacket and pushed open the door to the tiny living room. The heat hit her the instant she was inside. She worried about the gas bill but Georgie was always pointing out that babies need warmth, her look of disdain conveying better than words that that was something Von wouldn't know anything about. It was always there, the accusation, sometimes spoken but mostly implied: Von had wanted a career and had left Georgie to be brought up by her grandparents. She sometimes wondered what her parents would think if they could see her now, living with, and keeping, her daughter.

Georgie was dozing in the armchair, the baby asleep in the cot. The girl had inherited her mother's looks: pale skin and dark hair, which she wore in a short shaggy style. Von watched the gentle rise and fall of her daughter's breasts under the jumper, which bore traces of the baby's dinner. She skirted the cot and crept into the kitchen. The usual bomb site. Georgie lived on a diet of cheap ready meals, defrosted and heated in the microwave. From the smeared remains on the plate in the sink, Von recognised tonight's as Thai chicken. Beside it was a bowl full of baby bottles soaking in sterilising fluid. Another bone of contention: Georgie refused to breast-feed. Perhaps it was just as well, given the nicotine in her system and the junk she was eating. Von was tempted to throw the ready meals away and make something nourishing, even fill the freezer. But she knew Georgie's tastes. The girl would continue to buy that shit. And she didn't bother to defrost it properly and was constantly coming down with stomach upsets.

Von's eyes were gritty through lack of sleep. It was less the baby's night crying and more the constant tiptoeing around her daughter that was grinding her down. The problem was that, although she and Georgie had been living together for nearly a year, they were still strangers. She remembered the early weeks fondly, helping with her daughter's pregnancy, being present at the birth. And then, when the red-faced infant, shaking angry little fists, had been placed in her arms, her heart had twisted with love. It had been a time of such promise, a new start for them both. At what point, she constantly asked herself, had their relationship started to slide downhill?

There was a muffled sound from the living room. She lifted her head and listened. No, not the baby, Georgie had woken.

She took the last of the eggs from the carton and cracked them into a bowl. The girl had promised to restock the fridge, but of course she hadn't. Von scraped the mould off the cheddar and grated the cheese. What had made matters worse was that Georgie was dependent on her financially. That was what she was choking on, losing her independence, having had no choice but to turn to her mother for help. Yet Von had never made an issue of it, had quietly opened a joint account. They were managing on one income.

A minute later, Georgie came into the kitchen, drunk with sleep. She slid her arms round her mother's waist and gave her a squeeze. Von continued to tilt the pan on the stove, sliding the eggy mixture around. Georgie disentangled herself, took a clean tumbler from the draining board, and ran the cold tap. She thrust the glass into the stream of water.

'How was the baby today?' Von said, folding over the omelette. 'She sleep okay?'

Georgie drank deep from the glass. She put it in the sink and turned to go.

'I asked you a question, Georgie.'

'Chill out, Mum, the baby's fine. What do you want from me?'

'A civil conversation,' she said more sharply than she'd intended. As always, she found herself getting angry at nothing her daughter had said: it was what she thought the girl was going to say. She slapped the omelette onto a plate. 'One day, Georgie, we'll see daughters respect their mothers. I'll probably faint.'

The girl was fiddling with her ear piercings, working her fingers up the ear. 'I do respect you, Mum. The baby's fine,' she repeated, as a concession. 'She's always fine. What else do you want to talk about?'

'Well, you could tell me what you've been doing today.' Von

pushed open the door with her backside and flopped onto the sofa. She ate her supper savagely, conscious she was working herself into a state over nothing.

'The trouble with you, Mum,' her daughter said, her voice measured, 'is that you want everything wrapped up nicely like a chocolate box. But life isn't like that.'

'Oh? What is it like? Tell me, with your great experience of the world.' She bit down her anger. She'd told herself this morning that, in the interests of giving the baby a happy home life, she'd control her temper. All her good intentions were paving the road to hell now.

Georgie thrust out her lower lip, a gesture Von remembered from the girl's teenage years. 'You don't need to speak to me like that. You're not bossing your detectives around any more.'

Von laid her fork aside and stared at the wall. She imagined herself back at the Met, as Detective Superintendent, a post she'd turned down to be with her daughter. The road not taken. What would her life have been had she stayed? Better than the B-movie it was rapidly becoming. But that ship had sailed. She set her plate on the floor.

The baby stirred at the sound of her mother's voice and gave a little cry. Von leant over the cot and tickled the soft chin, making soothing noises, her anger forgotten. She couldn't get enough of her granddaughter, those trusting eyes in the tiny pink face, that crooked smile. She glanced up at Georgie. It was worth another try.

'Something's wrong, love. Tell me what it is and I'll try and fix it.'

Georgie avoided her eyes. 'I'm sick and tired of being sick and tired.' She pushed a lock of hair behind her ear. 'I want some "me" time. I want to go out and get Christmas-party drunk.'

For an instant, Von saw the rebellious teenager. And she also saw herself at that age. Yet she'd changed. She'd had to. But not her daughter, even though she now had a child of her own. The realisation that Georgie had never grown up filled her with dismay. 'I'll take tomorrow off, then,' she said quietly, 'and stop at home.' She watched the light rekindle in her daughter's eyes.

'Do you mean that, Mum?'

'I wouldn't have said it otherwise.'

After a silence, Georgie said, 'And could you let me have some money?'

Von met her gaze. 'Have you emptied the account again?'

'I did that last week,' her daughter said, lowering her eyes.

'You can't have. That jumper's new on.'

The silence lengthened. Georgie continued to look at the carpet.

'You know, love, when I was young, my mother taught me not to steal. Maybe that's out of fashion now.'

Georgie lifted her head and said with serene satisfaction, 'When I was young, my mother abandoned me. She didn't teach me anything.'

'For Christ's sake, Georgie, why can't you let it go? I feel like I'm being punished all the time. I have enough to do without all this.' She was suddenly bone-tired. She let her head fall back against the sofa.

Georgie was better at controlling her temper. And hiding her feelings. 'So are you giving me the money or not?' she said in a matter-of-fact way.

'I think we both know the answer to that question.' The current account was at an all-time low and Von had no intention of dipping into the savings. That money was for her granddaughter's education. She'd starve before she touched it.

'I don't need the attitude, Mum. I need the money.'

She gazed steadily at the girl. Her daughter, penniless, but with a row of designer dresses in the wardrobe, courtesy of the last man who'd shown a serious interest in her.

'If you need money, love, what about those clothes? Ever thought of selling them on eBay?'

'You know I can't do that.'

'Can't? Or won't?'

'I can't sell them,' Georgie said in a slightly tremulous voice. 'I loved him, Mum. Can you understand that?'

They were back to that, Georgie's great love. Always there between them. The elephant in the room. 'Yeah, yeah, I know all about it,' Von said, her emotions drained. 'Love at first fuck.'

She'd expected an acid remark in return, but Georgie looked away.

Von closed her eyes, and let her mind drift to her chance encounter with her former colleague. Steve, a ghost from her past and the last person she'd expected to see in Edinburgh. They'd had good times in the force, and he'd been rock solid as a buddy, saving her from her mistakes many a time. She felt the tension leave her shoulders.

'You'll never guess who I ran into today, Georgie? Steve English, my old partner from London.'

'London? So what's he doing here?'

'Working on a murder case.'

Georgie licked her handkerchief and rubbed at the stain on her jumper. 'Where did you run into him?' she said in a tone that suggested she wasn't interested.

'At a paintballing club.'

She had expected this to pique her daughter's curiosity, but Georgie said, 'I'm a bit tired, Mum. I think I'll have an early night.' She kept her eyes on the floor. 'I'll lock up.'

She left the room and Von heard the sound of bolts being drawn. Then another sound, fainter, but instantly recognisable. It was the slow unzipping of her bag. Georgie was taking money from her purse. The trust issues which Von thought she'd dealt with successfully were back with a vengeance. Her shoulders slumped. Her daughter had no idea how to manage money. It was too early to reinstate her credit card.

The girl returned and collapsed into the armchair. 'How about I make us a cup of tea, Mum?'

'I thought you wanted to turn in.'

'We can still have a cup of tea.' She got eagerly to her feet.

Von was too tired to make a scene. She studied her daughter's face. At least Georgie was capable of feeling guilty. 'Don't bother, love, I'm going to bed too. I'll help you with the baby.'

They carried the cot into Georgie's bedroom. Von glanced at the cheerless walls. When her missing persons was finished, she'd make time to decorate the room; the dark colours couldn't be good for the baby. She gazed at her granddaughter, lying on her side, her breathing so soft it was barely discernible. Her love for the child was so strong that it threatened to overwhelm her. It was at times like these that the thought crept into her mind to adopt the baby. But it couldn't work, she had to earn them all a living. And Georgie would never allow it. For all her faults, she loved the child.

Georgie was looking at her with a glimmer in her eyes. 'You're sure you've the time to stay at home tomorrow?'

'Yes,' she lied. 'I've the time.'

'Thanks, Mum. Night then.'

She stood at the door, her hand falling slowly away from the wall. 'Night.'

Chapter 11
Thursday, June 7th

'So why aren't you eating, Steve?'

'It's this afternoon.'

Von smiled sympathetically. 'Ah, I did wonder.'

They were having lunch in a café-bar on South Bridge. The fine weather was continuing, with only a smudge of cloud, and sunlight poured into the room. She had steered him to a table beside the open window, not because of the heat in the café, but because his complexion was like paste.

She watched him chase a piece of chicken around the plate. He never could face autopsies. He usually lasted until the Y-shaped incision was made and then he'd heave out the contents of his stomach. She, on the other hand, had no problem seeing dead flesh sliced. A part of her wished she could go with him but that was impossible. And he wouldn't want his hand held. Few men did.

'Have you voted yet, Steve?' she said, wiping her mouth with a napkin.

The general election of June 7th was expected to return Tony Blair to office in another landslide victory. It would make him the first Labour Prime Minister to serve a full second consecutive term, provided he didn't give up power to Gordon Brown.

'Ach, what's the point? We know who's going to win. Anyway, I never vote in general elections.'

'Right.' She put the napkin down. 'So how are you getting on with the case?'

'We've swept the woodland for the murder weapon and turned the clubhouse and adjacent buildings upside down.' He snorted. 'Waste of time and money. The DCI won't authorise a TV appeal to the public or a reconstruction. I agree with him. The crime scene's too remote.'

'How do you think the killer got there?'

'There are plenty of side roads where a car can be left unnoticed, and a perimeter fence with gaps where you can get in under the wire mesh.' He smiled ruefully. 'It's too dry for tyre tracks. That club's the perfect spot for a crime.'

'The killer had to know Bruce and Jamie would be there at that time, though.'

'Aye, that's for sure, which is why we're turning the spotlight on the members.'

'And have you found anything linking Jamie and Bruce?' she said guardedly. She wondered how much he was prepared to share. Strictly speaking, he shouldn't be telling her anything.

'They both worked for the Glasgow branch of Bayne Pharmaceuticals.'

'Sounds like you're well on your way, then.'

He pushed the plate aside. 'I met Jamie Dyer's twin sister a couple of days ago. She IDd her brother. Something interesting came out of that.' He leant forward. 'I told her we'd found Bruce Lassiter's body. She nearly had a fit.'

'Were they lovers?'

'Bruce Lassiter was gay.'

'What's really on your mind, Steve?' she said, after a pause. 'It's not the autopsy.'

He pulled out his notebook. 'Okay, listen to this, boss, and tell me what conclusion you come to. Here's what Ranald said about why they were playing: *The three of us were testing new equipment from a specialist American firm.*' He flicked forward a couple of pages. 'He said the same later: *As I said, Inspector, we're having a tournament soon and we needed to test new equipment from a specialist American firm.'*

'It's not unusual for people to repeat themselves.'

'Right, but listen to this now. This is from my conversation with Lexie later the same day: *We were testing new equipment from a specialist American firm.* Her exact words.'

'You've got my interest.'

'They agreed the wording in advance. No question.'

'Problem is,' Von said, chewing a piece of bread, 'how far in advance? Was it after the game, or before?'

'Lexie left after half an hour.'

She threw him an amused look. 'Who says?'

'She does, and so does Ranald. We checked her out, although given the time she was next seen she could have stayed the full hour.' He folded his arms. 'Here's what I think happened. They both played for the hour, got back to the clubhouse, then went searching when Jamie didn't return. They found his body, but couldn't just hoof it because loads of people knew they were out testing these new markers. So they called the police. They decided to get their story straight. Hence the identical wording.'

'It's possible,' she said vaguely. 'But then why wasn't Lexie there when you arrived?'

'Ranald was trying to protect her. They only needed one of them to find the body.'

'And what was the time of death?'

'Between half twelve and half one. For both Jamie and Bruce.'

After a pause, she said, 'I went to see Ranald McCrea after I left you at that wine bar. I quizzed him about Phil Pattullo. He recognised the name, although he said he'd never heard of him. He had a folder on the desk and there was something in it he didn't want me to see.' She traced a pattern on the tablecloth. 'After he left, I went back into his office and peeked inside.'

'I won't ask how you got back in without his being there,'

Steve said, a smile playing about his lips.

'Then I won't tell.' She laid a hand on his arm. 'Look, I need a favour. You said you're going to be checking out the paintballing-club members. I'm looking for ones who are young and work professionally. If you come across any, would you be prepared to pass on the names?'

He scratched his chin thoughtfully.

'I know you're not supposed to, Steve. But I can do a trade.'

'A trade, boss?'

'Stop calling me boss.'

He smiled. 'Sorry, but when your eyes shine like that it reminds me of the old days.'

'My eyes are shining because I got lots of rest yesterday. I was at home playing with the baby. That relaxes me better than a day at the spa.' She didn't add that she'd had an almighty row with Georgie who came home late, the worse for drink.

'So what's the trade?' he said, his smile widening.

'There was something interesting in Ranald McCrea's folder. A letter from the Calder Rifle and Pistol Club. Ranald's a member.'

'A shooting club?'

'On it was a list of shooting slots, which ones are free, and which aren't. Complete with names.' She didn't wait for a response. 'Well, aren't you going to ask me who else shoots at the Calder Rifle and Pistol Club?'

'Jamie Dyer,' he said emphatically.

'Wrong twin.'

His eyebrows shot up. 'So the two surviving paintball players are members of a shooting club? I suppose it's not surprising. Paintballing is only one rung down from using an actual firearm.'

'I take it you swabbed for firearm discharge residue?'

'We did Ranald, but we caught up with Lexie too late. The

Tox report's still to come in but, if Ranald shoots regularly, the results'll be worse than useless. The stuff'll never be off his hands. Or off Lexie's.' He rubbed his face. 'So they're both shooters.'

'I've done my homework. The Calder Rifle and Pistol Club's on the other side of the road, not that far from the paintballing place.' Her hand was still on his arm and she noticed he'd made no attempt to move. 'So, do we have a deal? About the names?'

'We have a deal,' he said, grinning. He glanced at his watch. 'Damn it, I need to get going.'

'Chin up, Steve,' she said, sliding her hand down his arm and squeezing his fingers.

He disentangled his hand and clasped hers. 'I've never understood how you do it, Von. I've always admired your behaviour at autopsies.'

'Iron constitution.' She looked at his meal, barely touched. 'And I never go into a cutting room on an empty stomach.'

He stood up but she pulled him back. 'Give me a call when it's finished. I'll be in town this afternoon.'

He threw her a baleful look, and dropped a couple of ten-pound notes on the table. With a brief wave that could have been dismissive but simply told her how nervous he was, he made for the door.

She watched through the window as he turned right and trudged up towards the University's Old College, his limp becoming more pronounced as he walked. Someday she'd have to press him on how he got that wound. 'In the line,' was all he'd said. She imagined him in the mortuary, slumped against the wall, trying to hold his breath as the pathologist eviscerated the corpse. No, he wouldn't call her afterwards. Men were like that. Steve, especially.

She leant out of the window for a last look. He was picking his way through the crowd. As he reached Chambers Street, a sudden gust flapped at the jacket of his navy suit. Before he rounded the corner, she'd made her decision.

She was in no doubt now that Ranald McCrea was the key to finding Phil Pattullo. And that he and Lexie were up to something together was also not in question. The two of them finding a corpse, then getting their story straight, wasn't a hanging offence. Many people did that out of panic. Lexie's reasons for wanting the police to think she'd left before her brother was killed might be innocent, although they betrayed a lack of knowledge of the precision with which the time of death could be determined.

The waitress brought the bill. Von glanced at it, then added a fiver to Steve's notes. She pulled on her denim jacket. Yes, she could imagine Lexie and Ranald huddled in shock over Jamie's corpse, rehearsing what they were going to say. Somehow, though, it didn't wash. She'd lay down good money that Lexie left early because she had a meeting to go to. What was more likely, and something which she was sure Steve had thought of too, was that Ranald and Lexie had agreed their story before Jamie and Bruce were killed.

And that could mean only one thing: they knew the murders were going to take place.

Chapter 12

The pathologist, the front of his surgical robe glossy with blood, lifted a pair of shears and leant over Jamie Dyer's corpse. He hacked at the chest, speaking to his assistant, who made notes.

Steve was staring fixedly at the wall. Dear God, how was he going to survive this? He'd only just held it together during the first hour when he'd watched the butchering of Bruce Lassiter's body. His worst moment had been seeing the bullets extracted with slimline forceps. The Procurator Fiscal seemed equally ill at ease, plucking nervously at the front of his gown.

The pathologist, the man with the tortoiseshell glasses, was an expert on gun wounds and had blethered on with a barely suppressed smile about the condition of the internal organs. The first bullet had perforated the pericardium and penetrated the left ventricle, killing Bruce Lassiter instantly. The second had smashed into the skull, forcing pieces of bone through the brain. The angle of fire indicated by the bullet furrows revealed that the assailant had fired horizontally into the back, suggesting Bruce had been standing when first hit, and had then fired downwards into the head. A double tap, as Steve had suspected. The pathologist dropped the bullets into a bowl of clear liquid, which his assistant placed in a machine. The man flicked a switch and Steve stared numbly as tiny strands of blood vibrated off the metal, leaving it clean and shining. He used his sudden overwhelming interest in the process as an excuse not to look when Bruce was turned over and his chest opened.

And now the pathologist was doing the same to Jamie Dyer. He'd extracted the bullets, cleaned and bagged them, and sent them to the Forensics lab along with Bruce Lassiter's. Jamie's corpse lay on the dissecting table, the skin semi-transparent, the tattoo on the left arm indecent in its vibrant shades. Two cherries on a stalk, just as Lexie had described. A thin dark scab at the edges reminded Steve of a child's drawing in which the contours are outlined in a darker colour.

The pathologist was peeling back the flesh of the torso, explaining that he preferred shears to the Stryker because of the large amount of dust created when a saw cut into bone. Steve knew the procedure: the bone on both sides of the chest cavity would be cut to allow the sternum and attached ribs to be lifted as one. The heart and lungs would then be exposed.

When the sound of cutting had stopped, he risked a glance at the body. The pathologist was using a scalpel to slice away the pink-white cobweb of tissue attached to the sternum. Steve felt his gorge rise. He stole a sideways look at the Fiscal. The man had let his head fall back against the wall and was staring at the ceiling.

'See this?' the pathologist said, looking up at the men. 'The bullet fractured two ribs, one of which punctured the right lung. Excruciating for the victim, but not fatal.'

The assistant placed the heart on the scales and noted its weight: 280 grams. Average for a man of Jamie Dyer's weight. Seconds later, he emptied the stomach contents into a bowl.

The pathologist leant over the mixture. 'Very little there. Not like the other one, who ate shortly before his death.' He stirred the contents. 'It's well digested so I'd say this fellow hadn't eaten for hours. Advisable if you're going to be taking strenuous exercise.' His eyes smiled at Steve over the mask. 'Is that not so?'

He moved the block from under the chest and placed

it beneath the neck. 'Are you sure you want to stay for this, Inspector?' he said, picking up the scalpel. 'Your ballistics expert will have the bullets by now. I'm sure you're more interested in what she has to say.' His eyes moved over Steve's face.

Steve hesitated. But he couldn't watch a second time as the flaps of scalp were pulled apart, the top of the skull sawn off, and the brain removed. What was worse was that the pathologist also knew it. He was grateful to the man for giving him a let-out.

'Aye, if I go now, I'll catch her,' he said, making a show of looking at his watch.

'Tell your DCI I'll have the report to him by end of play tomorrow.'

He felt guilty at abandoning the Fiscal, but the man had known what to expect when he took on the job.

In the corridor, Steve propped himself up against the tiled wall, breathing heavily. It had been bad. Two corpses. More than the sum of the parts. But at least he hadn't disgraced himself, thank God. He straightened. Maybe he'd finally got the hang of this autopsy thing. He'd call Von and tell her he'd survived two consecutives, something he'd not done before. She was the only one who'd never made a joke of his squeamishness. She'd be proud of him.

Suddenly, he heard the sound of the Stryker saw, a whine like a million mosquitoes. His stomach churned. A second later, the saw's tone changed as it bit into bone.

He bent over and, one hand against the wall, retched violently.

A short while later, Steve was on his way to the Forensic Science Laboratory. Fergus had broken the speed limit to meet him on Chambers Street and he was breaking the speed limit to get him to the Laboratory before they closed.

Steve had recovered enough from his nausea to take an

interest in his surroundings. He felt his colour return as he sipped at the soda water Fergus had had the foresight to bring. It hadn't taken the sergeant long to get the measure of his boss: he'd handed over the fizzy drink without a word. Aye, the man was a wee gem.

They were travelling south on the A701, the direct route to Howdenhall Road. It was Steve's first visit to the Forensic Science Laboratory, a building providing services to Lothian and Borders Police, which include the usual crime-scene examination and wet-laboratory services. The department he was visiting today, however, was ballistics.

'You think Miss Prince will be there, sir?' Fergus said into the mirror.

Steve suppressed a smile. Fergus had heard about the sexy new firearms expert from California. The ripples she'd made on her arrival in the Scottish police force had become waves. 'I'm counting on it,' he said, screwing the top back on the bottle. 'She has a two-hundred-percent hit rate when it comes to identification.'

'Perhaps "hit rate" is an inappropriate choice of phrase,' Fergus said, curving his lips.

'Actually, it's highly appropriate. She started out life in the Los Angeles police force. If anyone's fired a gun, she has.'

He saw the flicker of interest in the man's eyes burst into flame, and wondered again about Fergus. He knew little that was personal about his staff and liked to keep it that way. But he couldn't blame the man for his curiosity. The reputation of this American cop-turned-ballistics-expert had spread through Lothian and Borders like shot from a cannon.

They reached the Laboratory, a building well hidden behind tall trees, at a quarter to five. Fergus pulled up at the entrance, surreptitiously glancing at his watch.

The movement was not lost on Steve who knew that the

man's shift was coming to an end. 'I may be here some time, son. Get awa' hame, I'll take a cab.'

The sergeant threw him a look of gratitude before turning the car round.

Steve watched him go. Aye, that was the way to treat your staff; he'd be able to count on Fergus when the time came.

At reception, he flashed his ID and asked for Lina Prince. He saw the amusement in the girl's eyes. He'd nearly said, 'Lovely Lina', the nickname she was widely known by.

'She'll be along directly,' the girl smiled, putting the phone down. 'Please take a seat.'

He sank onto the sofa, hoping Lovely Lina wouldn't arrive only to send him away. The day's Scotsman was lying on the coffee table. He flicked through it. Mainly stuff about the general election. Bayne Pharmaceuticals was in the news because its share price was sliding. Something to do with one of its medications. He scanned the article, noting how gleefully the journalist had implied that the premature release of the drug was the reason for the shares' poor market performance. At the top of the page was the face of Bayne's American CEO, a man in his fifties who was prematurely balding at the temples. He was beaming into the camera as though he'd won the lottery.

'Inspector English?'

Steve glanced up, startled. A pair of bright green eyes looked coolly into his.

He sprang to his feet, but the action was clumsy and he fell back onto the sofa. A strong arm helped him to his feet.

'Miss Prince,' he said, embarrassed. He could see she was trying not to laugh. 'I've not come too late, have I?'

'I'm working the graveyard shift today.' She motioned with her head. 'The lab's this way.'

She sauntered down the corridor, occasionally glancing at him over her shoulder as though checking he was following.

He had difficulty keeping up because he was trying not to let her see his limp. She was slim with a pert backside which moved seductively under the white lab coat. It was how a model walked, and he wondered if she were doing this deliberately. He concluded he didn't care. Like all men, he enjoyed the show.

She ushered him into a room that was like a small classroom. On each table there was a computer screen and keyboard, a state-of-the-art microscope, and little else. Through the glass door at the back, he could see the stalls where weapons were test-fired.

'I figure you want to know how far I've got, Inspector.' She led him to a desk. 'Take the load off while I go get the file.'

She returned with a folder, and took the seat beside him.

'You'll be familiar with these because you were at the crime scenes,' she said, removing the photographs. 'When I examined them, specifically the edges of the wounds, I knew we were talking expanding ammo.'

'Why would the killer have used that kind of ammo, Miss Prince?' He knew the answer but wanted to hear her voice. It was liquid honey.

'When it comes to expanding,' she said, looking intently into his eyes, 'we're talking a bunch of things. First of all, that kind of ammo increases the chance of a slug striking a vital organ. Most people have to allow room for error because not everyone is Annie Oakley and can split a playing card edge on with a simple .22.'

He studied her admiringly. She had a clear pale complexion and a wide mouth. And an unblinking stare. Aye, she could be Annie Oakley, right enough.

'I know you know all this, Inspector, but I'll say it anyway for the record.' She nodded at the photographs, the movement causing the cascade of red curls to shake. 'Using expanding, even with a non-fatal hit, your victim will be incapacitated long enough for the perp to get in place for the killer shot. Long enough even for him to reload a fresh magazine.' Her expression hardened. 'But expansion is desirable not solely for incapacitation. The slug dumps its energy in one go and doesn't exit the target and hit someone else. It's why practically all law-enforcement agencies use some form of expanding.' She pulled a microscope across. After playing with the settings, she invited him to look.

He leant over, catching her scent, light and fresh with a touch of rose. As he adjusted the knob, the blue metallic image swam in and out of focus.

'You gotta admit, Inspector, it's a helluva thing.'

As far as he could tell, this was one of the bullets he'd seen removed at the mortuary. It was huge and distorted, like a shabby old mushroom with jagged edges. Little was visible of the base.

She pulled the keyboard over. 'A jacketed hollowpoint is what it is. I've been getting the images onto our system.' After a couple of taps she swivelled the screen so they could both see. There were four images, arranged in a square.

'From the two victims?'

'Uh-huh. The top ones are Jamie Dyer's.' She kept her eyes on the screen. 'So what do you see?'

'Well, they look identical to me,' he said warily. 'As near as damn it, anyway.'

'The slugs are all .45s. More specifically, they're ACPs.'

'Automatic Colt Pistol,' he said mechanically.

'Made famous by the gun that fired it, the Colt 45. If we had the casings I could tell you for sure. This calibre ammo, if it's well-made, often expands to .70 or larger. And that's what's happened here. With that level of expansion you could drop a dinosaur. It's a real son of a bitch.'

He examined the images, questions forming in his mind.

'When the hollowpoint cavity's so large,' she went on, 'you get extreme expansion, sometimes even fragmentation, on impact.' She waited until he looked at her. 'What I'm saying is that these slugs are so badly damaged, it may not be possible to get the make and model of firearm.'

'Not possible?' he said, dismayed.

'There's very little of the rifling marks left.' Her voice was measured and he sensed that some of her confidence had evaporated. 'I've checked the database of slugs used in UK gun crimes and there's no match. So it's not a weapon that's been used in a crime here before.'

'But you could get a match if you had the weapon?'

'Yes, even with slugs as distorted as these, there are markings on the base that can be compared in a test-fire.'

'And how many handguns fire .45 ACPs?' he said, staring at the screen.

'Here's the bad news, bud. It's such a popular cartridge that every major gun-maker builds pistols for it. Smith and Wesson even builds a revolver.'

He rubbed his face. 'So you're telling me that all we've got so far is a weapon that fires .45 ACPs?'

'Uh-huh.'

It was worse than useless. He looked away, not wanting her to see his disappointment. She was the expert and, if this was her best, they were well and truly fucked. 'What does it tell us about the killer?' he said.

She seemed to want to give him good news. 'Well, the .45 ACP is big and heavy. Some people find the recoil punishing. You need a larger size and weight of pistol chambered for this calibre. So, you're talking strong.'

'Could a woman fire one?'

She spoke dismissively. 'Sure, I've done it many times.'

'Well that's dandy,' he said, trying to show he was annoyed at her complacency. 'So where do we go from here?'

'Look, I get that you're pissed but, Jeez, you're the hotshot detective. Isn't there other evidence you can use?'

'Okay, where would you go from here?' Something made him add, 'If you were still a cop.'

The retort had hit a nerve. Her eyes blazed and he could see her struggling to contain her anger. He wondered about the circumstances of her leaving the LAPD. 'I'm sorry if I've spoken out of turn, Miss Prince, but I'd heard you were once a detective.'

'Yes I was. And you know something? I gave it up because I had so many cases like this. I saw hundreds of people blown to hell-and-gone by young punks using firearms they could buy in their local store. Everyone thinks it's a lead-pipe cinch that forensics gives you the answer to everything but, guess what? it doesn't, so I went into ballistics to try to make a difference.' She looked crushed. 'And I find I haven't although I've worked my butt off. I now know that what I do isn't worth spit. Anyways, what does it matter? I'm going back stateside in the fall. Back to that gun-loving country of mine.'

He stared at her wordlessly, astonished at her outburst.

'Oh crap, I've embarrassed you now,' she said, smiling. 'I never meant to, I swear to God.'

'You haven't embarrassed me, Miss Prince.' He returned the smile. 'You've rather humbled me.'

'No shit.' She glanced at his leg. 'You've been trying to hide that, but you got hit yourself, didn't you?'

'You can tell it's a bullet wound?'

'People shot in the leg tend to limp a certain way. I'm guessing less than a year ago?'

'I'm impressed.'

'Does it bother you much?'

'It gets stiff now and again.' He hesitated. 'Will the limp ever go away?'

'Show me where you were hit.'

He rolled up his trouser leg. She looked at the deep scar for a long time.

'It'll go away, Inspector.' But he could tell she was lying.

'Well, I'd better let you out,' she said, when the silence had become awkward.

The girl on reception had left, so Lina unlocked the front door. She nodded at his leg. 'If you'd ever like to talk about that, or anything else, you know where I am.'

He saw sympathy in the green eyes. And something else. Aye, she was interested in him, and no mistake.

'I will, Miss Prince. And thank you for your time.'

She smiled and locked the door after him. He peered through the glass, watching her sashay down the corridor.

He needed to call a cab and it would be a while before it came out to this neck of the woods. Maybe it hadn't been such a good move letting Fergus go.

It was as he was searching his jacket for his mobile that he realised Lovely Lina had slipped her business card into his pocket.

Chapter 13
Friday, June 8th

Von was hurrying down Princes Street in the direction of the Balmoral. There was no break in the warm weather, and the sky was clear with only a few powder-puff clouds. A lone piper stood outside the exit from the Gardens that was guarded by the bronze horseman with the bearskin hat. Von loved the sound of bagpipes and recognised the tune as the one from the Scott's Porage Oats advert. Had she not been tone-deaf, she would have hummed along.

Her intention was to drop by and see Mhairi; it had been three days since their chat about Phil. If she'd been thinking straight that Tuesday, she'd have set up a regular time and place for their meetings.

She reached the Balmoral, and was tempted to call in and speak to Mrs Pattullo. The woman would be on edge, waiting to hear about her son. But what was the point? There was no news. What did they say? No news is good news. Perhaps not for Mrs Pattullo.

The homeless boy with the puppy was sitting outside the Carphone Warehouse shop, cradling the animal. Von crossed the road, side-stepping through the traffic.

He lifted a sallow face as her shadow fell across him.

'All right?' she said softly, squatting on the pavement.

There was a flicker of recognition in the glazed eyes. She took a good look around, then pressed a Marks and Spencer's sandwich into his hand. He lowered his head, saying nothing, but the slight nod told her he'd registered the gesture.

A short distance from the Disney Store, a man in a gorilla suit was playing a set of drums. Mhairi was sitting outside the shop, nodding her head in time to the beat.

She greeted Von like a long-lost friend. 'Well, Von Valenti, my old darling, you're fast becoming my guilty pleasure.'

'How are you doing, Mhairi?'

The woman pushed her hair back and Von noticed her earrings, like little padlocks. 'Down but not out.' She gestured along the road. 'I see you've been looking out for my wee mannie.'

'I owe it to him. It was my fault he was roughed up the other day. So, fancy a coffee?'

'Not today.' She patted her stomach. 'Bladder's been playing up a bit.' She motioned to the pavement, seeming to take it for granted that Von would sit with her.

Von unzipped her red leather jacket and lowered herself onto the ground. She pulled a packet of cheese scones from her bag. 'You're quite safe,' she said, handing them over. 'I didn't make these.'

Mhairi ate one, then a second. When she was halfway through the third, she said, 'Not eating, my lovely?'

'I bought them for you.'

'Life is such a stinking sewer, but you're a breath of fresh air.'

Von laughed. 'Thank you, Mhairi, but it's just a packet of scones.'

'Here. Take the last one.' The woman thrust the scone into her hand. 'So how are you getting on, then?'

'My boss has come up with ideas to help me find Phil.' She bit into the scone. 'I hate it when he has ideas.'

'Well, forget that. You're closer than you think. I've seen him.'

'Seen Phil?' she said, nearly choking. 'Where?'

The woman glanced around but no-one was paying them any attention. 'I've been sleeping in the cemetery these last few weeks. There's a place outside the walls. Got old graves which no-one visits. The ground's soft and the bushes keep out the wind.' She kept her eyes on the passers-by. 'I wait till the place opens in the morning, then I get myself back to my patch here.'

'And you saw Phil when you were coming back?'

'I saw him in the cemetery.' The furrows on her forehead deepened. 'He was wandering around like a lost soul.'

Adrenaline coursed through Von's veins. 'It was definitely him?'

'Definitely.'

'What was he wearing?'

'Baggy jeans and that yellow sweatshirt. You know, the one with the logo, grapes and a red apple. Fruit of the Loom, I think. The words are on the front.'

'So what was he doing in the cemetery?' Von said, half to herself. 'Sleeping rough as well?'

'Could be. But it's the first time I've seen him there. And I'm there a lot these days.'

'Did you speak to him?'

'I called his name and he turned round, but then he stepped away into the bushes. When I got there, he'd vanished. I didn't stop and look for him. No point. If you want to hide in that place, no-one'll find you.'

'Is that like him? To ignore his friends?'

'He has moods which come and go, old darling. As do we all,' she added with feeling.

'How long ago was this?'

'About an hour.'

An hour. Von's pulse was racing. He might still be there. She scrambled to her feet.

'I wonder why he doesn't come back to see his Mum, moods or no moods,' Mhairi was saying. 'It's not as if the cemetery's miles away. Something's spooking him.'

'Spooking him? The wrong kind of angels?'

'Or the wrong kind of people. If you're going there, Von, watch yourself. I've seen him get violent.'

Von stared into the distance. A cemetery was a strange place to go to escape your demons. But maybe not. When you were tormented by the world of the living, what better place to find peace than the world of the dead? She put some notes into Mhairi's hand and curled the woman's nicotine-stained fingers round them. 'You're a godsend, Mhairi. One more question. Where is this cemetery?'

'Dean Cemetery? It's off the Queensferry Road.' Her face broke into a smile of genuine pleasure. 'Beautiful spot. It's where I'd be laid to rest if I had the dosh.' Her smile faded and her eyelids drooped. 'Amen to that, old darling.'

Half an hour later, Von was hurrying over Dean Bridge. Each time she crossed it, she couldn't help remembering what she'd heard somewhere, that the bridge's parapet had been raised a century earlier to discourage suicides. As she reached the Queensferry Road, slightly out of breath, she imagined the desperation in that final act, the step over the stone, the plunge into the unforgiving waters followed by the piercing knowledge that perhaps this was not the right decision after all.

She followed the curve of Buckingham Terrace until she reached Bristo Baptist Church. A large poster in the courtyard proclaimed that 'The Meaning of Life is – ' but the rest of the message had been torn away. Beyond the church, across a side road, lay Dean Cemetery. The black wrought-iron gates were padlocked.

She peered through the railings. A gravel path led deep into the grounds. Inside, on the left, was a sign warning visitors against dog fouling and advising them that the older graves had unstable headstones. To the right, rows of graves fell away into the distance, the bushes growing so thick between them that the stones seemed to be wrestling their way to freedom. Huge trees cast their shade over the graves, keeping the sun off the sleeping dead. If it hadn't been for the tombstones, she'd have thought this was a park.

But why was the place locked at this hour? And how had Mhairi got in and out? She ran her hands through her hair, swearing under her breath. Perhaps she could clamber over the railings. Perhaps not. The gates were in full view of pedestrians, of which there were many, and she pictured Steve's face when he learnt she'd been booked for unlawful entry into a cemetery.

She was considering her options when a black cab drew up. An elderly couple got out and approached the gates with such assurance that she wondered if they had a key. The woman, whose silky yellow-white hair was held in place with brown combs which were falling out, turned her haggard eyes on Von. She looked pointedly at Von's jeans, her lips curling in an expression of disapproval, and said something to her husband that Von couldn't hear. The plump red-cheeked man smiled in what could have been embarrassment and, taking his wife by the elbow, steered her towards a closed door tucked away at the side. He gripped the handle and the door opened, sliding over the gravel with a whooshing sound.

Von felt like laughing. She was losing her touch. How had she missed the door? She waited for a minute, preferring to distance herself from the couple, and then slipped inside.

Despite the noise from Queensferry Road, her first impression was one of peace. As a rule, she avoided cemeteries, but felt an inexplicable longing on seeing the laurel bushes and holly trees. She wandered between the rows, reading the inscriptions but keeping half an eye on her surroundings. If Phil Pattullo were here, how should she approach him? *Hello, Phil, your mother's worried to death about you. How about coming with me to see her?*

She passed funeral urns wreathed with stone garlands, and Victorian headstones decorated with elaborate carvings. The poetic epitaphs spoke of victory and reward after earthly trials.

There was a door to which I found no key.

There was a veil past which I could not see.

She'd read once that Christians are buried with their feet pointing east, to awake at the sound of the last trump, ready to greet Jesus Christ at the second coming.

He is not here for he is risen.

She paused at a grave whose headstone was in the shape of a teddy bear. Fresh bouquets had been placed in a neat pile on the uncut grass. She hadn't the heart to read the cards, knowing that this was the grave of a child. She moved deeper into the cemetery. *Where are you, Phil?*

The far wall was studded with memorial plaques set into the pink sandstone. The elderly couple were examining a bronze tablet, the woman swaying slightly, her lips moving either in prayer or mouthing the inscription. Her husband glanced at Von and smiled.

She followed the wall to where it ran back alongside Dean Path. Partway down, there was a wall pipe and tap with a hose attached. Someone hadn't turned the tap off properly and a dribble of water trickled from the hose, darkening the gravel. The clouds parted suddenly and sunlight bounced off the wall, blinding her. She paused to rub her eyes. As her vision cleared, she caught a movement in the distance. Something yellow flashed past the gate.

That yellow sweatshirt he wears. You know the logo, grapes and a red apple. Fruit of the Loom.

Phil.

She sprinted down the path and through the gate. She looked frantically up and down Queensferry Road. No sign of a sweatshirt, yellow or otherwise.

Dean Path and the roads around it were deserted. She hurried across Ravelston Terrace to Dean Cemetery's other burial ground. Surprisingly, the huge iron gates stood open in stark invitation. Had Phil slipped inside? She was about to go in, but something stopped her. Was it her imagination or had the birds stopped singing?

She was being foolish. The cemetery was like any other. She ran her hands down the side of her jeans, and went in.

The burial ground was twice the size of the first, and less cluttered, with islands of flowers and wide avenues lined with hedges. Bushes grew tall and thick, and giant chestnuts spread their branches, shading the paths.

If you want to hide in that place, no-one'll find you.

She began to search, exploring each row systematically, but keeping a watchful eye on the gates. Monuments towered above her: huge crosses rising from platforms, majestic statues of weeping women, a broken column symbolising a life cut short. And, strangely, a wall dividing the cemetery but ending abruptly as though the mason had simply run out of stone.

Without warning, the light vanished. The noise of the distant traffic dwindled until the only sound was the soughing of the wind. The temperature dropped.

And then she saw them.

Angels.

Everywhere, angels with flowing hair and open wings. One, the fingertips brushing the breast, another, the head inclined, the right hand raised. Fear seemed to reek from the stone. The air vibrated with it. It was choking her. Her legs buckled and she sank to her knees, her heart thudding painfully against her ribs.

A movement to her left made her look up sharply. A laurel bush was swaying. Was someone there? Or was it the motion of the wind? She felt a pricking on the backs of her hands. No.

Someone *was* there.

She staggered to her feet but her strength failed. She clutched at the nearest headstone, resting her head against it and letting her eyelids droop. Jesus, what was the matter with her? Why was she having another anxiety attack now? She took huge gulps of air in an effort to steady her breathing. The elderly couple were on the path. They stared in silence, and then turned quickly away. She thought of calling them back, asking if they'd seen anyone, but the words came out in a gasp.

The laurel bush had stopped swaying although the wind was still up, she could hear its hushing. Someone was there, watching her. She pulled herself along the mossy tombstones, scraping her fingers against the stone, until she reached the laurel. She peered through the tunnel of branches. Nothing but darkness.

There was a veil past which I could not see.

A sudden flash of yellow startled her. And, just as quickly, it was gone.

But, for one dizzying second, she'd seen a face.

'Phil!' she shouted into the bushes. 'Wait! I need to talk to you.'

She thrust herself into the foliage, trying to part the branches, but they were locked solid. She ran back past the gravestones until she found a gap in the hedge. Gasping with the effort, she squeezed through but caught her heel in the roots and crashed onto the path.

He was moving rapidly towards the gates. Yellow sweatshirt, baggy jeans. Just as Mhairi had described him.

'Phil!' she shouted. 'Don't go. Please!'

He stopped and, for an instant, turned to look at her, giving her a glimpse of cropped hair and a gaunt face with huge eyes. Then he hurried away and disappeared behind a monument.

She reached it in seconds. But he'd vanished.

Jesus, she should have followed him quietly instead of yelling at him like a lunatic. Shielding her eyes from the sun, she looked up at the memorial: a Pictish cross, names flashing across her vision. Where the hell had he gone? She slammed her hand against the stone. But she couldn't give up now, she was so close.

She ran onto the path, searching between the graves for that tell-tale flash of yellow.

The blow to the back of her head came as she reached a tall crumbling tombstone. Her stomach cramped with shock and she dropped to her knees, feeling waves of nausea engulf her. From behind the tombstone came the rustling of leaves, followed by the sound of running.

She blinked rapidly, hovering on the edge of consciousness, and gripped the tombstone. With a strength she thought she didn't possess, she clawed herself up and clung on, swaying with the effort.

The elderly couple approached. They made no attempt to help. She heard the woman mutter the words, 'blind drunk', and then their footsteps receded. With the last of her strength, she pulled herself upright, panting hoarsely. At her feet was a large piece of stone. It looked newly fallen.

Slowly, she became aware that there was an effigy guarding the grave.

The angel's wings were outspread, wide enough to enfold them both. The hand was raised, a finger pointing upwards, the sleeve falling back. The head was tilted, the hair impossibly waved. But it was the eyes that held her. Large. Expressionless. A cloud hid the sun, its shadow stealing across the grass and deepening the colour. It touched the statue's feet and crept up the stone until it covered the face.

She turned away, trembling. Perhaps she'd imagined it but, for the barest instant, she thought she'd seen something appear in the angel's eyes. Something that surprised her. An unflinching look of admonition.

Von was still shaking when she reached Princes Street. She'd thought of taking a taxi but they never stopped when you needed them. Not in London. Not here. She'd had to walk the length of Dean Path into the centre of town. And it was uphill, too.

So she'd seen Phil Pattullo. Of that, she was certain: Mhairi's description was spot on. But what was he doing in a cemetery full of angels? He was terrified of them. And now that she'd seen him, what was she supposed to do? Tell her boss at Swankie and Vale and get herself a new case? Tell Mrs Pattullo? And what would she say? *I saw your son in Dean Cemetery, Mrs Pattullo, but he doesn't want to be found. He tried to scare me away by hitting me on the head.* Perhaps she was being unfair. It may have been an accident. She'd examined the gravestone and found it deteriorating badly. It was the simplest explanation; she'd leant against it and a piece had become dislodged. She'd even seen a large chunk on the ground after she hauled herself up. And hadn't there been a sign warning visitors?

She ran a hand across the back of her neck. It felt as though someone was pounding away with a hammer. Strange how a blow to the head could result in pain there. And, of course, she was out of aspirin, having given the last of her tablets to Georgie.

Yet had it really been an accident? But why would Phil Pattullo hit her? Was he so desperate not to be found that he'd resort to clubbing someone? If that were the case, Mhairi had got off lightly. Lucky Mhairi.

Von was late. She'd agreed to meet Steve at half twelve and it was nearly one o'clock. He'd wait, but she hated not being on time. It was one of the things her Dad had taught her. She quickened her pace.

She spotted Steve sitting on the steps of the National Gallery. He got to his feet as she arrived. She mumbled her apologies but he brushed them away.

'Shall we get a bite to eat?' she said, collapsing onto the steps.

He sat down. 'No time. I have to be off shortly.' His eyes wandered over her clothes. 'Why do you look as though you've been dragged through a hedge backwards?'

'Because I have.' She let him pull leaves out of her hair. 'So how did you get on yesterday?' she said.

He looked at his feet. 'I barfed.'

'I meant what did the autopsy tell you?'

'Nothing I didn't already know.'

The one o'clock gun from the Castle sounded over Princes Street.

He rubbed his forehead. 'I went to see Ranald McCrea this morning. He said Lexie Dyer had told him we'd found a second body.'

'Then he'd have had time to compose himself.'

'Aye, right enough, but he still looked a wee bitty shaken. I tried to get a rise out of him by suggesting he was lying when he told me only he, Lexie, and Jamie had been playing. I implied he'd driven Bruce to the club himself, but he wasn't having any of it. He was expecting my question about how Bruce had got there. Gave me the same answer Lexie did.' Steve turned his gaze out to Princes Street. 'McCrea was Ice Man personified.'

She remembered the man's gentleness towards his father. 'I think he has a lot on his mind, Steve.'

'You got that right. Two people were found murdered at his paintballing club.'

She massaged her neck. 'So where was Bruce earlier that day?'

'Working in the Livingston branch. One of the cab companies had a record of a Bruce Lassiter phoning them first thing and making an appointment for later. We showed Bruce's photo around and got a positive ID. The cabby remembers the paintballing club and seeing cars parked outside.'

'Then the other three were already there, possibly even playing. Sounds as though they weren't telling porkies about that one.'

'But they may still have known Bruce was coming.'

'True. So is the Tox report in?'

'Aye, and we're getting nowhere fast. No blood spatter or firearm discharge residue on either Ranald's or Lexie's jumpsuits. No discharge residue on the victims' clothes or around the bullet wounds. Where we found it was on Ranald's hands. But thanks to your sleuthing we know he's a member of a gun club, so it's circumstantial.' He ruffled his hair. 'There's one glimmer of light, though. We checked the casts of the footprints we found near the crime scene against our database of treads. The trainer's an unusual make. Andrea Sibillini.'

'Never heard of it.'

'They're a bit like army boots. Give good ankle support, so ideal for dashing about where the ground's uneven. There was only the one set of treads on the path. We got the shoe size from the plaster cast. It's a men's twelve.'

'That's large.'

'Aye. Both Ranald's and Bruce's Andrea Sibillinis were size nine.'

'They had the same trainers?'

'Maybe the club recommends that model.'

'And what about Jamie Dyer?'

'He was wearing shoes. Must have forgotten to bring his Sibillinis.'

'So the killer has large feet,' she said with a shrug.

'Not necessarily.' He smiled wryly. 'All that the evidence shows is that someone wearing large trainers was there.'

'Touché. Could you tell anything about the degree of wear?'

'The treads looked even.'

'And what about the bullets?' she said, after a while. 'What did Ballistics have to say?'

'They were .45 ACPs. Hollowpoints.'

She winced. She could no longer remember the statistics from her time with the NYPD – a hollowpoint's expanded diameter, penetration depth, and average incapacitation time – but what she could remember were the photographs of the wounds and the autopsy sections showing crushed bone and mashed tissue. Hollowpoints gave her nightmares. And a .45 ACP hollowpoint was the most fearsome. Its stopping power was legendary. If this is what had killed Jamie Dyer and Bruce Lassiter, they were dealing with a particular kind of professional.

'Did you ever fire one in the States?' Steve said.

'I tried a Colt 45 once. Never again.'

'This isn't like your average gun crime in Scotland. This is something else.'

'More up-close and personal?'

'More carefully planned.'

'So what type of firearm was it?'

'The metal was so badly damaged that the ballistics expert couldn't tell.'

'Brilliant,' she said, pushing her hands through her hair. 'I don't need to tell you how many guns are chambered for a .45 ACP.'

'That's just what the ballistics lady said.'

She looked at him with interest. 'A lady?'

'From California. Anyway, you wanted to know about the paintballing-club members. Turns out most of them are young professionals.'

It was what she'd expected. And it made her job that much harder. 'Are you going to the Calder Rifle and Pistol Club?'

'I'm away to Glasgow to see if the dead paintballers were up to something that might have got them killed.'

She stared hard at the ground. 'Of course, you're not supposed to know that Ranald and Lexie are members of the shooting club. If the police go in there with guns blazing, pardon the pun, they're likely to get zippo. What you need is someone who's not a copper to go and sniff around. Perhaps someone who's thinking of joining and wants to know what sort of guns you can fire.'

When there was no reply, she looked at him.

His expression was hard to read. But there was no mistaking the sternness in his voice. 'Von, when I'm back from Glasgow, I don't want to find out you've been to the Calder Rifle and Pistol Club and asked whether their members can fire .45 ACP ammunition. And then to hear you've asked them if they keep large calibre weapons on the premises, chambered for that ammunition. And then to find out you've tried to discover who's learnt to fire those weapons.' He added, softly, 'Understood?'

She kept her expression innocent. 'Understood.'

Chapter 14

It was late afternoon by the time Steve arrived at the large glass-and-brick building on Glasgow's Pitt Street that was the headquarters of Strathclyde Police.

The desk sergeant, a big man with a blotchy face and a ridiculous comb-over, greeted him as though he'd never left. 'They're waiting for you, sir. Second floor,' he said. The corners of his mouth lifted. From what Steve remembered of the man, this was the equivalent of a beaming smile.

The smell of floor polish and stale coffee, mingled with aftershave, greeted him as he stepped out of the lift. He walked down the corridor, looking for the familiar sign: *If nobody is around, please knock two doors down.* Aye, it was still there.

He opened the door at the end of the corridor.

Several men (and they were mostly men on this floor) were sitting throwing paper aeroplanes across the room. No-one noticed him standing in the doorway.

'Six months and nobody's moved,' he said, grinning.

'Stevie!' someone shouted.

They were on their feet, clapping him on the back and dragging him to his old desk.

'Anyone here seen Kelly?' he said.

'Is that kay, ee, double ell, wy?' they chorused.

'Is this going to be the last time you bairns say that?'

The voice belonged to a slim woman in her mid-forties. She had short blonde hair and a heavy fringe that came down to her brown eyes and, had her face not been lined, she'd have been stunning. But she'd been a smoker since she was a teenager and, although she claimed to have weaned herself off the habit, from the smell of cigarette smoke on her boxy jackets it was transparent to the whole of Pitt Street that she still had the odd puff on the sly.

Steve's expression softened. 'Good to see you, Bridge.'

He'd worked with Bridget Kelly on and off throughout his career and, like most of his colleagues, was of the opinion that the woman was one of the finest detectives to grace Strathclyde Police. But Bridget had never risen beyond DI, which irked Steve, who'd entertained fond hopes of working under her when she was promoted to DCI. It was common knowledge she'd had a bust-up with the Chief Super, a difference of opinion that had resulted in her languishing at her current rank. A lesser woman would have worn her hairshirt on the outside, or even played the gender card, but Bridget was made of different stuff. Steve had once asked her whether staying a DI bothered her. Bridget had sneered, 'Nah, but what does annoy me is that that wee arsewipe is still in office.'

'Not tired of the place yet?' Steve said.

'Tired of all this?' came Bridget's good-natured reply. 'You can't be serious.'

'So what's going on? The car park's empty. It's never as quiet as this.'

'We're up to our necks in hot-and-cold-running auditors. The high heid yins are off to some swanky hotel for a wrap-up meeting. They'll be singing their looney tunes till the wee small hours.' She looked pointedly at her watch. 'We're just hanging on till bevvie time.'

'Still getting stoshus at the end of a shift, eh?'

'What else is there to do at the end of a shift?'

'And how's the work going?'

'Tell him about the dog,' someone said.

'Oh, you'll like this, Stevie.' A smile played about her lips. 'We got a call from a couple who'd been away for the weekend. Came back last Sunday night to their Kelvinside flat. Turns out a burglar had broken in on the Friday after they left. But here's the thing. They have a dog, a big black evil mutt.' She brought her face close to Steve's. 'The minute the burglar's feet landed on the sitting-room carpet, the dog jumped on him and sat on his chest. Whenever the man tried to move, the dog growled and made it clear he meant business. But, if the man lay still, he sat on him and didn't do anything except lick his face. He had to stay like that all weekend till the Mr and Mrs showed up. Worse than being banged up, the poor laddie said.' She was laughing openly now. 'Never seen anything like it in all my days.'

'Nice one, Bridge.' Steve's smile faded. 'So how are things with the DCI?'

'He's just so much piss and wind. Heard his latest idea? Dress Down Day.' She looked around the room. 'I'm not sure how anyone would tell the difference, to be honest.'

Steve ducked as a paper aeroplane flew past his head. 'And how's your daughter doing?'

'She's grand. The wee cracker's finally got her man. She's tying the knot next month,' Bridget added with pride.

'Tying the noose, you mean,' someone chipped in.

'Hold your wheesht.' Bridget Kelly's views on the sanctity of marriage were well known to her colleagues, most of whom were in live-in relationships. She'd been happily married for thirty years, a record by the standards of the force. 'So, Stevie,' she said, studying his face, 'how have you been, yourself?' She glanced at his leg. 'I couldn't help noticing the limp's still there.'

'I'm fine.'

She nodded, but Steve knew she wasn't fooled, she'd been with him when it happened. He turned away so she couldn't see his expression. They'd been tipped off that Triad gangster Tommy Teoh Lau was meeting with a member of a rival gang in a Chinese restaurant in the Garnethill area. Strathclyde police had infiltrated the restaurant and planted microphones, intending to record the conversation but, instead of making the collar, they found they'd been betrayed. Steve closed his eyes, remembering the screams as Lau's Chinese hardmen crashed through the flimsy partition. In the chaos, one officer was killed and Steve, ignoring orders to get the hell out of there, was shot in the leg. He would have died had his colleagues not dragged him away. Their last sight was of Tommy Teoh Lau being driven away in a black limousine.

Bridget's voice dragged him from his thoughts. 'You okay, Stevie?'

He turned to see her watching him, a surprisingly tender expression on her face.

'You're looking a wee bit peely-waly,' she said.

He smiled weakly. 'Nothing a glass of malt won't cure.'

'We'll get that hackit bastard one day, you know.'

'No, we won't. He'll get us.'

'Ach, pish. Tommy Teoh Lau's as good as in the bag.'

Tommy Teoh Lau. Except no-one called him that. He was known as Snake Eyes, a name that described perfectly his watchful unblinking stare. His Glasgow crime career began as an enforcer for the biggest and most powerful Triad gang. But it wasn't long before he tired of targeting Chinese restaurateurs for protection money, and cast his skin, leaving to form his own syndicate. Aye, and that had been the start of all their woes. Snake Eyes was smart enough to recognise the need for a legitimate face, and so he set up businesses in the entertainment industry, fronts for tax evasion and money laundering. Within a few years, he'd slithered up the ladder again, this time taking a large slice of the Glasgow drug trade, particularly the club drug,

Ecstasy, a growing market standing in the hundreds of millions.

'You any nearer to tracking down his source?' Steve said.

'We're following a lead.'

'And where's it taking you?'

'Here and there.'

He knew Bridget had nothing. Lau was getting his Ecstasy from somewhere in the far east, China most likely, and no-one had a clue how it was coming in. He straightened his shoulders. 'So what have you got for me on Jamie Dyer?'

She seemed glad of the change of subject. 'Orders came down from upstairs. We're working together on this one.'

'Suits me fine.'

She put on a pair of red-framed reading glasses and rummaged through her papers. 'When we heard that two employees from the same company had been murdered, we asked ourselves the obvious question. What links them? There's only the paintballing and the fact that they worked at the same plant.'

'They were killed while paintballing. It suggests that's the link. But maybe not. Anyone at work have a grudge against them?'

'We're still conducting the interviews. But, so far, they've come up squeaky clean. The victims were both well liked, although they didn't socialise much with the others. None of the workers at the plant could tell us much about them, to be honest.'

'If it was a contract, it's unlikely to be a simple grudge.'

'Our thoughts exactly, Stevie. Given the nature of the business, we thought maybe it was something to do with the medications they manufacture.' She handed him a folder. 'Here's the Fraud Squad report.'

He read the notes carefully. As Jamie Dyer was Bayne Pharmaceuticals' UK import/export manager, the Fraud Squad assumed the motive for the murder had to do with the theft of Bayne's medications. So far, they'd found no evidence to support their theory. If Dyer was guilty, he'd done a perfect snow job. Steve frowned. He was always out of his depth with white-collar crimes. Aye, give him a good clean aggravated assault any day.

'How do you go about stealing company drugs, Bridge? So it doesn't show up?'

'Don't ask me. The lady auditor I had a chat with, a bit of a nippy sweetie I should say, started to tell me all about the export trade, but it went over my head. All I know is that the Glasgow plant manufactures a huge range of medications, many of them expensive. Too expensive for our wee NHS.'

'If there's no evidence, why do the Fraud Squad boys think there was a medications theft?'

'It's what the DCI thinks. There's big money involved in pharmaceuticals and it would tie in with a contract killer doing the job.'

'The lengths some pharmaceutical companies go to to make money stick in my craw. I'm not sure whose side we should be on here.'

'There's only one side to be on, Stevie – the winning side.'

One of the sergeants approached them. He was a lad with ginger hair and a complexion that suggested he lived on a diet of bridies and beans. He looked young enough to be Steve's son. Aye, after six months away from the place, they all did.

Bridget waved the lad off. 'Away you go, now, the grown-ups are talking.' The sergeant grinned and left with the others.

Steve scanned the rest of the report. The Fraud Squad had also investigated Bruce Lassiter. He was an engineer who was responsible for the quality of the finished product and ensuring the correct batches were made ready for export. It was Jamie Dyer who handled the export paperwork and had everything made ready for shipping. Steve thought about the identical way they'd been killed. If they were working a scam together, and someone got wind of it and didn't like it, it would explain the murders. The mobile phone records were clean, though, and there were no repeated calls from one particular number. There was also nothing in either Jamie's or Bruce's bank accounts to suggest they were up to something, although if they were good enough to hide a medications scam they'd have little difficulty hiding the money. The problem was how to proceed. It was easier to drink the Clyde than to uncover an illegal racket in Glasgow. But something bothered him.

'They may just not be guilty, Bridge.'

'Guilty?' She rolled her eyes. 'Course they're guilty. Is the Pope a Catholic?'

'Something linked them, for sure, but it may not be anything to do with their work.'

'Maybe we'll have to dig deeper, then. Right down into their lives.'

Easier said than done. He knew what it would take to prise open the shell of Jamie Dyer's and Bruce Lassiter's private lives. In his many years as a detective, he'd discovered how little the next of kin and close friends know about the affairs of the deceased.

He handed back the report. 'We found a phone number in Bruce Lassiter's effects. It led us to a man called Gavvo Skelton.'

'We've had a chat with him. He and Lassiter were in a relationship. Skelton was fair cut up, although he seems to have got over it quickly. He was back at work the next day. I suppose he has to keep the gym going.' She shook her head. 'He's a puzzle to me, Stevie. We didn't really hit it off. You might do better. Skelton clammed up when I tried to probe. Grief perhaps. Or ... '

'He's guilty as sin.' Steve gazed out of the window across the ribbon of the Clyde, south towards the Victorian buildings and large green spaces of Pollokshields. 'So what's his background?'

'Until three years ago, he was in the SAS.'

'I'll go to the gym now. Boxing clubs are always open on a Friday night.' He hesitated. 'You coming?'

She took off her reading glasses. 'Sorry, Stevie, but my man is having his mother over. I need to get home.'

He nodded. He wouldn't want to get between Bridget and her man. Both of them hailed from a part of Glasgow whose people meant business.

She was frowning. 'You sure you want to go alone? Skelton got a wee bitty nasty when I tried to quiz him about his relationship with Lassiter.' She seemed to consider what she'd said. 'But a man like you could go ten rounds with him, no bother,' she added hastily.

'Yeah, right,' Steve said, smiling. 'It's okay, Bridge. I'll go on my own.' He shrugged. 'Who dares wins.'

Glasgow had been blanketed with thick cloud the entire day, and now the heavens surrendered and released a gigantic bucket of water over the city. Steve paid the cab driver who was shouting the fare over the drumming of rain on the car's roof. He tilted his face to the sky. His Mammy had always said you couldn't beat a cracking west-coast downpour. Aye, those softies in Edinburgh had no idea what feechy weather was.

Gavvo Skelton's boxing gym was off Springburn Road on the north side of Glasgow. Steve knew this area well, having been brought up in nearby Keppochhill Road. He also knew of this club, one of the oldest in the city.

The wind was strengthening, and curtains of rain blew across the street as he struggled up the steps of the rose-coloured Victorian building. Two lads who looked about fourteen ran past him inside. They didn't give him or his limp a second glance, something for which he was grateful. He followed them down a narrow white-tiled corridor past a sign to the Physiotherapy Room, and pushed through the swing door into

St Mungo's Boxing Club.

The room was large with a soaring ceiling but, despite the size, there was a strong smell of male sweat. Newspaper cuttings and autographed photographs of boxers in pugilistic poses covered the custard-yellow walls. A machine selling bottles of water and sports drinks stood near the fire exit, below a large sign warning the punters to wear gumshields and headguards at all times when sparring.

Swearing that blued the air mingled with the shouts and laughter. Teenage boys, some with hoods up, were working at a row of ceiling-mounted punch bags. Their trainer, an athletic grey-haired man, walked up and down behind them, adjusting their stances and bawling words of encouragement. A couple of lads punched away at free-standing bags shaped like torsos; others worked with pairs of pads held by their partners; and some trained on their own, hammering away at speed balls. Boys stood in rows in front of the wall-length mirror, watching their footwork and throwing punches with bandaged hands.

No-one paid Steve any attention. He joined a group seated around the blue-roped boxing ring.

Two men were sparring, watched by a woman referee. One spectator kept yelling instructions to someone called Lennie; they consisted of keeping his elbow up, pivoting on his back foot, and using his hips more. Judging by the scowls he threw the man, Lennie would be the one in the black-and-gold boxing shorts.

Steve followed the fight, curious despite himself. Lennie, clearly the younger and better built of the two, was no match for his companion. Steve watched in admiration as Lennie was outmanoeuvred and generally outboxed. Aye, it all came down to technique, with boxing as with everything.

The bout finished with a flurry of activity on the part of the older man. The woman stepped forward and, lifting his arm, declared him the winner. Steve caught the words, 'Well played, Gavvo.'

After giving Lennie a good-natured thump on the arm, Gavvo Skelton climbed out of the ring. He removed his gumshield and headguard, giving Steve a good view of the restless eyes, pockmarked skin, and pinched lips. It was a face only a mother could love. And maybe Bruce Lassiter.

'Mr Skelton?' Steve said, standing up. 'Could I have a word?'

Gavvo Skelton gave him the once-over while the woman untied his boxing gloves. 'I've already spoken to the Keystone Kops,' he said, taking a towel and rubbing it over his neck. 'I've nothing more to add.' His voice was like sandpaper. The London accent was like Von's.

'I'm from Lothian and Borders, Mr Skelton. Detective Inspector Steve English. I was there when they found Bruce's body.'

Skelton was slipping into a dressing gown. He stiffened, and then his shoulders sagged.

'Perhaps we could go somewhere and talk,' Steve said gently.

'Okay, mate. My office?'

'Lead the way.'

Gavvo Skelton's office was so small it could have been a broom cupboard. A glass partition separated it from the gym. Steve squeezed himself behind the tiny table and pulled out the rickety chair, his back to the glass. Skelton took the chair opposite.

A photograph of two men perched on the bonnet of a car was pinned to the noticeboard. Gavvo Skelton, in black jeans and brick-red sweater, had an arm round a smiling Bruce Lassiter. Lassiter was sitting with his knees under his chin. He was without socks and the laces of his plimsolls were looped round his ankles.

'That's a recent photo,' Skelton said, nodding at the wall. 'I think it's the last we had taken of ourselves.' He met Steve's gaze. 'You said you were there.'

Steve knew what he wanted to know. 'He died instantaneously, Mr Skelton.'

The man laughed harshly. 'Don't talk to me about death, mate, I've seen more of it than you ever will. I've spent my working life in Northern Ireland. For your information, death is never instantaneous.'

'You know the details of how Bruce died?'

'Yeah. Double tap.' His mouth tightened. 'Could have been worse, I suppose. He could have stepped on a mine.'

The man seemed in control but underneath he was a coiled spring. If touched the wrong way, he'd untwist and bounce off the walls.

'You were in the SAS, I understand. What made you leave?'

'That's easy. The Good Friday Agreement. Peace in our time, and all that. A lot of us left then. And not a day too soon,' he added under his breath. 'Seems like a century ago, but it was 1998. Three years ago.'

There was resentment in his voice and Steve wondered whether the peace agreement was the real reason he'd left. Maybe his mates had discovered his homosexuality.

'And that's when you met Bruce?'

'Yeah. I started up the gym.' Skelton smoothed his blond hair. 'He joined soon after.'

'He was interested in boxing?'

'I think he was more interested in keeping himself healthy. Fit as a butcher's dog, he was.'

'I expect Detective Inspector Kelly has already asked you this but why do *you* think he was killed?' Steve kept his expression open, hoping to win the man's confidence. 'You'll appreciate we're only at the start of our investigation.'

'There was no-one at the club who'd want to mark his dance card. As I said, he wasn't interested in sparring, he simply wasn't competitive that way. He came mainly to work out. Anyway, pissing up the wall higher than the next man isn't the kind of attitude I try to foster here.' He looked over Steve's shoulder into the gym. 'This part of Glasgow's like a demilitarised zone. We get a lot of young lads who are on the road to a life of crime. Learning to box gives them a sense of purpose, a sense of self-worth. I try to teach them to respect their opponents in the ring and not to hammer them senseless. All I can do is hope they'll take those values out onto the street.'

'I notice you have boys who can't be more than ten or eleven.'

'That's the age to catch them, mate. Before they learn to use a knife. Or start doing Es, or dealing. If I suspect there's any of that going on, I have a long talk with them.' He gave Steve a hard look. 'On the subject of Ecstasy, what's Strathclyde's finest doing about putting away that piece of Chinese filth? The one who's pushing his shit all over Glasgow.'

Steve gazed at the wall. Skelton made putting the Chinaman away sound so easy. But to send Snake Eyes down for a serious stretch, they had to link him to illegal drugs, and they still hadn't traced the source of his brand of Ecstasy. It was a version stronger than the usual stuff pushed on the streets, and its takers were prepared to pay well over the odds for the extra high.

'We're doing everything we can, Mr Skelton.'

'Sure you are.' The smile failed to reach his eyes, and Steve knew what the man had seen: the resignation on his own face. He felt like a total failure. Yet they'd tried everything, even turning to Snake Eyes' other criminal activities, the sex saunas and dogfighting rings, in the hope they'd find victims or witnesses to testify. But no-one ever made an official complaint. The Chinaman's name would induce instant amnesia. When he walked down the streets of Glasgow's Chinatown, pavements would clear like the parting of the Red Sea.

'We're like a family here,' Skelton was saying. 'Some of these kids have never had anyone in their corner. I'm the big yin, as you guys say. I look out for everyone. And I teach them to roll with the punches. That Liaison Officer they assigned after Bruce died keeps harping on at me to take time off, but how can I? The lads here depend on me. Anyway, work's the best way of coping. I learnt that in Northern Ireland.'

Steve needed to stretch his leg under the table but his knees were touching Skelton's. 'Let me ask you something, Mr Skelton. What was Bruce's and Jamie Dyer's relationship?' He chose the word deliberately.

'Bruce had no relationship with Jamie Dyer,' the man said, bristling.

'I meant at work.'

'Yeah, right.' He glanced at the photo as if to reassure himself it was still there. 'I can't tell you anything about his work. It's not a world I'm interested in.'

'But you've met Jamie Dyer.'

'I saw him at paintballing tournaments. I never met him. Or the others.'

'Which others?'

'Dyer's sister and that toff who lives in a church.'

'Ranald McCrea.'

Skelton snorted. 'Bruce was keen I meet them but I always managed to get out of it. From what he said, they struck me as the types who want to run with the big dogs and don't care how they do it.'

'And Bruce wasn't like that?'

He kept his voice level. 'Bruce wasn't like that.'

'Have you ever been paintballing, Mr Skelton?'

'Never could see the attraction. All that red paint . . . ' He wiped his mouth. 'But Bruce loved the game. He was mad about it.'

'Why didn't he join a club in Glasgow?'

'You know what the world of business is like, mate. You're always going from one office to another. Bruce worked a lot out of the Livingston place so he joined a club there. He always kept his trainers with him – everything else you get from the club.'

Steve's leg was aching badly. 'Sorry,' he said, smiling. 'I need to stretch.' He stood up and massaged his calf.

Skelton nodded at the leg. 'We can have a walk around, if you like.'

'I'm okay now, but thanks.' He squeezed himself back into the chair.

'I guess you're looking for a motive,' Skelton said, his voice flat.

'We're trying to establish what linked Bruce to Jamie. The work's the obvious thing.'

'I've asked myself that question a thousand times. Work and paintballing. That's what they had in common. Paintballing was the main event, though.'

'Who knew that Bruce would be going paintballing that Tuesday? If we knew that, we'd get somewhere. You realise, Mr Skelton, I have to ask whether *you* knew.'

'I didn't, as a matter of fact.' He smiled, not in an unfriendly way. 'Nice try but you'll need to get back into your corner and prepare for round two.'

'But you know how to deliver a double tap. A former SAS man is trained to kill professionally.'

To Steve's surprise, Skelton grinned broadly. 'You've come out fighting. Good on yer, mate. And I thought you were a bit of a lightweight. That's exactly the question I'd be asking. But I have a cast-iron alibi, I was here all day Tuesday.' He nodded towards the partition. 'There are any number of witnesses can testify I was in the ring at lunchtime.'

'I keep coming back to where Jamie and Bruce were killed,' Steve said, after a pause. 'Don't you think it's funny that a professional would come all the way from Glasgow to do it?'

'Funny, mate? I'm having hysterics.' He looked at Steve as though amazed the detective hadn't worked it out for himself. 'That's an easy one. The killer would have come from Edinburgh. A shooter wouldn't lug a piece from Glasgow to Edinburgh and back again.'

It made sense. And suddenly Steve knew that Skelton was right. Whoever had made the contract had found himself a local man.

'Want to know how I'd do it?' Skelton was saying, 'I'd be watching the mark's movements till I knew him better than he knew himself. Then I'd choose the spot for the kill. That's right, mate, a pro job is never left to chance, it's always the killer who chooses the time and the place.' He sneered. 'You're used to dealing with, what do you call them? crimes of passion. Some missus doing in her old man with a rolling pin, or a husband losing it and killing his wife's fancy man. Bet you catch those every time.' He shook his head slowly. 'But this guy planned it well in advance. And he's going to be a bugger to track down.'

'But there were two marks.'

'And that's much harder because you can't guarantee they'll be at the same place at the same time. If it were me, I'd take them out at separate times and in different places. Or, if it had to be done simultaneously, I'd get in a second man. But from what your DI told me, they were killed one right after the other and in the same place.' His eyes narrowed. 'That would take extraordinary planning.'

When it was clear the man was saying nothing more, Steve got to his feet. 'I think that's everything, Mr Skelton. You've been very helpful.'

'No, I haven't, mate.'

Steve opened the door to the gym. 'I don't suppose you know anyone who'd take a contract, either in Glasgow or in Edinburgh?' He tried to keep his tone light, knowing the question was likely to give offence.

'You think some of my former SAS pals are in that line of business?' Skelton said, following him out.

'Are they?'

'I wouldn't know. I've cut my ties with all that. I don't even go to the reunions.'

They were standing by the mirrored wall.

'You married, Inspector?' Skelton said suddenly.

He smiled. 'Not even a bidey-in.'

'Bruce and I were as good as. He was a lovely man. Very caring. When I met him, I thought I'd finally found the person I'd spend the rest of my life with. You know, go the distance? But killing someone like him, it's enough to make you get religion.' Despair filled his eyes. 'There's never a right time for anyone to die, is there? There are so many things I wish I'd said to him. I'd give anything to bring him back and just have a five-minute conversation. Five minutes. That's all I'd need. And I'll never have that.'

He collapsed into a chair and gave himself up loudly to his grief. A hush descended in the gym as people stopped what they were doing. They stared, some openly, some with sidelong glances, at the hard man, the former SAS soldier, sobbing like a woman.

Steve walked across the room, banged his fist into a speed ball, and left.

Chapter 15

After Steve had left for Glasgow, Von lingered outside the National Gallery, enjoying the sun on her face. She'd rung Swankie and Vale and left her boss a message reporting the sighting of Phil Pattullo, but they both knew the case would remain open until she brought Mrs Pattullo face to face with her son. The chances of that were looking increasingly unlikely. Even if she found Phil again, there was no guarantee she could persuade him to see his mother. The alternative, less appealing, was to take Mrs Pattullo to Dean Cemetery. But would he greet his mother with open arms? She pictured the scene: Phil fleeing, Mrs Pattullo crying after him in desperation, confusion on her face, the stone angels looking on.

She brushed the dust from her jeans. Whatever she decided, she had to let Mrs Pattullo know her son was alive and well.

A few minutes later, she was outside the Balmoral's revolving doors. Across the road, next to the statue of the Duke of Wellington, a troupe of Latin American Indians was playing drums and panpipes, drowning out the trendy bagpipe music from the Scotch House. She glanced towards the Disney Store, hoping to catch a glimpse of Mhairi, but the crowd of lunchtime shoppers was too thick.

Inside the Balmoral, she asked the receptionist if she could have a few words with Mrs Pattullo who worked as a chef. The man, tall and narrow-shouldered, with close-set eyes, looked at her as though she were something stuck to his shoe.

'Mrs Pattullo is busy.' He smiled coldly, and drew himself up. 'We're serving lunch.'

She tried to look perplexed. 'But I rang ahead,' she lied, 'and the manager told me it would be okay because she'd be on her break.'

He drew his brows together, tapping a pen against his teeth.

'Perhaps you could phone the kitchens and ask her to come up. I need five minutes, no more.' She opened her eyes wider. 'Or maybe I should speak directly to the manager?'

That did it. The receptionist sighed theatrically and put the call through. As she waited, leafing through magazines, she felt the man's eyes boring into the back of her head.

A minute later, the lift doors opened and an anxious Mrs Pattullo appeared. She wore a white coat, buttoned to the neck, her name embroidered in red on the pocket. Her hair was hidden under a chef's hat.

Seeing Von, her look of anxiety turned to one of terror.

'Phil's fine,' Von said quickly, steering the woman away from the reception. 'I've just this minute seen him.'

'Oh, thank God,' Mrs Pattullo said, closing her eyes. Her face was sickly grey. She leant against the table, disturbing the newspapers.

'I saw him at Dean Cemetery. Do you know why he'd want to go there?'

'Dean Cemetery? I've no idea. You're sure it were him, like?'

Von described Phil's clothes and his general appearance.

'Yes, that's me Phil all right.' The woman took out a handkerchief and wiped her eyes. 'I don't know how to thank you, Miss Valenti.'

'Well, don't thank me till we've got him back. I'll go there again and see if I can find him.'

She seemed to realise what this meant. 'He didn't want to come back, did he?'

Von ran a hand over the back of her head. A nice lump was forming. 'I think he has his reasons for wanting to stay hidden,' she said gently. 'Mrs Pattullo, is there anything you haven't told me? About the cemetery, maybe? It would help if I knew why Phil was there.'

'The cemetery? I think he goes because it's a peaceful place. He told me once the angels weren't like the others. Full of love and happiness. I went meself to see what he was talking about.' She smiled weakly. 'It's pretty, Dean Village, isn't it? We do the odd private catering there. There are some grand houses on the other side of Dean Path, like. Buckingham Terrace and Belgrave Crescent.'

'Did Phil ever mention going paintballing?'

'Not to me. Why do you ask?'

'Word on the street is he made some friends who were going to take him. There's a place out near Livingston.' She stopped herself in time. She had no intention of telling Mrs Pattullo the name of the paintballing club. The deaths of Jamie Dyer and Bruce Lassiter were all over the newspapers, and the last thing she wanted was his mother jumping to conclusions.

'He's made some friends, then. That's something, isn't it?' The woman seemed lost in her reverie. A cough from the receptionist brought her out of it. 'You will let me know when you've brought him back, like? Doesn't matter what time of day or night.'

'Of course,' Von said, squeezing her arm.

She watched the woman hurry towards the lifts. Something about their conversation stirred a forgotten memory.

Buckingham Terrace and Belgrave Crescent.

Belgrave Crescent.

She laid her Edinburgh streetfinder on the table. Belgrave Crescent was a stone's throw from Dean Path and Dean Cemetery. But she hadn't been down that street this morning;

she'd gone to the cemetery via Dean Bridge and the Queensferry Road. No, she knew Belgrave Crescent in another connection entirely.

She stared at the map for several seconds, and then pulled out her notebook.

And there it was. The address. Ex-directory, but she'd traced it the day before.

Her heart was clubbing away in her chest. For the first time since she'd taken this case, she saw a chink of light.

She was sure now, as sure as she was that Phil Pattullo was alive, that there was a link between her case and Steve's.

Half an hour later, Von was nearing Lexie Dyer's house. The sun was high, the light touching the curving sweep of amber-coloured stone. Belgrave Crescent, one of Edinburgh's most elegant streets, glowed in the early afternoon.

Von's original plan had been to visit Lexie at work, but a call to Bayne Pharmaceuticals told her that Ms Dyer had taken this Friday off. Was she playing the role of the grieving sister and stopping at home? That could work to Von's advantage. Far better to beard her in her den; Lexie in her natural habitat would disclose more about herself.

On the pretext of checking her phone, she leant against the railings of the Crescent's communal gardens and examined the building opposite. Lexie's flat consisted of the basement and ground floor of the house at the corner with Belgrave Place. A pair of boot scrapers stood at the top of the steps, partly obscured by pots of lobelia. Ivy climbed up the walls, past the front door, and twined around the balustrade of the first-floor balcony.

She crossed the street and glanced over the wrought-iron railing. The basement window boxes were planted with pink and white surfinia. A curled garden hose lay in the lane connecting the terrace's buildings. She turned left, and sauntered nonchalantly past the houses until the pavement ended at a cluster of hydrangea bushes and a rough stone wall. Standing on tiptoe, she looked over. A grassy slope. And then Dean Path. She was close to the cemetery.

Back at Lexie's flat, she peered into the windows. There was no-one home. She climbed the steps to the front door and tried to see through the engraved glass.

An engine sputtered behind her. She wheeled round and saw a large van with the words, We Cater For Everyone – Frankie Goes To Houses. The vehicle stopped and a girl in a black shirt and trousers jumped out. She smoothed strands of dark hair away from her face.

'Are you Iris? Steph's friend?' she said in a ringing voice. Without waiting for a reply, she threw open the van's back doors. 'Steph wasn't sure if you'd got her message.'

Her companion scrambled out of the van. She had cinnamon-coloured hair and was similarly dressed. The two girls began to unload trays of food.

'Come on, Iris,' the first girl shouted, 'give us a hand. We've a lot to do before Miss Dyer's party gets back.'

Miss Dyer. It was risky, but . . . 'No problem,' Von said, taking a tray.

'I'm Frankie, by the way. And this is Elen.'

They exchanged smiles.

'Hold on, you can't go in wearing that,' Elen said, motioning to Von's leather jacket. 'I guess Steph didn't tell you about the dress code. What have you got on underneath?'

Von slipped off her jacket.

The girls looked doubtful.

'The black jeans will be okay, I suppose,' Frankie said, 'but the white T-shirt is a bit of a no-no.'

'We keep a spare black shirt in the glove compartment. Half a tic.' Elen ran round to the front and returned with a blouse.

'Her bust's too large,' Frankie said promptly.

Elen tilted her head. 'Is that all you, or are you wearing padded?'

'All me,' Von said. She fingered the blouse. 'It's a zip, not buttons. Provided I don't do anything too athletic, I'll be okay.'

The girls grinned. 'You can change in the house,' Frankie said. She climbed the steps and inserted a key into the lock.

The door opened onto a long corridor fitted with a deep-blue Persian carpet. The carved chairs lining one wall were reflected in the bevelled mirror opposite.

Frankie turned left into a sitting room that could have contained Von's flat twice over. Von stared into the pink ceiling with its ornate white cornice. A crystal chandelier hung from a gigantic ceiling rose.

'There's a loo down the corridor if you want to change there,' Elen said in a tone that suggested Von get a move on. She and Frankie laid the trays on the sideboard and left to fetch the rest.

The loo was at the top of the stairs leading to the basement. The toilet, bidet and wash-hand basin were in aquatint colours and the walls were decorated in pale green Toile de Jouy wallpaper. The toilet seat was up.

Von changed quickly, wondering what she would say if the real Iris phoned or even showed up. It sounded, though, as if Steph hadn't made a firm arrangement. She decided that, if Iris arrived, she'd say she was unemployed and saw a chance for some work. She was getting Frankie out of a hole, and maybe the girl would appreciate that.

She took a deep breath and zipped up the blouse; it was tight over her bust but not outrageously so. She joined the girls outside, throwing her handbag, T-shirt and jacket into the back of the van, and they hurried to transfer the trays and boxes to the sitting room.

When everything was to Frankie's satisfaction, she said to

Von, 'You know what to do?'

'Steph did tell me, but remind me again?'

'Nothing to it. If no-one's eating, circulate with the trays but don't keep pestering people. Above all, though, make sure glasses are kept filled.'

'Got it.'

'Look pleasant but don't smile too much. Remember they've come back from a memorial service.'

A memorial service. So Lexie was honouring her brother today.

Frankie prowled around the room, straightening trays and giving the glasses a polish with the hem of her shirt. 'Right, Iris, we need to get rid of the boxes. We'll stash them in the kitchen.'

The kitchen, at the end of the corridor, was only slightly smaller than the sitting room. It could have been a showroom; the surfaces were spotless, the chrome gleaming. 'Don't you just love this?' Frankie said, running a hand over the oak table. Von wondered if Lexie ever used it, the smell of polish was so strong. It was more likely she ate from the breakfast bar, assuming she ate here at all.

'Now, Miss Dyer's particular about her carpets,' Frankie was saying. 'If there's a wine spill, and it always happens, this is where you'll get the stuff to deal with it.' She tapped a large salt cellar. 'Salt for red wine. If it's white, use detergent.'

'Copy that.'

She glanced at her watch. 'We've got fifteen minutes.' Her eyes rested on Von. 'Take a look around if you like, but be back by three.'

'Will do.'

In the corridor, Von peered into the Adam-style dining room, seeing her tentative reflection in the fine gilded mirror above the fireplace. The curved walls were decorated with elaborate plaster swags in pastel shades of pea green and lemon yellow. Arabesque vine scrolls curled across the ceiling.

She went systematically through the rooms on the ground floor. Of the two bedrooms, the one at the back was unused. The front bedroom was a large en-suite with an eau-de-nil colour scheme. The occupant was either a bit of a slob or had been in a hurry that morning. The quilted bedspread was nearly off the bed and the crumpled peach nightdress was on the floor, partly covering the fur-trimmed mule slippers. An Escada perfume bottle sat on the dressing table amid the scatter of Chanel cosmetics. Wardrobes had been fitted along two of the walls. One was crammed with colourful designer dresses of the kind you see on a catwalk, and the other contained sober business suits. She ran a hand over the material of a strapless cream dress, enjoying the sensation of silk on skin. But where did Lexie keep the clothes she wore at the weekend? Probably in the spare bedroom like everyone else.

She was leaving the room when a flash of metal caught her eye. A pair of green-and-gold trainers lay under the chair. She crouched to get a look at the label. Andrea Sibillini. Lexie Dyer took a size six-and-a-half.

Frankie caught her in the corridor. 'Rattle your dags, Iris, the cars have arrived.'

Dark forms were climbing the steps to the front door. She hurried into the sitting room and took her place at the sideboard.

Elen gave her a grin. 'All right?'

'Fine.' People were milling in the hall. 'How many are we expecting?'

'Dunno, but it always feels like hundreds.'

As the first guests drifted through the door, Frankie stepped forward with a tray of filled glasses.

'So who are they all?' Von murmured.

'People from work, I think. But see that guy? The gorgeous

one with the hair gel?' Elen glanced at her, smirking. 'Eyes back in, girl. He's a famous paintballer. You wouldn't think it to look at her but Lexie Dyer goes paintballing.'

'And which one is Lexie Dyer?'

'The blonde in the killer dress.'

She followed the direction of Elen's gaze. A tall high-breasted woman in a knee-length black dress and slingback shoes was greeting people. Her hair was piled up in the style that looks as though it's about to come down, which meant she'd have spent ages on it. Her face, all eyes and mouth, was set off to best advantage with smoky eye makeup and pale-pink lipstick. Frankie approached with a tray. Lexie lifted a languid hand, the fingers tipped with acrylic nails, and took a glass.

'Does she live alone?' Von said.

'As far as I know.' At a nod from Frankie, Elen nudged her. 'Come on, Iris, we need to look sharp. You take this half of the room and I'll do the other.'

Von picked up a tray of open seafood sandwiches and offered them around, trying to make herself as inconspicuous as possible. The guests chatted in hushed tones and no-one gave her a second glance. She and Elen continued to serve food and fill glasses for the best part of an hour and, as the wine hit the spot, the mood of the room became noticeably lighter.

After she'd completed a particularly slow circuit, Frankie caught her eye and signalled to the window. The guests there were standing with empty glasses, and Elen had left the room.

Von picked up a bottle and made her way over. A tight group, which included the gel-haired paintballer, was listening to a small-boned man with a droopy moustache. The paintballer motioned to her and stepped back, holding out his glass. In the split second he took to lift his arm, she saw the man standing next to him. Ranald McCrea had his eyes on the speaker. And he was playing with an empty glass.

She caught her breath. Jesus, she should have known he'd be at this reception. If he saw her, the game would be up; no amount of invention would get her out of this one. She was tempted to ditch the bottles and run.

The paintballer tapped McCrea's arm. 'Top-up, Ranald?'

Ranald was turning his head when there was an almighty crash. Elen was standing at the door, fingertips pressed against her lips, eyes squeezed shut. She'd dropped a tray of glasses. From the colour of the spill, they'd held red wine.

'Gosh, that was spectacular,' Lexie said into the silence.

Von seized her chance. She ducked her head and pushed through the guests. 'I'll deal with this, Miss Dyer,' she said, taking the trembling Elen by the arm. She steered her out of the room and into the kitchen. 'You get the salt, Elen, and I'll clear up the glass.'

They returned to a room full of guests chatting contentedly. A pink-cheeked Frankie was moving amongst them with a tray of tiny coffee meringues. She threw Von a thin-lipped smile. Ranald McCrea was still riveted by Moustache Man. He brushed the hair off his brow, nodding thoughtfully.

Von dropped to her knees and swept up the shards of glass. A shadow fell across the carpet. She looked up to see Lexie Dyer holding a wineglass. Close to, the woman was seductive with the sort of cold beauty that attracts men. Her eyes were clear and unnaturally bright, and she didn't look like a sister mourning her brother.

'I don't think there's any damage done, do you?' Lexie's expression changed to one of gratitude. 'You were awfully quick to act. You've saved that carpet, you know.'

Von smiled, saying nothing.

'You're new, aren't you?'

'Iris, Steph's friend,' she said, hoping this strand of the conversation would go no further.

'Ah, yes. Steph.'

She held up the dustpan. 'Well, I'd better get rid of this.' But Lexie was already moving away.

Elen was shaking salt over the carpet, her shoulders slumped. She rolled her eyes at Von and mouthed, 'Thank you'.

Von dumped the glass into the kitchen bin. She tiptoed into the corridor and listened. A satisfied buzz came from the sitting room. No-one would miss her for a few minutes.

She made for the stairs.

The basement ceiling was low and only a little light filtered from under the closed doors. These would be the original servants' quarters.

She had no time to lose. Opening doors systematically, she glanced into the rooms. The first was piled floor to ceiling with garden furniture: green rattan chairs, a torn parasol, a croquet set. A door in the far wall led to the basement lane; she could see the window boxes with the pink and white flowers. The second room was filled with functional bookcases stacked with encyclopedias.

But she was in luck with the third. It was what she called an IKEA bedroom, with white wood furniture. A crumpled pair of pyjamas and a scrunched red duvet lay on the floor beside the single bed. On the ledge above the wash-hand basin, there was a tube of Boots toothpaste and a shaving-foam aerosol. She glanced into the rubbish bin. Disposable razors.

A cheap desk and computer chair had been pushed into the corner. A PC sat on the desk, the screen glowing.

She opened the desk's left-hand drawers, starting from the bottom and leaving them open: biros, printer paper, a box of staples. The compartment on the right-hand side was tall enough to store box files, but it was empty. She tugged at the single shallow drawer. It was locked and the key was missing. She stared at it for several seconds. Then she closed the drawers with one decisive push of her arm.

The movement of the desk caused the screen to light up. As she leant over for a better look, she thought she felt something behind her. She whirled round. The door to the corridor was wide open. Yet she'd left it only slightly ajar.

Someone had been in the room with her.

The blood pounded in her head. Had someone followed her to the basement? But who? Lexie? Ranald McCrea? One of the guests?

Whoever it was had made no sound on the thick-piled carpets, had slipped down the stairs behind her, watched her open doors and nose around the rooms. Her sense of foreboding deepened. She remembered the cemetery and the same feeling of being watched, and saw again the crumbling tombstones, the swaying laurel branches, the brooding angels. And now, in this room, her fear returned with unexpected force. She stared through the door. The blackness of the corridor was like an open mouth. Was someone there? Was he waiting for her?

She crept across the carpet and forced herself to peer out. There were plenty of shadows where an assailant could be lurking. A voice in her head told her not to be ridiculous, that nothing would happen to her, but another voice told her to stay in the room.

She sat on the bed, massaging her temples, her eyes on the dark corridor. Was it her imagination or did she see the outline of a shape pass by? She sprang to her feet and rushed out of the room, beating at the blackness.

At the top of the stairs, she collapsed against the wall. Lexie was hurrying into the sitting room.

A hand was placed on her arm. 'You okay, Iris?' It was Frankie.

Von was gasping for breath and didn't answer immediately. 'I'm fine,' she murmured. 'Just a bit dizzy. No lunch.'

'They're beginning to wrap it up. I think there'll be a speech, followed by a toast, and then everyone's away.' Frankie looked at her searchingly. 'If you like, you can start loading the boxes in the kitchen. Elen and I can finish up in the sitting room.'

Von made a point of working slowly, ensuring she'd be in the kitchen until after the guests had gone. From her position at the table, she could see into the corridor. Ranald McCrea was the last to leave. He kissed Lexie on both cheeks, then whispered into her ear and they both laughed. Something made him glance in Von's direction but he looked away immediately. Had he seen her? He couldn't fail to have. But had he recognised her?

She helped Frankie and Elen load the boxes into the van. Lexie stood on the pavement watching them, a glass of white wine in her hand.

'Lovely flat, Miss Dyer,' Von said, meeting her gaze.

'It is, isn't it?'

'Do you live here alone?'

Her eyes widened. 'Gosh, that's rather direct but, yes, I do.' She paused. 'Why do you ask?'

'It seems too big for one person, that's all.'

She laughed. 'Well, thanks for helping out, Ellis,' she said, dismissing both her and the conversation. She straightened her sandal strap, and then tripped lightly up the steps.

Frankie had loaded the last of the boxes and was holding Von's handbag and clothes. Elen started the engine.

'No need to undress in the street,' Frankie said, smiling. 'Here's my card. You can drop the shirt off at the office.'

Von slipped into the jacket. 'Thanks.'

'You're not Iris, are you?' the girl said, counting out some notes. 'I don't know what your business is except that it's none of mine. You did a cracking good job in there and, as far as I'm concerned, that's the end of it.' She looked Von full in the face. 'I don't know what investigative reporters earn but if you're ever short of cash I'd hire you again. I'm sure it goes without saying that you'll slip the name of my firm into your article. We could use the publicity.' Her lips curved into a smile. 'So, I'll see you around.' The smile widened. 'Iris.'

Von watched the van drive away, relieved she'd been let off the hook. She ran a hand over her hair, wondering what aspect of her behaviour had raised Frankie's suspicions.

The sun had moved round the side of the building and was casting long shadows across the pavement. She stood for a while listening to the breeze, feeling it strengthen and set the garden's great trees swaying.

She thought back to her experience in the basement. Why had Lexie given no indication she'd followed her downstairs? Maybe she'd thought it too trivial to bother about; hired help nosing around the gentry's manor was hardly a hanging offence. But perhaps it was simpler than that: Lexie hadn't come from the basement, but had been coming out of the loo on the ground floor, and it had been someone else. As Von made her way into the centre of town, her mind drifted to what she'd seen through the railings as she was loading the van – the faint imprint of a face staring at her from a basement window. A face which had melted away.

She'd seen it before, in Dean Cemetery. Its owner had worn a yellow sweatshirt and baggy jeans.

Chapter 16

The sun was close to setting as Steve paid off the taxi. The downpour had spent itself, and the sun's last rays were skimming the underside of the clouds, painting them gold. There was a freshness after the rain, the scent of evergreen in the air.

When they were kids, Steve and his sister had taken the train to Kelvinside. Their eyes had widened on seeing grand houses, swanky cars, and children in fur-trimmed coats and leather shoes, but what had impressed him most was the absence of the outside cludgies with cut-up news-sheet for toilet paper. Somehow he couldn't see the coalman shouting 'coal and brickets' outside these houses. Aye, you had to be fair minted to live in Kelvinside. But that was the only visit he and his sister had ever made here: he could still remember how, when they returned, his Mammy had skelped his airse for buying train tickets with the money she'd given him for the messages.

Jamie Dyer's house in Cleveden Gardens was a two-storeyed rose sandstone villa set back from the road. It was built higher than its neighbours, as though saying, 'Look at me, I'm the king of the castle.' The garden consisted of a lawn sweeping down to immaculately-trimmed box hedges and a drive covered in translucent chipping, the chips so large they could have been ice. Unlike the other buildings in the street, which were screened from prying eyes by thick-packed clusters of trees, you could see up to the house. Which meant, of course, that the occupant could see anyone approaching from the road.

Steve climbed the short flight of steps behind the pillared gateposts and crunched his way to the front door. A solitary basket hung from a hook under the porch, the parched orange flowers straggling over the sides.

The brass knocker was in the shape of an *en pointe* ballet pump, a strange choice for a man, but maybe it had come with the house and Jamie simply hadn't got round to changing it. Steve unlocked the door and stepped into a hall tiled in black-and-cream squares. The room was comfortably large but the Venetian-red paint, bleeding away from the white-plaster coving and into the walls, made it look smaller.

He stopped and listened. An oak longcase clock with a face painted in delicate colours stood against the wall, ticking insistently. The two keyholes in the dial told him this was an eight-day clock, which required winding only once a week. No-one had thought to stop it after Jamie died. There was nothing else in the hall other than a coat-stand with integrated boot rack.

Steve opened the door to the living room, his eyes drawn immediately to the pink-and-black-spotted velvet curtains held back with pink-and-black-striped velvet ties. He looked away quickly so as not to get a migraine. The pale-pink carpet looked newly fitted (he thought of his own, stained and threadbare), with the pile so thick he was reluctant to step on it. He skirted the black glass coffee table, seeing his moving reflection in the polished surface. The lacquered pink baby grand in the bay window was positioned so the light would fall on the keys. But the lid was locked. Maybe Jamie couldn't play and the piano was for show. The room had that self-inflated look that said: I've got money and I don't care who knows it. He doubted he'd be the only person to find the pink-and-black colour scheme tasteless.

There were no books or magazines, no back numbers of newspapers, and no hi-fi. So what did Jamie do in this room? The bar in the corner and the wide-screen television above the blocked-off fireplace said it all. Yet the place looked newly decorated. There were no stains on the carpets, no marks on the pale-pink wallpaper. He inhaled deeply, as if he could absorb the very essence of the man and thereby uncover his secrets. Air freshener mingled with the faint smell of cigar smoke. But the black onyx ashtray was not only empty, it had been washed.

He crossed the hall to the dining room. It was more elegantly furnished, with painted apple-green walls and a dining suite in pale wood. An antique chicken-coop dresser leant against a wall, the space intended for chickens filled with linen.

The adjacent room had been set up as a study. There was a single object on the mahogany desk. He peered at the inscription on the silver trophy – Jamie Dyer's team had won the club's paintballing tournament the year before.

The walls were covered in bookshelves. Aha, so Jamie Dyer was an avid reader, like himself. The man had suddenly jumped a notch in his estimation. Steve had so many nineteenth-century novels that he'd had floor-to-ceiling bookcases built into the walls of his Garry Street apartment. After a long day at the station, he'd collapse onto the seat at the window and lose himself in Dostoevsky. He peered at the titles, noticing they repeated after a while. What he'd assumed to be rows of books was simply leather-embossed wallpaper. Dyer had kitted the room out only to look like a library.

The desk drawers contained the usual documents: old bills, television licence, and letters from the council. Motor vehicle documents were at the bottom. Steve raised his brows when he saw the insurance for the Maserati. Amongst the personal papers, he found a passport. He studied the photograph of the young man with the severe expression. The passport was due to expire in three months.

The kitchen was spotless. Everything had been put away. Even the tea towels had been laundered and folded into a neat pile. If he hadn't seen the documents in the study, he'd be asking himself whether anyone had ever lived here.

There were three bedrooms on the first floor. In two, the beds had been stripped. He pulled back the sheets in the third. They looked newly changed. He bent low, smelling floral washing conditioner. A large wardrobe in white lacquer towered over the rest of the furniture. He brought the sleeve of a light-grey jacket to his face and smelt the faint odour of dry-cleaning fluid, and then went through the suits, finding the same smell on them all. In the wardrobe's drawers, the vests and T-shirts had the same floral scent as the sheets. In his first year at Pitt Street, he'd had to question an obsessive-compulsive woman who couldn't stand dirt. Her house had been like this one. The minute he was out of the door, he heard her using the vacuum cleaner. He wondered what Bridget had made of this place.

The bathroom was predictably immaculate. The walls were lined with soft-focus photographs of nude women in sexual poses. In the centre of the room, an enamelled bath stood on clawed feet, a silver candlestick on the floor, the candle burnt to a stub. Against the wall, there were two free-standing wash-hand basins shaped like commas and, on the wooden rack underneath, a pile of folded towels. The unused shaving soap and bath gel on the shelf were by Carolina Herrera. The reek of disinfectant hung in the air.

He stared at himself in the mirror and a tired man stared back. Leaning in close, he studied the grey complexion and the tiny red threads in the eyes. The face swam in and out of focus. His eyelids started to droop.

The noise jolted him awake.

He listened, his nerve-endings jangling, and then took the stairs two at a time. It took him only a second to identify the source of the sound. He flung open the study door.

The phone stood on the floor behind the desk. It was one of

those retro Bakelite models with a front dial. But who would be phoning a dead man's house? For an instant, he thought it was Bridget, but dismissed the notion. Bridget phoned him on his mobile. And Bridget didn't know he was here.

He brought the receiver to his ear. Silence. And yet . . . Was it his imagination or could he hear the gentle rise and fall of someone breathing?

'Who is this?' he said.

A click. The phone was disconnected. In the sudden stillness, the ticking of the hall clock seemed unnaturally loud.

He sat in the chair, cradling the receiver to his chest, staring at the olive-green carpet. Someone didn't know that Jamie Dyer was dead. But who? The paintballers knew by now, as did his work colleagues. Then who had rung him? And why call the house? Why hadn't they tried him on his mobile? Ach, he was losing his touch. Of course, the police had Jamie's mobile. The caller must have tried that first, then called the house when there was no reply. He replaced the receiver. There would be a simple explanation: a friend or acquaintance who hadn't read the obituaries.

Tiredness was creeping up on him. Time to go home and crash out.

He was opening the front door when he noticed the coat-stand. A beige cashmere coat hung next to a green Barbour jacket. On an impulse, he searched the pockets. They were empty. No credit card stubs or cashpoint receipts. Not even a paper handkerchief. Blue wellingtons stood in the foot rack beside a pair of green-and-gold trainers.

Andrea Sibillinis.

What had Gavvo Skelton said? *Bruce worked a lot out of the Livingston place so he joined a club there. He always kept his trainers with him – everything else you get from the club.* Jamie, then, would also have paid special attention to his trainers, remembering to take them with him whenever he was playing. But he'd left these here on the day he was testing out new equipment, equipment which could have given him an edge in a tournament. *He was mad on paintballing.* Lexie's words. Aye, right enough, for someone mad on paintballing, who took every opportunity to play, picking up his trainers on the way out would have been second nature. Yet the one thing he'd needed to bring, he had left behind. What, then, was preying on his mind so much that day that he'd forgotten his Sibillinis?

Chapter 17
Saturday, June 9th

Von switched off the engine and jerked up the handbrake. She rested her hands on the steering wheel, studying the unimposing building behind the car park. Calder Rifle and Pistol Club was a two-storeyed red-brick box sitting amongst acres of grass. It was a Saturday and the place was at its busiest; she could hear the sound of pistol shots, even with the Ford's windows up. She'd done her homework and knew the club had an outdoor as well as an indoor range, but how long shooting would continue outside was anybody's guess – grey clouds were building up from the west.

Her appointment was with the chief instructor. She'd come early so she could think how best to make her approach because she had only a vague idea of why she was here. Yes, anything she learnt about the weapons and ammunition would help Steve but her main concern was Phil Pattullo.

She couldn't shake the feeling that something bizarre was going on. What in God's name was Phil doing staying at Lexie Dyer's? It explained his appearance at Dean Cemetery. All he had to do was nip along the basement lane, scramble over the wall, and follow Dean Path. Lexie wasn't keeping him a prisoner, that much was clear; he'd returned to Belgrave Crescent after whacking Von on the head. She could understand someone in his position battening like a leech onto a rich nob but what was going on in his life that he wanted to do it? More to the point, what was going on in Lexie's that she had a homeless person living in her house? They weren't lovers, of that she was sure – two beds on different floors had been slept in. And he was an unlikely lodger, assuming he had the money to pay rent. No, Lexie had a plan for him. The problem was, what?

And Ranald McCrea was in on whatever they were hatching. He'd recognised Phil's name when Von had mentioned it. She recalled his defensiveness over the folder with the application forms. And yet, could it have been instead the letter from the Calder Rifle and Pistol Club that he was anxious to keep from her? The more she thought about it, the more convinced she was that this shooting club held the clue to what was happening – or what was about to happen – to Phil. The pieces of information shuffled around in her head: Phil told he'd be going paintballing, Phil disappearing, Jamie and Bruce shot while paintballing with Ranald and Lexie, Ranald and Lexie members of a shooting club, Phil living with Lexie. She ran her hands through her hair. She could make no sense of it. But on one point she was clear: she wasn't bringing Phil in to reunite him with his mother until she'd got to the bottom of this. What was the point? He'd only do a bunk again.

She had ten minutes before her appointment. She glanced through the day's Scotsman. The headlines were all about – yawn – Tony Blair's second-term win for Labour. Bayne Pharmaceuticals was in the news again, its share price falling steadily and dragging the FTSE 100-Share Index with it. She skimmed the text. The editor was putting the blame fairly and squarely on the poor performance of Bayne's new medication, Lazinex. This miracle wonder-drug was supposed to combat various types of rheumatoid arthritis. Although the company's scientists had predicted side effects, they reassured the public they would be mild, and released the drug. But everyone was unprepared for what happened to the people who took it. Victims presented with a variety of symptoms. The most common were violent mood swings, but they included schizophrenia, and depression so severe that one person had attempted suicide.

She threw the paper onto the back seat, locked the Ford, and followed the path to the clubhouse.

'I'm looking for Mr Toby Hilliard,' she said to the spiky-haired young man at reception.

He smiled, showing uneven teeth. 'Is he expecting you?'

'I have an appointment with him for ten. Von Valenti.'

He peered at the computer screen. 'Toby's finishing a lesson. He won't be long.'

'No problem.'

The walls of the reception area were covered in posters advertising shooting matches and other competitive events. She glanced over them, noticing the regularity with which they were held; the Calder Rifle and Pistol seemed a popular club. A couple of youths came in. They looked no more than fifteen but she knew they couldn't be younger than eighteen.

In a corner, there was a glass cabinet with a sturdy lock. She studied the collection of rifles and handguns. None was a weapon she immediately recognised.

'Miss Valenti?' The voice was confident, as though the owner were used to giving orders and having them obeyed.

She spun round, feeling like a schoolgirl caught peeping at a dirty magazine. A tall, muscular man in combat fatigues was standing at the desk. His ear protectors were round his neck and he'd pushed his goggles up onto his head, messing up his dark hair. He reminded her of an aviator.

He smiled, extending a large-knuckled hand. 'Toby Hilliard.'

'Von Valenti,' she said, putting her hand into his and watching it disappear.

'Nice to see you here, Miss Valenti. We often have no-shows, people getting cold feet and not turning up.'

'Good heavens, why on earth do they make an appointment, then?'

'It's often the partners who make the appointment. You know, as a birthday or anniversary present. But they don't know their loved ones as well as they think they do.' He glanced at her left hand.

She smiled to herself. He was looking to see if she wore a ring. 'I made the appointment myself, Mr Hilliard.'

'Toby, please,' he said with a nod. He slipped his hands into his trouser pockets. 'So you want to learn to shoot.'

She hesitated. She'd be required to complete an application form. Shooting clubs vetted their members thoroughly, notifying the police of new applicants, and Toby Hilliard would discover her background. Best to come clean now.

'I've fired weapons before. I used to be a detective.' From the corner of her eye, she saw the receptionist's head shoot up.

A smile spread across Toby's face, deepening the cleft in his chin. 'Then I expect you've not come for a lesson. What sort of shooting would you like to do?'

'What do you have on offer?' she said, thinking rapidly. It was a long time since she'd fired a weapon.

'Easiest if I showed you around so you can see for yourself.'

'Tell me about these first,' she said, turning to the cabinet. 'They look vaguely familiar.'

'They're collector's items, all deactivated.' He pulled a bunch of keys from his pocket. 'If you watch Second World War films, you'll see these.'

As he leant down to unlock the cabinet, his US-style dog-tags fell forward from his shirt. He removed a firearm with a dropped wooden stock. 'You'll know this one. Thompson sub-machine gun. Favoured by gangsters. It's the gun that put the Roar into the Roaring Twenties. Here, feel the heft.'

She'd fired mostly handguns so found it heavy. 'Nice,' she said.

'And this,' he said, removing a rifle, 'is the famous M1 Garand.'

'Used by American servicemen?'

'I'm impressed, Miss Valenti.' He looked at her appreciatively. 'The first semi-automatic rifle ever to be issued to the infantry.'

She was grateful that one of the cops she'd met during her year with the NYPD had also been a collector of vintage firearms. During a boozy evening, he'd shown her his collection, thinking he could wow her into bed. Von, who had a good memory for trivia, had listened politely before excusing herself and taking her leave.

'Everyone's heard of the M1,' she said, injecting admiration into her voice. 'Didn't someone say it was the greatest battle implement ever devised?'

'George Patton.'

She ran a hand over the oiled wood. 'What sort of ammo does it fire? I can't remember now.'

'This takes the original .30-06 Springfield cartridge.'

'Of course.' She motioned to the back of the cabinet. 'And that pistol there? Behind the bigger pieces?'

'That's the pearl in our oyster, you could say. The Colt M1911.'

'Ah yes, the famous Colt 45 designed by John Browning.'

'You know your firearms, Miss Valenti.'

She threw him a quick smile. 'It's Von.'

'Von.'

'So where did you get these?'

'They're not mine, unfortunately, they belong to the club owner.' He replaced the firearms and locked the cabinet. 'He often comes to look at the collection. The Colt is his favourite. He loves handling it.'

'He must be an American.'

His voice had a slight edge. 'Dewey Croker.'

She knew the name, knew that he was a multi-millionaire businessman. And that he was CEO of Bayne Pharmaceuticals. So the owner of this gun club ran the company that employed Ranald McCrea and Lexie Dyer. Was that significant? Everything was significant until proven otherwise.

Toby was looking at her enquiringly. 'I see the name means something to you.'

'I read about him just today, in The Scotsman.'

'Lazinex, I'm guessing.'

'That's right.'

He leant in so close that she could smell the smoky woody scent of his aftershave. 'If you have shares in Bayne's, Von, now's not the time to sell.'

'I don't have shares in anything, actually.'

'Good girl. So, shall we take a look around?'

She followed him down a narrow corridor. The sound of firing grew louder.

He opened a door into a visitor's gallery. Through the double-glazed window, she counted ten shooting bays. The occupants, all middle-aged men, wore ear protectors and goggles and were firing at bullseye targets.

'What's the range?' she said, trying to show interest. In her time in the States, she'd fired in similar galleries and could have made an educated guess.

'For indoors? Twenty-five metres.'

'And what are they using?'

'Our members use the club's firearms because, as you know, the law has made it almost impossible to own a handgun. We stock a variety. Are you interested in one in particular?'

She needed to know whether the club owned large-calibre weapons. Would Toby Hilliard find it strange that a short woman wanted to fire something heavy? But, nothing ventured . . . 'I quite fancy a large calibre.'

He ran his eyes over her body. 'Don't take this the wrong way, Von, but you need muscle for that.'

'You're suggesting I use a peashooter, then?'

She could tell from his face that he wasn't sure if she was joking. She smiled warmly.

He seemed embarrassed to have misunderstood her. 'Well, if you really want to try, I'll need to give you a lesson and show you the right way to stand. The recoil packs something of a punch.' He took her hands and ran his fingers over them. 'Your hands are small,' he said.

'Is that a problem?' She noticed he made no attempt to release her.

'The pistol grip is longer and wider than that of a smaller-calibre model. Makes it difficult for shooters with small hands. Sure you want to do it?'

'Absolutely.' She imagined him standing behind her, their arms extended, his hands round hers. The thought made the blood throb in her temples. 'So what's the biggest calibre ammo you use?'

She knew the answer before he told her. 'We don't go above a .45,' he said, releasing her.

'Then let's go for broke. What pistols do you have that will fire, say, the ACP version of a .45?'

He seemed no longer surprised at the extent of her knowledge. 'We have Smith & Wesson Model 25s, Taurus Trackers, Ruger Blackhawks and we've got one or two Webley revolvers that have been converted to .45 ACP.'

'Are they popular?'

'Very. The .45 ACP is our most in-demand cartridge. Almost all the men have fired with it. I know, because I've instructed them.'

'Men?'

'As I said, you need strength for large calibre.'

'Do you have many women members?' she said, genuinely curious.

'We have some. But it tends to be a boy's sport.'

'So where do you store your firearms? I expect security's a nightmare.'

'As a club approved by the Home Office, our security has been vetted. Come on, I'll show you.'

They left the gallery, and he led the way down a series of corridors. She found it difficult to keep her eyes on her surroundings. Toby Hilliard had the body of an athlete and the confident walk of a trained soldier. She wondered what his background was and what had drawn him to guns.

They entered a windowless room. A Bambi-eyed girl with long wavy hair was sitting behind a desk. She looked up from the computer screen, an intimate smile creeping onto her face as she saw Toby.

'I'm showing a prospective around,' he said. He turned to Von. 'This is Megan. She signs the firearms in and out. Megan, Von Valenti.'

'Hi,' Megan said, her smile fading as she checked Von out.

'Hi, Megan.'

On the left-hand wall was a sign saying, Gun Store. Toby unlocked the door and stepped back to let Von enter. The room was roughly twenty feet square, its walls lined with the type of shelving that displays firearms. Half the space was given over to pistols.

'As you can see,' Toby was saying, 'we have rifles as well as handguns. All newish models.' He ran a hand down the stock of a small-bore rifle. 'As well as indoor shooting, we offer a range of experiences outdoors. You might find rifle-shooting more to your taste than using a pistol.'

'And to fire one of these, I ask Megan? I tell her what I want, she fetches the gun and I sign something?'

'That's it. If Megan's on a break, someone else will be here. This area is never left unattended.'

'After shooting, the gun is signed back in?'

'If it's not, Megan calls me or one of the lads and we go searching. But that rarely happens.' He looked at her without blinking. 'It's my responsibility to ensure that all firearms are here by closing time. Two staff members then go through the shelves systematically and tick off each firearm.'

'Sounds like a secure system,' she said, trying to look impressed. 'And do all your staff have keys to the gun room?'

He thrust his hands into his pockets. 'As a former police officer, you'll know that key-holders have to be registered. Only a few staff have keys. So does Mr Croker.'

She'd have to tread more carefully: he might be thinking she was using her police knowledge to trip him up. 'Just curious,' she said, smiling. 'And the ammo?'

He indicated a room leading off the gun room. 'Ammo cans are stored here. The cabinets are to British Standard as are the shelves for the firearms. And it's the same protocol with the keys.' He looked steadily at her. 'Once you've signed out a piece, Megan fetches the ammo. She has a database which tells her which guns fire which cartridges. But she's an expert shooter herself so rarely needs to consult it.'

Megan, who was hovering at the door, inclined her head modestly. She said nothing but the look in her eyes was unmistakable: *Hands off, Valenti.*

Von glanced around the gun store. If the firearm that had killed Jamie Dyer and Bruce Lassiter belonged to this club, it would be in this room. Yet, given the level of security, she doubted the murder weapon came from here. The murderer, on the other hand, may well have.

'We've time to take a quick look outside,' Toby was saying. 'Saturdays are our busiest so all the stations will be in use. You'll find it interesting.'

Whatever else Toby Hilliard was, he was competent and self-assured. Von, whose experience of men ran to the indecisive and clinging, found herself happy to let him take command. She followed him through doors with heavy locks down corridors humming with alarms. Megan's office and the gun and ammunition stores were in the heart of the building. To get to the guns, for example at night, the alarm system would have to be disabled. Even then, it would be impossible without keys. As it should be.

They had to cross an area of rough grassland to reach the outdoor shooting range. People in goggles and ear protectors were lying on the ground, firing rifles at targets shaped like human bodies. Further along, the shooters were sitting on chairs, their rifles resting on tables. Many were wearing grey hooded sweatshirts with the words Calder Rifle and Pistol Club in red letters.

'We find the ladies prefer to sit,' Toby smiled, nodding at an elderly woman with a red baseball cap over her white hair. Seeing Von's face, he added hastily, 'but I suspect you're not into precision shooting with static targets.' He lifted an eyebrow hopefully. 'We do advancing man on a railroad track.'

'When I was in the States, I saw shooting drills where you fire in all four directions in turn. And scenario shooting.'

He was looking at her with renewed interest. 'We do that here too. Cops, military, eliminate the bad guys. That sort of thing.'

'Mazes in the dark?'

'You're really up for it, aren't you?' he said softly.

Oh, in more ways than one. She gazed into his brown eyes, her attention slipping as she wondered what his body was like under the fatigues. 'So, when can I start?' she said.

'You understand we can't do a turn-up-and-have-a-go. Home Office restrictions.'

'Of course.'

'You need a Firearms Certificate, which you won't get without being a bona-fide member of the club. In other words, you have to serve your probationary and become a full member.'

'And the annual fee?'

'£90. Cheaper if you join with your partner.' He hesitated. 'Will you be doing that?'

Clumsy. For that, she wasn't telling him. 'It's just myself who'll be joining,' she said sweetly.

'Then let's get the paperwork started, shall we?' He led the way back into the building.

In his office, he took a thick application form from the desk drawer. 'I won't ask you to fill this out here and now. I'm afraid I have a lesson in a few minutes.'

'No problem. I'll drop it in tomorrow, shall I?'

'Or you could let me have it tonight.'

'Tonight?'

He smiled slowly. 'I thought we could explore your reasons for wanting to join a gun club over a few drinks. Shall we say 8.00pm in the Caledonian bar?'

'You're taking a lot for granted.'

'It's the best way.'

There was a brief silence. 'Fine,' she said.

He drew a card from his pocket. 'In case you can't make it.'

She glanced at the card, and then at him.

Of course she intended to make it.

Von was pulling up outside the flat when her mobile rang.

'Mum?' said a stricken voice. 'It's me, Georgie. You need to come down to Jenners.'

'Why? What's happened?' Her stomach clenched. *Oh Jesus, not the baby.*

'It's okay, I'm all right, Kylie too. But you need to get here.

Now.'

She closed her eyes. *Not again, Georgie. Not again.* 'I'm on my way,' she said.

It took her only minutes to drive into the town centre. Miraculously, she found a parking space at the south end of St Andrew Square. She ran down the street and into Jenners' side door.

A white-faced Georgie was sitting on a stool at the Clinique area, cradling the softly whimpering baby. The girl behind the counter was looking everywhere but at Georgie. Von recognised the older woman standing stiffly with her as the store manager. Her eyes were cold.

Seeing Von, the manager's expression cleared. 'Thank you for coming over so promptly, Miss Valenti. I've refrained from calling the police in view of your association with us and the excellent work you did as a store detective.' She cast a sidelong glance at Georgie. 'I'm afraid your daughter has been caught stealing.'

Von massaged her face wearily. 'Georgie,' she murmured, 'what were you thinking?' She addressed herself to the manager. 'What did she take?'

'Nancy saw her slipping something inside the baby's buggy. We stopped her outside and removed these from behind the pillow.' She held up lipstick and eye-shadow.

Von struggled to keep her anger in check. 'I'll pay for those,' she said, opening her handbag automatically. 'And of course you must keep the items.'

'That won't be necessary. But I'd like an assurance that your daughter won't visit this store again.'

Georgie had been listening to the exchange, tight-lipped. Realising she'd been let off, she got to her feet and put the baby in the buggy. 'Don't worry,' she muttered, 'I'm not coming back to this poxy place.'

Von gripped her daughter's arm. 'You little idiot. Don't

you know that this lady has every right to call the police? But she hasn't. And instead of being ashamed of what you've done, you're behaving like a spoilt brat. The very least you can do is apologise.'

Georgie glared, saying nothing.

'Apologise, Georgie, or, by God, I'll call the police myself.' Her eyes bored into her daughter's. 'I mean it.'

The girl bit her lip. She hesitated, then turned to the manager. 'I'm really sorry for what I've done,' she said, trying to make it sound as if she meant it. 'And I promise I won't come here again.'

'Was that so hard to do?' Von said.

Georgie shook her arm free. 'Can we go now?'

The manager was looking sadly at Von. 'Miss Valenti, you do realise that if we see your daughter here again I'll have no option but to call the police.'

'I do. And you can call them with my blessing.'

Something passed across Georgie's face, a look of comprehension. She released the brake on the buggy and made for the door.

Von mouthed, 'thank you', to the two women and followed her out.

'Where's the car, Mum?'

'Up here.' Von was trying to hold it together until they got home. But her simmering anger boiled over the minute they were inside the Ford. She stared into the rear-view mirror. 'What the hell are you playing at, Georgie? It's bad enough you steal, but involving the baby?' She slammed her hands against the steering wheel. 'How *could* you?'

Georgie pushed a lock of hair behind her ear. 'There's no need to be so melodramatic. I didn't involve the baby. She's not a criminal.'

'You realise that if you get a custodial sentence they'll take her away from you?'

'For stealing some Clinique stuff? Get real, Mum, they won't send me to prison just for that. And anyway, you'll swing things so I get off. Like you did just now.'

'I won't do it again, Georgie. I swear it. You need to take responsibility for your actions.'

'Like you did at my age?' came the soft reply.

'Oh, for God's sake, climb down from the moral high ground. At that height you'll get a nose bleed.' She stared through the windscreen at the Roman column, towering over the office-block buildings bordering St Andrew Square. 'You don't have a divine right to lecture me, Georgie. Well, maybe you have. But that's no reason to behave the way you do.'

'I know I shouldn't have done it, Mum,' the girl said in a conciliatory tone. 'It was wrong, I do know that. But I had a good reason,' she added eagerly, as though that made it acceptable.

Von rested her head on the wheel. 'Go on.'

'You're not going to believe me.'

'Say it anyway. I like to hear you tell it.'

'I've met someone. I'm seeing him tonight.'

'That's nice. Who is he?' Her head jerked up. *Tonight?* 'You can't, Georgie, I'm going out myself tonight.' She caught the fleeting look of disappointment on her daughter's face.

'It's too late, Mum, I've made a date. If you're going out, you'll have to take Kylie with you.'

'I can't do that.'

'Well, neither can I. And I'm going on my date.'

'Over my rotting corpse.'

They'd reached their usual impasse. Except it never was an impasse. Von always capitulated. She felt the lassitude that followed arguments with her daughter settle in her bones. 'Fine,' she said wearily. 'I'll stay in.'

Georgie rested her head against the seat. 'Thanks, Mum.'

She studied the girl in the mirror. Georgie always was careful how she spent her gratitude. Pity she didn't take the same care with money.

'And did you do the shopping, Georgie?'

'It's in the fridge. That's why I had nothing left for the Clinique.'

'Look, love, all you had to do was ask. If you've run out of makeup, then of course I'll buy it.' A sudden thought came into her head. Perhaps the Clinique counter wasn't the only part of Jenners her daughter had visited. 'What are you wearing tonight?' she said suspiciously.

'One of my dresses, what else?'

Of course, the designer dresses. Perhaps this wasn't the time to bring up the subject of selling them. In the Grassmarket, she'd seen a vintage clothes shop that was paying good money for second-hand clothes. Any one of those dresses would provide Georgie with spending money for months. Yet her daughter didn't think that way.

'Who's this bloke you're seeing, then?'

'His name's Norrie.'

'Does he have a surname?'

'If he does, he didn't tell me.'

'Well, try to find out.'

'So you can check up on him with your police pals?'

'Don't be silly.' But it wasn't the furthest from her thoughts.

'Let's drop it, Mum. He's nice and I think you're going to like him.'

She started the engine and pulled out into the traffic.

'I'll be home late,' Georgie said, as they reached the flat.

'I realise that. How late?'

'I don't know.'

No, of course she didn't know. Any more than Von would

have known how late she'd have been after her evening with Toby. She hauled the buggy inside. She'd have to call him and tell him she couldn't make it. She imagined the short silence, the polite way he'd take the news, her suggesting another date, his letting her down graciously as a gentleman would do, and then disconnecting and calling Megan. In the kitchen, as she watched her daughter drinking orange juice straight from the carton, she imagined another scenario: Toby devastated at her news, rushing over with a take-away and a bottle of cava, helping her feed, wash and dress the baby, and then the two of them making love on the sofa.

It was a nice fairy tale.

Chapter 18
Sunday, June 10th

It was late afternoon the following day and Von was driving as fast as she dared down the A71. The sunlight slanted through gaps in the trees, dazzling her briefly before disappearing again. She'd wound the window down because the Ford's air-conditioning was broken and it was stifling inside, and now, with the air streaming in, the smell of hawthorn was overpowering.

She'd made her peace with Georgie, who'd come home at 1.00am with wine spilt down the front of her Stella McCartney dress. She was determined her daughter would no longer inflict her behaviour on her, wresting a promise from the girl to stay in for the rest of the day so she could ferry her completed application form to the Calder Rifle and Pistol Club.

Toby had been unavailable to take yesterday's phone call. Her apology (and don't they always sound lame on the phone?) that she'd had to cry off the drinks date had gone straight to voicemail. She'd decided to wait until the club was closing today in the hope he'd still want to take her for a drink, and she could suggest they go now. She was clutching at straws, but what else could she do? For a middle-aged woman living with her daughter and granddaughter, straws were all that was left.

And now, the traffic was building up on the A71 where roadworks had started. She felt like screaming. To the sound of horns, she overtook recklessly and made it to the gun club with minutes to spare. As she pulled up in the car park, she saw a light-blue car driving off. She glanced at the occupant, and then ducked her head. Ranald McCrea was at the wheel of his Ascari. Had he seen her? She couldn't tell.

She ran inside and threw herself at the mercy of the spiky-haired receptionist. 'Is there any chance I could see Toby? I'm Von Valenti. It really is urgent.'

She could see he was trying not to smile. 'That's what all the ladies say.' But he put the call through.

She waited impatiently, hearing only his side of the conversation. He shot her a doubtful glance that made her draw in her breath, and then put the phone down.

'This way, Miss Valenti,' he said, pushing back his chair.

She breathed again. As he led her down the corridor, she wondered miserably whether Toby would see through her plan, and whether that was a good thing or not.

The receptionist knocked at the office door, and then opened it and ushered her in. 'Want me to lock up, Tobe?'

Toby Hilliard was on his feet. 'Yes, please,' he said, smiling at the young man, 'and then get off home. I'll let Miss Valenti out.'

The door closed behind her.

'It's all right for me to be here after hours?' she said.

'Provided you're with the chief instructor. Rank has its privileges.' He looked at her closely. 'I was wondering, after your phone message, whether I'd see you again. We get people who take the application form away and then think better of it.'

He was letting her off, making it seem as though her no-show for drinks was to do with second thoughts about shooting. She took the form from her bag. 'All done. And I've attached the cheque and passport-sized photos.'

'Excellent. I can have your ID badge ready for your next visit.' He glanced at the form and then threw it into a tray. 'So, about that drink . . .'

'Is now a good time?'

'Now is always a good time,' he said, his eyes resting on hers.

'The Caledonian?'

'Too quiet on a Sunday. Do you know Federico's?'

'Where is it?'

'The Grassmarket. They do decent grub.' He added, 'assuming you like to eat early?'

'Fine,' she smiled.

An hour later, they were sitting in the type of cocktail bar she hadn't drunk in since her move from London: subdued lighting, teardrop chandeliers, yellow leather seats. An archway separated the bar area from the restaurant. She decided against her usual vodka tonic and went for the cocktail Federico's was famous for, Gin Rickey. Toby ordered cognac over ice.

'How did you find this place?' she said.

'Through a friend. She comes here a lot. Lexie Dyer.'

She tried to keep her tone level. 'Lexie Dyer?'

'One of the club members. You sound as though you know the name.'

She thought quickly. 'It's been in the newspapers. In connection with the murders at that paintballing club.' She had a sudden vision of Ranald McCrea glancing in her direction as she stood in Lexie's kitchen. Both Ranald and Lexie were members of the Calder Rifle and Pistol Club and would know Toby. But she felt sure neither of them had told him anything about her. Why would they?

'A bad business,' he said. 'It was one of the members who found the bodies. A double tap, according to the newspapers.' He took a deep swallow of his cognac. 'Do you know the origin of the double tap?'

She frowned. 'Wasn't it invented by the police?'

'It originated with the British Special Operations Executive.'

'Wartime agents?'

'Now it's used world-wide by special forces.'

'And contract killers,' she said softly.

'I've no idea where the police are in their investigation but we've been told the paintballing club will be open by next Saturday.' He lifted his glass. 'Thank God for that.'

'What's so important about Saturday?'

'The tournament. We're all playing.' He said it as if it were the most natural thing.

'You're a paintballer?'

'Most of the gun club members are.'

She dropped her gaze, hoping he hadn't seen her expression. So, Toby Hilliard was also a paintballer. Nothing surprising in that. And the two clubs were practically on each other's doorsteps.

He was watching her with the hint of a smile. 'Have you ever tried paintballing, Von?'

'Never.'

'You should.'

'What's the attraction?'

'It's the closest you get to shooting at live targets. You must have played Cowboys and Indians as a child. Remember that feeling when you took aim and fired?'

She did. It had been a game popular with her two brothers. But she'd been less interested in killing and more in solving crimes, and she'd soon tired of it and moved them on to playing Cops and Robbers.

He took her silence for assent. 'Paintballing's better. You look unconvinced.' He stretched his legs out under the table. 'Why don't you come and watch the match? As my guest, of course.'

'How exactly do you play in a paintballing tournament? I mean, how do the spectators see what's happening? It takes place outside, doesn't it?'

'Come on Saturday and your questions will be answered.'

'And you're taking part?'

'You can cheer for me.' His eyes wandered over her body.

'Provided you wear a short skirt and wave pompoms.'

She laughed at the frivolous remark, all the funnier because it had come from such a serious man. 'Done,' she said.

He caught the barman's attention and, without asking if she wanted another cocktail, signalled they needed their glasses refilled.

'You mentioned you used to be a detective,' he said. 'So what made you leave?'

She didn't reply immediately. It was a part of her life she was trying to forget. 'I suppose it was mainly because I no longer believed in what I was doing.' She kept her eyes on her drink. 'Everyone has to have something to believe in.'

'And why Scotland?'

'I came to be near my daughter and her baby. They live with me.' There. She'd said it. Her eyes rose to meet his.

He was smiling. 'You must hear this all the time but you don't look nearly old enough. So, shall we order something to eat?'

They took a table inside the archway and, over supper, he told her about himself. He'd been in the army and had fought with the 1st Armoured Division in the Gulf War.

She put down her chicken-and-sun-dried-tomato wrap. 'Okay, now it's my turn to ask. What made you leave?'

'After Desert Storm, I'd had enough of the army. I wanted to travel so I went to the States.'

'Doing what? Touring around?'

'To begin with. Then I found work in a shooting club. It's where I met Dewey Croker.'

'Is that where you got these?' she said, flicking his dog-tags playfully.

'The club has a strong World War Two theme. All the members have them.' He smiled. 'I've even got some American army boots. But I'm not as bad as Dewey. He's named his three sons, Able, Baker and Charlie.'

'Good grief, that's a bit over the top.'

'I agree. Anyway, Dewey told me he'd be opening a shooting club after he relocated to Livingston. He offered me the job of manager. The money was too good for me to turn down.'

'Why did he relocate here?'

'The money was too good for *him* to turn down.'

'He'll be finding the attitude to guns in the UK very different.' Her experience with the NYPD had shown her how ingrained was the belief by many Americans that they had a God-given right to own guns for self-protection. In her time there, she'd learnt enough about firearms and the different types of wounds inflicted by them to develop a deep mistrust of a society that allows its citizens to legally carry instruments that can kill with the flick of a finger.

'From the minute Dewey arrived,' Toby was saying, 'he complained about Britain's gun restrictions. He has a big collection in the States which he had to leave behind. As you've guessed, he collects World War Two firearms.'

He spoke with contempt and she wondered about the men's relationship. 'I get the impression you're not best mates,' she said.

He made a gesture to indicate he was weary of the subject. 'Dewey's fine when it comes to the club,' he said, putting down his venison burger. 'I mean he's a decent boss. But I don't like his business practices.'

'The CEO of a big pharmaceutical company?' she said with heavy irony. 'What's not to like?'

'He's not just the boss of the one in Livingston. He's the capo di tutti capi, and anyone who crosses him ends up sleeping with the fishes.' He smiled faintly, as though he'd spoken out of turn. 'I don't mean that literally.'

'How did he become the capo di tutti capi?'

'He has a huge business brain and he's ruthless when it comes to competition. He's quick off the mark, knowing when to merge and when to acquire. It's not difficult to find these things out. He's always profiled in magazines.'

'This fiasco with their new drug means that Bayne's will be taking a knock, surely.'

'I don't doubt it. But he'll be looking for his next big challenge. He'll pull out of Bayne's and go home soon. CEOs of pharmaceuticals don't last long, with or without a fiasco. Every few years, the toilet flushes and a new one comes along.'

'What's he like as a person?' she said, sipping her Gin Rickey.

His features tightened. 'He's a category-ten hypocrite. Tells the world how his drugs are going to help mankind and all that tosh, yet he sets the price so high that only the richest countries can afford them. Occasionally you see them on the NHS but not often.'

'But this new drug is available on the NHS.'

'Lazinex? That was part of his look-what-a-wonderful-benefactor-I-am game plan but I bet the government paid well over the odds to get it onto the NHS lists.' He smiled unpleasantly. 'Dewey made a huge mistake with Lazinex. Pharmaceutical companies are like software houses. They push their products out before they're ready so they can maximise profits. It's not life-threatening to find a bug in your email system but you want your medication not to kill you.'

'Is that what Lazinex does?' she said, shocked. 'I thought the main side effect was severe depression.'

'Depression is only one of them. Did you read about the man who thought he could fly? His colleagues pulled him away from the window just in time.'

'Jesus, that can't have made Dewey popular.'

'His admirers could meet in the back of a van, there are so few.'

'So why do you work for him? You obviously feel strongly about his moral values.'

'It's a question I often ask myself. But the job's a good one. And I'm hoping to buy the place when he leaves, which he will eventually. The way things are going at Bayne's, it'll be sooner rather than later.' He waved a hand dismissively, as though he could dismiss Dewey as easily. 'Anyway, enough about Croker. Tell me more about yourself. I saw on your application form that you're a professional investigator now.'

'It's not as glamorous as it sounds and please don't do a Humphrey Bogart impression.'

He smiled. 'What's the job like?'

'You wear out a lot of shoe leather following suspects, and photographing and videoing them while they're meeting people they shouldn't. Then there are the other types of surveillance work. I once had to gather evidence against nuisance neighbours. That was fun. Turned out they were using their premises to hold swingers parties. I've still got the videotapes.' She wiped her mouth with her napkin. 'And I get the odd bit of legal work from solicitors where I take witness statements to do with accidents or crimes.'

'So are you working on a case just now?'

'I'm on a missing persons.'

He gave a serious nod.

'I do quite a bit of those,' she went on. 'Usually we're contacted by worried parents.'

'And do you find their children?'

'If the parents are well-heeled, their kids have usually emptied their bank accounts and gone to London.'

'And if they're not?'

She thought of Mrs Pattullo and the anguish in her eyes as she begged Von to find her son. Her heart clenched. 'Then they haven't.'

Her mind was drawn back to that glimpse of Phil's face at Lexie's window, and to Ranald's defensiveness when he'd learnt she was looking for Phil. Her brain made a sudden connection with what Mhairi had told her. Yes, Lexie and Ranald were the professionals who'd taken Phil under their wing. And, if they were taking him paintballing, maybe they'd be taking him shooting too. But that was unlikely. He'd have to fill out that weighty form and be vetted by the police, and she couldn't see his application being accepted. This wasn't a line worth pursuing. She'd learnt as much as she was going to from the Calder Rifle and Pistol Club. Steve would have to do the rest. She was back to the paintballing. A thought struck her. Maybe Phil would be at this tournament on Saturday.

Toby was watching her, his expression lazy. 'So when do you think you'll be having your first lesson?'

'I'm not sure . . .'

His eyes were mocking her. 'I know it'll be your first time firing .45s, so I'll be gentle.'

She laughed. 'Well, in that case . . . To be honest, though, I'm going to be pretty busy over the next few days.' She saw the disappointment in his eyes. 'But I'll try to make time this week.'

'Good. But in case you can't, I still expect to see you at the tournament and I won't take no for an answer. I'll leave your name at the gate and you come in as my guest. I'll find you there,' he added softly.

They looked at each other for a long moment. 'I have to be getting home,' she said. 'I promised my daughter I wouldn't be late.'

'Then I'll call us a cab and I can drop you off.'

She could have told him she could walk – she lived not far from Lothian Road – but the thought of the shared cab ride was too much to resist. She had a soft spot for cabs, especially the back seats. Her first romantic encounter had occurred when she shared a taxi with one of her brother's friends. The driver had schlepped halfway around London before they told him to stop.

She picked up her leather jacket. 'I'll just pay a visit to the little girls' room.'

She was under the arch when she heard his mobile ring. Force of habit made her pause to listen. She stood out of sight of their table, head bent over her bag, pretending to look for something. From her position, she could hear his side of the conversation clearly.

'What? Are you absolutely sure?' Pause. 'How the devil did . . .' Longer pause. 'So what do you suggest we do?' Pause. 'I hope you're not thinking of . . .' Pause. 'Ranald, do you really think that would work?'

A waiter hurrying through the archway collided with a swaying customer and dropped a tray of food. The crash echoed through the bar, deafening her, and she missed the rest of what Toby was saying. All she caught was the final part.

'Look, I don't want you to . . .' Short pause. 'Okay. Got to go.'

She ran to the loo, cursing the waiter.

When she returned, Toby was paying the bill. 'The taxi's on its way,' he smiled.

'Please let me pay my share.'

He brushed the suggestion aside. 'Come on, let's wait outside. It's a beautiful evening.'

The sun was sinking into a gap between the buildings, turning the sky blood-orange, its light reflecting off the bright swollen moon rising opposite. The evening was warm and the smell of dust and beer rose from the cobbles. Shouts of laughter came from the Grassmarket's noisy wine bars.

Toby took out a packet of cigarettes and shook one loose. He offered it to her.

'Thanks, I don't smoke.'

'I'm restricting myself to one a day,' he said, pulling matches from his pocket. 'Giving up something as pleasurable as smoking is hard to do.' The match caught with a hiss. He blew the smoke from the side of his mouth, studying her. 'I'll have to replace it with something better.'

He smoked quickly, taking long deep drags, spilling glowing ash onto the sleeve of his jacket. She guessed he wanted to finish the cigarette before the taxi came. He was just throwing the butt into the wall-mounted ash tray when it arrived. They settled in the back and he sprawled next to her, an arm lightly across the back of the seat. If she was going to make the first move, this was as good a time as any, but she had other things on her mind. It was clear from Toby's conversation with Ranald that they were rattled about something. The comment: *I hope you're not thinking of . . .'* was what interested her most. There'd been a warning tone in Toby's voice. And: *'Ranald, do you really think that would work?'* suggested that, whatever they were planning, Toby wasn't one hundred percent behind it. Her mouth went suddenly dry. Could Toby be part of this thing that involved Phil?

The cab pulled up in Gardner's Crescent. 'This is me,' she said, gazing at him in the half-light. 'It's been a great evening, Toby.'

'I hope we'll do it again.'

She smiled. 'Me too.'

He held the smile, then leant across and kissed her lightly on the lips. 'Just marking my place,' he said.

She was tempted to kiss him back but his actions suggested he wanted to take things slowly. Perhaps it was just as well. She could hardly invite him in with Georgie there, and she'd outgrown those sticky gropings in the back seats of cabs. She wasn't sure what she wanted from him. Sex? Yes, it would be great and it was a long time since she'd taken a man into her bed. But did she want more?

'Night, Toby,' she said, getting out of the cab. 'And thanks again.'

She watched the taxi disappear, and then let herself into the building.

The living-room lights were on although there was no sign of Georgie. Von felt her anger rise. The girl never switched anything off. Why bother? She wasn't the one paying the electricity bill.

The baby's cot was against the wall. Von tiptoed over and gazed down at her granddaughter. She ran a finger over the heavy cheeks, listening to the faint breathing. The baby had dark lashes that were so long they almost curled over themselves. She turned her onto her side and kissed the nape of her neck. Delicious. But why hadn't Georgie taken the cot in with her? A glance at the small bottle of vodka on the coffee table told her.

No matter. Her granddaughter could sleep with her. And it wouldn't be the first time. She knew the routine when the baby wakened, where to find the bottle, how to make up Baby Formula. She pushed the cot into her room, taking care not to wake the child.

She was tempted to draw a bath and lie in it for hours listening to Pink Floyd, but she'd be up in four hours' time and then again after that; the baby always woke at least twice in the night. And Georgie wouldn't stir. When she hit the bottle knowing her mother was home, it would take an ice-pick to get her out of bed.

A sudden draught blew through the bedroom. The living-room window had been propped open, something Georgie did when she was smoking surreptitiously. Rage surged through her. Why the hell her daughter thought this fooled anyone was beyond her. She was a detective, for Christ's sake. She closed and bolted the window, wondering how she could improve relations between the two of them.

She pressed her brow against the cold glass and shut her eyes, feeling an anger towards Georgie that astonished her.

The girl had no business getting drunk and leaving her child unattended. What if something had happened and Von had been unable to get back? The baby could have been crying all night while Georgie lay in a drunken stupor. No, this couldn't go on. She'd have to have it out with her. She could hear what the girl would say. How could Von talk about abandoning a child when she'd done the same thing to her own daughter? Well, she was tired of that argument; it was time Georgie started singing a different tune. Once again, she asked herself whether formal adoption of the baby wasn't the right thing. Could she invest so much love in another woman's child? But the baby was her flesh and blood too.

Darkness was falling. She reached across wearily to draw the curtains.

A figure was standing across the road, staring up in her direction. He was several feet from the street lamp and it was too dark to make out his features. The hairs rose on the back of her neck. She switched off the light and slid behind the curtain. Could this be Toby? But the taxi had left a good half hour earlier. And why would he return to her flat and watch her?

A sudden fear gripped her. Whoever it was knew where she lived. And knew where her daughter and granddaughter lived. She was shaking inside, her hand clutching the curtain. The switching off of the light must have signalled something because the figure turned away and moved down the street. She watched him open a car door. It was too far away to catch the make or registration number but the car was pale-coloured, silver perhaps. The faint purr of the engine reached her across the still night. A second later, the car disappeared.

She let her hand drop and fell into the armchair. She couldn't stop shivering. Her mind was in turmoil. Maybe she was being neurotic and the figure hadn't been looking at her window. There could be any number of reasons why someone stood and stared upwards, none of them anything to do with her. It could have been a star-gazer. The moon was full and bright and who knew what planets were visible in the sky? Yes, that would be it.

She rose and checked the bolts on the front door.

In the bedroom, she undressed and slipped between the sheets. A faint noise came from Georgie's room. It was a smothered laugh. Not her daughter's voice, deeper, a man's. So that was why Georgie had left the cot in the living room. She listened as the laugh turned into grunting, then a rhythmic creaking of the bed. After it was over, and her daughter's room had grown silent, she found herself imagining Toby on top of her, heaving in the darkness, thrusting expertly. Slowly, she slid her fingers between her legs, feeling the moist warmth, and began to knead the flesh.

A moment later, the baby whimpered, and started to cry.

Chapter 19
Monday, June 11th

Steve winced as he took a gulp of coffee. The brew was just as he remembered it, scalding and bitter, a feature of Pitt Street which hadn't changed in the months he'd been away. Bridget drank it by the gallon with no apparent ill effects.

'Slainte.' She blotted her mouth with a paper hankie. 'Okay, Stevie, what do you think of Dyer's house, then?'

'Not a décor I could live with. But there's something odd about the place, wouldn't you say?'

'I would.'

Steve massaged his face wearily. 'It was cleaned thoroughly. Put to bed. The sort of thing you'd do to a place if you had a mind to sell it.'

'Or a mind to leave it for a long time.' She nodded. 'That's right, we're back to the medications scam. I'm convinced Dyer had done something he shouldn't with Lassiter and the two of them were planning to leg it.'

'Do you think Lassiter would go without Gavvo Skelton?'

'Skelton may or may not have been in on it.'

Steve swallowed another mouthful. 'There's something I need to run past you, Bridge. About the murders.'

'Go on.'

'How did the killer know that both Jamie and Bruce were paintballing that Tuesday lunchtime?'

'I take it there's some sort of booking system? So, maybe the killer's someone with access to it.'

'Right, except that, according to the IT crowd at Lothian and Borders, only Jamie, Ranald, and Lexie made a booking onto the database. It was over a week before the knockabout. But Bruce made no booking for that day. The others didn't know he'd be playing.'

'You're sure about that?'

'Ranald and Lexie were genuinely gobsmacked when they discovered Bruce had also been out. Either that or they're Oscar-winning actors.'

Bridget shrugged. 'Then Bruce must have told someone and news got around. And the killer got to hear of it. But there's another way it could have happened, one that's more likely.' She gazed at him steadily. 'The killer set the whole thing up.'

Steve remembered Gavvo Skelton's words: *A pro job is never left to chance, it's always the killer who chooses the time and the place.*

'He's a club member,' she went on, 'and knows how people will play in the woodland, what route they'll take. That gives him plenty of time to decide where best to lie in wait.'

'Aye. But someone still has to get Bruce and Jamie there. That's easy, though. These new markers. Everyone's falling over themselves to test them.'

'So the killer maybe suggests to Jamie that he should test them out with Ranald and Lexie. They make the booking.'

'But Bruce isn't there. Maybe that's part of the cunning plan. The killer is careful not to leave a trail that will point to him. Someone might remember him huddling with Jamie and Bruce.'

Bridget was nodding slowly. 'He tells Bruce later.' She hesitated. 'But then why doesn't Bruce make a booking?'

'Could be any number of reasons. Maybe he forgot, maybe he wanted to surprise his pals.'

'So who is this killer who's also a paintballer, Stevie?'

He remembered what Ranald had told him. 'Most of Bayne's

are members of the paintballing club.'

'There you have it, then. Someone from Bayne's.' Her mouth formed into a smile. 'It must be the medications.' She paused. 'I meant to ask. What did you think of Skelton?'

'I liked him. He seems genuinely concerned for his boys. Gave me an earful we're not doing enough to solve our Ecstasy problem.'

'Our luck's got to change soon, Stevie.'

'But we don't have the manpower, do we? And the Chinaman knows it.' At the thought of Snake Eyes, Steve's leg ached as though he'd been shot all over again. Whenever Tommy Teoh Lau came up in the conversation, his stomach turned over. That fateful afternoon at the Garnethill stakeout, the man had seen him. He'd looked through the window as his car rounded the corner and stared at Steve with expressionless eyes. He was said never to forget a face. Steve felt like a dead man walking.

'Anyway, let's get back to the medications scam,' Bridget said. 'I've made an appointment for you to see Cally Cockrill, the auditor lassie I told you about. Here's where you'll find her.' She handed him a business card. 'Maybe the both of yous can figure out what Dyer and Lassiter were up to.'

There was one question Steve hadn't asked. 'Did either of the victims leave wills?'

'Lassiter had a fair sum put by. He left everything to Skelton.'

'Enough to get offed for?'

'Some people in this fair city would kill for it, that's for sure.'

'And Jamie?'

'Dyer's worth a wee bitty more. He didn't leave a will. His sister, as his only living relative, gets it all.'

So Lexie Dyer was the beneficiary of Jamie's will. Nothing surprising there. Would a sister kill her brother for money? It had been done before.

Steve blew on his coffee. 'Someone called the house when I

was there, Bridge.'

'Did they, now?'

'I checked it out. It was from an unregistered pay-as-you-go. Must have been someone who doesn't know Jamie's dead. But here's the interesting thing. There was no prior call made to his mobile. I can understand someone not knowing he's dead, but why ring the house and not try the mobile first?'

She shrugged. 'Could be a businessman who thought Dyer would be working from home and tried the landline.'

'The people Bayne's deal with wouldn't be using a pay-as-you-go. And it doesn't explain why he didn't try the mobile.'

'Perhaps the caller didn't bother with it because he knew the polis had it.'

'Doesn't wash, Bridge. If he knew we had it, he'd also know why. And that means he'd know Jamie wouldn't be at home. He'd be in the mortuary.'

'That's for sure.'

They looked at one another.

Her gaze sharpened. 'Time to stop footering about.' She nodded at the business card in his hand. 'Take a closer look at Bayne's exports. Follow the paper trail.'

An hour later, Steve was standing outside Cally Cockrill's apartment. She lived on the ground floor in a new apartment block, part of the riverside development around Glasgow Green.

He leant against the bell. A second later, the door was opened by a statuesque brunette. She wore tight black jeans and a silk waistcoat embroidered with the Scottish saltire. Her braids were divided at the nape and hung over her breasts.

He was conscious he was staring. 'Miss Cockrill?' he said, holding up his warrant card. 'I'm Detective Inspector Steve English from Strathclyde Police. I believe you're expecting me.'

'You're a Detective Inspector?' She continued to gaze at

him, making no move to let him in. 'Now I'm feeling young.'

She looked about sixteen but had to be older. He guessed mid-twenties from the clear complexion and brightness of the eyes. The tilt of her head and the finger in her mouth suggested he wasn't worth her time. 'Nippy sweetie' was what Bridget had called her. Aye, and she might not be far wrong.

He straightened. 'Well, are you going to let me in?'

A smile played on the girl's lips, and she stepped back just enough that he had to squeeze past, which he suspected was her intention. As he brushed against her, he caught a trace of scent, sweet like sherbet.

Her front door opened onto a large low-ceilinged room created by knocking out two walls. It was decorated in wax-crayon colours. There was a pink sofa, a yellow coffee table and an enormous green lampshade. In a corner, silver branches, with winking white lights instead of leaves, grew out of an orange-coloured pot. Three of the walls had been painted black. The fourth consisted of a gigantic picture window with a view over the Clyde that doubled the value of the apartment.

'Nice,' he said doubtfully.

When there was no reply, he turned to look at her. Her dark eyes were running over his body.

'Detective Inspector Kelly suggested you may have something for me,' he said.

She laughed, showing straight white teeth. She was young enough to be of the generation that doesn't have fillings. He thought of his own, each wisdom tooth, molar, and pre-molar plugged with amalgam.

'DI Kelly said that? That I've got something for you? Sweet. But first things first. Would you like a drink?'

He hesitated. His insides were awash, although it would be nice to get rid of the taste of the Pitt Street brew. 'Coffee will be fine.'

She screwed up her face, and then shrugged. The yellow table was in her way. Rather than going round it like a normal person, she stepped onto it, and disappeared into the kitchen.

'Milk and sugar?' she shouted through.

'Neither, thanks.'

He wandered over to the red DVD rack and scanned her collection: Black Christmas, Scream Bloody Murder, and Friday the 13th. She was into slasher movies. He ran a hand over his face.

She returned so quickly he guessed she had a pot constantly on the brew. She handed him a mug, and then poured herself a drink from a dark-coloured bottle on the navy-blue sideboard. 'Sure I can't interest you in a little muscatel?' she said over her shoulder.

It wasn't even noon and she was on the muscatel. He wondered how much they were going to get done at this rate. But Bridget had made it clear he mustn't piss Cally off. When it came to rooting out a swindle, the girl was 'pure dead brilliant'.

He sipped at the coffee, his spirits rising. It was smooth and rich, just as he liked it. If she made it as good as this then things were looking up. 'Excellent coffee, Miss Cockrill.'

'I'm Cally. And I'm calling you Steve,' she added curtly. 'I'm not standing on ceremony because you're a detective.' She regarded him from under long lashes. 'Detectives are just policemen with smaller feet.'

He wasn't arguing. 'Fine by me.'

She gulped her muscatel, and poured herself another.

Bridget had told him little about Cally, but the comment that the girl had made a living as a commodities trader had caught his interest. 'I hear you worked in the City,' he said, studying her as he sipped.

'I dealt in industrial metals on the London Metal Exchange. Then I moved up to Glasgow and managed straight investments.'

'Was that fun?'

She pulled a face. 'It became boring pretty quickly. I decided to become a freelance auditor, specialising in fraud investigation.'

'Bet the pay's not as good,' he said, grinning.

'As an investment manager, I made enough to retire on. The pay's not the issue,' she said in a matter-of-fact way. 'It's the thrill of the chase that floats my boat.' She looked into his eyes. 'I'm a poacher-turned-gamekeeper.'

He returned the gaze. They were about to put that statement to the test, right enough. 'So, do we work here?' he said, eyeing the yellow coffee table dubiously.

'The kitchen. I'm set up and ready for you. You know, you're not at all what I expected,' she added suddenly.

He resisted the urge to ask what she had expected and why he wasn't it. In his experience, the answer was never favourable. He smiled wanly.

'Come, Steve.'

To say that the kitchen was decorated in a minimalist style was an oversimplification. Everything except the floor, which was covered in black lino, was white, including the table and chairs. The vibrating colour of the living room wasn't much to his taste but the complete absence of it here made his head swim. The only item that wasn't white was the clock. It was large with a circular red face from which red butterflies were escaping. An industrial-strength coffee-maker, which was steaming gently, stood on the working surface. There were no pots, pans, or utensils, suggesting Cally was either super-efficient in her tidying up or she simply didn't cook. He thought of his Mammy's kitchen and how she polished the range with blacklead once a week.

The table was set up with more computer equipment than he'd seen in one place. Several screens were arranged around a huge PC. 'Is this, um, a mainframe?' he said.

'Don't be daft, Steve. This is a high performance workstation.'

'I don't see any cables.'

'Have you heard of wireless, by any chance?'

'Why are there so many screens?'

'I'm running several jobs.'

'So where do you eat?' he said, gazing at the machines.

She looked puzzled. 'I eat out, of course.' She sat down and patted the chair next to hers. 'Sit.'

He stared wide-eyed as she tapped away at the keyboard and moved the mouse. There was activity in every screen, with lines of data scrolling hypnotically. He felt any confidence he had in computers slipping away.

'What do you know about fraud, Steve? Particularly financial fraud.'

He tried a joke to cover his vast lack of knowledge. 'To make a small fortune on the stock market, you start with a large fortune.'

'Very good. You'll go far.'

He set down his mug. 'Cally, I'll be honest with you. I know next to nothing. No, cancel that. I know absolutely nothing.'

She stared at him for a while. 'You've got gorgeous eyes.' She turned back to the keyboard and hammered away. 'But we're not talking about the markets. We're talking about defrauding a company of its assets.'

'Its assets being?'

'Medications.'

He studied her profile. The bushy tips of her braids rose and fell as she breathed. Her skin was pale and without a trace of makeup. That and the dark hair and eyes reminded him of Von. 'Look, you're better placed than I am to answer these questions,' he said. 'Fraud's your area. And you've worked in the private sector.'

'I have. And I was good.' She peered at one of the screens. 'But not as good as Jamie Dyer.'

'How do you know?'

'Because he was up to something and I can't find what. And it's bugging me. I won't sleep till I do.'

'How are you so sure he was up to something?'

'Don't you have cases where there's no evidence but you know who the bad guy is? You just know?' She put her hands over her stomach. 'You know here?'

He stared at the long slim fingers interlaced over the saltire. 'Aye, all detectives have cases like that.'

'Well, it's the same for me. I've been looking through Bayne Pharmaceuticals' data. Every so often, something doesn't feel right.' She swivelled a screen round. 'See for yourself.'

He peered at the jumble of words and numbers. 'You're going to have to explain this to me.'

'What do you know about the import/export trade, specifically pharmaceuticals?'

He looked at her helplessly.

'Let's go back to basics. Stop me when I start to lose you.' She threw the braids over her shoulders. 'Bayne Pharmaceuticals manufactures every type of medication conceivable, as a pill, capsule, nasal spray, or injection.'

'And Jamie and Bruce were stealing them?'

'Don't get ahead of yourself, Steve.' She looked at him with steady eyes. 'How do you think pharma companies make so much money?'

'The way all businesses do? They sell at a profit?'

'Correct.' She tapped the screen. 'This is data that's in the public domain. It's the profit after taxation made last year by the major multinational pharma companies.'

He glanced down the list, searching for Bayne Pharmaceuticals.

'Let me help you. Bayne's is here,' she said, pointing.

He stared at the number, unbelieving. 'It's in the billions,' he murmured.

'These figures are in dollars. In case you can't do the maths, the profit in sterling is still in the billions. And Bayne's is by no means the largest company.'

'How do they do it? I mean, why are they so much more profitable than, say, Marks and Spencers?'

'Because they sell not just to people who need medication but to people who only think they do.'

'Okay, so you're saying they oversell.'

'More like overdose. But there's another thing. They keep their prices so high that only the richest countries can afford their drugs.'

'Fine. What's next?'

'Lesson number two.' Her eyes were dancing. 'If you want to defraud a pharma company, how would you go about it?'

'Steal their drugs and sell them yourself. Theft, pure and simple.'

'And where would you sell them, Steve? Which is the biggest market?'

He looked blank.

'The biggest consumer of medication is the US. The pharma companies there have learnt how to "manage" disease. So they say to consumers, "You have a non-threatening but treatable disorder? That's okay. You can live just like everyone else if you take this little tablet once a day for the rest of your long life."'

'So they have a guaranteed market which they've created themselves?'

'You cotton on quickly. And here's the clincher. Medication costs are higher in the US than anywhere else in the world.'

'Ah, so I steal the meds and sell them to US companies at lower prices than they'd pay legitimately?'

'Bravo, Steve,' she said, smiling mockingly. 'Honest-to-God stealing and selling from the back of a lorry. Only on an epic scale.'

'And you think Jamie and Bruce did this?'

'The Fraud Squad think they did it a lot. I discovered that, before Jamie worked in the import/export department, he was a salesman. He travelled all over the world to find customers for Bayne's products. It would have been straightforward to tip someone the wink that he could sell some of the products at a discount. He could have set up a nice little group of clients.' She motioned to another screen. 'These are the electronic records showing Bayne's sales for the last year. Almost all of them go to the US. I'm thinking that's where the bulk of Jamie's personal clients will be.'

He rubbed his face. 'Look, Jamie would have known there'd be a paper trail, right?'

'Right. Everything pharmaceutical companies do is scrutinised. There's paperwork, real and electronic, for every part of the process.'

'DI Kelly told me you checked and found no evidence of theft,' he said, exasperated.

'Not me, Steve. The Fraud Squad. Having met their experts, I'm not surprised they found zilch.'

'How do you mean?'

'They only scratched the surface. What the Fraud Squad boys did was a very superficial check of what medications went out versus what money came in. And they found no discrepancies.'

'Jamie and Bruce were squeaky clean, then.'

'There are different ways you can swindle a company. Bruce was involved in quality control of the finished product. He could have labelled perfectly good product as sub-standard, diverted it somewhere, and then sold it on the black market. The Fraud Squad boys didn't think of that.'

She was looking at him so intensely that, for an instant, he wondered if she were talking from experience.

'Well, did he?' he said, holding her gaze.

'He didn't. That's the first thing I checked. Everything sub-standard was accounted for and disposed of.'

'So, what other ways are there?'

She put a finger to her mouth and considered him. 'Here's one. The obvious one, actually. The medications are shipped out but diverted en route.'

'But what about the regulations? And the paperwork? Won't the people at the receiving end notice?'

'If small numbers of batches are missing in any one shipment, it's possible that no-one bothers to chase them up. It wouldn't be worth the effort. But Bayne's send out so much that, over time, it comes to a considerable amount.'

'Aye, right enough. So, how do we establish that's what Jamie and Bruce were up to?'

'Start by checking the data. Examine the mirror statistics.'

He ruffled his hair. What the hell was she talking about?

She motioned to the screen. 'I have Bayne's manufacturing and export records going back years. Batch numbers, expiration dates, the lot. I intend to compare the quantity of all the medications which Bayne's declares that it exports to the US with the corresponding quantity which the US declares that it imports from Bayne's. It's straightforward enough because Bayne's ship directly so there's no need to check, for example, import/export records of any third-party countries.'

'You're going to do the checks electronically?' he said, stupefied.

'No, I'm going to use my magical superpowers. Yes, dummy, of course I'm going to do the checks electronically. As well as my degrees in business management, I have a Masters in Software Engineering from MIT.'

He closed his mouth, hoping she hadn't heard the two

clunks as his balls dropped off.

'The code-cutting, dry runs, and debugging will take no time at all,' she said, twirling the braids in her fingers. 'But I'm also working on a couple of other contracts just now. So shall we meet again here, same time tomorrow?' She turned back to the keyboard. 'You can let yourself out.'

He was at the kitchen door when she said, 'Oh, and Steve?'

'Yes?'

'Lose the tie,' she said, peering into the screen.

Chapter 20

Von was on Lothian Road, slouching outside a kebab shop, her mobile phone to her ear. It was late afternoon and she had things to do. If Steve didn't pick up, she'd have to abandon it because this wasn't a message she intended to leave on voicemail.

She yawned, feeling the tiredness settle in her limbs. The baby had woken several times in the night. In the morning, she'd run into a narrow-chested young man who smelt of hair gel and cheap cologne, and had a towel wrapped round his waist. They stared at one other, and then the towel slipped, exposing the man's nakedness. But she'd long since lost the ability to blush. He grinned, informing her his name was Norrie, and then had the cheek to ask her when breakfast would be ready. She emerged from her shower to the smell of frying bacon. He laid the table for three and, to her amazement, set down a cooked breakfast of bacon, eggs, mushrooms, and tomatoes.

As they chatted, he told her he worked in construction as a surveyor. The job was good and so was the money. She knew enough not to pump him about his intentions regarding her daughter, and was impressed by the readiness with which he helped move the cot into the living room, and the gentleness with which he lifted out the baby. She left for work before Georgie wakened, having extracted a promise from Norrie that he would make sure her daughter went shopping for food because she'd not be back until late.

'Von?' Steve had picked up the phone. 'How are you doing?'

'I'm fine, and I've got some intel for you. I've been to the Calder Rifle and Pistol Club. They have several types of firearm that take a .45 ACP cartridge. The chief instructor told me most of the members have fired with it.'

There was a pause. 'What's the security like?'

'Forget it, Steve. For a gun to go missing, there'd have to be a big conspiracy. The firearms are signed in and out and the list double-checked against their collection before the place closes.'

'What about the ammo?'

'Both the guns and ammo are stored in windowless rooms in the centre of the building. At night, you'd have to go through several locked doors. And the placc is heavily alarmed. Anyway, give up the idea of finding the ammo there. You won't get expanding ammunition in British clubs.'

She could hear the frustration in his voice. 'But you can buy expanding for shooting deer and vermin.'

'Yes, but I've never heard of .45 ACPs being used for killing animals. It's usually smaller calibre. I think the ammo used to kill Jamie and Bruce was brought into the country illegally.'

'Okay, but from where?'

'Most likely the States. It's widely available. A propos that, Steve, I have a lead for you. The owner of the gun club is none other than Dewey Croker. As an American, he'll have access to firearms that shoot .45 ACPs as well as the ammo itself. As I said, he can get all that easily in the States.'

'His name's vaguely familiar.'

'If you're reading the newspapers these days, you'll have seen it in connection with this drug that's causing so much fuss. He's the CEO of Bayne Pharmaceuticals.'

She heard the low whistle. 'The company Ranald and Lexie work for?' he said, adding, 'And Jamie and Bruce.'

'It's a connection we can't afford to ignore. I'm about to go online and see what I can find out about him. Oh, and there's one other thing. Many of the gun club's members also belong to The Paradise World of Paintballing.'

He was silent for so long she thought they'd been disconnected. 'Steve?'

'Still here.'

'Sorry. I know it means more cross-checking.'

'Aye, all in a day's work. And what about your missing persons? You any nearer to finding your laddie?'

'I caught a glimpse of him so I know he's alive.' She ran a hand through her hair. 'I'm convinced he's mixed up with Ranald and Lexie somehow.' What she didn't tell Steve was what she intended to do later. It was strictly illegal and, if he knew, he'd stop her. 'So when are you coming back?' she said. Something made her add, 'I'm missing you.'

There was a brief silence. 'Wednesday.'

'And are you coming to the paintballing tournament this Saturday?'

'Aye, I suppose so. After all, you never know who'll be there.' A pause. 'Got to go, Von.'

She snapped the phone shut. Yes, of course he'd be coming to the tournament. If anyone was going to be there, it was the killer.

Von strolled down Lothian Road to the Internet café, and booked a couple of hours. She sat down beside a glassy-eyed teenager who threw her an unfriendly glance before continuing with whatever game he'd been playing. She logged on and fired up Internet Explorer.

As a first attempt, she typed 'Dewey Croker' into Google. The results that came back were recent postings about Lazinex. She scanned them quickly. Nothing she didn't already know. One article from CNN International had a videoclip of an interview with Croker. She pulled her earphones out of her bag, put them on, and clicked on the link.

A thick-set man was sitting, legs crossed, in an attitude that suggested he was supremely in command of the situation. He smiled disarmingly, running a hand over his iron-grey hair as the female interviewer asked her questions. His voice was deep but soft, with a Southern burr. Von took an immediate dislike to him, not because she saw through his apple-pie smile, but because of what he was saying.

'So you refute what the press have written about you in the papers, Mr Croker?'

'I just don't buy it. There's no evidence the Lazinex series has caused these unfortunate symptoms.'

'Despite the fact that the majority of the sufferers took Lazinex for rheumatoid arthritis?'

'Look, all these guys were taking a cocktail of medications. I've had my people look at what else they were prescribed and they're due to report back in the fall. I'm betting five gets you ten that the side effects were due to some of those other drugs. Someone needs to play hard-ball with these firms. They're pushing their stuff out too quickly. We at Bayne's, on the other hand, did exhaustive testing before we released Lazinex.' He leant forward and looked the woman resolutely in the eye. 'And we've kept the price deliberately low so that countries less fortunate than ours can afford it.' He smoothed his brow with both hands, a look of self-importance on his face.

Countries less fortunate than his? Self-righteous prick . . . Von closed the videoclip before she exploded. She ran her eye over a couple of leading articles. The editor of Glasgow's Sunday Herald had cut through Croker's defence like a cleaver, claiming that not only had Lazinex caused the symptoms but the CEO had known about it. In other words he'd sinned against the light. Ballsy. She hoped the editor knew what she was talking about because that kind of statement was liable to land her in court.

The game-playing teenager seemed to have won because he jumped up suddenly and punched the air with a 'Yes-s-s-s!!!'

Von suppressed a smile and typed in 'Bayne Pharmaceuticals'. A couple of clicks from the company's web page and she was reading Croker's biography. She'd half expected the author of the piece to lionise him but the account was surprisingly impersonal. Croker had been born in 1950. A poor boy from Biloxi, Mississippi, he'd won a scholarship to Princeton, become an entrepreneur before completing his education, and a millionaire by the time he was thirty. He was married to a New York heiress with whom he had three sons. Her photo showed a full-lipped woman with washy blue eyes and straight blonde hair that fell down to her shoulders. Bayne Pharmaceuticals had snapped up Croker and he'd moved to the Livingston branch as CEO two years ago. There was no mention of his interest in firearms, but one thing caught Von's eye: he'd donated heavily to charity, specifically those helping children in Third-World countries.

Von studied the photograph of Croker chewing on a wet cigar. He looked as though he'd once been fat and his diet had left him just on the wrong side of plump. He had a small bump in his nose, and deep indentations on either side of the bridge that indicated he wore reading glasses.

She brought up Google again and entered, 'Dewey Croker' + 'guns'.

The results spilt onto the page. She followed links at random. Dewey Croker was proficient with every type of firearm. He was a crack shot and had won shooting competitions, both pistol and rifle. One photograph showed him looking seriously into the camera, holding a Colt M1911, the muzzle pointing upwards. In another, he was speaking with the President of the National Rifle Association of America. The caption read: 'Mr Dewey Croker, a firm supporter of the Second Amendment of the United States Bill of Rights, vows to continue his work to promote firearm safety and the responsible use of firearms by United States citizens.'

Responsible use of firearms? She'd be prepared to bet good money that Croker was being paid a fistful of dollars by the NRA to be a 'firm supporter' of the gun lobbyists. The way he was standing, you'd think it was his destiny to take on the role of sole protector of the Second Amendment. His rigid neck muscles and unsmiling expression gave off the message that, provided you did as he did, you'd stay within the law and (more importantly) the law would protect you. She remembered a case in New York in which a disabled man had been shot by the police because they thought he was reaching for a gun. What they saw in his cold dead hand when they turned his bullet-ridden body over was his disabled person's card. He was a deaf mute and had been reaching into his jacket for his ID.

Her time was up. One more click and she was out of here. She brought up a photograph of Dewey Croker demonstrating to a group of schoolchildren the correct stance when firing at an assailant. He was holding a revolver two-handed, arms extended, and was aiming at a man on the ground. The caption read: 'As part of a demonstration on how to use firearms safely, Mr Dewey Croker aims his prized Ruger Blackhawk at an assailant who has been incapacitated with a shot to the chest.'

She'd handled a Ruger Blackhawk in the States but couldn't remember the details. A quick trawl with Google, and she found the page on a handguns website: 'A Ruger Blackhawk is a single-action revolver whose cylinder can be removed and replaced with one chambered for different cartridges.'

It was impossible to tell from the photograph whether Croker was holding the Convertible model of the Ruger, but she remembered that one cartridge for which cylinders were available was the .45 ACP. She looked at the angle of Croker's arms. There was no mistaking it – he was aiming at the man's head. A chest shot, followed by a head shot. A double tap.

Her heart was pounding. Dewey Croker owned a revolver capable of firing the same calibre bullets that had killed Jamie Dyer and Bruce Lassiter. And a revolver didn't eject cartridges.

Von was skulking behind a rhododendron bush in Belgrave Crescent's communal gardens. She was dressed in a warm sweater and black trousers, and had exchanged her red jacket for a dark heavy-duty padded number. And she was wearing gloves. Summer nights in Scotland can be chilly. She adjusted the zoom lens of her camera, set up on a tripod so she could watch who came and went from Lexie Dyer's house. So far, only Lexie had arrived, from work judging by her sharp suit. There was no sign of Phil. He might be on his nocturnal wanderings in the Grassmarket or maybe he was haunting Dean Cemetery.

It was a mild evening. Just as well, as she'd be here for hours. After leaving the Internet café, she'd phoned Steve and told him what she'd discovered about Croker, telling him everything, including the photo of the CEO demonstrating a double tap. He'd said nothing, but that could mean anything with Steve.

She unscrewed the cap of the Thermos and took a swig of coffee. The tuna sandwich she'd bought before Marks and Spencers closed was squashed at the bottom of her rucksack. She munched slowly. This was a side of investigating she was well used to. As a detective, she'd taken part in many surveillance operations. The trick was not to fall asleep. Easy when you had your partner with you, not so easy alone. Pity Steve wasn't here. As a surveillance buddy, he'd been the best, keeping her awake with tales from his Glasgow childhood. Times had been hard for him, as they had for her. It was what had helped form their strong bond, the realisation that their upbringings hadn't been so different. He'd joined the police force as a way out of the poverty that had ground down his parents. His Da had started as a fitter's assistant at the North British Locomotive Company, his mother stopping at home to raise him and his sister. Von smiled to herself, remembering his account of how his Mammy would take them all to the 'pawn'. She'd wheel her washing basket pretending she was going to the steamie but no-one was ever fooled.

A sudden wind blew through the gardens, stirring the trees and harrying the branches of the rhododendron. A glance at the sky told her the weather was on the change. She rubbed her arms briskly. It was nearly 9.30pm. Damn it, it didn't look like Lexie was going out tonight. Still, there was the rest of the week. She'd told Georgie and Norrie she'd have to work late for the next few days. Georgie had simply nodded, but Norrie had assured her he'd be on hand to help out and she wasn't to worry. He was proving to be a godsend. What he saw in the rebellious Georgie was beyond her but perhaps her daughter was rebellious only with her. She pulled her coat tighter. She'd give Lexie another hour, and then pack it in.

Half an hour later, a light-blue car coasted into the sweep of Belgrave Crescent. She recognised Ranald McCrea's Ascari. She checked her camera and took a few snaps of him leaving the vehicle, going up Lexie's steps, and ringing the bell. He looked over his shoulder and his gaze swept the gardens. But her balaclava was down and her lens had an anti-reflective coating. No-one could see her through the leaves.

A minute later, the door opened and Lexie appeared. Von took a couple of snaps. The woman was dressed in a pink jacket and tight black-leather trousers, and her face was expertly made up, her hair falling over her shoulders in loose curls. But it was the slim figure in jeans and a dark-brown corduroy jacket that made Von's pulse quicken. A black baseball cap was pulled low over his eyes but, from the build and the way she'd seen him walk, this was Phil Pattullo. She would have taken a photo of his face but too little of it was visible.

The three of them got into the Ascari, and it pulled away smoothly.

She sat back on her heels. Interesting. So, where were they going? Mhairi had said Phil's posh new friends took him places. Perhaps they were off clubbing. Lexie was certainly dressed the part. Von waited another half hour before dismantling the tripod and packing everything into the rucksack. She left the bag in the bushes, and climbed over the railings into the street.

Twilight was falling but it was still light enough for someone to see her. Although the street was deserted, who knew what was happening behind the curtains? Keeping to the shadows, she crept along to Lexie's house.

As a professional investigator she'd seen most types of burglar alarm and had learnt how to disable them. The box on Lexie's was one of the more common models. She removed a cable and screwdriver from her jacket and, after a glance around, climbed onto the side railing. It took her less than a minute to remove the casing, fiddle with the inside, and attach the cable so as to bypass the part of the circuit that rings when the alarm is triggered.

She jumped down and made her way to the end of the street. Shallow steps led into the basement lane. She hunched over so as not to be visible from the windows, and hurried down the steps and along to Lexie's. There were three rooms on this side of the basement, she remembered from her afternoon as 'Iris'. She examined the lock of the first, the one stacked with garden furniture. *There was a door to which I found no key.* It was a simple pin-and-tumbler model. Her guess was that the same key fitted all three basement doors and, if it was anywhere, it would be in Phil's. She took out a pick and tension wrench, and set to work. The lock was stiff but she was well practised.

A minute later, she heard the faint click as the last pin set and popped out of the cylinder. The door was partially blocked with furniture. She pushed it gently, wriggled inside, and closed it behind her.

The beam of her pencil torch illuminated the rickety towers of tables and chairs. One false step and they'd come crashing down. She slipped past, hugging the wall. A second later, she was in the corridor. She made her way softly past the room with the bookcases and stopped outside Phil's door. She paused to listen, holding her breath. Nothing. She turned the handle slowly and pushed. The door slid over the carpet with a whispering noise.

The curtains were drawn. She peered into the gloom, reluctant to use her torch. The place was tidier than she remembered: the duvet was spread neatly over the bed and the pyjamas were folded on the plumped-up pillow.

The PC was switched off. It took an age to boot and, as she'd expected, it was running the Millennium Edition of Windows. She shut it down, took a CD from her pocket, and inserted it into the drive. The machine booted into MS-DOS mode from the CD. A few key presses later, she started up Windows without being prompted for a password, congratulating herself silently on her foresight in taking her agency's computer courses.

There was enough light from the screen for her to see what she was doing. She moved the mouse rapidly, her hands ghostly white in the glare. The icons were familiar: My Computer, My Documents, Internet Explorer. Nothing out of the ordinary. She glanced through the My Documents folder. It was empty. She searched through the other folders systematically but found only letters that Lexie had written to Edinburgh local council, and a few PDF files stamped with Bayne Pharmaceuticals' logo. She opened a couple at random. They were about employment law.

She sat back, picking her lip. This was clearly Lexie's computer. But was Phil also using it? What would he be doing? Surfing the net? She launched Internet Explorer and checked the browsing history. In the last week, Lexie (or Phil) had connected to a number of world news sites, sites hosting computer games, and a couple of soft-porn sites. She reordered the browsing history to show the pages most visited. Top of the list, visited daily, was a web page showing Bayne Pharmaceuticals' logo. When she tried to get in past the welcome page, she was prompted for a password. Lexie must be doing some of her work from home.

Whatever Phil was up to with Lexie and Ranald, she wasn't going to find the answer on this machine. She was about to power it down when her gaze drifted to the drawer. It was the one on the right-hand side of the desk.

The one that was locked.

She hesitated. If she unlocked it, Phil would know someone had been here. She was prepared to leave the door to the basement unlocked because it might be months before anyone discovered it. But the drawer was different. Phil was here every day and was the likely holder of its missing key. He'd notice if it was unlocked. But would he? He might think he'd simply forgotten to relock it. She weighed the pros and cons, then, holding the torch in her mouth, she pulled out her tools.

It was even easier to open than the basement door. She peered inside the drawer. There were two items. The first was a small fat key, the type that fits into a left-luggage locker. The second was a passport in Phil Pattullo's name. She glanced at the back page. Phil's serious face stared back at her. The passport was two years old and she didn't have a recent photo of him. She took out her tiny digital camera and, with the torch still in her mouth, took a couple of snaps. She laid the passport and key exactly as she'd found them in the drawer.

As she dipped her head, the torch's beam caught something at the back, something that reflected the light. She pulled her gloves off and slipped her fingers inside, touch-feeling her way.

They brushed against something with a smooth metallic finish.

It was a CD.

The PC was still on. Her heart was pumping as she slipped the disk into the drive. With a few deft mouse movements, she brought up the CD's contents. There was a single file called PA.XLS. A quick double-check of the hard drive confirmed what she already knew – this file wasn't on the PC. That it was on a CD in a locked drawer made it soar in significance.

With trembling fingers, she doubled-clicked on the file. The spreadsheet opened to reveal three columns of data. The first contained eight-figure numbers. The cells in the second held five-character alphanumeric data: the first three characters were numbers, the last two, letters. The final column contained words of variable length. They looked Spanish, possibly Italian. There was nothing to tell her what the columns represented. She stared at the words, trying to decipher their meaning, and then brought up an online foreign language translator. No joy. She slammed her hand against the desk. The screen wobbled, making the words dance. Damn it, she'd never been good at codes and secret messages. She'd have to think about this later. She removed the boot-up disk, replaced it with a clean CD, and did a drag-and-drop of the file.

She put everything back the way it had been and powered down the machine. The screen's glare died, plunging the room into darkness. She was sitting thinking about the CD when she heard the purr of a car engine. It was followed by the slamming of doors. She felt a prickle of anxiety. The luminous dial of her watch told her it was nearly eleven. This couldn't be Lexie and the others. They'd been out for only an hour.

Suddenly, she heard the sound of feet on the front steps.

She hurried to the window and peeled back the curtain. Black clouds obscured the moon. Thank God for the darkness. If they'd glanced up and seen the cables hanging out of the burglar alarm, she doubted she'd get away before the police arrived.

Heavy feet thumped across the low ceiling. They were going into the sitting room. She caught the faint sound of words. Ranald's voice, followed by a woman's laugh. Then a voice she hadn't heard before, a man's voice, higher in pitch than Ranald's and slightly nasal. Despite the urgency of the situation, she paused to listen. But she couldn't make out the words. And padding up to the ground floor and putting her ear to the keyhole was out of the question.

The talking stopped and someone marched purposefully across the room. The sitting-room door opened and closed. Her stomach cramped with shock. Someone was coming downstairs. With a feeling of unreality, she ran out of Phil's room and rushed into the one stacked with furniture. The footsteps were in the corridor now. She pressed herself against the wall, trying not to make a sound, and squeezed past the tottering stacks. The footsteps stopped. Whoever had come down had halted outside Phil's room. Too late, she remembered she'd left the door open. And Phil had left it closed.

She tugged open the basement door and, pushing herself through, almost fell out of the building. She dropped into a crouch. The light came on in Phil's room, seeping through the thin curtains and washing the basement lane with an eerie light. She pictured the scenario: Phil, his suspicions raised by the open door, looking to see if anything had been disturbed. It was a matter of seconds before he'd try the locked drawer. Jesus, she'd messed up. Big time. There was a sudden muffled cry from the room, and footsteps thundered back up the corridor. Game over.

She turned to run, but caught her foot in the garden hose and kicked over the watering can. The noise after the silence was deafening. There were shouts from above and she realised with a jolt of fear that she was directly below the sitting room. They couldn't fail to have heard the racket, and Phil would be there by now, telling them there'd been an intruder. She abandoned her initial plan of reassembling the burglar alarm – what was the point? – and sprinted up the lane. She took the steps two at a time and rushed into Belgrave Place. But Phil had been quick. There was a relentless pounding of feet behind her. If she could make it to Queensferry Road, she had a chance. Even at this hour, there would be people and traffic and she could melt into the street.

She raced up the street towards the junction with Buckingham Terrace. Her breathing was coming in painful gasps and she had to will herself to keep going. She was slowing on the approach to the corner when she felt something heavy land on her back. She lost her footing and fell sprawling, throwing her arms out reflexively to protect her face. Her assailant was strong enough to pin her down, and was turning her over when she heard the sound of a car coming towards them.

He sprang back into the shadows. She scrabbled to her feet and launched herself into the bushes. In a second, he'd be after her. She crashed through onto Queensferry Road and, ignoring the blaring of horns, rushed across the street. She reached the pavement and turned to see him on the other side. He was trying to watch her and get across the road without being run over.

A cab was coming towards her. She made a big show of hailing it, and then ducked down. She pulled her balaclava up off her face.

'Where to?' the driver said.

She thrust a twenty into his hand. 'Just drive,' she yelled. 'Like your life depends on it. I'm being followed and I need you to draw him off.'

The man frowned, pushed the money back into her hand, and sped off.

She yanked the balaclava down and crouched behind the bus shelter, watching through the glass. Her assailant had stopped halfway across the road and was waving down another cab. He got in and the cab drove away, passing so close to the shelter that had it not been dark she would have seen his face.

She straightened, shaking with relief, only then becoming aware of the pain in her knees. Jesus, they throbbed so badly she felt like crying. She pushed the balaclava up onto her head and limped down the road. A third taxi passed. She was sorely tempted to flag it down but she couldn't go home yet, much as she craved a long soak in a scented bath listening to Pink Floyd. She hobbled along Queensferry Road, following the curve of the pavement towards Dean Bridge until she came to the intersection with Belgrave Crescent.

After a glance around, she slipped into the gardens and limped towards the rhododendrons. She was slinging the rucksack over her shoulder when a light came on in one of the houses. She dropped to her knees automatically, smothering a groan at the sudden stab of pain.

She peeped through the leaves. Three figures were standing silhouetted in Lexie's doorway. Why three? Her assailant would be halfway across town, chasing after the empty cab. Had the police arrived while she was being pursued? She parted the branches for a better look. There was no squad car. And somehow she doubted Lexie had called the police. The officers would see Phil and, whatever Lexie and Ranald were up to, she was sure they wanted to keep it secret. She was fumbling with the zoom lens when one of the figures detached itself from the group and trotted down the steps. He turned into Belgrave Place. He was a biggish man, not Phil's build. He slipped his hands into his trouser pockets before fading from view and, in that single action, she recognised him. She felt suddenly dizzy.

The two figures were still standing in the doorway. The taller moved his head and she saw Phil's features. He murmured something to his companion who looked up at the burglar alarm, the light falling on her long blonde hair.

So the man who'd come after her was Ranald.

But, while he'd been giving chase, Lexie and Phil had had a visitor. Or had they phoned him when they realised there was an intruder? He'd have had to live on their doorstep to get there so quickly. Another thought slipped unbidden into her mind. Perhaps they'd brought him back with them from wherever they'd gone clubbing. Nothing strange in that. Toby was a paintballer too and he'd admitted to knowing Lexie. And he knew Ranald; she'd heard him on the phone at Federico's.

Her heart was beating painfully as she remembered how he'd waved at Lexie and Phil.

Phil. He knew Phil.

Her hands were shaking so much that she had to put the camera down. If Toby knew Phil, then whatever was going on had to involve him too.

Chapter 21
Tuesday, June 12th

Steve was leaning against the wall, watching a Labrador copulating with a Dalmatian while their owners chatted away oblivious. The door opened. Cally stood in the doorway, fiddling with the hem of her shirt, which was white and patterned with tiny sunflowers. She was wearing black tights under a short light-blue denim skirt, the hem fraying more by design than by accident. He suspected the whole outfit, including the clumpy shoes, would have cost him a month's wages.

'Hi, Steve.'

He greeted her with a weak smile. 'Hi, Cally.'

'You don't look so hot.'

'I had a bad night.' His leg had played up and he'd thrashed about in bed.

She said nothing, nodding as if she knew all about it. Maybe she assumed he'd been out on the razzle. Aye, he'd leave it at that and let her think he was a big girl's blouse, and couldn't take his drink. Better than telling her the truth, that he'd been shot on duty through carelessness and his wound was constantly giving him gyp.

She combed her fingers through her hair. It was loose today, pushed to the side and cascading in waves over her shoulder. 'Come, Steve.'

He followed her in.

'We're good to go,' she said when they were in the kitchen. 'I've tested everything on my own data. But before I run the job

I need to tell you what the code does.'

His face wore a martyred expression. 'Is that necessary?'

'Now, now, be nice. If you don't know what the programme does, you'll have no faith in the results.' She leant in so close to him that he could smell the muscatel on her breath. It was 10.00am. Perhaps she drank it for breakfast.

'First though, I'll get you some caffeine. Black, no sugar, right?'

'Right.'

She seemed pleased with herself for remembering. She poured from the monster coffee-machine. 'I got this going earlier. And I've bought blueberries.'

'Blueberries?'

'Brain food. I eat them all the time when I'm working.' She took a large ceramic bowl from the fridge and placed it in front of him. 'They keep me sane. Have you ever seen anyone with code rage, Steve?'

He shook his head, smiling.

'It's not pretty.' She jerked her head at the wall. 'Look what happened last month.'

A chunk of plaster was missing from the white wall behind her.

'Don't be alarmed,' she said quickly. 'I only ever attack inanimate objects. Although you're not far off it today. Shall I give you a Thai massage? I've been on the course.'

'Thanks, but there's no need.' He raised his mug in mock salute. 'I'll be going like the clappers once I've had this.'

She opened her mouth to speak, but must have thought better of it. She took the seat in front of the workstation. 'So, are we sitting comfortably?' When he said nothing, she added, 'Then I'll begin.'

She smiled at him so warmly that he felt his spirits rise.

'Okay, so this screen shows the import/export records

from Bayne's Glasgow plant, going back yonks.' She traced the columns of figures. 'This is the data of interest, the export data. These records show which medications were made, when they were made, and in which quantities. This column here shows how much was of sub-standard quality and hence was discarded. The final column gives the quantity that was batched up for export. With me so far?'

'Aye.'

'The data is on Bayne's main server, which I've been given access to. Don't tell anyone but I've copied it all to this.' She tapped the side of the workstation. 'The jobs will go that much faster if the processing isn't slowed down by the I/O.'

'Of course,' he said, trying to look intelligent.

'The shipping manifests are also on Bayne's server. They have the batch numbers, destinations, customer details. That sort of thing.'

'So these statistics you were talking about . . . '

'Mirror statistics. I've managed to get hold of the import data from the relevant US shipping companies. In other words, what they say came in, down to the last pill. My code will compare the stats at either end. If there's any discrepancy, even one batch gone astray, it will flag it up.'

It seemed straightforward the way she explained it. He suspected she was giving him a grossly simplified version of what the code actually did. But he was grateful she wasn't patronising him.

'So tell me about the case,' she said suddenly.

'I can't.'

'You can, though. I've signed the police's hush-hush documents. The more I know about the case, the better I'm placed to help.' There was a look of challenge in the brown eyes.

'Aye, okay. The two people who were out paintballing with Jamie and Bruce also happen to work for Bayne

Pharmaceuticals.' He paused to see what effect this had but her face was expressionless.

'You think something's going on at Bayne's?' she said.

'It's possible. The CEO, Dewey Croker, hasn't been in post long. He'll be keen to make his mark . . . '

' . . . so he wouldn't want any sort of scandal involving Bayne's. The damage to Bayne's reputation would be enormous . . . '

He nodded at the computer screen. ' . . . and if he found out somehow that Jamie and Bruce were swindling him . . . '

' . . . he might be angry enough to take matters into his own hands.' She tilted her head. 'You think Dewey's the shooter?'

He hesitated. 'We've no evidence it's him.'

'But?'

'Jamie and Bruce were shot with expanding ammunition. That's not easy to get hold of here but it is in the US. And Croker's an American who happens to own a gun that can fire that type of ammo. From what I've been seeing of him online, he knows how to kill.'

She leant back in her chair, studying the ceiling. 'Dewey is based in Bayne's Livingston branch. That's not far from where the bodies were discovered. He could have slipped out, done the dastardly deed, and then gone back to his board meeting.'

'Aye, it's possible.'

'It means that his gun has to be in his office somewhere.'

It was something he'd considered after Von had told him what she'd uncovered about Croker. But they'd need more than the mere suspicion of Dewey's complicity before the Fiscal would grant them a warrant to search his office.

He scratched his neck. 'Let's get back to Jamie and Bruce. I understand you've checked their bank statements. Anything funny there?'

'All fine and dandy. But that's what you'd expect. If they were skimming the profits, there's no way the money would even have touched the Royal Bank of Scotland.' She put a finger to her mouth. 'You said there were two people out paintballing with Jamie and Bruce. Are they in the frame?'

He remembered Ranald's and Lexie's identical words about testing the new paintball markers. And they were members of a gun club practically on the doorstep of The Paradise World of Paintballing. Briefly, he told Cally what he knew, including the aborted phone call to Jamie's landline, and the house, cleaned as though he intended to leave the country.

She was silent for a while. 'Are you going to check out the guns at the club?'

'Something makes me think it's too obvious, the murder weapon coming from there. It's the first place the police would look.'

'And yet you haven't.'

She was right. And for all he knew, his boss, as Senior Investigating, had already taken away the handguns. But he was convinced it would be a wasted effort. 'It really is the obvious place, Cally. And the security is second to none.'

'Come on, Steve, security is intended to keep out Joe Public. But what if you're not Joe Public? What if you're Dewey Croker, the owner, who has keys to every door and knows how to switch off the alarms and dodge the cameras? It's like walking around your own house.'

She had a point. 'But the killings were done during the day. And the guns have to be signed out.'

'And I bet Croker knows how to get round that.' She folded her arms. 'Think of it from his point of view. He plans to commit murder, takes a little-used weapon, doctors the database – I'm assuming it's a modern club with digitised records – and removes all trace of the firearm.' She shrugged. 'It's how I'd do it.'

He doubted Dewey had the knowhow to fix the computer's logs to hide the transaction. But it was a mistake to assume that what he himself couldn't do with computers couldn't be done by others.

She was watching him. 'What do you think the killer did with the murder weapon?'

'It'll be at the bottom of the Forth.' He smiled crookedly. 'It's how I'd do it.'

'If we find evidence there was a grand theft, what will you do?'

'Look for evidence that Dewey knew about it. It'll be a motive for murder. Find the motive, and you find the murderer.' It was the maxim Von lived by. Had lived by: he'd forgotten she was no longer a police detective.

'Where did you hear that, Steve?'

'My old boss at the Met used to say it.'

'A woman.'

'How did you know?' he said in surprise.

'The expression on your face changed,' she said softly. 'You've got a bit of a thing for her, haven't you?'

He said nothing.

But she'd lost interest. 'Have you considered that Dewey may not have actually fired the gun?'

'Aye,' he said, rubbing his eyes. 'I'm wondering whether there was a contract killer.'

'Maybe these two other paintballers did it. They were on hand. They work for Bayne's. Perhaps dark forces hold sway there.'

'We've checked them out. There's no evidence. One of them had firearm discharge residue on him but it's circumstantial because they're both gun-club members.'

'The presence of residue would be suspicious if they *hadn't been members*. Having it always on their hands makes them ideal candidates.'

She was smart, he had to give her that. 'One of the paintballers was Jamie Dyer's sister,' he said.

'And you think sisters don't murder their brothers?'

He recalled Lexie's shock at seeing Jamie's corpse. Could she have been acting? She'd said they weren't close. *I didn't know him terribly well.* Aye, she or Ranald could have killed Jamie and Bruce on Dewey's orders. Lexie could have left early to dispose of the murder weapon, leaving Ranald to call the police. But why? For money? Maybe. Yet wouldn't Dewey have arranged for a faceless contractor to do it, rather than embroil his employees in a capital crime? Would he, when he could even have done it himself, put into their hands the means by which they could blackmail him?

He could see Cally was drawn taut as a bow, wanting to turn her great intellect to the problem of who had killed Jamie and Bruce. But he needed her to start the code running. He gestured at the workstation. 'Let's get the show on the road.'

'Our mission, then, is to see if there's a mismatch between Bayne's exports and the US buyers' imports and, if so, how much Bayne's has lost as a result.' She moistened her lips. 'How far back shall we go?'

'Twelve months to begin with. How long would that take?'

'Given the other jobs that are running simultaneously, I'd say two to three hours.' She hesitated. 'You don't have to go back to the cop shop, do you? I need to stay here and check on progress. And I thought we could watch a film.'

'Well, I'm not sure . . . ' he said, remembering the rows of slasher movies.

'You can choose the film.'

'Aye, fine.'

'Right. Let's start then.' She brought up some text on the screen. He sat slack-jawed as she made edits. What the hell programming language was she using?

She glanced at him. 'I'm making sure the code references only the US companies that buy from Bayne's. We don't want it going all round the houses.' She pressed a button and sat back.

The screens sprang to life simultaneously. He sat bolt upright.

She threw her arms round him as though to prevent him from taking off. 'Woah, Steve, I see the caffeine's hit the spot.'

'So what's happening?'

'This status bar at the bottom tells us how far along we are. And this screen here' – she tapped the one beside her – 'samples the data so I can see whether we're getting gibberish.'

'Gibberish?' he said, peering at the scrolling rows of numbers. 'How can you tell?'

'Believe me, I can tell.'

'You're making a list. You're checking it twice, eh?' he grinned.

'I only check lists once, Steve.' Her eyes rested on his. 'So? The film?'

In the living room, he ran a finger along the spines of the DVDs, hoping to find something other than a slasher. But he was out of luck. In the end, he chose April Fool's Day. It seemed appropriate, somehow.

He sprawled on the sofa as Cally worked the player.

She refilled his mug and fetched the bottle of muscatel from the sideboard. 'Don't let me drink too much,' she said, flopping down next to him. 'Half a bottle and I begin to recite limericks.'

'Fine by me.'

The opening scene, showing a blonde with big hair being interviewed by someone off camera, flashed onto the television screen. He closed his eyes and nodded off.

A movement woke him. Cally was clambering over the yellow coffee table towards the kitchen. He levered himself off the sofa and followed her.

She studied the rows of data. The status bar was a third of

the way along.

'It's been going for about an hour,' she said, a finger at her mouth.

An hour? He'd been asleep that long? It explained why he felt so refreshed. He wondered if she'd noticed. With luck she'd been too engrossed in the film.

'And is it working?' he said.

'Listen, chum,' she replied good-naturedly, 'my code always works, all right? I test to destruction.'

'I didn't doubt it for a minute.'

'Yes, you did.' She smiled. 'Are you hungry?'

'I could eat.'

'What do you do for lunch?'

'I usually get a poke of chips.'

She looked at him thoughtfully. 'Just before you woke up, I ordered some Indian food to arrive in an hour's time.'

'Why an hour?'

Her eyes were steady. 'Now that you've had your little sleep, you're finally good for something.' She started to unbutton his shirt.

He gripped her fingers.

'Do you mind?' she said, searching his face. 'You can say no, and we'll still be friends. If it's any consolation, I've been turned down more often than the beds at the Glasgow Hilton.'

He laughed loudly. 'I find that hard to believe.' He still couldn't get over how like Von she was. The same humour in the eyes.

She linked her fingers through his. 'I should tell you that I'm spectacular in bed,' she murmured. 'And I have a feeling you are too.'

'So, no pressure then?'

He let her take him into the bedroom. They stood looking at one another.

'Aren't you going to take your clothes off?' he said.

'You do it.'

He slipped off her shirt, and then the tiny lace bra. He knelt and took a nipple in his mouth, sucking gently as he pulled down her skirt.

Steve rolled over with a groan. The room was spinning. God, the girl was good, he hadn't had sex like that since he'd left London. He turned towards her, smiling, and ran a finger down her flushed face.

'Lovely, Steve,' she said softly. 'I've always thought that having sex is like making money. It's how you get there that counts. And you kept your funds in without any premature withdrawals.'

He laughed, smoothing her hair out over the pillow to frame her face. She pulled him towards her and his mouth came down hard on hers.

After a few seconds, she pushed him away. 'We've time to do it again before the Indian food man comes.' There was a mischievous look in her eyes. 'Although I should warn you that past performance is no guarantee of future success.'

He was reaching his climax, Cally straddling him, her hand cupping his testicles, when the doorbell rang.

She swore under her breath. 'Keep going, Steve. He'll wait.'

A minute later, she threw her head back, gasping. 'Okay, okay, you can get the door now.'

He wrapped the duvet round himself and fumbled inside his jacket for the wallet.

The delivery man, a lean-framed giant with a baby face, handed over the plastic bag, scarcely giving the duvet and Steve's obvious nakedness a second glance.

He returned to find Cally in a white dressing gown. She was tying up her hair. 'We'll eat before we shower,' she said. 'I'm always starving after sex.'

She followed him into the kitchen.

'Aha,' she said, leaning over the table, 'I overestimated how long this would take.' She indicated the status bar. 'I think another half hour and we're done. Let's eat.'

'And, where . . . ?' he said, frowning at the table loaded with equipment.

'In bed, of course.'

'Cally . . . '

'Don't worry. I can't manage again so soon, either.'

In the bedroom, she spread the cartons out on the two giant Rubik's cubes that passed for bedside tables. 'Tuck in, Steve.'

She picked at the food, watching him as he shovelled it away. 'You're eating like it's going out of style,' she said. 'I like a man with an appetite.'

She left the room and returned with the bottle of muscatel and two glasses.

'No thanks,' he said, 'not my tipple.'

'Don't tell me.' She went into a Sam Spade impression. 'You're a bourbon man, like every hard-boiled cop.'

'Close. I drink malt whisky.'

She leant across the bed and picked something off the floor. It was a business card. 'This fell out of your jacket. Who's Lina Prince?'

Lovely Lina. He'd forgotten he had the card. 'A firearms expert from California. She examined the bullets retrieved from the victims.'

'And she gave you her card?'

He smiled innocently. 'She did.'

She made a claw and ran it lightly down his chest. 'You're not going to make me jealous, are you?'

'I saw her once. It was business. And it's not likely I'll be seeing her again.'

'Then you won't need this.' She tore the card into pieces and threw them into the air. 'Shall we check the job? It should be done by now.'

In the kitchen, they huddled together in front of the main screen. She tapped a key and the rows scrolled down. They contained words which meant nothing to him.

'This is what's known as an exception report, Steve. It compares the mirror stats I told you about and only makes a record when there's a discrepancy.' She was frowning as she read. 'The first bit is the header. The stuff that's of interest is at the bottom.'

He waited, his heart thumping.

'I don't believe it,' she said finally. 'It's kosher.'

'What do you mean?'

'My comparisons show that the meds that left Bayne's are exactly the same as those that reached the US ports. Exactly the same. Batch numbers, quantities, the lot.' She stuck out her chin. 'But something was going on. I'm convinced of it.'

She sounded like a petulant child. For a second, he thought she was going to throw a tantrum.

'Cally, is it possible you made a mistake?'

'I tested the code on my own data,' she said, anger flaring in her eyes. 'There's no mistake.'

'Well, then, that's it. If there's no evidence of theft, we have to look for a motive elsewhere.' He suddenly felt tired.

'No, Steve, that's not it. There's more analysis I can do on these records.'

'Such as?'

She raised a tense face. 'I don't know yet.'

She was determined not to let this go. A thought struck him. 'You said Bayne's also sell to other countries.'

She looked guilty, like a child who's been found out. 'Of course I could examine all their buyers. But the US is by far their largest customer.' She returned his gaze. 'Do you know how people become millionaires, Steve?'

'You're asking the wrong person.'

'By going for the big time. Which is why the scam must involve the US in some way.'

He looked at the screens, all static now, the cursors winking asynchronously. 'And your report to DI Kelly . . . '

' . . . will say that my results are, as yet, inconclusive.'

'Aye, fine, but don't you think that, even if you do look at all the data, it'll be a dead end and you'll get the same results you've got now?'

'I've never been wrong, Steve.'

He was tempted to say, 'There's always a first time'. He massaged his face. 'How long do you need for this further analysis?'

'A day, maybe two. Or three. How long is a piece of string? I won't know till I've done it.' She brightened. 'You're not heading back to Edinburgh, are you?'

'Why?'

She tugged at his duvet, pulling it down. She ran her fingers through his chest hair. 'Have you ever had a threesome, Steve?' She looked at him hopefully. 'The Indian food delivery man and I are good friends . . . '

Chapter 22
Wednesday, June 13th

Von was sitting in Princes Street Gardens watching tourists taking photographs of each other. She was waiting for Mhairi. The woman wasn't at her usual post outside the Disney Store. But at 9.30am she'd still be shuffling into the centre of town from wherever she'd chosen to spend the night. Had she been at Dean Cemetery with its high walls and sheltered corners? What did the homeless do when the weather grew too cold for stopping outdoors? Von shivered, and stared into the sky. A feeble sun forced its light through breaks in the clouds; the threatened rain had come to nothing.

She'd slept badly since the night in Belgrave Crescent gardens. Not because her skinned knees were giving her hell but because she'd seen Toby leaving Lexie's house. Had she been quicker off the mark, she'd have followed him. Some investigator she was turning out to be. She'd agonised all day yesterday about what to do next. A part of her didn't want to bring him into the equation but she'd be failing at her job (and failing Mrs Pattullo) if she didn't. And, for her own peace of mind, she needed to know that Toby was simply a casual friend to Ranald and Lexie and wasn't mixed up in whatever they were doing. But she wouldn't think about that now. She had something else planned.

She thrust a hand into her pocket, checking again that her press pass was there. The previous day, she'd persuaded an old editor friend to let her masquerade as one of her staff. The woman had thrown up her hands, but had backed down on being told that her magazine would be getting the exclusive of Von's interview with Dewey Croker. It wasn't the first time she'd played journalist and the editor was up for it because (she confessed reluctantly) her own requests for interviews with Croker had been turned down: the man was trying to keep out of the public eye. The reason was obvious – that morning, Radio 4's Today programme had discussed the Lazinex fiasco, informing listeners that Bayne's shares were at an all-time low.

Von had thought long and hard about how to make her approach to Croker's office to ensure she be granted an interview. Anything to do with the Lazinex drug would slam the door in her face. And she couldn't say she was interested in his gun collection, because a woman's magazine wanting an interview about that topic simply wasn't credible. In the end, she tried the only angle that had a chance of succeeding: she told Dewey's press secretary that she wanted to profile him and his work with children's charities. To her surprise, she'd been told that Mr Croker could give her an hour at 11.00am the following day. The editor had been over the moon. She'd also let slip that, minutes after Von had put the phone down, her office had been contacted by Bayne's, ringing to check on Ms Valenti's credentials.

Von had a little time before she needed to schlep out to Livingston. Her hope of finding Mhairi was fading. No matter, she'd catch her later.

She was at the west end of Princes Street when she spotted her. The woman was limping heavily. A young man in a hurry pushed past her, spinning her round and causing her to drop her carrier bags.

'And who said chivalry was dead?' Mhairi shouted after him. Seeing Von, her face brightened. 'You're a sight for sore eyes, old darling.'

Von was about to run after the man but Mhairi grabbed her arm. 'Not worth it, Von. He'll belt you in the mouth, I know the type.' Her eyes roamed over Von's face. 'I thought you'd stopped coming to see me.'

'Why would I do that?'

'The homeless are like bad luck. People want to forget them.' She smiled, as if to mitigate the effect of her words. 'You got any news of Phil, then?'

'I know he's alive. I don't know what he's up to.'

'You think he's up to something?'

'Isn't everyone?'

Mhairi looked thoughtful for a moment. 'He's not stopping at the cemetery any more. I've just come from there.'

Von wondered how much to tell the woman. She decided to keep to herself that Phil was staying at Lexie's. If Mhairi learnt he was living in a degree of luxury she could only dream of, she might be less inclined to help. Von could hardly blame her. She took the photos from her bag and showed Mhairi the ones she'd taken of Lexie and Ranald during her evening vigil. 'I'm certain these are the people who made friends with Phil. Have you seen them before?'

Mhairi blinked at the images. Von could see her interest was raised: Ranald and Lexie were standing on the steps of a fine Georgian house. 'Dunno,' Mhairi said. 'They don't look familiar.'

'Here's one of Phil.' It was a print of his passport photo, the contrast digitally enhanced.

'Not a brilliant shot of him. Looks washed out. And he's normally smiling.'

'Can you show these photos around? Ask what Phil and these other two do together? Is there a place they go to more than any other?'

The woman nodded, her eyes on the photo of Phil.

Von unfolded a flyer from the Calder Rifle and Pistol Club. 'I'm particularly interested in this man,' she said, tapping the thumbnail of Toby. 'Can you ask if anyone's seen him with Phil too?'

Mhairi's gaze sharpened. 'A gun club? What's this got to do with anything?'

'Just a hunch.' She pressed some notes into the woman's hand. 'This is a retainer for your services, Mhairi.' She grinned. 'It doesn't mean we're engaged or anything.'

'Amen to that. I'll try to get up to the Grassmarket today.'

'There's enough for a cab there and back as well as a few square meals. For your friends too.'

'Oh, I know who my friends are, old darling.' She lifted the wad of notes. 'They're all right here.'

After Von passed the sign to Bonnington, the landscape grew flat. Nothing but hedgerows and a patchwork of ploughed fields. But her interest was growing by the minute. Where she was headed was just a few miles from both The Paradise World of Paintballing and the Calder Rifle and Pistol Club.

This was her second visit to Livingston, a new town built in the sixties. A few months earlier, she'd been engaged by an IT company who suspected a rival firm of industrial espionage. Her work required her to bug the rival's conference rooms, something which left her with a sour taste as she discovered the depths firms go to to gain a competitive advantage. Both companies were now struggling, and joining the decline hitting many of the technology companies of what had once been dubbed Scotland's Silicon Glen. The pharmaceuticals, however, were thriving.

She turned off the A71 onto Alderstone Road and, a couple of roundabouts later, saw the sign for Almondvale Business Park. She found Bayne Pharmaceuticals without difficulty. It was one of the largest complexes in the Park, having been built a decade earlier at a cost of a billion pounds. The company's website boasted the links with Edinburgh University, giving it a badly needed research edge and helping it become a 'centre of scientific excellence in the global pharmaceutical market'.

In the car park, she paused to study the map of the area. Croker's offices were in Bayne Tower, the multi-storeyed building straight ahead, and the largest for miles. The research labs were housed in the adjacent white complex. Several vans were parked in front, Bayne's sprawling logo painted on the sides.

The reception area of Bayne Tower stretched endlessly in every direction. Von was met by a tall blue-eyed woman whose pale-pink lipstick matched her jacket. She threw Von a practised smile, introduced herself as Croker's personal assistant, and led the way to the waiting lift.

As they climbed to the top floor, Von cast a sideways glance at the woman's tailored jacket and pencil skirt. She herself was wearing her best professional outfit, an indigo-coloured trouser suit she'd bought in Marks and Spencer's when she became an investigator.

A second later, the lift doors opened with a faint hum.

The assistant motioned to the toilets opposite. 'In case you need to wash your hands,' she said smoothly.

Von guessed that only Croker and his assistant occupied this floor. A quick look at the doors as she followed the woman down the wide corridor confirmed her suspicions: they opened onto meeting rooms. The assistant had her desk outside a door marked with the name, 'Dewey Croker'. There was no mention of who he was in the organisation. There was no need. Von wondered why he hadn't given the woman an office of her own. Was he so important he had to have his secretary literally on his doorstep?

Von was ushered into the sort of office she'd seen only

in films. One wall was covered in a Byzantine-like mosaic in glittering shades of brown and gold. The wall opposite contained an embedded flat-screen showing the leading shares and their fluctuating prices. In the centre of the room, a low coffee table was surrounded by sofas and, to the right, there was an oval conference table large enough to take a dozen chairs. The room left a visitor in no doubt that this was the white-hot centre of Bayne Pharmaceuticals.

Dewy Croker was sitting behind an oak desk, the phone to his ear. He seemed more relaxed than when interviewed by CNN International and beckoned to Von to take a seat at the coffee table. Her feet sank into the thick pile as she made her way across the duck-egg-blue carpet.

Although unimpressed by his apparent unwillingness to cut short the call – she was not early, and he'd set the time of the interview – she was glad she had this opportunity to study him. His face was tanned and, when he smiled, he flashed expensively capped teeth. He wore a pearl-grey silk tie and a black suit. Looking at the cut, she thought wryly that it's not manners that maketh man, but clothes from Gieves and Hawkes. He swivelled to face the huge window which afforded an uninterrupted view of his empire, the light glinting off the statement Rolex watch. Seen from the back, the broad shoulders and sharp haircut said everything about him.

'Knock it off,' he said into the phone, so loudly that she flinched. 'Just answer me yes or no.' A few seconds later, he put the receiver down firmly.

'I apologise for keeping you waiting, Miss Valenti,' he said, getting to his feet. He came round the desk, beaming, hand extended. 'It was a last-minute conference call and I couldn't put it off.' He said it with such sincerity that she felt ashamed of her earlier conclusions.

She put her hand in his, feeling the cool strong grip as his fingers closed round hers. He had a lawyer's face with a firm chin, and eyes that were continually blinking. It was a handsome face. The newspaper photos didn't do him justice.

A tray arrived. The assistant slipped out of the room, leaving her boss to fuss over his guest. Croker handed Von a china cup in an exquisite blue-and-gold pattern.

'So, you're a journalist, Miss Valenti,' he said, stirring his coffee. 'I must confess to not reading your magazine although my wife's a great fan.'

She wondered if that were true, or whether he was practised at putting people at their ease. His next comment surprised her.

'I like journalists. They always look as though they've just lost something.' The expression in his eyes was not unfriendly.

She had no idea how to reply.

'I believe you're here to profile my work with underprivileged children,' he said, stroking his tie. 'So, shall we dance?'

She'd recovered her composure. 'You don't mind if I record our interview to back up my notes, do you?' she said, opening her bag.

'Not at all, but in return I'll ask to see your article before it goes to press. I have the agreement here.' He pushed a sheet of paper across.

She'd seen this type of document before and signed without a murmur, knowing the magazine editor would make good on it. Watching Croker pen his signature below hers, she wondered what a handwriting expert would make of the scrawl.

She switched on the recorder. 'Before we talk about your foundation, Mr Croker, perhaps you could tell me a little about yourself. What brought you to Scotland?'

He sat back, crossing his legs. Her eyes were drawn to his large buffed-leather shoes and the knife-edge crease in his trousers. 'I was starting to get itchy feet,' he said. 'I heard there were huge business opportunities here in Livingston. So I put out feelers, and Bayne Pharmaceuticals offered me the job. It's one of the world's leading pharma companies and I felt I couldn't really turn it down.'

'And what do you think you bring to the table?'

'It's no secret I have a reputation for turning ailing companies round.'

'I had no idea Bayne's had been ailing,' she said, making her eyes wide.

'They were blundering forward like the third day at Gettysburg. The share price was rock bottom.' He smoothed his brow with both hands. 'I've boiled the place down for fat, and it helps if you get a good point man, but we've a ways to go before we join the Big Pharma guys.'

She couldn't resist a glance at the TV screen. Bayne's share price stood lower than it had at the start of the morning. The red figure in brackets indicated it had dropped 5.5 percent in the last twenty-four hours.

He'd seen the glance. 'We're not doing so well just now but, hey, the markets go up and down. I'm not going to Crazy Town every time the share price wobbles.' He looked squarely at her. 'The smart money's on Bayne's, and you can quote me verbatim on that.' There was something taunting in his expression.

'And what sort of policies did you introduce to turn the company round?' she said with genuine interest.

Something passed across his face, a look of caution. She'd tugged at a nerve.

'It was a bit of a doozy but I managed to convince the board that we needed to invest in research and development. There are many medical conditions doctors simply aren't able to treat. My mission was, and still is, to rectify that. I've forged links with Edinburgh University and brought in the best scientists money can buy. My top man, Dr. Ranald McCrea, runs the biochemistry department here.' He said it with an air of quiet triumph, and she wondered why he hadn't realised a quick-witted journalist would make the link with Ranald and the recent murders of Jamie Dyer and Bruce Lassiter. Hardly good publicity for Bayne's, having its number-one-scientist finding two more Bayne's employees shot in his own paintballing club.

'And how is this investment funded?' she said, writing.

'You know something? We did it primarily through efficiency gains.'

Spoken like a true politician. She tried to keep the contempt from her voice. 'Surely not only through efficiency gains, Mr Croker.'

'I know the press are breaking my balls over our prices but they don't realise that everything has a cost. You have to turn a profit to keep a business going. And you can't turn a profit if your prices are kept artificially low. Even for medications. Especially for medications. Have you any idea how much funding is required for research and development? I'm sorry, but sentiment in business is what cost the South victory.' He leant forward. 'Weak pharmaceutical companies are always fighting off takeover bids, Miss Valenti. You get a multinational coming along, smelling the blood in the water . . . '

Her eyes rested on his, and then she had it. *And there are younger sharks ready to feast on your carcass.* That was what he feared most, the older man's dread of screwing up and being replaced by someone fresh out of business school. She wondered how he slept nights.

'But we're losing the subject,' he said, holding up a hand. 'I'm sure you have other questions for me.' It was a statement which carried with it the hint of a command.

She threw him her most brilliant smile. 'Let's move on to your work with children's charities. Tell me how you got involved with that.'

For the next twenty minutes, he described how he and his

wife had taken a vacation to India, and been appalled at the widespread poverty and the exploitation of child beggars. On their return, they'd set up a foundation to channel funds into those charities working directly with children. And not just in India; he reeled off a list of countries that his organisation was helping. His wife was now chairman and worked full time, visiting schools and hospitals. Von remembered the Internet photo of the blue-eyed blonde with the red lips, and wondered where his wife's office was, here or in the States. She listened intently, watching the play of emotions on Croker's face. He seemed genuinely moved when he spoke of the horrors of life for some children. Once or twice, he raised a hand to his eyes, as though wanting to brush away what he'd seen. She couldn't make him out. A rara avis. Who was the real Dewey Croker? The hard-headed businessman? Or the marshmallow-centred philanthropist.

He finished speaking and poured her another coffee. He kept his eyes on hers, as though wanting to gauge her reaction.

She removed the tape and flipped it over.

She kept her voice matter-of-fact. 'I understand you like to shoot, Mr Croker,' she said, lifting her head. 'I believe you're something of a marksman. Didn't I see a photo of you on the web where you were demonstrating how to fire a Ruger Blackhawk?'

She thought he'd go misty-eyed and start to talk lovingly about his guns. But he stiffened, saying nothing, his expression steady.

Interesting. It wasn't the reaction she expected. 'You must find our gun restrictions frustrating,' she pressed.

'You'd be surprised.'

'Surprise me.'

'I happen to agree with the British stance,' he said, smiling suddenly. 'You've made firearms difficult to own and your gun-crime rate has plummeted.'

She decided to bait him. As a way of getting information, it often produced results. 'That makes me feel all warm inside, Mr Croker,' she said, injecting irony into her voice. 'Why aren't you doing the same in the States?'

That knocked the smile off his face. 'Our Second Amendment – '

'I hear the melody but I don't believe the lyrics. Amendments can be amended.'

He frowned. 'Miss Valenti, I can do nothing about our gun laws. The best way forward is to promote the responsible use of firearms.'

'Isn't that yesterday's solution to today's problem? I'd have thought that someone who cares so much about children in Third World countries would also care about those in his own. Why aren't you lobbying Congress?'

He looked at her for a long moment, and then reached across and switched off the recorder. He made no move to get up. 'You're quite a lady, Missy,' he said, raising an eyebrow.

She held his gaze. 'All part of the package.'

'Now that we're speaking off the record, what brought on this sudden change?'

She decided on a gamble. 'I used to be a detective. I spent time with the NYPD. I've seen every type of gunshot wound this side of Perdition.' After a silence, she gathered up her things. 'I don't expect a member of the NRA to understand that but someone has to tell the truth about guns.' She lifted her head. 'It must have been hard leaving your Ruger Blackhawk behind in the States.'

For the barest instant, something crossed his face, a look that gave her her answer.

'I'll let myself out, Mr Croker.' She stood up. 'I'm grateful for your time.'

He was on his feet. 'Goodbye, Miss Valenti.'

He held out his hand. She paused, then slid her hand in his. He squeezed gently, a new respect in his eyes.

In the corridor, she thanked the assistant for the coffee and walked towards the lift. She pressed the button and waited, rocking back and forth on her heels and glancing now and again in the assistant's direction. The woman's phone rang and, as she answered, she dipped her head so that Von couldn't hear. The lift doors opened. Von backed away and slipped into the ladies' room.

She pulled a piece of loo roll from inside a cubicle and, standing under the smoke detector, set fire to the tissue. When it caught, she stood on tiptoe and held it high. A few seconds later, the smoke reached the ceiling and an alarm sounded that could have woken the dead. Simultaneously, jets of water burst from above, drenching her in seconds.

She put her ear to the door. Over the sound of the alarm, she heard running feet, Croker shouting, doors opening and closing. She smiled to herself. Yes, if the fire alarm went on the top floor of a building next to biochemical research labs, she'd be getting a move on, no question.

After waiting a full minute, she stepped into the corridor. A glance through the fire door, and she ran to Croker's office.

Croker's Ruger was in this room somewhere, she'd bet good money on that. The man had struck her as the type who'd keep it close, and this would probably be where he spent most of his time. Convenient for the Calder Rifle and Pistol Club, too. There were precious few places he could have hidden it. He must have had a safe installed. No pictures, though. Just the huge mosaic. It had to be behind that, there was nowhere else. She passed a hand over the edge, feeling for irregularities that suggested a hidden switch. In a distant room, a telephone rang unanswered. She tugged at the mosaic but it didn't budge.

It was unlikely, but not impossible, that he kept the gun in a hidden drawer. Fortunately, none of the sets of sprinklers was directly over the desk, something she'd noticed at the interview. There were three drawers. The bottom two were empty. The top drawer contained a folder labelled Stannard HealthSolutions. She pushed it aside and felt around. Nothing. She knelt behind the desk and ran a hand underneath.

The fire brigade would be here any minute. She slammed a hand against the desk. Damn it, where the hell was it?

The wail of a siren told her she was out of time. She jumped to her feet, dragged the hem of her shirt over everything she'd touched, and rushed out of the office.

She was pushing against the fire door when she saw a shadow move in the stairwell. Jesus, the men were here already. She sprang back, her heart hammering, and ducked into the ladies. Feet thundered down the corridor. A quick peek round the edge of the door, and she was creeping out, when a heavy hand on her shoulder caused the air to leave her lungs.

She whirled round.

A well-built fireman was glaring at her. 'What are you still doing in here, lass?'

'I had to make a phone call,' she stammered. It was the first thing that came into her head. Had she hesitated, he'd have smelt a rat and had the police on her. She wondered if Bayne's system was smart enough to tell the firemen exactly where the fire had started. Obviously not, as they were running past the toilets.

'Get down those stairs and keep going till you reach the car park,' the man said sternly. He pushed her towards the fire door. 'Go on, now.'

Minutes later, she reached the ground floor.

In the car park, a large crowd was staring up at Bayne Tower. A fire engine was unloading ladders, the men shouting instructions to one another, watched by Croker and his white-faced assistant. Von knew that Ranald McCrea would be here somewhere. She couldn't risk being recognised, although so far no-one had noticed her. She slipped into the crowd, keeping her head down, and pushed her way to the edge of the group.

The Ford was directly in front of her, next to the exit onto Almondvale Way. She took a step forward, and then froze. A few feet away, Lexie Dyer was getting out of a red BMW. She stared up at Bayne Tower, lifting a hand to shade her face, her eyes wide, her mouth half open. While Lexie's attention was on the building, Von crept towards the Ford, trying to make herself invisible.

She was fumbling for her keys when an ambulance screamed through the entrance. Every head swivelled in her direction and, for the barest instant, Lexie's eyes locked with hers. There was no mistaking the girl's expression. She lifted a hand to point at Von, turning her head away, presumably to catch someone's attention. Von yanked the car door open and fell inside.

A second later, she was through the entrance, pedal to the floor.

She glanced into the rear-view mirror. Lexie was standing staring at her, her mobile phone to her ear.

Von let herself into the flat. Consecutive broken nights and the events at Livingston had left her drained, and all she wanted to do was curl up and sleep. A sudden smell of curry reached her. Not the usual greasy smell from one of Lothian Road's takeaways, but a rich spicy aroma that made her salivate and reminded her she needed to eat.

Georgie and Norrie were sitting on the sofa playing with the baby. They looked up as Von entered, the surprise on their faces turning to shock.

'What on earth happened to you, Mum?' said Georgie. 'Did

you fall in the fountain?'

'Something like that. Happens all the time. Nothing to worry about.'

'Norrie's taken the day off,' her daughter said defensively, as if needing to justify his presence there on a weekday. 'He's made us all curry.'

'Let me get you some, Mrs Valenti,' Norrie added, springing to his feet.

A steady job, he was good with the baby, and he could cook? She studied Georgie. The girl seemed happy enough. She was taking more care with her appearance and her complexion was improving, no doubt thanks to a better diet. She was cooing over the baby and nuzzling her. Things were looking up.

Von changed into casual clothes and towelled her hair briskly. She thought of running a hairdryer over her head but her rumbling stomach was pulling her in another direction.

Norrie handed her a fork and plate. 'I thought you'd prefer to eat here in the living room,' he said. 'I've still to sort out the kitchen.'

She stared at him in wonder. She'd never known a man sort out a kitchen. Not the male members of her family and certainly not her lovers. What did it say about her that she'd quietly accepted the role of the little woman, whereas Georgie hadn't?

She tried a forkful of curry. It was lamb with chick peas and a vegetable she couldn't identify. Sweet rather than spicy, with yoghurt added to make it creamy.

'Delicious, Norrie,' she murmured. 'Where did you learn to make this?'

'Ma taught me. Said boys should know how to cook.'

Von glanced at her daughter. And girls.

If Georgie had interpreted her mother's look correctly, she gave no indication. 'We're taking the baby out for a walk, Mum. Is there anything we need from the shops?'

'Loo paper, love,' she said, gratified by the pleasantness in her daughter's voice. Norrie was proving to be a good influence where manners were concerned.

Von ate the curry slowly, hoping there was more, while Norrie busied himself tidying the kitchen and Georgie got herself and the baby ready.

After they'd gone, Von made coffee. She was about to call Steve when she noticed she had voicemail.

Toby's deep bass had a tinny edge. 'Hope I've got the right number, Von. You've not yet set up a lesson so I've taken the liberty of booking an appointment for you for 10.00am on Friday. If you can't make it, do get back to me.'

Bit of a cheek. But she felt a warmth spread through her stomach as she realised he hadn't forgotten about her. When had their supper date been? Sunday. And today was Wednesday. And he'd invited her to the tournament on Saturday.

Her thoughts drifted to their evening at Federico's, specifically his cryptic one-sided conversation with Ranald McCrea.

'What? Are you absolutely sure?' Pause. 'How the devil did . . . ' Longer pause. 'So what do you suggest we do?' Pause. 'I hope you're not thinking of . . . ' Pause. 'Ranald, do you really think that would work?'

Pity she hadn't heard the rest. Bloody waiter.

But the tone of Toby's voice made it clear that something was wrong. Something involving Phil, perhaps? Was he in danger and he was at Lexie's because they were trying to protect him? And yet they'd taken him out for the evening. Maybe she should ring the doorbell and demand to speak to him. But a voice inside her told her it would be counterproductive. If he were mixed up in this double killing, who knows what avalanche such an approach would set off? No, where Phil was concerned, it was softly, softly, catchee monkee.

She sat at the kitchen table and removed the plastic sleeve from her bag. Inside was the printout of file PA.XLS that she'd made at Swankie and Vale's. PA.XLS was a mystery. Did the letters 'PA' stand for something? Filenames were usually significant. It occurred to her that 'P' and 'A' were the first two letters of Phil's surname. But wouldn't a filename like that be too obvious? What else, then? Personal Assistant? Press Association? Privacy Act? Public Address? The list was endless. Better to concentrate on the data itself. Columns in a spreadsheet were linked, so each of the eight-figure numbers in the left-hand column was connected to the corresponding cell in the column of five-character alphanumeric data, as well as to a Spanish-sounding word.

She sipped her coffee. Perhaps the long numbers were phone numbers. But she'd never come across a phone number with eight digits; they usually had eleven. Ah, but the second column had three digits followed by two letters. Did those three digits belong to the eight digits in the first column? None of them started with a '0', although they all had at least one '0' in them. If these were phone numbers, they were well and truly scrambled. What was the number of permutations of eleven digits? Something astronomical.

She turned her attention to the letters. A foreign-sounding word in the third column and two letters in the second column. She picked at her lip. Two letters, then a word. Could this be someone's name? A list of names and a list of jumbled phone numbers. And if the numbers were rearranged for security reasons, then the letters would be too. She hadn't a hope of deciphering this on her own. She thrust the sheet back into her bag.

So why had Phil locked away the CD with his passport and the left-luggage key? And where was this locker, anyway? Few public places had lockers now. If she'd had her wits about her, she'd have examined the key for make and serial number. She toyed with the idea of breaking in again – they wouldn't be expecting it – but chances were that Lexie had had the basement doors fitted with ultra-secure locks.

Lexie. Maybe this was her file and not Phil's. That password-protected web page suggested she worked from home so perhaps the data in PA.XLS was something to do with Bayne's. Von stared into the mug. Another mystery unsolved. They were stacking up, and she needed expert help. She gulped the rest of the coffee.

It was time to talk to Steve.

Chapter 23
Thursday, June 14th

Steve stared at Von. 'You did what?' he said softly.

They were walking from Waverley station towards Princes Street. Earlier in the day, Von had taken Steve's phone call asking her to meet him off the Glasgow train. She'd been in bed when he rang, trying to catch up on sleep. Norrie had taken up residence and when he and Georgie were deep in their post-coital slumbers they didn't hear the baby cry, and she was the one who had to deal with her granddaughter's needs.

She'd finished her account of her search of Dewey's office, leaving out the telling little detail that she'd set off the fire alarm. Both activities were illegal but, of the two, poking about a person's office was less illegal than tampering with fire equipment.

Steve ran a hand over his face. 'And how is all this supposed to help me?'

'Dewey Croker has a revolver that can be chambered for .45 ACPs. I thought he'd keep it in his office.'

'So?'

'It could be the murder weapon.'

'Look, Von, nobody with half a brain keeps hold of a murder weapon.'

'I realise that, but this gun is a prized possession. There's no way he's chucking it, murder or no murder.'

'I can't go investigating every American in Edinburgh just because he's a gun enthusiast. Okay, suppose you'd found it. He would simply deny it was his. He could say it was planted.

Could we prove otherwise? Anyway, we'd never get a warrant to search the place.'

'You would if you had something else on him.'

'Aye, and maybe I do.'

'You've got a lead?'

He told her about Cally's suspicions that Jamie and Bruce had been up to something that might give Croker a motive for killing them.

'Croker did strike me as someone ruthless enough to do anything to keep Bayne's at the top. He might well have been tempted to take out a contract. Or do it himself.' She felt a headache coming. 'Pity I didn't find the Ruger.'

'And he'd have known it was you and called us in.'

'But at least you'd have established that it was the murder weapon.'

'Aye, and you'd have been in the clink for theft.'

'And he'd have been in the clink for murder.' She paused. 'It's behind that wall mosaic, I know it is.' She was so tired she could have stretched out on the pavement and slept. 'This Cally person, you say she's a problem-solver and an IT whiz too?'

He looked at the ground. 'She's got a software-engineering degree,' he said quietly.

Von reached into her bag. 'Then ask her if she'll take a butcher's at this.'

'What is it?' he said, taking the CD.

'A spreadsheet. I can't make head nor tail of the data.'

'Where did you get it?' he said, giving her a cool look.

It was clear from the way he thrust out his chin that he wouldn't give Cally anything unless Von came clean. 'Lexie Dyer's house,' she said.

'Legally?'

'Look, Steve, Phil Pattullo is staying with her. I took this CD from his bedroom.' She ignored his sharp intake of breath.

'It was in a locked drawer along with his passport and a key, possibly to a left-luggage locker.'

'Sounds as though your man is thinking of leaving the country.'

'I doubt it, he hasn't got the money.' But the thought had crossed her mind. Maybe he'd persuaded Lexie to fund a trip abroad. Maybe he thought he wouldn't see the bad angels there. But why would she help him financially? And why hadn't he gone already?

Steve turned his gaze out to Princes Street. 'We searched both Lexie's house and Ranald McCrea's the day after the bodies were discovered. I was there. I'd have remembered a passport belonging to someone else. Phil must have arrived some time after.' He glanced at her. 'So what's he doing at Lexie's? And what has he got to do with my murder case?'

'Perhaps nothing. But the contents of that CD may tell us.' She knew what he was thinking: she'd gone rogue and broken the law. She fixed her eyes on the knot of his tie and said, 'I didn't damage anything when I took it.'

His lips twitched. 'Delighted to hear it,' he said, the twitch growing into a smile.

'I'm thinking there may be names and phone numbers on the spreadsheet, but they're scrambled. This Cally lady might be able to make sense of them.'

She'd gone as far as she could with her investigation. Without another lead, she was walking in ever-decreasing circles. It bothered her she needed Steve's help, and she was conscious she was jeopardising his career by involving him. Perhaps this was the time to bow out. Yet, if she did, she'd be giving up. And giving up was an experience new to her.

At the end of Waverley Bridge, she slowed her pace. 'Stop a minute will you, Steve?' She leant against the wall of the Shopping Centre.

'And I thought I was the one out of condition.' He studied her more closely. 'Aye, you don't look well, and no mistake.'

She avoided his eyes. 'It's nothing.'

'Something's wrong.'

'Everything's fine.'

'You never could lie to me, you know.' He lifted her chin. 'What's bothering you?'

She felt like crying from exhaustion. 'Everything's getting away from me. I need someone to talk things over with and you're the only one on the short list.'

'Perhaps a wee bevvie would help. I know the sun's not yet over the yardarm but we could talk about it over a vodka tonic, or three. There's a cocktail bar in the Grassmarket. Federico's.'

Federico's was where Toby had taken her. 'How do you know Federico's?'

'I went there with Lexie Dyer after she identified her brother.'

'Okay, but can we take a cab?'

A short while later, they were seated in Federico's bar area, away from the window. She'd decided against alcohol so early in the day. Her coffee lay on the table, untouched. Steve had stuck to his usual, a single malt.

As he sipped, she told him about Toby's phone conversation with Ranald McCrea. When she described the figure she'd seen outside her flat, he set the glass down sharply.

'What type of car was it?' he said.

'Couldn't tell.'

'Colour?'

'Silver? Could have been light blue.'

'Light blue. Ranald McCrea has an Ascari that colour. If Hilliard spoke with him earlier, then he might have given him your address.'

Yes, Toby knew where she lived from her application form.

She thought of the conversation. *'So what do you suggest we do?'* Pause. *'I hope you're not thinking of . . .'* If it had been Ranald taking up vigil outside her house, what exactly had he been thinking of? And had Toby been trying to warn him off? She hoped that, whatever they were all mixed up in, Toby wasn't heavily involved. She so wanted to believe he was genuine. He'd been good with her, not like the men she'd known, most of whom belonged to the caveman school of how to treat women. Yet, if Steve was right, he'd passed on her address to Ranald.

'I think they're on to me, Steve. Lexie saw me outside Bayne's. And I'm sure Ranald saw me arriving at the gun club. There's Georgie and the baby to think of.' Now she'd said it, she realised her anxiety hadn't been for herself: it was for her daughter and grandchild. The feeling of dread had been growing in her subconscious, pushing into her thoughts, draining her of energy.

He took her hand. 'How much sleep have you been getting lately?'

'Not much. I usually feed the baby when she wakes.'

If he thought this arrangement irregular, he said nothing.

'You think I'm being an Olympic-class idiot and imagining things, don't you?'

'I don't think that at all. Your instincts have always been correct.' He took a gulp of whisky. 'Can Georgie and the baby stay somewhere till your case is over?'

'Not really.' She was loath to tell him that renting another place for Georgie would break the bank. 'She's got a new boyfriend, name of Norrie. He seems reliable enough.'

'Could they stay with him?'

'I think he's living with his mum.'

He took her arm firmly. 'Look, Von, being worried for Georgie and the baby is one thing, but you're the one who's blown your cover. I want you to watch yourself.'

'You sound like my Dad.'

'You need to listen to me.'

'Now you sound like my husband.'

In the uncomfortable silence, he released her and finished his malt. 'Swanky place,' he said, running a hand across the yellow leather of the sofa. 'And Hilliard brought you here for a drink, you said?'

'He brought me here for supper.'

He smoothed back his hair at the sides and got heavily to his feet. 'I need to be getting on.'

At the door, he turned briefly in her direction. She thought he was going to say something but he didn't. She couldn't let him go like this. 'I'll be seeing you,' she said.

He smiled, the corners of his eyes creasing. 'In all the old familiar places.'

Steve headed back into the centre of town.

He felt strangely out of sorts. He tried to tell himself it was because he was worried about the state Von had slipped into, but he knew it had more to do with her having had supper with Hilliard. It was none of his business, of course, but it irked him that she might be becoming romantically involved with someone.

He left Victoria Street, his leg aching from the climb, and turned onto George IV Bridge. No, what he should be more concerned about was Hilliard's obvious connection to Ranald McCrea and, by extension, Lexie Dyer. If they were all up to something and thought Von suspected, it would explain why they'd tried to put the frighteners on her, if that was indeed what had happened. As a former police officer, she had the nouse to recognise danger and know how to keep out of it. But she wasn't thinking straight. Having Georgie and the baby living with her was tiring her out, physically and mentally. And that meant her budding relationship with Hilliard was likely to go nowhere.

He experienced a sudden warm rush of satisfaction, and then felt immediately ashamed of his thoughts. What right had he to think like that? He'd slept with Cally, hadn't he? But he'd have to be a selfless saint to want to see Von in a loving relationship with another man. And he was no saint.

He trudged glumly down The Mound, past the National Gallery, and into the Gardens.

Head bent, he walked slowly through the trees, paying scant attention to his surroundings. As he reached the huge fountain with the naked woman at the top, a familiar voice dragged him out of his reverie. Lexie Dyer and a dark-haired woman were standing at a trestle table, pouring from large Thermos flasks. A ragged group of homeless had gathered and people were pushing each other to get to the front.

Lexie was handing out styrofoam cups. 'No need to jostle,' she said brightly. She pushed back a wisp of hair that had escaped from the tight ponytail. 'There's plenty of soup to go round, you know.' Turning to her companion, she said, 'Can you open this Thermos please, Frankie? The top's a bit stiff.' She delved into a box labelled, We Cater For Everyone – Frankie Goes To Houses, and removed a number of clingfilm-wrapped packets.

Steve watched the women pour soup and hand out sandwiches. Near the front, a young fair-haired lad with a dirty face stood clutching a wriggling black-and-white puppy to his chest. He kept his eyes on the ground while Lexie spoke to him, apparently reluctant to leave. She smiled and tickled the puppy's floppy ears, and then leant forward and ran her fingers through the boy's hair. He flushed with embarrassment or delight, Steve couldn't tell which. As he turned away, she slipped him a second sandwich, motioning to the dog.

Something made her glance over to where Steve was standing, as though suddenly conscious of being watched. Her friendly expression vanished. She plucked at the front of her maroon-coloured shirt, a troubled look in her eyes. But she recovered quickly, pasting the smile back onto her face.

'Are you here for some free soup, Inspector?' she said, tilting her chin.

'Thank you, Miss Dyer, but no.' He motioned to the table. 'Is this one of Bayne's charities?'

'Miss Dyer pays for this out of her own pocket,' the girl called Frankie said in a defensive tone.

He studied the group at the fountain. They were cramming sandwiches into their mouths, their eyes darting back and forth as though afraid the food would be snatched away. The blond boy was tearing into the clingfilm. The puppy had trampled his own sandwich, and was barking at one of the fountain's lion-head water spouts, its gold paint dull in the shadows from the Castle Rock.

'How often do you do this, Miss Dyer?'

'As often as I can manage.'

'Two or three times a week,' Frankie chipped in. 'Sometimes weekends as well.' She was gathering up the empty cups and packing them into the box.

So this act of generosity was Lexie's. The woman could just as easily have left Frankie to get on with everything but she'd chosen to come and help. Not something he'd have expected of her, either footing the bill, or the personal involvement. Aye, people were a constant surprise to him.

Lexie was running a hand down her black jeans, studying his face. There was a nervous flicker in her eyes. She'd be wondering how far on he was in his investigation, but he could see she was unwilling to ask him in front of Frankie. The caterer left to gather up the discarded wrappers. Lexie glanced in her direction, and then back at Steve. She opened her mouth to speak but seemed to think better of it.

'How are preparations going for Saturday's paintballing

tournament, Miss Dyer?' he said.

'Oh, you know, coming along. Will you be there?'

'I don't think so. I'm working.' He was watching her closely, thinking she'd ask about the investigation, but she didn't rise to the bait. 'Well, I'd better be getting up the road,' he added.

Frankie returned and started to pack up the boxes. 'Come and see us again,' she said. 'We're often here by the fountain.'

He smiled, and headed towards the path.

'Maybe next time you'd like to give us a hand,' she shouted to his retreating back.

Cheeky wee besom. Without turning round, he lifted an arm and waved in acknowledgement.

Von dropped her bag and collapsed onto the sofa. The place was quiet. Too quiet. Georgie and Norrie must be out with the baby. It was after six, so maybe they'd met up at his office and gone for a bite to eat. But they wouldn't be away long, the baby needed to be fed. She, herself, couldn't face the idea of eating. What her body craved was sleep, the kind of dreamless sleep where you're more or less unconscious. She'd leave a note for Georgie, and then crash out.

She was searching for a pen when she heard a faint sound from her daughter's bedroom. She felt a strange uneasiness. Was Georgie at home? But where was the baby? The cot stayed in the living room until it was time for bed but there was no sign of it. With a rising sense of panic, she rushed over to the bedroom, snatched at the handle and hurled open the door, banging it against the wall.

The noise she'd heard was the baby mewling in the cot. Georgie was lying face down on the bed, motionless, her head buried in the pillow. Von stared in mute horror at her daughter's body, the arms outstretched, the legs splayed. Oh Jesus, she was dead, someone had pushed her head down and smothered her.

Georgie lifted her head and twisted round. 'Mum?'

Von slumped against the wall, weak with relief. Anger, fuelled by fatigue, surged through her. 'For heaven's sake, Georgie, I thought something had happened to you. What the hell are you doing lying there like that?'

The girl's blotched face was streaked with tears. 'Mum,' she wailed. 'It's Norrie. He's gone. He's left me.'

Von was tempted to tell her daughter to mop up her bleeding heart, that another man would come along as, in her case, he always did. She couldn't deny it gave her a certain bleak satisfaction that the saintly Norrie, paraded by Georgie as a trophy – something Von had failed to win – had turned out to be more of a sinner. But then she felt ashamed of her feelings. She wasn't so old she couldn't remember the sharp stab of rejection. 'It's all right, love,' she said, sitting on the bed and stroking the girl's hair, 'it's not the end of the world.' If Norrie was gone, Georgie probably hadn't eaten that day. 'I'll phone for a takeaway, shall I?' When there was no reply, she added less patiently, 'Come on, Georgie, let's not make a long day longer.'

The baby, hearing the tone in her voice, started to bawl. Von picked her up, making soothing noises, and took her to the kitchen.

Holding her granddaughter to her shoulder, she made up the baby's formula. She fed, bathed, and clothed her, and then settled her back in the cot. Georgie was sobbing softly.

'Oh, Mum, everyone leaves me.' She sat up, snivelling, wiping the tears with her fingers. 'First you, then every man I've ever loved, and now Norrie. I don't want to end up on my own.'

The words hit Von like a slap in the face. The recriminations about her abandonment of Georgie were nothing new, it was a tune she'd listened to many times. But the self-pity over losing men was something she'd not heard before. She'd thought the girl was made of stronger stuff, yet she realised with a twinge of sadness that Georgie was more like Von's own mother, who hadn't been able to get through life without a man at her back. When had Georgie become so emotionally dependent?

She took her daughter's hand. 'So what happened, love? Did you have a row?'

'No, nothing like that. We were supposed to meet in town but he didn't show.'

'And you think he's left you?' She rubbed Georgie's arm. 'There could be any number of reasons why he wasn't there. Maybe he's running late at work. Have you considered he might be ill? Or his mum?' She searched the girl's face. 'Have you rung him?'

'I get number unobtainable.'

'That doesn't mean anything. He might have got himself a new phone.'

'Oh, look behind you, Mum,' Georgie wailed.

Von swivelled round and saw what she'd missed earlier. The doors to the long fitted wardrobe were open.

'He's taken my dresses.' Georgie was sobbing again.

Von stared at the row of empty hangers, comprehension dropping into her mind with a thud. The designer dresses, even second-hand, were worth thousands. 'How did he . . . ?'

'I gave him the spare key. He asked me to.'

'What's his address, Georgie?' she said, feeling her anger swell. 'I'm going there right now.'

'I haven't got his address. We never went to his.'

'Well, what's the name of his construction company?'

Georgie pushed a lock of hair behind her ear. 'I never asked. For all I know, he made that up.'

So the marvellous dependable Norrie had feet of clay. She wondered what Georgie was really grieving about: the loss of Norrie or the theft of her dresses. But she had no intention of letting this go. 'I'm phoning the police,' she said.

'Oh, what's the point, Mum?' Georgie was shouting. 'I don't even know his last name.' She covered her face with her hands and gave herself up to her grief.

Von felt her heart constrict. 'Hush, love, it's not as bad as all that.' She listened to her daughter's crying, wondering how she could distract her. 'Do you remember that time I took you to the Natural History Museum?'

Georgie looked up, wiping her eyes. 'The one on Exhibition Road?'

'You were eight and it was a week after your birthday. I'd just come back from a training course at Hendon and had a few days off, so I came over to Grandma's to take you out for a treat. I hadn't seen you for ages and I thought you were so grown up. Your hair was much longer and you had it in a ponytail. And you were wearing the new trainers I'd sent you for your birthday, the ones that light up at the sides when you walk.' She wondered how much of this Georgie remembered. Her visits to her parents had been few and far between in those early years, but she always sent her daughter something for her birthday. In a box in her room, she still had the thank-you letters the girl's grandparents made sure she wrote. 'Do you remember that central hall?'

'With the big dinosaur skeleton?'

'And can you remember what you did?'

Georgie smiled. 'I sat on its tail.'

'You tried to make it rock like a see-saw.' She could still recall the look of horror on the museum attendant's face. 'And then you started to climb up the tail. Your trainers were flashing. I think that's what did it. The man pulled you off and shouted at you.'

'We had to go to someone's office, didn't we?'

'The Director's. He was none too pleased.' The man had glowered at them, but melted when Georgie slipped her hand into his and promised not to do it again.

'When we got home, I drew a picture of the dinosaur and sent it to him. Dippy. That's what the dinosaur was called,' the girl added, sniffing.

It had been one of their best days together. They had giggled about the episode on the tube home.

'Was it you with me, though, Mum? I thought Grandma took me that time.'

'No, it was me.' She turned away so that Georgie couldn't see her face. She had only herself to blame if her daughter's memories of her grandparents eclipsed those of her mother. Her career in the police force hadn't been worth the sacrifice, she knew now.

'Mum, Norrie's got a key.' Georgie was whimpering again. 'We'll have to have the locks changed.'

Von slipped an arm round her daughter's shoulders. 'Leave me to worry about the locks. You try to get some sleep.' When there was no reply, she added, 'Shall I make us some supper?'

Georgie shook her head. She gripped Von's hand, fresh tears streaming down her cheeks. Von pushed off her shoes and lay down next to her. When she heard the sobs turn into regular breathing, she pulled the duvet off the floor and dragged it over them both. She stared out of the window, watching the sun sink slowly below the rooftops.

She couldn't blame her daughter for her error of judgment. After all, she herself, someone who prided herself on being able to read people, had also failed to see through Norrie. How long had the relationship lasted? Not even a week. Georgie was murmuring something Von couldn't hear. She put her ear to the girl's mouth, but the words made no sense. Strange, she didn't know Georgie talked in her sleep. But why should she? She'd been absent for so much of her daughter's life. She nestled closer. The moon slipped from behind a cloud, casting a band of creamy light across the duvet.

She studied her daughter's face, washed sickly pale in the moonlight. Poor Georgie, she'd fretted about changing the locks. Of course, they'd have to get it done. It was an expense they could ill afford, although she knew someone who'd do it cheaply. But she doubted Norrie would be back. What was there left to steal?

Chapter 24
Friday, June 15th

'So, Inspector, how many firearms are we talking about?'

Steve smiled. 'Not sure, Miss Prince. From the database, I'd say over a hundred.'

Lina Prince was looking at him from under her lashes. He'd forgotten those green eyes. And the unblinking stare. 'It's the .45 ACPs, right?' she said.

'Just those. How long will it take?'

'Jeez, you're one cop in a helluva hurry. You guys never cut me any slack.'

'Sorry.' His smile was becoming forced. 'So when can you make a start?'

She nodded at the van. The last few pistols were being loaded in. 'As soon as they've taken the truck to Howdenhall Road. I'm having three staff working round the clock. You do the math.'

'Not by tomorrow, then?' he said, hoping his tone showed he was joking.

'I won't be working tomorrow, bud. I've got something else planned.' Her eyes were steady, their expression daring him to ask her what it was. 'You never did come to see me about that,' she added, motioning to his leg.

He thought of the business card she'd slipped into his pocket. The card Cally had torn into little pieces.

She seemed disappointed. 'Well, I'd better get my sorry ass over to the lab.' She swung round, her charcoal-coloured skirt swirling, and climbed into the van.

'I'll be seeing you,' she shouted through the window.

He nearly replied, 'In all the old familiar places.'

The van sped away with a squeal of tyres.

Von swung the Ford into the car park. She was late for her 10.00am lesson. About half an hour late. She'd risen early after a fitful night and left Georgie sleeping while she dealt with the baby. But, as she was leaving the flat, Georgie had dragged her sleep-drugged body into the kitchen and begged her to stay. Von could hardly say no. She'd drunk a cup of coffee with her daughter, desperate to get going.

Georgie's state of mind worried her. The girl was subdued, not even showing an interest in her child. Von had cooed over the baby under Georgie's watchful but vacant eyes. The girl showed emotion only when Von put on her jacket. Now, rolling in late for the shooting lesson, she wondered what excuse to make. She decided to tell Toby the truth, that there was a crisis at home because her daughter's boyfriend had left her. Men understood that kind of crisis.

A van accelerated past her, a red-haired woman at the wheel. She gave Von barely a glance as she turned onto the A71.

The car park was full of police. Steve was standing talking to an officer. Seeing her, he waved to her to stop.

She wound down the window. 'Hi, Steve. What's going on here?'

'We're taking the pistols for test-firing. And we're checking the database to see if anyone's tampered with it. It's possible our murder weapon was taken from here and the record of it erased.'

She felt a twinge of irritation. For God's sake, hadn't she been over this with him? 'You're wasting your time. The gun that killed Jamie and Bruce isn't here.'

It was his turn to be irritated. 'And you know this how?'

'Because it's impossible to steal from here. Or almost

impossible,' she added.

'Aye, it's that word "almost" that's driving this.'

'I'm surprised the Fiscal granted you a warrant.'

His look of exasperation turned to one of amusement. 'Hasn't it occurred to you that it mightn't have been a thief, but was an inside job?'

Of course it had but she'd pushed the thought away: as one of the few people with full access, Toby was a prime contender. 'I take it the place is closed,' she said, looking anxiously towards the building. Was Toby inside? Or had he been sent home as soon as the police arrived?

'The manager closed it himself. It's your Toby Hilliard, isn't it?'

'He's not my Toby Hilliard.'

'Well, he's inside. I take it that's why you're here,' he added, his voice level.

'I have a lesson,' she mumbled. The comment sounded defensive, although there was no reason why she should feel this way. 'Who was that redhead in the van?' she said, wanting to change the subject.

His lips curved upwards. 'The ballistics expert I told you about. Lina.'

The front door opened suddenly and Toby appeared. An officer stepped forward and said something to him but he pushed past angrily. Seeing Von getting out of the car, he stopped, a look of uncertainty on his face.

She felt a rush of disappointment: he'd forgotten their lesson. She raised a hand in greeting, hoping he wouldn't apologise in front of Steve for his lapse of memory.

'Von,' he said, hurrying towards her, 'have you been waiting since ten? I'm so sorry, I should have phoned. We'll have to take a rain check on our lesson.' He looked at Steve and his features hardened. 'As you can see, we're being raided.'

She tried to keep the relief from her face. But she was secretly pleased she wouldn't be spending her morning shooting.

Toby rounded on Steve. 'I hope you and your plods know what you're doing. Those firearms are valuable. I'll be royally pissed off if I find even one of them scratched.'

'Our insurance will cover us,' Steve said lazily.

It was the wrong answer. Toby's dark eyes flared and, for a second, Von thought he was going to take a swing at Steve. If he did, Steve was likely to come off worse. Toby had thirty pounds on him and Steve was no longer agile on account of his leg injury. Toby took a step forward, his dog-tags flashing, but Steve held his ground.

The men glared at one another. She was about to intervene when Toby turned away, taking her by the elbow. 'Come on, let's get out of here,' he said, loudly enough that Steve would hear. 'I need a drink.'

'Fine,' she murmured.

He steered her towards his black S-Type Jaguar. 'We'll take mine,' he said. 'I'll bring you back later.'

She was glad they weren't going in the Ford. It was months since she'd cleaned it and the back seat was covered in baby litter.

As they drove onto the main road, she risked a last glance into the car park. Steve couldn't fail to have seen her looking but he stood motionless, watching, not lifting a hand in farewell.

She could feel the white heat of Toby's anger radiating through his checked shirt. He was bound to be furious at the closure of the gun club. A police raid after two fatal shootings in the vicinity was hardly going to be good for business. Her experience of men told her to say nothing and wait for him to make the first move.

They took a side road off the A71. The words, The Paradise World of Paintballing, in large blue letters, jumped out at her.

'I need to do something here, Von. Do you mind? They're

erecting the stands for tomorrow's tournament and I promised Ranald I'd check everything's going to timetable.'

'No problem.'

Checking on building work on Ranald's behalf suggested the men were more than mere acquaintances. And yet he seemed relaxed about telling her, not bothered by her response. He behaved like a man with nothing to hide. She thought back to the night in Belgrave Crescent gardens. Maybe he'd run into Ranald and the others at Federico's and come back with them for a nightcap. He may have met Phil there for the first time. Perhaps she was wrong about him and he had nothing to do with anything. On the other hand, perhaps she was fooling herself. It had happened before. Especially where men were concerned.

They drove in through a high gate. A short while later, he stopped the car outside a single-storeyed building.

Her heart was beating hard. She recognised the place from the press coverage of the murders.

He must have seen the expression on her face because he said, 'This is where it happened.' He smiled wryly. 'Are you curious?'

'Wouldn't anyone be?' she said, shrugging self-deprecatingly.

'Ranald told me where the first body was found. The field behind the clubhouse.'

'That was Bruce Lassiter?'

'It was – ' He paused, as if searching his memory. 'Jamie Dyer. Bruce's body was found in the woods, by the stream.'

They left the car and followed the path that ran round the side of the building.

There was a large structure behind the clubhouse, a barn that had seen better days. 'That's the farmhouse,' he said. 'You'll have seen pictures of it in the newspapers.'

Beyond the farmhouse was the field of tall grass where Jamie

Dyer's body had been found. Further still, there was a mass of yellow bushes. Was Toby taking her that way? Her detective's instincts hoped he would but he turned sharp left.

'The tournament area's behind these trees,' he said, 'so watch where you put your feet. The ground's a bit damp in places. Try to keep to the path.'

The woodland was matted with undergrowth and she kept stumbling. It grew dim, the light filtering uneasily through the latticework of leaves, the foreshortening of perspective making the trees seem closer than they were. As they moved in deeper, she heard the sound of running water. She followed Toby's footsteps faithfully, grateful for his knowledge of the wood and its paths.

The trees thinned and it grew lighter. The woodland gave way to open ground and she saw, directly ahead, a mesh of metal scaffolding. Workmen were erecting a huge wooden structure which disappeared into the distance.

Toby gestured to the rigging. 'This is where the spectators will sit for some of the games. Or rather, where they'll stand. No-one sits during a paintballing tournament.'

'It's that exciting?'

'You can tell me after the game tomorrow,' he said, meeting her eye. 'By the way, I'm hoping you'll be my guest for dinner afterwards.'

She thought of Georgie, conscious suddenly of the way their roles had been reversed: her daughter had been abandoned by her man while she, Von, might soon be doing the fandango with Toby. She realised how the girl would feel about being left alone on a Saturday night. 'I'm not sure, Toby,' she said cautiously.

He studied the rigging. 'You've got family commitments to sort out, so no need to say anything now. Tell me after the game.'

She felt a flush of pleasure at this show of consideration, and was determined to find a way to make the date, even if it meant engaging a babysitter so Georgie could go out too. Assuming she still wanted to.

A workman waved at Toby and shouted something she couldn't catch.

Toby waved back. 'I need to go up and speak to them. I won't be long.'

'Fine.'

'Don't wander off and get lost,' he smiled over his shoulder. 'The trees go on for miles.'

He climbed into the scaffolding. A moment later, he and the men were deep in conversation. They seemed like best mates, although it was clear from their body language that the workmen deferred to him. He was a natural leader, a type she was unfamiliar with, a completer-finisher who'd make sure his men inspected every inch of rigging. He waved, indicating by tapping his watch and holding up both hands, fingers splayed, that they'd be another ten minutes. After a while, they walked along the rigging away from her.

It was now after eleven. She peered into the wood. Although the path looked newly-made, the trees, mostly oaks, were ancient, suggesting the area couldn't have been planted especially for paintballing. She walked a little way in, running a hand over the thick mossy bark. Bracken grew in clumps between the trunks, the bright green foliage stippled with light. She heard a sudden rustling overhead and looked up. A pair of grey squirrels were chasing each other over the branches.

The ground was covered in dead leaves and gave off a smell of damp earth. Something snapped loudly underfoot. The sound reverberated through the wood, followed by the urgent flapping of crows' wings. She tried to recall the newspaper diagrams showing where Jamie Dyer and Bruce Lassiter had been paintballing before they were murdered. They'd been running through this part of the wood, trying to reach the bridge that would take them to the field. It was an ideal place to lie in wait, easy for a killer to conceal himself behind bushes or wide trees. Had the police scoured this entire area? She doubted Lothian and Borders had the resources. It wasn't like the Met.

Five minutes later, she realised she'd wandered off the trail. The thought slipped uneasily into her mind that she could get lost here; the woodland looked the same in every direction. She searched for the path, stepping over ferns and skirting the bushes. A sudden wind stirred the branches, making the canopy of leaves sway rhythmically.

Without warning, the ground gave way and she found herself falling. She hit the earth with a thump, striking her head on the mat of leaves. As well as knocking the breath out of her, the jolt caused pain to shoot from the back of her head to her neck, reminding her that the injury sustained in Dean Cemetery hadn't healed completely. She looked around in a daze. Somehow, she'd fallen onto her side. Her right leg was stretched out in front. Her left leg had disappeared.

A shadow fell across her and she looked up, suddenly afraid. A large figure blotted out the light. In that instant, she saw what Jamie and Bruce had seen in their final moments: a man towering over them, ready to deliver the killer shot of a double tap.

'So this is what you've been up to?' The voice was not unfriendly. 'I leave you for one second and you go wandering off. I'm beginning to think you want to avoid me.'

'Toby,' she said, relieved.

He gripped her arm and tried to haul her to her feet. 'Your leg's trapped,' he said. He put both arms round her waist and lifted her clear. Her leg reappeared, covered in soil.

'What the hell happened?' she said, bending to examine the ground. 'It's caved in.'

He was frowning, his hands thrust deep into his pockets. 'The soil can be soft around here.'

'Soft? Are you kidding? There's a gaping hole.' She dropped to her knees to get a better look, but he pulled her up, keeping his hand on her arm.

'Let's go, Von.' There was an urgency in his voice that took her by surprise.

She let him guide her back to the path, noticing how he was careful where he put his feet. They reached the farmhouse and, a minute later, were inside the Jaguar.

He started the engine. 'I should have warned you about the soil.' He looked at her. 'Forgive me, I never thought to ask, you didn't hurt yourself when you fell, did you?'

'Nothing was hurt but my pride. And even that was only slightly dented.'

He smiled, the movement of his mouth deepening the cleft in his chin. 'So. Coffee.'

'Federico's?'

'I thought we could go to mine. I've got salmon steaks for lunch.' He paused. 'Unless you've things to do?'

She thought of Georgie and felt a twinge of guilt. 'A quick lunch, then.'

'In that case, we'll pick up your car en route. You can follow me in. You know how to tail a car without getting lost, right?'

She laughed. 'Right.' It was a skill she had in spades, having done a fair amount as an investigator.

At the gun club, he pulled up next to the Ford. 'My address, in case,' he said, fishing a business card out of his pocket. 'It's near the Queensferry Road.'

She glanced at the card. Something stirred in her memory. She'd been down that street before.

He waited until she'd started the Ford before driving onto the A71. He drove slowly and she had no difficulty keeping up. But that address. It annoyed her she couldn't remember and she was unable to concentrate fully on the road. At a set of traffic lights, she slowed deliberately on the amber so she'd be held up when it turned red. Toby sailed on. By the time the lights turned green, he'd disappeared from view.

At the first opportunity, she pulled over, and took out her streetfinder. A second later, she'd found Toby's street. She stared at the map, her breathing shallow. The street was a five-minute walk from Belgrave Crescent. Maybe it wasn't significant. But everything was significant until proven otherwise.

She drove slowly to his address.

She'd hardly taken her finger off the bell of the small town house when the door opened. Toby was wearing a green-and-white-striped plastic apron.

He threw the door wide, evidently pleased to see her. 'You made it. For a while there, I thought you'd had a change of heart.'

She tried to look embarrassed. 'I missed the lights, I'm afraid. I had to stop and check the map.'

'Well, do come on through.'

He ushered her into a large modern kitchen. A dish containing salmon steaks in a fiery red sauce stood on the working surface.

'Piri-piri,' he said, following her gaze. 'Quick and easy. I'm not much of a cook. Anyway, take a seat.' He placed the dish in the oven, and stirred the contents of a couple of saucepans. 'Can I tempt you to wine? Or do you not drink and drive?'

'A small glass won't hurt.'

'I've Pinot Grigio open. But if you prefer red, I'll fetch a bottle.'

'White will be fine.'

She watched him pour two small glasses but her mind was on other things. She was anxious to get away now, not just because of Georgie, but because she needed space to think. She'd eat quickly, make her apologies, and leave. She picked up The Scotsman. The front page carried an article on a merger between Bayne Pharmaceuticals and Stannard HealthSolutions.

Stannard HealthSolutions. She'd seen a folder with that name in Dewey's desk drawer.

'Who are Stannard HealthSolutions, Toby?'

'A US multinational.' He glanced at her. 'You've seen the piece about the merger, then. Stannard obviously think they and Bayne's make a good fit. It'll be the saving of Livingston.'

'How so?'

'You know Bayne's shares have been falling.'

'Because of this medication thing?'

'Lazinex, yes. The merger will rescue Bayne's and save thousands of local jobs. The share price is already climbing. Investors are buying like mad. If you've any spare cash, now's the time before the price stabilises.'

She felt like laughing. *If you've any spare cash.* The way her finances were going, she and Georgie would soon be sleeping under bridges. She put the paper down. 'Why would anyone merge with Bayne's?'

'Maybe Stannard want Bayne's expertise. That's what mergers are usually about.'

I've forged links with Edinburgh University and brought in the best scientists money can buy. My top man, Dr. Ranald McCrea, runs the biochemistry department here. Dewey's words. He knew about the merger at that interview, he'd even hinted at it. *The smart money's on Bayne's, and you can quote me verbatim on that.* 'I suppose Dewey Croker will be cock-a-hoop,' she said.

Toby said nothing but she guessed what he was thinking from the way he tensed: Croker had released a drug prematurely with disastrous results, and now he was going to rake it in because he'd saved the company and turned Bayne's water into wine. She couldn't begin to imagine the size of the man's bonus. Yet Dewey Croker wasn't all bad.

'Do you know about his charity work?' she said to Toby's

back.

He snorted. 'Charity work? Dewey?'

She told him briefly about the foundation (without saying how she'd come by the information).

'Great story,' he said, spooning potatoes and broccoli onto dishes. 'I could almost set it to music.'

He brought the plates to the table, and refilled their glasses without asking if she wanted more.

She tasted the salmon. 'Delish, Toby.'

'It's simple. You pour the sauce over everything and shove it into the oven.' He lifted his glass. 'Anyway, bung ho. What shall we drink to?'

'Success at tomorrow's tournament?'

'You bet.'

As they ate, he told her more about the event: the rules, the type of battle scenarios to expect, the custom-built equipment. The team he was playing in was called the 'Yellows' on account of the players' yellow kerchiefs. She listened, saying little, not because she had nothing to say but because it was difficult to get a word in. Paintballing seemed to be what Toby lived for, even more than shooting with guns.

When they'd finished eating, he brought over a tub of amaretto-flavoured ice-cream. 'I thought we could forget about bowls and just share,' he said, handing her a spoon.

He tasted the ice-cream, then lifted the spoon to her lips. She was taken by surprise and allowed him to slide it into her mouth. But she didn't want this. She sat back, the movement causing his hand to drop. 'Toby . . . ' she began.

He placed a finger to her lips. 'It's okay. I know. I'm going too fast.' He smiled faintly. 'I'm no good at this, am I?'

'It's not you. It's just that I'm not sure I'm ready for this. I've got problems at home.'

'I'm a good listener.'

'There's not much to tell. My daughter's broken up with her boyfriend and I need to be there for her.'

'And who's there for you, Von?'

She looked into his eyes. That one was easy. No-one. No-one had ever been there for her.

He got slowly to his feet. 'I'll put the coffee on.'

'That'll be great,' she said, meaning it. A caffeine hit was exactly what she needed.

He busied himself at the machine. 'It'll take a while to percolate.' He hesitated. 'The trouble about cooking is that your clothes end up smelling. Do you mind if I take a quick shower?'

She suspected it was less the clothes and more that he wanted a breathing space to get over his embarrassment. 'Not at all,' she said quickly.

He smiled. 'Make yourself at home.'

She watched him through the kitchen door. He walked briskly along the corridor. A second later, she heard the dull thump of someone mounting the stairs.

Her thoughts tumbled over one another. Having a shower took a while.

First, she looked in the less-used bottom cupboards. Cleaning materials and a dustpan and brush. She gave the top cupboards a casual inspection; they were full of tins. If this were her house, where would she keep a pistol and ammunition? The law said they had to be kept locked but not every killer would let an inconvenient Act of Parliament bother him.

She crept into the hall. To her right was the living room. A glance inside told her she'd be wasting her time there: the only piece of furniture where anything could be hidden was crammed with glasses and china. Yet something told her to look again. Her old governor had taught her that the best place to hide something was in plain sight. But the room had few ornaments or knick-knacks. Unless Toby had hidden a piece in the upholstery or under the floorboards, what she was looking for wasn't here.

That left the cupboard under the stairs. She paused to listen. From above came the faint sound of running water.

The cupboard door opened onto a small space. She saw a vacuum cleaner and ironing board, and the sort of junk you store away: old CDs, videotapes, and used paperbacks. Behind the door were beige army boots of the kind worn by GIs in war films. She opened the door wider to let in the light and caught a metallic flash of green and gold.

A pair of trainers. She'd nearly missed them. She recognised the make, having seen a similar pair in Lexie's bedroom: Andrea Sibillini. The treads were a mix of circles and lines enclosed in a figure-of-eight. The trainers hadn't been cleaned and bits of mud and leaves were sticking to the rubber. She brought them into the corridor for a better look. They were a size twelve.

There was just the one set of treads on the path. We got the shoe size from the plaster cast. It's a men's twelve.

She'd been holding her breath, and it came out in a rush. Toby had a pair of trainers which could have made the footprints found at the murder site. So what? There would be countless members of the paintballing club who had Andrea Sibillinis in the same size. And wouldn't the terrain where the bodies were found be covered in footprints? To suggest, on these grounds, that a club member was the murderer would be ludicrous. She'd found no hard evidence of Toby's involvement in either the murders or anything to do with Phil Pattullo. She should have been relieved. So why was something in her gut worrying her?

She was so lost in her thoughts that she didn't see the figure beside her. It was when Toby spoke that she realised he must have been standing watching for a while. She was surprised she could hear him over the thudding of her heart.

'Thanks, Von, I'd wondered where I'd put my Sibs.'

He was in jeans and the gun club's grey hooded sweatshirt with the words Calder Rifle and Pistol Club in red letters. He was holding a towel. Her tongue felt thick. 'I didn't hear you come down,' she said.

'I can see that.' He rubbed his hair with the towel. 'You're like all the women I've ever met. They want to know everything about a man before considering getting involved with him.' He nodded at the trainers still in her hand. 'But you've done me a favour. I thought I'd lost those.'

She handed him the Sibillinis without a word. What was there to say? He'd outed her as a snoop but at least he'd been gracious enough to make light of it. She tried to remember whether the police had released the fact about the trainer treads and the size of the shoe that had made them. It was the type of detail police keep to themselves.

She wiped the perspiration from her upper lip. She felt like one of his squaddies, discovered in the act of going through his officer's foot locker. The simplest thing would be to leave. 'I'd better get going,' she said quietly.

He slung the towel across his shoulder. 'Not staying for coffee?'

She thought she detected something in his voice. His eyes were expressionless.

'I really do need to go, Toby.'

'You're still coming tomorrow.' It sounded like a command. 'Starts at ten.'

'I haven't forgotten. You said you'd give them my name at the gate?'

He smiled, and she felt herself relax; he'd be pleased she remembered that little detail.

'I'll find you inside, Von. If not before the game, then after.'

'Great,' she said cheerfully. 'Well, I'd better get going. Thanks for lunch. I really enjoyed it.' She was tempted to put a seal on her restoration to his good books by telling him she'd have dinner with him after the match, but something stopped her.

He waited a second, and then moved aside. In the narrow corridor, she had to brush past him to get to the door. She smelt his soap, sharp and masculine.

In the car, she waved briefly before pulling away. She drove around the web of streets until she found Queensferry Road, her mind not fully on her driving. So she'd found no guns or ammo although she'd searched only the ground floor. But, if Toby were the killer, would a pro like him keep weapons at home? Sure he would, if he had few or no visitors. Yet it was he who'd invited her back so, either he kept them well hidden, or they were in a room he didn't expect to take her into. That excluded the bedroom, she thought wryly, remembering how he'd slid his spoon into her mouth.

And he lived practically on the doorstep of Belgrave Crescent. Close to Lexie and Phil. For the first time, she found herself entertaining the thought that Phil's demon angels had prevailed, and he'd become a killer. It would have been easy for Ranald and Lexie to groom him for the task, taking him paintballing to show him where and how to do it. Or maybe it was Toby, with his expertise in guns, who had schooled Phil in the art of delivering a double tap. And now Phil was in hiding, a packed suitcase hidden in a locker somewhere, his passport in the desk drawer, at the ready. Ready for what, though? If he was going to go, why hadn't he gone? Why wait around?

No, it didn't add up. It was a co-incidence that Toby lived so close to Lexie. And it was also a co-incidence that he lived on the street adjoining Ranald McCrea's; she'd passed the church on the way to his house.

Her thoughts turned then to the other Ranald McCrea living in that church, the kindly gentleman with impeccable manners, his mind a fog, who'd thought he was in Stamford

Bridge and she was his sweetheart, Daphne. And suddenly she felt like crying, not just for the man whose life had been destroyed by dementia, but for herself and her daughter, and the way they could all have been living their lives like normal people but instead were mired in unhappiness, unable to communicate.

Chapter 25
Saturday, June 16th

The road was thronged with cars trying to get into Livingston's sporting event of the year: the annual tournament at The Paradise World of Paintballing. Steve manoeuvred the Peugeot through the wide gate and past the billboard with the blue letters. It was so different from his first visit when he and Fergus had cruised into the deserted site looking for a dead man. Now, having to drive himself because his sergeant had the day off, Steve was dodging vehicles, and was finally forced to slow to a crawl and trail the car in front.

A large grassy area had been set aside for visitors. Despite his early arrival – it was 9.00am and the first match wasn't due to start till ten – the car park was crowded and he was shunted to an overflow area.

He locked the Peugeot and followed the crowd. White jumpsuits stamped with the word, Marshal, were ushering visitors away from the clubhouse. Aye, that made sense: the building would be out of bounds to all but the players; he could hear laughter through the open windows.

Behind the clubhouse, more marshals guided him to the path through the woods. He paused briefly to look past the farmhouse towards the tangle of broom bushes, the yellow so bright in the clear air it was painful to the eye. The tents, the flag markers, all trace of the police had vanished. There was no indication a corpse had been found at the bottom of the field and, if the visitors knew, they were acting as though they didn't.

They trudged along in single file, keeping to a well-marked path, and anyone who thought to stray into the trees was directed back by the white suits.

He had a full day ahead of him; there were matches in a variety of venues. Von would already be here. She'd have most likely risen with the baby and got in early enough to avoid the traffic. He hadn't seen her Ford in the car park but then he hadn't looked. Perhaps she'd spent the night with Hilliard and had come in with him. He bristled at the thought of the two of them together. Hilliard had behaved as though he owned her, taking her away like that. And she'd let him. It rankled but it was no business of his. Ach, he had no chance with her, never had. It was time to put it away.

The crowd parted and he found himself in a large area bustling with people. There were food stalls, and stalls selling drinks, which he noticed were all soft. The rich smell of burgers reached him on a stream of blue smoke. He wondered what else they sold. He was here for the day and burgers weren't his thing. A long row of portaloos stood behind the stalls. He grinned to himself. Aye, they'd want to discourage people from peeing in the woods.

He blinked into the sun, studying the colosseum-like structure before him. Twenty feet up, spectators were sauntering along a walkway behind stiff meshing.

He was climbing up the wooden steps when his mobile rang.

He snapped it open. 'Steve English.'

'Hi there, lover boy.'

'Cally! Where are you?'

'Right behind you.'

He spun round, nearly falling off the steps.

She was leaning against a tree, holding a phone to her ear. 'I've been watching out for you, Steve. Glad you came early.' She formed her lips into a pout. 'Didn't expect me here, did you?'

She was wearing flesh-coloured trousers in a stretch material, the weave so fine they could have been her skin. The white shirt was the type that closed with a zip. Her hair was caught up in an asymmetric ponytail, falling over her left cheek.

He limped down the steps. 'I didn't know you were a fan of paintballing.'

'I'm not. But I couldn't resist coming to see the place.' She nodded at the trees. 'Is this where it happened?'

He rarely answered such questions directly. His Senior Investigating was one to keep the public in the dark and expected his officers to do the same. 'How did you know I'd be here?' he said.

'Got the intel from DI Kelly. I wouldn't have come otherwise.' Her expression softened. 'I'm hoping we can get together afterwards.' She must have seen his hesitation because she added, 'You're going to tell me that was a mistake, aren't you? But some mistakes are too much fun to only make once.'

She looked greatly pleased with herself and he found himself smiling. Aye, sure enough, she was right about that. 'So, Miss Cockrill, dare I ask where you are with your investigations? DI Kelly told me you've been examining the victims' laptops. Did you finally find evidence of criminal activity?'

'Still looking.'

'And the mirror stats?' he said, hoping she'd be impressed he remembered the expression.

'Still crunching the numbers.' She brought her face close to his and he smelt the muscatel. 'But I'm now more convinced than ever that Jamie and Bruce were up to something.'

'You have found a discrepancy in the figures?'

'It was the file you sent me via DI Kelly. The one on the CD. PA.XLS,' she added, when he continued to look blank.

The CD Von had found in Lexie's house. But it didn't belong to Jamie. It was Lexie's or Phil Pattullo's. Cally had jumped to this conclusion because Bridget had. Steve had hinted obliquely that there was stuff relevant to the Jamie Dyer and Bruce Lassiter killings there, otherwise Bridget wouldn't have given the disk a moment's consideration. But this wasn't something he could tell Cally. 'Go on,' he said.

'It was a bit of a no-brainer. The filename gives it away: PA is the two-letter country code for Panama.'

'Panama?'

'Once I grasped that, the rest of it fell like ninepins.' She paused for effect. 'The first column consists of bank account numbers.'

He stared at her. 'And the second column?'

'Passwords, I'm guessing. It would explain why Jamie and Bruce kept the file on a CD. That kind of information simply isn't safe to keep anywhere but offline. As for the last column, I'm not sure. Could be the names of the account holders, but it's unlikely. If these are in a Panama bank, they won't be nominated accounts.'

'So they're numbered accounts.' He rubbed his scalp. 'If that last column isn't names, what is it?'

'I've been trying to think how I would go about hiding money. Big money, because the fact we're talking several accounts means there's too much to put into the one. I'd be laundering the money first. There are many ways you can do it, but one method is to set up front companies in a country where companies pay no corporation tax. I think that last column has the names of these companies.'

'And what would their business be?'

'Oh, they could conduct legitimate business like' – she puffed out her lips – 'well, anything, really. The laundered cash could then be siphoned into the Panama accounts.' When he said nothing, she added huffily, 'You're not as delighted as I'd hoped you'd be.'

'Which Panamanian bank would these accounts be in?'

'Got me there, Steve. There's nothing on the file. Chances are that Jamie and Bruce kept that little piece of info in their heads.'

'Are there many banks in Panama?' he said after a pause.

'Fraid so. And here's the bad news. They're lightly regulated. Even if you tracked down the bank, there'd be no record that those accounts are associated with those companies or with Jamie and Bruce. Panama's like that. No registration. No tax treaties with other countries.'

'Remind me again why I should be delighted?'

'It means you have that all-elusive motive for Jamie's and Bruce's murders,' she said peevishly. 'Stealing on a grand scale.'

He'd acted badly. 'I'm sorry, Cally. You're quite right. And I am grateful.' But his mind was only partly on what he was saying. Von had found the CD with Phil Pattullo's passport and a locker key. The natural assumption was that all three objects belonged to Phil. But was that necessarily true?

Cally was watching him, a finger to her mouth. 'Okay, I know what you're going to say. All this means is that money is likely to have been laundered, but it could be Jamie's or Bruce's own money, earned legitimately. Or maybe one of them won the lottery. I still need to get irrefutable evidence the two of them swindled Bayne's, right?'

'It would help.'

'Have no fear. My machines are churning away as we speak.'

The openness of her expression made her look like a little girl. He ran a finger down her cheek. 'To make up for my bad manners, may I take you to dinner tonight?'

She didn't answer immediately, she was going to make him work for it. But he needed to know one more thing. 'Cally, can you remember when the file was created?'

'No, but I know it was last modified a month ago.' She folded her arms. 'Where did you find the CD? Answer, Steve.'

He hesitated. 'In a drawer at Jamie's sister's.'

She made a tutting noise. 'A drawer in someone else's house? Can't have been for safekeeping. He wouldn't have given that kind of data to anyone but an accomplice. Whatever he's doing, his sister's in on it. And maybe it hasn't come to a full stop just because Jamie's died.'

The girl had a point. If anyone else was in on the scam, it would surely be Lexie and not Phil Pattullo: from what Von had told him of Phil, he wouldn't have had the ability, let alone the opportunity, to pull off something as complex as stealing and selling medications.

'You know, Cally, I saw Jamie's house. It looked the way a house does when you're about to sell it. I've been thinking all along that he was going to do a runner with Bruce Lassiter.'

She tilted her head. 'But maybe it's his sister, Lexie, he was going to flit with.'

Aye, and was Ranald also a partner? Perhaps Cally would have to extend her investigations.

'So, tonight, Steve. Seven-thirty for dinner at the Balmoral.'

'The Balmoral?'

She looked at him meaningfully. 'It's where I'm staying.' She stroked his tie. 'The Indian food delivery man is staying there with me.'

Von was watching Steve and the twiglet. She had no idea who the girl was but they seemed more than just good friends. She wondered if they were in deep or if it was simply a fling. Not like Steve to have found someone young enough to be his daughter but, well, good for him.

She buried her head in her programme in case they spotted her. She was wearing a baseball cap low over her forehead, the biggest pair of sunglasses she could find, and clothes that were nondescript and which she hadn't worn for weeks. It was the best she could do and, although Steve might recognise her, she hoped that neither Ranald nor Lexie would. They were both playing in the first event, which was starting in fifteen minutes.

Toby had been as good as his word. She hadn't had to pay at the gate and someone in a white jumpsuit had guided her to a reserved car-parking space. Nice of Toby to be so thoughtful. There was a full schedule of games planned so, unless he managed to sneak away between matches, she wouldn't see him until the tournament was over. She'd watch the first game so she'd have something to talk about. Then she'd start searching for Phil.

She climbed into the viewing rig, transformed from the metal monster it had been yesterday into something resembling an arena. Below her, through the wire netting, was a jumble of sheds, trucks, and military vehicles. A bright yellow flag hung limply from the turret of a rusting tank.

This was Game Zone No. 1, according to her programme sheet, and the first match was called Capture the Flag. There were two flags, one for each team, and whichever side captured the opposing team's won the match. It seemed straightforward, but she guessed that both attacking and defending would require chess-like tactics and someone to co-ordinate the players.

She edged round the high walkway, squeezing through the noisy crowd, looking for somewhere to sit. There were seats in the front row, but most of the spectators seemed to want to stand. Toby was right: it was essential to walk around to see the match properly; the opposing team's flag was somewhere beyond her vision.

There was a sudden frisson, and a group in green camouflage jumpsuits and yellow kerchiefs, and carrying their face guards, strode into the playing area. They stopped not far below where she was standing. She recognised Toby instantly; he wore his kerchief Rambo-style round his forehead, the only team member to do so. Then she saw Ranald and Lexie, and automatically shrank back against the rigging. But there was no need to make herself invisible: the players were oblivious to what was happening above them.

Lexie's hair was tied back in a ponytail and she wore little or no makeup. She seemed in command and marched around the course checking the layout, the others following her like bees. Her inspection over, she called the team and they huddled together, their arms round each other's shoulders, talking in low tones. Suddenly, a figure looked up and stared directly at Von. It was Megan, the girl with doe eyes and long curly hair who signed the firearms in and out of the Calder Rifle and Pistol Club. Next to her was the spiky-haired receptionist. Were all the gun-club members here?

The girl's attention shifted to the entrance. The opposing team was strutting in like a company of gladiators. A glance at the programme told Von they were called Angels With Dirty Faces. Their brown jumpsuits were printed front and back with red angels with outspread wings and golden haloes, although the figures on the back were largely obscured by the players' paraphernalia. Jesus, red angels? She thought of Phil's drawings and the stone effigies in Dean Cemetery.

She had that strange feeling of being watched and looked around anxiously. But the crowd's attention was on the players. She scrutinised the spectators' faces. Phil's wasn't amongst them. Yet something told her he was here.

Lexie's voice made her turn. It was shrill with anger. Toby was speaking into a mobile phone, a hand up, as though warding her off. Clearly annoyed, the girl let her arms fall to her sides in a gesture of impatience. The call finished, he replaced the phone inside his jumpsuit and zipped it up. Only then did he give his full attention to the blue-jumpsuited referee who was explaining the rules and safety regulations.

The players put on their face guards and tightened the straps. Then everyone dispersed to take up position. The Angels moved to the far end of the arena while the Yellows returned to their flag.

At a signal from the referee, who shouted something through a loudspeaker, the game began. Everyone moved at once, rushing to take cover behind vehicles. Any doubts Von had about Lexie's role were gone: the players kept their eyes on her, waiting for instructions. She made jabbing motions with her hand, shouting 'Go, go, go!', directing half the team to defensive positions near the flag, while the others moved forward using the objects as cover. Von found herself caught up in the excitement and rushed round the walkway with the yelling crowd. In the centre of the playing area, the two sides were firing on their opponents, the steady put-put-put of the paintballs drowned out by the shouting of the players. In minutes, every tank, truck, and jeep was splattered in paint.

Lexie bellowed out orders, hopping in a crouch from one place of cover to the next. To the crowd's delight, she executed a perfect one-handed cartwheel, bringing her body down behind a covered truck. Von watched, fascinated. Was this the same Lexie Dyer she'd seen when she was 'Iris'? Lexie stopped to reload her gun from a container at her waist, and then ran out again, firing. Two of her team had been hit in the chest. They raised their paintball guns and left the field. Toby, whom Von recognised by the kerchief round his head, had been hit high in the leg. A white suit examined the paint splodge and then patted him on the back. He was allowed to stay in the game.

The play continued with each side gaining, and then losing, ground. The Yellows were surprised in a flanking attack. Lexie took shelter behind an upturned jeep, shouting 'Pull back! Pull back!' More players were hit and had to leave the field, including Toby. He shrugged when ordered off by a marshal but left gracefully enough, lifting his gun to acknowledge the spectators' applause. As the sun climbed into the sky, the sharp smell of paint drifted on the air.

The battle moved to the far end of the arena where the Angels had their flag. The spectators hurried there, wanting to be in at the kill. They screamed at the players whom they knew by name, everyone siding now with the winning Yellows. The game reached its climax when one of the Yellows ran onto a wall and grabbed a large red flag with an angel on it. He picked up a bugle and brought it to his lips. The sound signalled the end of the game.

The player lifted the flag high, removing his mask with his free hand. It was Ranald McCrea, his face shining with exhilaration. Below him on the ground was one of the Angels. He, too, removed his mask, and Von recognised the man with the gelled hair who'd so taken Elen's fancy at Lexie's drinks reception.

The man grasped Ranald's outstretched hand and let himself be helped to his feet. He grinned at the victor, clapping him on the shoulder.

'Quite exciting, isn't it?' The voice came from Von's right.

She looked into the speaker's eyes. Her heart was banging in her chest. It was the last person she'd expected to see.

'Mrs Pattullo,' she said.

'So, what do you think, sir? Should we get up a match at Lothian and Borders? I'm sure the Chief Super would dig deep.'

Steve turned to see Fergus smiling at him. 'Didn't know you were a fan of paintballing, Fergus.'

'I'm not really, sir. But the smart money tells me this is the place to be.'

'And why is that, then?'

'The last time there was a match here, two people were murdered.'

'You're becoming a bit of a ghoul, lad,' Steve said, lifting an eyebrow.

'Human nature, sir.'

'So did you see the match?'

'Thrilling, wasn't it?'

Steve hadn't found it particularly thrilling. For an instant, as he'd watched a player lift his marker to his shoulder, he was back in Glasgow at the scene where he'd been shot. 'You here on your own?'

'Actually, no, sir.'

The woman he'd taken for a spectator turned round from staring at the arena. 'I thought you'd be here, Inspector,' Lina Prince smiled. When there was no reply, she added, 'Those Yellows are something else, huh? They took the Angels like Grant took Richmond. If I were a betting woman, I'd be putting my money on them.'

'How are you, Miss Prince?'

Her green eyes were sparkling. 'I'm good. You?'

'All the better for seeing you. How's the test fire going?'

'I was wondering when you'd get round to that.' She paused, not offering anything more.

'And?'

'And my staff are on the case. You want me to call them and see how far they've got?'

'I'm sure they'll ring you the minute they find something. And then you'll ring me.'

'Uh-huh.' She removed her baseball cap and her curls fell over her shoulders. She shook them out, releasing a musky rose scent.

Fergus had been listening to the exchange. 'Shall I get us some coffee? How about you, sir?'

'Not for me,' he said with an acknowledging tilt of the head. 'Mine's on the way.'

The man smiled, and left.

'Can you tell me if you're close to catching your perp, Steve? On the QT?'

'We have a motive.'

Her expression changed as she looked past him.

Cally was holding a large styrofoam cup. 'Your coffee, Steve,' she said, glaring at Lina.

He made the introductions, noticing the way Cally slipped a proprietary arm through his. 'Miss Cockrill has been helping us with our investigations,' he said to Lina, amused at the woman's polite smile.

'Pleased to meet you, Miss Cockrill,' Lina said.

'Likewise,' Cally replied, looking her up and down with undisguised hostility. 'You're the gun lady, right?'

'Right.'

Cally pressed herself against him. 'The next match is starting soon. It's a bit of a trek from here so we should get a move on.' She rubbed his arm. 'Come, Steve.'

'You go. I'll catch you up.'

The girl looked uncertainly at Lina. But she was smart enough to know when to back away. She gave him a peck on the cheek, tossed her ponytail, and left.

'Nice ass,' Lina said, watching her go. 'She looks like a twice-on-Sundays sort of girl. So why aren't you showing me your happy face?'

'Find me the murder weapon and I'll be happy. Isn't there anything at all you can tell me?'

'The pistols we fired yesterday afternoon didn't return a match. There's no way to dress it up, bud. I don't think the ones we're testing today will either.'

They both knew that without a murder weapon crimes involving shooting were tough to solve. 'I don't believe it,' he said. 'You're looking but you're not seeing.'

'I'm looking but I'm not seeing?' she repeated, incredulity

in her voice. 'Don't give me that, Steve. You don't think the murder weapon is in that club any more than I do. Fess up, you're just ticking the boxes. Take it from someone who was once a cop, this isn't an enigma wrapped in a paradox. Work on the motive, for Chrissakes. Here endeth the lesson.' She seemed embarrassed at her outburst, adding more quietly, 'You'll have my report on Monday.'

Aye, he'd get the test-fire results, right enough, and they'd show up the exercise for what it was: a waste of time and money. Von had been right. Von was always right. He wondered why he'd let her think the Fiscal had granted the police a warrant to search the shooting club. The truth would surprise her – Dewey Croker himself had contacted Lothian and Borders and asked them to turn the place upside down.

Fergus arrived with the coffees.

'Not going to join your girlfriend?' Lina said.

Steve shook his head.

'Paintballing's not of that much interest, huh?' She glanced knowingly at his leg.

After some more small talk, she and Fergus moved away.

He threw the half-full coffee cup into a bin and spread out his crumpled programme. The next event, at 11.30am, was deep inside the woodland. He followed the crowd through the trees to Game Zone No. 4 where the hulk of a downed plane loomed above them. The top half of the fuselage was missing so spectators in the treetop walkways could see the action. Around the plane were scrub, and trenches you could hide in if you lay flat. The same teams, Yellows and Angels, were already lining up. He didn't bother to read how the game would be played. And he wasn't climbing into the trees.

He looked around for Cally but couldn't find her in the mêlée. He was considering leaving when he became aware of someone watching him. Across from the playing area, a man was standing motionless, ignoring the people bumping against him. Seeing Steve's fixed stare, he made his way through the trees towards him.

Gavvo Skelton wasn't someone Steve wanted to speak to. With his tormented eyes and agitated manner, the man was on a hair trigger. Although an SAS-man-turned-boxer ought to be able to control himself, Steve knew that one wrong word and the hair trigger would be released.

He braced himself. 'Mr Skelton, what brings you here?'

'Is that a serious question, mate?' The voice was so harsh that Steve winced. The man didn't improve on second acquaintance.

'I take it you're here to honour Bruce.'

'He'd have been playing in this tournament. I'd made arrangements to get time off.' He compressed his thin lips into a line. 'Saw no reason to cancel.'

'Did you watch the first match?'

Skelton laughed but there was no mirth in the sound. 'Those lightweights, they have no idea of tactics. I could have shown them how to win in half the time and without the casualties.'

'Your SAS training?'

'Yeah. I gave Bruce a few pointers. Hoped to see him put them into practice today.'

He had a way of shifting his weight from foot to foot which Steve found irritating. He pulled a packet of Camel cigarettes from his pea jacket. Without offering the packet to Steve, he fixed a cigarette in the corner of his mouth and flicked the lighter. 'Found your contractor?' he said, blinking through the smoke.

When Steve didn't reply, he sneered, 'That's what I thought.' He looked at the plane, surrounded now by Yellows and Angels. Lexie Dyer was deep in conversation with the referee. 'You're on the ropes with this one, aren't you? You should have called in an expert,' he added.

Steve was growing tired of people telling him how to run

the case. 'An SAS man, like you, you mean? Is that why you're here, Mr Skelton? You did say we'd find the killer in Edinburgh.' He fixed his eyes on the man's pitted skin, flaking around the mouth. 'Are you intending to track him down yourself?'

Skelton was pale with anger, his neck muscles bulging. 'And what, give him a good fucking over? Yeah right, like I'd admit to that, mate.'

'But you have to agree that disposing of someone in this wood would be child's play to a man with your skills.'

'Disposing of anyone anywhere would be child's play to a man with my skills.'

The men faced off. For an instant, Steve wondered whether Skelton still had his service revolver.

'Isn't there anything you can tell me, Inspector?'

'I really can't discuss details of the case with you.'

A hunted look came into the man's eyes. 'I just need you to say you haven't thrown in the towel, that there's been progress.'

Steve was about to tell him that Cally had found a motive, but he realised Jamie and Bruce may have had an accomplice. Not for the first time, he found himself wondering how Gavvo Skelton had found the cash to start up his boxing gym. Yet Bridget had checked his finances and the man was mortgaged to the hilt. If Bruce had been swindling Bayne Pharmaceuticals, he hadn't passed on the fruits of his labours to his partner. He suddenly felt sorry for Skelton.

'Aye, Mr Skelton, there's been progress.'

'Good on yer, mate. That's all I wanted to know.' He tossed the half-finished cigarette onto the ground.

A gust of wind blew through the trees, catching his fair hair and lifting it at the crown. Without giving Steve a second glance, he walked away, his shoulders drooping.

Von looked around, hoping Mrs Pattullo had her son with her.

But she was alone.

'I nearly didn't recognise you, Miss Valenti. So did you watch the match?'

'I did. But what are you doing here?' Stupid question. The woman was there for the same reason she was.

'I've been looking for me Phil. You said he was going paintballing in Livingston. I checked Yellow Pages and this is the only place.' She seemed unsure and gazed at Von as though for confirmation.

'You're right. There's nowhere else round here.'

'I don't get Saturday off as a rule but when I told Chef I was looking for me son, well . . . She understood, she's a mam herself.'

Von realised what it had taken for the woman to come here. There was a new bruise on her cheek, not completely covered by the pan-stick makeup. 'I couldn't help noticing you've had your hair done, Mrs Pattullo.' The wispy ponytail was gone, replaced with a soft bob. 'It suits you.'

It was the first time she'd seen Mrs Pattullo smile. It took years off her. 'I thought if I run into me Phil I don't want him feeling ashamed, especially if he's with them new friends.' Her voice wavered. She glanced down at the navy blazer. 'I bought meself a new jacket. I wanted to look dead smart, like.'

'Anyone would be proud to have you as a mum,' Von said, sick at heart.

People were bumping past them, drifting away from the game zone in the direction of the woods. Mrs Pattullo watched them go. 'I've been here since opening time, Miss Valenti, and I've not seen hide nor hair of him.' She turned tear-filled eyes to her. 'Do you think he'll ever come back to me?'

'I know he will, Mrs Pattullo.'

The remark and the conviction with which it was said seemed to carry the woman over her disappointment. She smiled bravely. 'Well, I'm going to stop at the big gate. It's the only way out. He'll have to come by sooner or later.' She started to walk away.

'Mrs Pattullo,' Von called after her, no longer able to bear the woman's misery. She pulled a scrap of paper out of her bag and scribbled on it. 'This is where Phil's staying. It's a flat on Belgrave Crescent.'

The woman stared at the address. 'I know the street, like. It's not far from Dean Cemetery.' She lifted her eyes. 'But he could never afford a place like that. Is this where his friends live?'

'One of them.' Von hesitated. She could see the question on Mrs Pattullo's face: Why had Von not contacted her sooner with this information? 'I was hoping to speak to him first, you see. Tell him how worried you are. And then I was going to get in touch with you.' It sounded pretty lame. But the woman seemed to accept it.

'Thank you, Miss Valenti.' Tears of gratitude coursed down her cheeks. 'Perhaps you could send me your final invoice.' She hesitated, fear in her eyes. 'Best if you post it to the Balmoral.'

Von nodded miserably. The woman didn't want her husband finding out where his wife's money was going.

Mrs Pattullo folded the scrap of paper and put it into her bag. She turned away and moved through the wood, the dappled sunlight making shifting patterns on her jacket. She looked constantly to left and right as though slowly shaking her head at the strangeness of life, searching for her son with hope and bewilderment.

Von watched the woman's dwindling frame slip in and out of the trees until the wood swallowed her. She removed the sunglasses and wiped her face.

So the case was closed, technically anyway. But what would Mrs Pattullo do if she couldn't find Phil in the Paradise World of Paintballing? She'd go to Belgrave Crescent and hammer on the door. And then what? Beg him to come home? Would he tell her the angels he saw at Lexie's were different from the ones that lived at his mother's? She pushed the damp hair off her forehead. Had she done the right thing in telling Mrs Pattullo where she could find her son? Not if Phil had taken his passport and the left-luggage locker key and slung his hook. She'd have achieved nothing except getting his mother's hopes up unnecessarily. Yes, well done, Von. Note to self – next time, put your brain into gear before engaging your mouth.

She lifted her face to the sun, feeling the sweat evaporate in the soft air. The case might be over, but she still wanted to talk to Phil. It was time to start looking seriously. She'd seen him outside Lexie's flat wearing a dark-brown corduroy jacket. Given today's heat, though, chances were he'd be in his Fruit of the Loom sweatshirt. And, if he were here to cheer on Lexie and Ranald, he'd be wherever the Yellows were. She dismissed the thought he'd be playing with them: from what she'd seen of the game, the members of Lexie's team had been paintballing for years.

She hurried with the crowd to Game Zone No. 4, arriving at the same time as the players. Seeing Lexie, she stopped dead and turned away. But the girl's attention was on her equipment; she was loading her gun with paintballs. A broad-shouldered man in dark-blue slacks and a cream polo shirt detached himself from the crowd. He stopped beside a tree and beckoned. At first, Von thought he was signalling to her.

'Lexie,' the man shouted.

It was Dewey Croker. He was here as well? On the pretext of stopping to fumble in her bag, Von slipped behind a large oak and watched.

Lexie hurried over. When the spectators had gone, Dewey gathered her in his arms and they shared a long kiss.

Lexie pulled away. 'I've got to go, darling,' she murmured, running a hand down his shirt.

'I know, honey,' Dewey said. 'But I wanted to give you this. It's a little good-luck charm.' He pulled something long and glittering from his shirt pocket. Von was too far away to see what it was but, from the way Lexie cooed, he hadn't bought it in a high-street department store.

Lexie gazed up at him. 'So, can you come tonight?'

'Sorry, Lexie. It's not possible.'

'Oh, sweetie.' She slid a hand down his stomach and between his legs. 'Just this once?'

'I have an evening meeting with the board of Stannard's. It's important and it'll go on till late.' His voice was husky. 'And you know our rule. I don't sleep over.'

She let her arm drop, saying nothing.

'I don't like it either. To make up for it, I'll buy you one of those lobster dinners you love so much.' He ran a finger over her lips. 'It won't be long now before it's over and we can put this behind us.'

She nodded. 'And thank you so much for this,' she said, lifting the necklace. 'You spoil me terribly. You really shouldn't have, you know.'

'You're worth it, baby.' He looped an arm round her waist and kissed her, lightly at first, then more passionately, until Von thought they'd rip each other's clothes off and copulate against the tree.

It was Dewey who pulled away, his face contorted.

Lexie was fumbling between his legs. 'Come tonight, darling. Just this once. I need you inside me.'

He took a couple of steps back and Von could see from the rigid set of his jaw that he wasn't caving in. Lexie started to move towards him but he stopped her with a calming motion, assuming the same authority Von remembered from the interview. With a firm nod, he left the girl and headed towards the spectators. Lexie waited until he was out of sight, and then followed the path to the playing area, slapping her paintball gun against her thigh in obvious frustration.

Von watched her go, unsure of the significance of what she'd witnessed. So Dewey Croker and Lexie Dyer were having an affair. Not something she'd have guessed, but then she hadn't seen them together before. But it was an affair he was keen to keep quiet for obvious reasons – he was CEO of a huge corporation going through a well-publicised merger, to say nothing of having a wife who was chairman of his charitable foundation. *You know the rule. I don't sleep over.* But his wife was in who-knows-what part of the world helping the poor. He was being cautious in the extreme in not spending the night with his mistress.

And his words: *It won't be long now before it's over and we can put this behind us.* What would soon be over? What were they hoping to put behind them? Something involving Phil? Or involving Ranald and Toby. The number of combinations of people involved in whatever was going on was large. Too large to think about now. She was on a quest to find Phil. And she felt sure that, once she did, everything else would fall into place.

It was late afternoon and everyone was heading for Game Zone No. 2. This was a wide area, mainly woodland, in which the two teams who'd made it to the finals would be playing. The last match of the tournament would start from a muster point under some camouflage netting. It was to be a reenactment of a battle, one which Von had never heard of.

'Miss Valenti!'

Mrs Pattullo was running towards her. She reached the netting and leant against a wooden post, out of breath. 'Oh, Miss Valenti, I've found him. I've found me Phil.' She was clutching her side, wheezing.

'You've found him?' Von clasped the woman's hand, sharing

in her excitement. 'Where is he?'

'In there, in the wood. I was on my way to the exit when I saw him. In the distance. He was just standing in the trees. I called out to him. He turned and I think he smiled, like, and then he waved. He was looking so well, Miss Valenti, I think he's put on weight. Them friends of his must be looking after him.' She continued to gabble. 'It's a good sign, isn't it, that he's no longer on the streets. Anyway, I wanted you to know I'm going to call on him soon.' She looked at Von pleadingly. 'Do you think he'll come and live with me again? Maybe not immediately, but after a while?'

She seemed to want to be reassured. 'I'm sure he will, Mrs Pattullo.'

The look of hope died on the woman's face. The angels with the burning eyes were there in her house, waiting for him.

'Well, I'd better leave you to get on, Miss Valenti. I wanted you to hear me good news.'

'What was Phil wearing, can you remember? Was it a yellow sweatshirt?'

'It was brown, not yellow. Come to think of it, it was a jacket. That's it, a brown jacket. Can't remember what colour kecks he had on. Blue, I think. Denims. Why do you ask?'

'In case I run into him myself. I'd like to meet him.' *And I've a few questions to ask him.*

'He looked really happy,' Mrs Pattullo said wistfully, moving away. 'Really happy.'

Yes, I bet he did. She doubted Phil appreciated the misery he'd caused his mother, to say nothing of the expense she'd been put to in hiring an investigator. He hadn't even gone over to speak to her. Were all children so selfish? Von wondered, thinking briefly of Georgie.

People were arriving. Suddenly, she heard a deep voice.

Toby was talking to another Yellow. They were adjusting the

ropes around the netting. The job done, the other man left.

Before she could move away, he glanced up and saw her. 'Von,' he said, his face breaking into a smile. 'You made it.'

She smiled back. 'Wouldn't have missed it for the world.'

'What do you think, so far?'

'I see what you mean about not wanting to sit down. Everything moves so quickly.'

He raised a hand to his brow and adjusted the yellow kerchief. His dark eyes were shining; he could hardly keep still. 'We're on course to win. Even if we just draw this last match, we've got the tournament. It'll be champagne tonight. Nothing but the best for you. I thought we could go to the Sheraton.' He stuffed a map into his pocket, and slung on a harness containing paintball cylinders. 'Is seven-thirty good for you?'

'I need to check with Georgie. Let me phone her.' But Von had no intention of calling her daughter. She was playing for time so she could think how to let him down gently. 'I'll find you after the match.'

'Why don't I ring you once we've finished? I'll drive us into town and we can start on the champagne.'

'Fine.' She intended to slip away before the game ended.

'So who was that lady you were talking to?'

'Mrs Pattullo?' she replied without thinking, taken aback by the change of subject. 'My missing persons case. It's her son who's vanished.'

Too late, she remembered he knew Phil; she'd seen them both at Lexie's house the night she broke in.

The change in him was remarkable. The excitement drained from his face. His eyes swept the trees. 'Your missing persons?' he said, his gaze finally settling on her.

She had no option but to continue. 'Mrs Pattullo engaged me to find her son. But he's no longer missing. She told me she saw him just now.'

He looked hard at her. 'Here?' He licked his lips nervously. 'She said Phil's here?'

So he didn't know Phil had come to the tournament. 'She saw him in the woodland. Anyway, the case is closed. He's alive and well and his mother's seen him.' But something made her wade in deeper. 'How do you know her son's called Phil? I don't remember telling you his name.'

'You must have.' There was an unmistakeable edge to his voice. 'How else would I know?'

It struck her that they were alone. And there was dense woodland behind her. 'Yes, of course, I must have,' she said slowly.

They stared at one other. He moved in so close she could feel his breath.

Voices came from the distance, growing louder. Relief washed through her. Toby wouldn't try anything here.

She needed to find a way to leave. 'You know, Toby, I don't think dinner tonight's such a good idea. I really need to get back to Georgie. I'll call you next week, shall I?'

A look of regret crossed his face. 'If that's what you want, Von, then let's leave it. It was a mistake. I see that now.' He turned away, his body rigid.

She could distinguish individual voices now, Ranald McCrea's among them. In a second, the Yellows would come round the corner. There was no time to lose, and no chance of a graceful exit. As the players sauntered into view, she scurried under the netting and jumped into the bushes. Their excited chatter reached her from a few feet away.

She parted the branches carefully, and peered through the netting. Ranald McCrea was unscrewing the top of his water bottle.

Toby grasped his arm. 'She knows, Ranald. She knows everything.'

'What? Listen, you idiot,' Ranald hissed, 'this isn't the time and the place to talk about it.'

'Phil's mother's here. She told her she's seen her son. She recognised him.'

'Jesus, what the hell's he playing at? We told him to stay out of sight. And he's come here, of all places.'

'Look, forget him for a minute and listen to me. I don't want anything happening to her. I mean it, Ranald.'

Ranald's voice was soothing. 'Of course nothing will happen to her. I told you that before.' He paused. 'But I need to think how to handle this. We'll talk about it later, all right?'

'All right, but when?'

'Can't be after the match. I have to get home. My Dad's not well.'

'Sorry to hear that.'

'I'll call you tomorrow.'

The men moved away, mingling with the other players.

Von sat back on her heels. *She knows, Ranald. She knows everything.* The problem was that she knew next to nothing. But she'd learnt something from the men's exchange: Phil's appearance at the tournament had spooked them. *We told him to stay out of sight. And he's come here, of all places.* So, what was significant about this woodland? Only that two men had been murdered not far from where she was sitting. *I need to think how to handle this.* So Ranald, not Toby, was in charge. She pulled off her baseball cap and ran a hand through her hair. Damn it, she should have kept the dinner appointment and tried to find out more, although the way Toby's behaviour had changed had frightened her. Anyway, it was too late now. She wouldn't be seeing him again.

She squinted through the branches. The teams had assembled and the referee was going through the rules to the evident boredom of the players. The game would be all over this area and there were so many places where spectators could stand and watch that her chances of finding Phil were close to zero. She might as well jack it in and go home.

There was a sudden shout and people raced off into the wood. She crouched further into the shrubbery, letting them go past. Toby and Ranald, followed by Lexie, ran so close to her that she felt the bushes move.

She waited another minute, and then stood up and brushed soil from her jeans. The skinny girl with the wonky ponytail was standing on tiptoe at the camouflage net. Steve wasn't with her. She must have caught the movement because she turned and stared. Von ignored her, acting as though hunching in bushes was normal behaviour.

She consulted the programme. To get from Game Zone No. 2 to the car park involved a trek to the food stalls, and then a longish walk to the exit. She was putting the programme away when she spotted the figure in the wood. He was wearing a brown jacket and blue denims and had his back to her. But then he moved his head as a group of players ran past, and she saw the thin face and huge eyes. She felt a rush of excitement. So Phil was still here. Well, this time, she was going to have that little chat.

The playing area was cordoned off and out of bounds to spectators. After a glance around, she stepped quickly over the tape and slipped into the wood. She heard the thump of running feet and the steady put-put-put of the paintballs, and sprang behind a tree. A couple of paintballers ran past, so splattered with paint that it was only by the green-and-gold Sibillinis that she recognised them as Yellows. It occurred to her that, from a distance, she could be mistaken for a player, and wondered what a sting from a paintball felt like, and whether the paint would wash out. Too bad, she was here now. An Angel ran past. Seeing her, he shouted a warning and ran on. She waited before setting out again.

Damn it. Phil had disappeared. But he couldn't have gone far. In which direction, though? That was a no-brainer, it would be wherever the play was. The problem was that the play seemed to be everywhere. The paintballers, some in groups, but most in twos and threes, were taking different paths through the wood. She followed what she thought was the main direction of travel, trying to spot Phil and keep out of the way of everyone else.

The shouts from the players and the noise of the paintballs diminished steadily, and she became aware of the sounds of the wood: rustling in the bracken, the sudden overturning of dead leaves, the cawing of rooks. A while later, she heard running water and her feet squelched into boggy ground. She pulled out the map. There was no stream anywhere. She was totally disorientated. *Don't wander off and get lost. The trees go on for miles.*

Brilliant. She never did have much of a sense of direction. She considered retracing her steps but that would be counter-productive: routes back always look different and she could roam around for ages. There was no point looking for Phil now, there wasn't even a paintballer in sight, she may as well press on and try to find the exit. She lifted her feet out of the mud, cringing as she saw the state of her trainers. Something stirred in her memory. Trainers. The Sibillinis. It was near a stream that Steve had found those size-twelve footprints. It meant she was close to the site of the murders. Despite the day's heat, she found herself shivering.

But this could work in her favour. The newspapers had printed sketches of the area around the crime scenes. Across the stream there was a bridge that would lead to a field, then a large outbuilding, and finally the clubhouse. From there, it was a short hop to the car park. All she had to do was follow the water.

Guided by the sound, she struck out through the trees,

wading through the undergrowth until she reached the bank. The light made moving shapes on the water as it trickled over the stony bed, fast in places, but slowing to near stillness where it grew deep. She gazed up into the trees. Beyond was a roof of pure blue.

She followed the stream as it looped through the wood. How long had she been walking? She seemed to have lost all sense of time. The trees thinned and she was suddenly dazzled by the light flashing off the water. Where the hell was the bridge? She peered into the distance, ignoring the jumping light. Yes, there was a shadow on the water that didn't belong there.

The foot-boards looked as though they wouldn't take her weight but they'd taken Jamie Dyer's. And his killer's. She crossed the bridge and moved into the wood, searching for the path to the field. Something made her pause and listen. Strange. The woodland was still. The birds had stopped singing. Her breathing grew faint. Time to find the way out of this godforsaken place.

She scanned the ground, looking for the path. A sudden bang from a car back-firing made her heart lurch. It was followed closely by another. A startled duck flew up from the water, flying so close that it dropped a clot of mud onto her face. She watched the bird labouring into the sky, remembering then that somewhere near here was the main road to Bonnington. If she crossed back over the bridge and headed into the trees, she'd find the stone wall that marked the perimeter. All she had to do was follow it to the entrance, and she'd get to the car park. A part of her was tempted, but another part – the detective – wanted to see the field where Jamie Dyer had been murdered.

The path, when she finally found it, was well trodden and less muddy than the bank. The trees gave way to a patch of yellow gorse and, behind it, a dilapidated fence, breached in places, marked the edge of a clover field. She recognised the large barn in the distance from the photos in the papers. Toby had referred to it as the farmhouse.

She pushed herself through the nearest gap in the fence. The grass was thick and the terrain uneven. She'd walked only a few feet when she found it: a dusty brown stain on the grass. Her heart was banging in her chest. She'd wanted to see it, and now she had.

Where she was standing was where Jamie Dyer's lifeblood had leaked away.

Chapter 26
Monday, June 18th

'There's a young lass for you, sir,' the duty constable said, grinning. 'Won't give her name but you'll want to see her.'

Steve looked up from his desk. 'Show her in,' he said gruffly.

He was in a bad humour. And it was only 10.00am. Lina Prince had just rung him. None of the pistols she'd test-fired had returned a match with the bullets that had killed Jamie Dyer and Bruce Lassiter. He could still hear the ill-concealed satisfaction in her voice as she'd added that neither the database nor its backups had been tampered with. He scrubbed his scalp. His boss had been fizzing, both at the negative result and the expense, and had given Steve and the rest of the team an earful. Well, hard cheese. The man could have said no to Dewey Croker.

The door swung open and Cally breezed in. A hush descended on the open-plan office as several pairs of male eyes followed her across the room. She sat down on the edge of Steve's desk and swung a leg seductively. She was back in braids today, and wearing a see-through white blouse and short kilted skirt in shades of lilac and green. A pebbly leather handbag hung off her shoulder. There was something fresh about her, a bloom on her skin that made Steve feel old and withered by contrast. He suspected it was the glow of recent sex.

'So this is Lothian and Borders?' she said, looking around the room. 'Even more of a dump than that place on Pitt Street.'

'Nice to see you too, Cally.'

'I have something for you, Steve.'

He raised an eyebrow, ignoring the guffaws from the room.

'Jamie's laptop,' she said, lowering her voice. 'There was a file on it that was deleted, but wasn't, if you see what I mean.'

'I don't.'

'When you delete a file, it doesn't actually go unless you reformat the disk or run a utility.' She wagged a finger in admonishment. 'Jamie hadn't done that. He left a calling card.'

He sat up straight. 'What did you find?'

'Things he'd rather we didn't.' She slid along the desk, so close that, had she come any closer, she'd be in his lap. 'You see, I tried a bit of lateral thinking.' She smoothed her skirt. 'We've been busting our guts assuming the theft was to do with the medications. In other words, it was perpetrated at the export end. But it could also have been perpetrated at the import end.'

'You've lost me.'

'I asked myself what else do Bayne's do other than sell medications. The answer was staring me in the face. They import the raw materials to manufacture them.'

'Raw materials?' He frowned. 'Like what?'

'The composition of medications is always a closely-guarded secret. But there's a limited list of raw materials. And they come from all over the world. Actually, it's from wherever they're produced the most cheaply, and that's the far east.'

He waited, unable to see where this was going.

She brought her face close to his. 'It struck me that it's far easier to perpetrate a scam involving countries that are not well regulated, especially when it comes to chemicals. What with all the travelling Jamie did, he could easily have gone to these countries and arranged for some of the drums containing the base chemicals to be mislabelled.'

'So what would be in them?'

'Listen carefully, Steve. The deleted file has data about

special consignments from China. There are batch numbers, dates, and other shipping information. And numbers for containers at Greenock Ocean Terminal.' She paused for effect. 'The consignments are always the same. The drums contain PMK or piperonyl methyl ketone, a precursor chemical used in the manufacture of MDMA.'

'Dear God,' he said softly. 'Ecstasy.' He felt the blood surge through his veins. He gripped her by the arm. 'Cally, have you told anyone else about this?'

'Nope. You're the only one.'

'Then, for the love of God, keep it that way.'

Something in his tone must have registered because her expression changed. 'Okay,' she said slowly. 'But why?'

'There's one man in Glasgow who controls the Ecstasy trade. Tommy Teoh Lau. Better known as Snake Eyes.'

He wondered how much to tell her. Snake Eyes' brutality was legendary. He was said to crucify his victims by nailing them to the floor. After hours of shooting them in various parts of the body, he would finish them off with a shot through the anus. This wasn't something he left to his hardmen. He did it himself.

But she had a right to know. Her life depended on it. 'The man's a vicious thug who likes hurting little girls like you,' he said. 'Killing is something he does for recreation, and he's very imaginative in how he does it. He's one of the Triads. I take it you've heard of them.'

She tossed her head, as though impatient with what he'd told her. 'Of course, lover boy, everyone's heard of the Triads. But surely they import their Ecstasy ready-made. There are loads of factories around the world that make it.'

'The Ecstasy doing the rounds of Glasgow is a version far more potent than anything you get elsewhere.' With a sudden rush of clarity, he realised that he and Bridget had been barking up the wrong tree. Snake Eyes wasn't bringing Ecstasy in from abroad. He was manufacturing it himself. He tightened his grip on her arm. 'Cally, if Jamie and Bruce have been illegally importing PMK via those special consignments from China, then this thug will be their number-one customer. Probably their only customer.'

'Okay,' she said, disentangling herself from his grasp, 'so where does he make the tablets?'

'Clandestine labs can be set up in a living room, dismantled, and moved. Even if we find them, they can be rebuilt elsewhere for pennies. Look, was there anything in Bayne's records to show what happens to those consignments?'

'I traced the batch numbers but the records show that the drums come into Greenock as chemicals other than PMK. My guess is that, somewhere, cash changes hands, paperwork gets forged, and records are altered.' She stroked her hair, clearly no longer interested in this thread of the conversation. 'So how do you think this Snake Eyes gets his hands on the drums?'

'The containers are craned from the dock onto special lorries which take them to warehouses. They're unpacked and the drums distributed. In our case, to Bayne's Glasgow plant. Greenock Terminal is only half an hour from Glasgow.' His thoughts were spooling around in his head. 'There are several ways that the drums could be diverted. They could disappear from the ships, from the containers waiting at the dock . . .'

'Or the lorries going to the warehouses. Or the ones on their way to Bayne's.'

'Aye, right enough. My money's on the deliveries to Bayne's. If Jamie passed on to Snake Eyes the dates the shipments arrived and the location of the warehouses, it would be a piece of piss to intercept the lorries on a quiet road somewhere.'

'So how do we get him, Steve? It won't be via the money trail. You already know that anything Jamie and Bruce made from this will never have touched their bank accounts. It'll have been laundered till it's whiter than white before being deposited in Panama.'

He rubbed his face. Von had found that spreadsheet on a CD at Lexie's house. Her assumption was that it belonged to Phil Pattullo. But it was more likely now that it was Jamie's. He'd have done his money transfers from there, logging in from Lexie's home computer. 'Can you tell how long this has been going on, Cally?'

'The deleted file has data for the last twelve months. But Jamie and Bruce have been working at Bayne's for longer than that. It's likely this racket goes back years.' There was a touch of wistfulness in her voice. 'They'll have trousered more money than you and I can ever imagine.'

'So Bruce was definitely in on it?'

'There's no evidence but I'm guessing he was. They were both killed together, weren't they? They must have got greedy and tried to sting Snake Eyes for even more money, and he hired a killer to get them.' She leant across and kissed him lightly on the lips. 'Either swindling him or blackmailing him would provide a cast-iron motive, lover boy.'

He threw her a crooked smile. 'Aye, right enough.' Yet something bothered him. Killing with a double tap wasn't the man's style. Snake Eyes would have taken a more exquisite revenge. 'We may have a cast-iron motive, Cally, but we still need cast-iron evidence that Snake Eyes is involved.'

'Then catch Snake Eyes or one of his henchmen in the act.'

'It's too late. The special consignments have stopped with Jamie's death.'

'In the best pantomime tradition, Oh no they haven't.'

He stared at her.

'You really are a dumbo, Steve. It takes ages for chemicals to come by sea from the far east.'

He felt his heart pound. He grabbed her by the shoulders.

'When is the last of Jamie's consignments due to come in at Greenock?'

Her eyes were gleaming. 'In two days' time.'

Von was hurrying down Princes Street, avoiding the midday shoppers. Mondays were always bad, families rowing over nothing and sharp-elbowed women diving into clothes stores. Why people couldn't do their high-street shopping at the weekend, as she did, was one of the great mysteries of the universe.

Now that she'd seen Phil and told his mother where he was staying, she should be contacting her agency and asking for more work. But the conversation between Toby and Ranald had piqued her curiosity, and she couldn't rest until she got to the bottom of it. *She knows, Ranald. She knows everything.* What was it they thought she knew? Why such panic in Toby's voice? She'd sent Steve an email describing the conversation and the men's state of mind but there was no reply.

She passed a shop selling television sets, all showing the same channel. It was the BBC News, and the feature was still the announced merger of Bayne's and Stannard HealthSolutions. The reporter was talking about the frenzied buying of Bayne's shares, the price of which over the last few days was displayed on a board behind her. Von was no mathematician but the initial slow rise had accelerated to what seemed to her an exponential rate. Nice for the people who owned shares in Bayne's.

The boy with the puppy was absent from his usual spot in front of the Carphone Warehouse. That was a bad sign. Or was it? She made a mental note to check out the fountain in the Gardens.

She found Mhairi sitting on her jacket outside the Disney Store, sunning herself, a hand round a bottle of water. The woman was wearing a faded red T-shirt and creased cargo trousers, and her wiry hair was hidden under a patterned headscarf.

One eye opened as Von sat down beside her. 'Ah, Von, my old darling.'

'How are you these days, Mhairi?' She handed the woman a piece of asparagus quiche wrapped in cellophane. 'I bought this from Jenners' food court.'

'Jenners?' the woman said, pulling the wrapping off with stained fingers. 'You are manna from heaven, Von Valenti.' She broke off small pieces of quiche and stuffed them methodically into her mouth. Any crumbs that escaped her maw were carefully picked off her T-shirt and eaten.

Von waited until Mhairi had finished before speaking. 'So, what news?'

Mhairi leant forward slowly, wincing as her knees creaked. 'I've been up to the Grassmarket. Showed those snaps of yours around.' She shifted her weight and pulled the photos out of her pocket. 'People are remarkably bad about remembering faces. Not many have seen these two,' she said, tapping the images of Lexie and Ranald with a greasy finger. 'And the people that have can't remember if Phil was with them.' She screwed her face up and blinked into the sun. 'Hold on, my lovely. I'm forgetting myself.' She paused to take a sip of water.

Von kept the smile glued to her face, hoping it would mask her impatience. But there was no hurrying Mhairi.

The woman screwed the cap back on the bottle. 'Molly saw them all going into a shop. Phil and the people in your photo.'

'What kind of shop?'

'Dunno. But she wrote down the address when I showed her the spondulicks. She knows the woman who owns it, you see.' Mhairi produced a crumpled scrap of paper.

Von spread it out. The shop was in Candlemaker Row.

'They were going in at night,' Mhairi said.

'The shops in the Grassmarket are open at night?'

'This one's open all hours, I hear.'

'You don't know what it sells?'

'Sorry, my lovely, I didn't ask. But Phil and his pals were having a right old time, laughing and such. They'd been drinking, Molly said.'

'Thanks, Mhairi, you've been a big help.' She slipped the paper into her pocket. 'And the other man? The one on the gun-club programme?'

'No-one's seen him. With or without Phil.'

It hardly mattered now. There was no doubt that Toby knew Phil. He'd said so himself.

'You want the photos back?'

'Keep them. I've got copies.'

Mhairi looked at her enquiringly. 'You're not your usual cheery self, old darling. Anything up?'

'Oh you know, problems at home. My daughter.'

'Ah, yes, daughters are fantastic on a good day but they can make your life a misery.'

'She's broken up with her man and she's taking it badly. Not just that, he stole her clothes.'

'He a trannie, then?' Mhairi said, looking at her quizzically.

'They were designer dresses. He took them to sell.'

'A double whammy, eh?'

'You know, Mhairi, I sometimes forget how simple life looks to the young. What I need are a housekeeper, a babysitter, a huge injection of cash, and a steady job where I work nine to five. If only wishing made it so.'

'Not forgetting the power of prayer.'

She looked at the woman with envy. 'You're always so jolly. What's your secret?'

'Clean living.'

'I'll have to try it sometime.'

It was late afternoon when Steve returned to the police station.

Bridget had nearly done the Highland Fling when she'd learnt about the file on Jamie's laptop. She'd notified the Drugs Squad and Cally had sent them the data on the PMK consignment, specifically the one arriving in two days' time.

Steve took Cally by the arm and pulled her out of his chair, where she'd been sitting surrounded by male officers. He took her to one of the interview rooms, and sat her in front of a computer monitor and keyboard.

'What's with the attitude, Steve?' she said petulantly.

'Those men are supposed to be working.'

'They were. I was teaching them how the markets operate. It'll be useful background for their next white-collar crime case.'

'Aye, excellent. They'll be leaving to become bankers now.'

A gleam of irony came into her eyes. 'What's the collective noun for a group of bankers, Steve?' When he said nothing, she added, 'A wunch.'

'That's mildly funny, right enough,' he said, trying not to smile. He unzipped a large soft bag and pulled out a PC's base unit, taking care not to drop it. He attached it to the monitor and keyboard. 'What do you need to get under the surface of this?'

'Everything I need's in my handbag,' she said, clearly intrigued. 'Whose PC is this?'

'Lexie Dyer's. Our boys say there's nothing of interest on it but I don't believe them.' He could see her salivating. 'So, apart from what's in your handbag, Cally?'

She pulled the keyboard towards her greedily. 'Just an Internet connection. And blueberries. Loads of blueberries.'

'One of the tech guys will set up the connection. I'll bring some coffee.' He held up his hands. 'No muscatel. And I'll send someone out for the berries. You work in here, no interruptions.'

'What am I looking for?'

'Your challenge is to tell me where the money is.'

'Forget it. That's impossible.'

'See if Jamie began the money transfers from this machine, then,' he said with irritation.

'That's doable. But why do you want to know about the money? Do you really think there'll be a record of Snake Eyes doing a bank transfer?'

'Snake Eyes runs several legitimate businesses,' he said patiently. 'There's an outside chance Jamie and Bruce were paid that way.'

'Okey dokey. See you in a tick.'

One of the constables accosted him as he entered the office. 'No luck with Toby Hilliard, guv.'

The DCI had decided they should pull Hilliard in for questioning and the constable had been dispatched to find him.

'We tried the gun club as well as his house,' the man went on. 'None of the members has seen him. And they're moaning they can only fire rifles. They asked when the handguns are coming back.'

'Was Hilliard due at the club today?'

'He had several lessons booked. They've had to cancel. No-one's been able to get him on his mobile. They've decided to close the club for the time being.'

'And yesterday?'

The constable shrugged. 'The same. Sunday's one of their busiest days but he was a no-show.'

'Have you talked to his neighbours?'

'Not yet, guv.'

'Well, get onto them. See if anyone's seen him pack a bag. Look through his windows, for God's sake.'

'The last known sighting of him was at that tournament on Saturday. His car's still at the paintballing club.'

'He could have taken a cab home. Or to the airport. You know what to do, so get on with it.'

Steve returned to the interview room with two coffees,

passing the tech guy on his way out. Cally was hunched over the computer.

'I'm just taking a quick peep at the markets,' she said, glancing up. 'I get jittery if I'm not looking at the FTSE.'

He smiled. 'What would you do if the sun exploded and you weren't near a computer, Cally?'

'I'm never more than eight minutes away from one.' She scrolled down the page. 'Ah, here we are.'

He stood behind her, looking over her head at the columns of figures.

She sat up so sharply that her head banged against his chin. 'That's odd,' she murmured. 'Bayne's shares are falling.'

'Why is that odd? Don't the markets fluctuate?'

'Not like this they don't. They've been rising steadily since the announcement of the merger. The whole world has rushed to buy shares.'

The tremor in her voice made him wonder why she was so disturbed. 'Are you invested in Bayne's, Cally?'

'I bought in when the share price was low. Not enough to hurt if they fall. But still, no-one likes to lose money.'

'So why's it happening?'

She pulled up a news channel. 'The merger talks are on hold. It'll be some technicality. They'll start up again.'

'And the share price will rise?'

'You got it.' She removed a CD from her bag and inserted it into the disk drive. 'Right, let's look at what's on Lexie's PC.'

Her good humour seemed to rise and fall with the value of Bayne's shares, and he wondered idly how much she had invested. She ran the mouse over icons and scrolled through windows. The constant tap-tapping threatened to lull him to sleep, and his mind wandered to the conversation with the constable.

So Toby Hilliard was missing. He tried to remember when he'd last seen the man. It was at that paintball tournament;

Hilliard had played in Lexie Dyer's team. Steve hadn't stayed till the end, he hadn't even bothered to look for Von. But, if anyone had seen Hilliard last, she had. He imagined the two of them under the sheets and toyed with the idea of sending the constable to her flat. He'd got her email with the text of a conversation between Ranald McCrea and Hilliard. *We told him to stay out of sight. And he's come here, of all places.* Aye, it mattered to them that Phil was at the tournament, and no mistake. But why?

Cally had been working for the best part of an hour. He wondered if he should invite her home now that the Indian food delivery man had returned to Glasgow. He was glad he'd not taken up her offer of staying the night: she'd let slip that the delivery man had a police record (he'd been arrested for crawling under pub tables looking up women's skirts). Steve had had a lucky escape. Ach, and a threesome just wasn't his thing.

'Bingo,' Cally said finally. 'I've got you.'

He pulled his chair over.

'Okay, Steve, look at this. It's Internet Explorer's browsing history.' She ran a black-painted nail down a list. 'This page here is the one most visited.' She double-clicked the link and brought up a screen showing the Bayne Pharmaceuticals logo. She was prompted for a password. 'I've used a software utility I wrote myself to crack this,' she said, entering something which appeared as black dots. 'I'm now into Bayne's main server as superuser. I can change to another account and roam out over the Internet.'

'And Jamie did this?'

'He removed the logs of what he did. But not all of them. He's been a tad careless. I found a link to a company in the Channel Islands.'

Bayne's server. 'Could Lexie have done this?'

'What's her role at Bayne's?'

'Human Resources Director.'

'Not a hope in hell.'

After a silence, he said, 'So what next?'

She let her breath out in a rush. 'You know, I've just this instant realised something.' She pointed at the screen. 'The timestamps for accessing the Channel Islands' company are all since June 7th. What does that tell you, Steve?'

It took a couple of seconds for him to get it. 'It can't be Jamie Dyer. He died on June 5th.'

Chapter 27

Von was finishing the washing up. Supper hadn't been a huge success but then she'd never made a secret of her inability to cook. She and Georgie had prepared a fry-up together. The smell of bacon and onions had spread through the house where it would linger for days. The meal hadn't been a patch on Norrie's but at least it wasn't defrosted or out of a packet. Georgie was hunched in the armchair, wearing the new clothes Von had bought her that afternoon. The baby was asleep in the cot.

She studied her daughter's reflection in the window. As if conscious of her mother's scrutiny, Georgie stirred, stretching her arms above her head. She paused, turning her head slowly, then froze as she saw her mother's back to her. Von knew what was coming. Georgie slipped silently out of the armchair and padded to the sofa. She slid a hand inside Von's bag. As she removed the purse, Von turned, dropping suds onto the floor.

'There's not much there, love. I spent most of it on those new clothes. Remember?'

The girl paused, her hand on the purse.

'The way our finances are going, Georgie, we'll soon be wearing bin bags.' She pushed her hair from her face with her forearm.

At least the girl had the grace to hang her head. 'It wasn't me, Mum. The little voices made me do it.'

'Oh, don't talk such crap.' Von wiped her hands on a kitchen towel. 'I've a good mind to take those clothes back to the shop.'

'You can't do that, Mum. Please. I won't take money from your purse again.'

'You said that the last time.'

'I promise.'

'You said that the last time, too.'

Georgie flopped into the armchair. She was more subdued than she usually was when caught thieving. 'I don't like myself very much, Mum.' She pushed a lock of hair behind her ear. 'I think that means no-one else does, either.'

When her daughter was in this mood, Von swithered between anger and compassion. The girl's self-pity came not just from Norrie's rejection but from his cunningness in stealing the only thing of value she had left: her designer dresses. And yet Von had parted with a small fortune in an attempt to cheer her up, money she could ill afford to spend.

She threw the towel onto the kitchen table. 'I have to go out to work.'

'At this hour?' The girl played with her ear piercings. 'I bet you're off on a jolly.'

'I told you earlier there's something I need to do. For Christ's sake, Georgie, I could have done it this afternoon but I took you shopping instead.'

Tears rolled down her daughter's cheeks.

'Georgie, the last thing I want to do is upset you,' Von groaned. 'But you do need to understand that it's my job that puts food on the table.'

'And clothes on my back.' The girl wiped her face with her hands. 'You were going to say that, weren't you?'

'I won't be long,' Von said wearily. She picked up her jacket and left.

It was after nine, and the sky was sliding from blue to purple as Von trudged through the jumbled streets of old Edinburgh.

She followed the Grassmarket in the direction of the Cowgate, seeing George IV Bridge ahead and above her; she never could get her head round the many roads in this city that crossed other roads on bridges. Candlemaker Row swung up to the right.

She peered through the iron gates into Greyfriars Kirkyard, seeing the steep flight of stone steps and the tops of grey-green headstones. A lorry sat abandoned on the cobbled path, newly lopped branches stacked in the back.

The ancient cemetery was famous both for the ghost of Bloody George Mackenzie who'd persecuted Covenanters and displayed their severed heads on the prison wall, and for the resurrectionists who'd exhumed the recent dead to supply the local medical college with corpses. Von had passed the cemetery several times but had been in only once, when Georgie, in one of her lighter moods, had suggested they go and find the tomb of Jock Gray, owner of faithful terrier, Greyfriars Bobby. They'd taken a guided tour and, although Von could remember the cemetery's history, she had little recollection of the layout because the place had been crowded with tourists.

Her mind drifted to her visit to another cemetery with its stone angels and Victorian inscriptions:

There was a door to which I found no key.
There was a veil past which I could not see.

As a rule, she avoided burial grounds.

The high walls of the kirkyard eclipsed the dying sun, deepening the colours of the buildings opposite. The words HARVEY'S FURNITURE STORES, visible as a ghostly imprint above a shop selling comic books, were slowly fading in the failing light. Next to it was a boutique with quirky hats in the window.

There was little to Candlemaker Row – she could see the statue of Greyfriars Bobby at the end of the street – and she guessed that the address she was after was at the curve in the road. A chill wind, funnelled by the high buildings, blew through her bones as she trudged up the street. A minute later, she was outside the shop. It shrank from the road as though it didn't want to be found.

There was no name on the front but a glance through the window told her what went on inside.

This was no shop. It was a tattoo studio.

The strip-light blink-blinked on and off as she pushed open the door. If it hadn't been for the dark-inked drawings pinned to the wall of the low-ceilinged room, the sterile smell would suggest that she was in a dentist's surgery. A photocopier stood in the corner next to a desk spread with bottles and jars and, in the centre of the room, there was a low bed covered in a clean white sheet.

A muscular woman in a sleeveless T-shirt, and with blue tattoos on her arms, was sitting at the desk. She had blonde hair shading into brown but the grey at her temples and the flesh under her chin put her on the wrong side of fifty. She looked up from her reading. Seeing a potential customer, she laid the magazine aside and took a pair of black gloves from a drawer.

'Evening,' she said. 'What can I do you for?' Her eyes roamed over Von's body, lingering at the face and throat. 'You got lovely white skin. Sure you want to mark it?' She had a soft voice and an English accent.

'Do you ask everyone that?' Von said, surprised.

'I do, as a matter of fact. Most folk haven't made up their minds when they come in. Don't want them leaving all upset, know what I mean?'

Von motioned to the drawings on the wall. 'Are these your own designs?'

'They are.' The woman lifted an eyebrow pierced with metal studs. 'See anything you like?'

'I'm not here for a tattoo.' Von looked into the deep-set eyes, the brown of the irises enhanced with liner. 'I'm hoping you can help me.'

'In what way?'

'I'm looking for someone.'

The woman returned her gaze.

'Would you take a gander at these photos?' Von said, opening her bag.

'You police?'

'I'm an investigator.' She pulled out her ID. 'I'm searching for a missing person, a man.'

'You think he was here?'

'A friend saw him come into your parlour.'

'Lots of people come into my parlour, know what I mean?' The woman leant forward, her body-language not unfriendly despite the veiled suggestion that she might be responsible for a man's disappearance. 'Let me see those photos.'

Von handed her copies of what she'd given Mhairi. The woman spread them out and looked through them methodically, playing with the studs in her lip. She returned to the passport photo of Phil Pattullo. 'This one,' she said, running over it with a red nail, 'came in for a tattoo.'

'Can you remember when?'

'Two, three weeks ago. Something like that.'

'Was he alone?'

'He came in with some people. I remember because they were bladdered. But merry with it. As a rule, I don't tattoo people who are drunk but he wasn't nearly as gone. The woman paid for everything cash on the nail.'

'What did this woman look like?' Von said, knowing the answer.

She indicated the photo of Lexie. 'That's her. Wouldn't forget a posh bird like that.'

'How many people altogether?'

'Including him and the bird?' She rubbed her chin. 'Four.' She nodded at the chairs. 'While I was doing the tat, the others waited there.'

'So, him, the woman . . . '

' . . . and two men.' She tapped the photo of Ranald. 'He was one of them. Big geezer. Didn't say anything. But he took in everything that was going on, know what I mean?'

Von unfolded the flyer with Toby's thumbnail image. 'Was he the fourth? Take a good look.'

'Nope, not him. Before you ask, yes, I'm sure.'

Von stared, uncomprehending. Phil had come in with Lexie and Ranald but not with Toby. And yet there'd been one more. A man. 'This fourth person, this man . . . '

'He already had a tattoo.' The woman tapped her left arm. 'Rolled his sleeve up and showed me. Wanted it done to your guy on the same part of the arm. Everything had to be exact. Size, position, colours.'

'You gave him the same tattoo?'

'Copied the pattern. Drew up a stencil. Then I traced it onto the skin and razzed away.'

'What was the pattern? Can you remember?'

'Usually I keep a stencil in case somebody else likes it. But the bird was keen I destroy everything. She was paying. Customer's always right, know what I mean? But I can remember it.' She reached into a drawer and produced coloured pencils and a pad. With feathery strokes, she drew two cherries with leaves on a stalk. She pulled off the sheet. 'My compliments,' she said, handing it to Von.

Von studied the drawing. Why would Ranald and Lexie get Phil a tattoo? And why this specific design on someone else's arm? 'This fourth man,' she said, 'can you describe him? Draw him, even?'

'No need.' The woman tapped the photo of Phil. 'He was a

dead ringer for this guy. Sat on the bed and rolled up his sleeve. And your guy sat next to him while I did him. I got a good look at them both.'

The blood pounded in her head. A dead ringer.

'Not identical,' the woman went on. 'But the same short hair and eye colour, and shape of face. I notice faces.' She gestured to the drawing of the cherry tattoo. 'And with identical tats, you couldn't tell them apart, know what I mean?'

At the words, Von's brain made a sudden connection. And then it was so obvious that she wondered why she hadn't realised it before. She rested her head against the wall and let her eyes close.

'You okay?' the woman said.

'I'm fine. Just a bit tired. But you've helped me enormously.' She opened her purse. 'Can I give you something for your trouble?'

'I don't charge for information.' The woman stared past her through the window. 'Listen to me. Don't look round now. Have you got someone waiting for you outside?'

'No,' she said, her chest suddenly tight.

'There's someone with a hood up. He's been waiting across the street. In the shadows. Been there ever since you got here.'

'Can you see his face?'

'No, but he's tall and well-built.'

Von turned slightly and picked up a drawing. She lifted it to her face and, pretending to examine it, looked through the window. The light was failing, but she saw the figure slouching against the wall. He was wearing a hooded sweatshirt with writing on the front and, although she couldn't make out all the letters, she thought the first word was Calder. He shifted his weight, and then slipped his hands into his pockets. Toby . . .

But what was he doing standing there? Why hadn't he come in? She felt a sudden constriction in her chest. He must have followed her.

Her instincts told her to get out of there. And she always trusted her instincts. He was standing just a few feet away, and she doubted she'd get far if she tried to run past him towards the Grassmarket. Although there were pubs beyond the curve of the street, this part of Candlemaker Row was deserted.

'Know who he is?' the woman said.

'I think so.'

'Trouble?'

'He's followed me here and I don't know why.' Von's eyes darted around the room. 'Is there a back way out?'

'Yes, but you need to be quick. I think he knows you've rumbled him.'

Von glanced through the window. Toby had straightened, and was looking up and down the street, the way you do before you cross it.

The woman dragged her towards the back and, lifting a curtain, pulled her through. 'There's a bit of a clutter,' she said, letting the curtain drop. 'Here, take my hand.' She grasped Von's fingers and led her through what felt like a cupboard. There was a strong smell of machine oil. 'I live over the shop. We're going up one floor.'

'Upstairs?'

'There's a way out. I won't put the light on so watch your step.'

They climbed quickly, Von stumbling several times and glad of the firm grip on her hand.

She stood in the tiny bedroom as the woman, swearing softly, struggled to open the sash window. She gave the frame a final desperate tug and the window jerked up with a crash. 'Greyfriars Kirkyard,' she said, gazing out.

In the dying light, Von made out murky headstones and trees with twisted trunks. Unlike cluttered Dean Cemetery where the tombstones fought with each other, each grave here kept a respectful distance from its neighbour. The few trees stood like sentinels, guarding the dead.

She craned her neck and looked down. Below the window, close enough that she could touch it, was a memorial stone flush against the wall. The wall of the house she was standing in, she realised with a shock, was also the wall of the cemetery.

'I take it you're not afraid of ghosts,' the woman said, throwing a glance at the door.

'Should I be? Are you?'

'George Mackenzie and I have an understanding. I don't bother him and he don't bother me, know what I mean?' She pointed to the memorial. The pediment was inches away. 'If you can get onto that, you can swing yourself down.'

'How do I get out of the cemetery?' Von said, trying to gauge the distance to the ground. It was a fair jump but, if she rolled as she fell, she might get off with skinned knees. She was beginning to wonder whether she wasn't overreacting.

'There are two ways in and out. See that big dark shape? That's the church. Opposite it is the main entrance.'

'And the other way?'

'Down there, to the right, past the Monument.'

'There are steps leading to a gate,' she said, remembering.

'If the gates are locked, there are places in the cemetery wall where you can climb over. Behind the Flodden Wall, near the school, the stones have come away.'

If the gates are locked. Jesus, what if she couldn't get out? She'd be trapped in a graveyard with Bloody George Mackenzie.

'Once you get out,' the woman said with a confidence Von didn't feel, 'go down to the Grassmarket. It'll be heaving with folk this time of night.'

'I don't think you're in danger. If he's after anyone, it's me. But you should call the police.'

'Don't worry about me, I can take care of myself. Ever felt

the weight of tattoo equipment, know what I mean?'

Von squeezed the woman's arm. She sat on the sill and slipped a leg through the window. After finding a secure foothold, she swung the other leg out and then lowered herself onto the sloping pediment. But the angle was steeper than she'd estimated and she lost her balance. With a cry, she slid off and landed heavily on her backside.

She looked up to see the tattoo artist peering at her, but it was too dark to see her expression. Von waved to signal that she hadn't seriously damaged herself. The woman nodded and waved back. A second later, her head disappeared and the window was pulled shut.

Von dragged herself to her feet. The moon was lying on its side, casting a strange light over the ground. She blinked into the gloom, trying to get her bearings, her elongated shadow stretching faintly in front of her.

The Flodden Wall was directly opposite, but she decided her best bet was to try the gates.

Beyond the Martyrs' Monument, there was a privet hedge enclosing a triangular piece of ground. She slipped behind it and hurried towards the steps. A glance at the gates told her they were padlocked. If these had been secured, the main gates would have been too. Yes, well done, Von, she should have paid more attention on Candlemaker Row.

That just left the Flodden Wall. A light wind stirred the branches as she stole past the steps and across to the cemetery's northern boundary. She clung to the shadows, listening above the sighing of the trees for the sound of running. An eternity later, she came to the Flodden Wall. Straining into the dark and alert for any sudden movement, she stumbled over the graves until she found the archway. Through it would be the short path to the gates of George Heriot's School. She could climb those gates easily. She could climb any gates if she had to.

As she turned onto the path, a shot rang out. She saw a flash, and heard the bullet ricochet off the arch and whine away into the darkness.

The air rushed out of her lungs. Christ, he had a gun. She dropped to her knees. Lights went on in a couple of windows.

She crawled back behind the wall, but not before she'd glimpsed the hooded silhouette. He was at the gates, on the other side, in the school yard.

Suddenly, she heard a clanking. She risked a glance through the arch. He was climbing the gates. He'd be in the kirkyard in less than a minute.

In blind panic, she sprang to her feet and bolted across the opening. There were places she could hide but her best chance was to choose somewhere no sane person would be in after dark.

She cut across the grass, keeping to the trees as much as possible. Behind the church, the small shell-decorated rotunda of George Mackenzie's tomb was washed ghostly grey in the moonlight. There was no question of going inside – the council had kept the tomb locked since hearing reports of strange happenings within – but she could hide behind it.

The wind had blown last year's leaves through the railings, bunching them into piles. She climbed in and, kicking aside an empty milk carton, squeezed herself between the rotunda and the cemetery wall. At her feet was a small opening, too narrow for her to push through. She knew from the guided tour what was inside: a grate in the floor leading to a stairway. Several coffins, including George Mackenzie's, lay in a vault amongst scattered human remains. Rumour had it that Bloody Mackenzie could never find rest after his atrocities.

She put her head slowly round the rotunda but the trees and headstones were swallowed up by the dark. She dropped into a crouch and waited, peering into the night.

The moon crept from behind a cloud.

He was standing facing the church, both hands round the gun. He turned so he had his back to her and moved his hooded head slowly, surveying the cemetery. After an age, he dropped his arms and loped away towards the Flodden Wall. A second later, he melted into the heavy shadows.

She couldn't take the risk he'd given up, thinking she'd found a way out. But where could he be hiding? The moon had flooded the cobbled paths with light and it would be suicide to cross. She would leave on the side away from the Flodden Wall. If she skirted the perimeter, which was shrouded in thick blackness, she'd find an exit. She counted to one hundred, her eyes never leaving the headstones.

She was about to make her move when she heard the sound. It was a grinding creaking noise and it was coming from inside the rotunda. All of a sudden, the ground began to shake. Without another thought, she was over the railings and sprinting towards the church. A second later, she'd shinned up the main gates.

There was a party in full swing in Greyfriars Bobby's Bar. She fought her way through the revellers and collapsed onto a seat in the corner.

The kilted man sitting opposite was sucking his pipe, studying her. 'Looks like you've had a wee bit of a shock, lass,' he said. 'How d'you get that nick on your face?'

She gazed at her reflection in the window. An angry mark had appeared on her chin. She ran a hand over it, feeling it throb.

'Your feller did that to you?'

She shook her head. 'I've been in Greyfriars Kirkyard. George Mackenzie's mausoleum.'

The colour left his face. 'You were there?' He drew back, as though what she had was contagious. 'And did you hear anything from inside?'

She nodded.

His breathing grew shallow. 'Aye, it would be Bloody Mackenzie.' His eyes flew to her chin. 'The ghost of Bloody Mackenzie.'

Yes, maybe Bloody Mackenzie's ghost had marked her face. But the man who'd fired at her was flesh and blood.

Chapter 28
Tuesday, June 19th

Steve was looking over Cally's shoulder. 'So how's the share price today?' he said.

'Bayne's shares are still depressed. And all in the space of less than twenty-four hours. I don't understand it.' She straightened. 'So, Steve, to work. Do you want me to dig deeper or what? We know this isn't your man.'

Since the discovery that Jamie Dyer couldn't have been the person hacking out from his sister's computer, Steve's theory about the motive for the murders was unravelling. He'd slept badly, partly because of his worry that he'd been barking up the wrong tree, and partly because of the god-awful film (The Slumber Party Massacre) that Cally had made him rent out. Even the female nudity didn't make up for what could only be described as a sickening gore-fest.

He'd dragged her out of bed and into the station so she could work on following money in and out of Snake Eyes' many legitimate businesses, but he was seriously doubting it was worth the effort. And his boss was already making noises about the size of her fees. Aye, maybe their best bet was to tail Jamie's last shipment and collar one of Snake Eyes' hardmen.

An officer popped his head round the door. 'Someone to see you, guv.'

'Show him into the office. I'll be there directly.'

'It's a lady. Gave her name as Von Valenti. Said it's urgent.'

His head shot up from the screen. 'Then bring her in here.

Now,' he shouted, when the officer was reluctant to tear his gaze from Cally's milk-white thighs.

A second later, Von entered, pale and dishevelled. She seemed flustered and there was a nasty bruise on her chin. She threw Cally a glance, and then addressed herself breathlessly to him. 'I've found something, Steve.' She paused, uncertain, and looked again at Cally.

'I'm working with the police, Miss Valenti,' Cally said smoothly before Steve could open his mouth. 'Cally Cockrill. You can speak in front of me,' she added warmly.

The expression on Von's face told him that the name had registered; this was the person she'd asked him to give the CD to.

'Fine, pleased to meet you,' Von said. She looked from one to the other. 'Okay, I'll make this quick. I need to know whether Jamie Dyer had a tattoo.'

Steve frowned. 'I saw it on his arm at the PM.'

'His left arm?'

'I think so. Why is it important?'

'Have you got the pathologist's report? There'll be a photograph.'

'Von, strictly speaking . . .'

She made an impatient gesture. 'Yes, I know, strictly speaking you're not supposed to let me see but I won't tell anyone if you won't.'

'And I certainly won't,' Cally chipped in. Her eyes were wide with interest.

He hesitated. 'Aye, fine,' he said with the weariness of someone who knows when he's defeated. 'Wait here.'

He fetched a folder from the office and returned to find Von and Cally studying one another candidly.

'It's like he doesn't think I'm potty-trained,' Cally was saying. 'But he's great in bed so I don't really mind. I call him the Laser. He's set to stun.'

Steve had no idea if she was referring to him or to the Indian food delivery man, and decided he didn't want to know. He extracted a photograph and laid it on the desk. 'This is Jamie Dyer's tattoo.'

Cally leant over for a better look. She stared in fascination at the photo of the left arm. The tattoo was so bright against the bloodless skin that it seemed to glow.

'Let's have a butcher's,' Von said, taking the folder. She skimmed through it and pulled out two photos of Jamie Dyer: one taken at the crime scene, the terrified eyes open, and the other at the mortuary, with the eyes closed. 'This is Jamie?' she said, glancing up at Steve.

He nodded, swallowing hard. It was a while since he'd seen these images. The photograph of the tattoo brought back the afternoon of the autopsy as though it were yesterday. There was a sudden pounding in his head and his stomach somersaulted.

She pored over the photos, and then stared straight ahead. Suddenly, she hunched over, her head in her hands. Her shoulders were shaking and she seemed to be trying not to laugh out loud.

'Care to share the joke?' he said, annoyed.

She looked up and he saw his mistake. Her stricken face was wet with tears. He felt his heart twist.

'Sorry,' she said, pulling out a handkerchief, 'not had much sleep lately.'

Cally poured coffee from a pot and pushed a mug across, making sympathetic noises.

Von removed a photograph from her bag and laid it next to the ones of Jamie Dyer. 'Take a good look. This is Phil Pattullo. A missing person I've been trying to track down,' she said to Cally.

The girl picked up the photos and examined them. Her gaze sharpened.

'Aye, right enough,' Steve said, 'they look pretty similar.'

'They're not similar, you numpty,' Cally said from the side of her mouth. 'They're identical.' She gestured to the photo of Phil Pattullo. It was a blow-up of the back page of a passport. 'If this document is genuine and this man's name is really Phil Pattullo, then the dead man with the tattoo is also Phil Pattullo.'

'That's impossible,' Steve said, his mind reeling. 'The dead man with the tattoo is Jamie Dyer.'

The women were looking at him curiously.

'Listen, Steve,' Von said, 'last night, I followed a lead. It took me to a tattoo studio in the Grassmarket. The tattoo artist told me that, a few days before your murders, she gave Phil Pattullo a tattoo.' She pulled out a drawing and laid it next to the mortuary photo of the tattooed arm. 'This one.'

The designs were identical: cherries on a leafy stalk. 'Can someone explain what's going on, please?' he said in a small voice.

'When did Jamie Dyer get his tattoo?' Von said.

He thought back to the drink he'd had with Lexie. *There was that time at Uni when Ranald got Jamie drunk. When Jamie woke up the next morning, he had a tattoo.* 'His sister said it was when they were students.'

'So, what, ten years ago?' She pushed the mortuary photograph under his nose. 'See the dark bit on that cherry? That's a scab. A ten-year-old tattoo would have healed by now. This tattoo was done recently. It can't be Jamie's.'

'Bravo, Miss Valenti,' Cally said admiringly. She looked at Steve. 'Ergo, the corpse lying in the mortuary is Phil Pattullo and *not* Jamie Dyer.'

It was several seconds before he spoke. 'The autopsy. I saw the tattoo. Why didn't I realise?'

'You're not at your best at post mortems,' Von said, trying to include Cally in her smile. 'It was an understandable mistake.'

'Understandable? The Chief Super won't think so. He'll hang me by my thumbs.' He groaned. 'How could I have been so incompetent?'

'Let me count the ways, lover boy,' Cally said airily.

'So how did it happen?' he said, looking at Von. 'The identical tattoos?'

'The tattoo artist told me that one of the people who came in with Phil rolled up his sleeve and told her to give Phil an identical tattoo. It had to be the same size and in exactly the same place. She said he looked just like him.'

Steve searched through the folder and found the imprint that Bridget's boys had taken of Jamie's passport. He laid it next to the passport photo of Phil. 'Aye, they could almost be twins.'

'The tattoo artist identified Lexie Dyer and Ranald McCrea as the people who came in with Phil and this other man.'

He cast his mind back to the scene at the mortuary. Lexie, fainting, having to be supported by the Liaison Officer. But then, at Federico's, laughing and joking as though her brother would be walking in through the door. And he thought she was just trying to be brave. 'It was Lexie who identified her brother. By God, she did it deliberately. She willfully mis-identified him.'

'Of course she did it deliberately,' Cally said impatiently. 'It's obvious what's been going on.' She addressed herself to Von, as if Steve were too dim to appreciate what she was saying. 'The three of them, Lexie, Ranald, and Jamie, were in cahoots. They made Phil get that tattoo for one reason only. They intended to make Jamie disappear but in such a way that no-one would ever look for him.'

Steve stared at Cally.

'Think about it, lover boy. They wanted everyone to think Jamie was dead. If he disappeared, there would always be doubt. But, dead. And buried . . . '

Von gripped his arm. 'You said yourself you knew that Lexie and Ranald were up to something when they told you about testing that new paintballing equipment. They used identical wording. They agreed it in advance.'

Aye, right enough, he could see it now. They agreed the wording when they were plotting to have Phil murdered. And how readily Lexie had talked about Jamie's tattoo, knowing that the man lying on the slab – Phil – had an identical pair of cherries on his arm.

'The question is, why did he do it?' Von said. 'Why did Jamie want to disappear?'

'Oh, it's so sweet,' Cally said, clicking her fingers. 'Let me tell her, Steve.' Briefly she filled Von in on their discovery of the illegal PMK imports from China and their theory that the buyer was Snake Eyes. 'Jamie must have double-crossed him. No-one plays games with the Triads and gets away with it.'

'And Bruce?' said Von. 'Did he fake his own death as well?'

'His mother and his partner identified him,' Steve said. He remembered Lexie's reaction at Federico's when he told her they'd found Bruce's body: the spilt Coke on her blouse, the blood draining from her face. Whatever they'd planned with Jamie regarding Phil hadn't extended to Bruce. So why had Bruce been killed?

'And you think the money's now in a Panama bank?' Von said.

'Yes, Miss Valenti.' Cally tilted her head, looking at her approvingly. 'It was you who found that CD, wasn't it?'

'In a highly illegal operation,' she said with a faint smile. 'Everything makes sense now. It's Jamie who's been hiding out at Lexie's, so stir crazy that he's taken to roaming Dean Cemetery. He fooled Phil's mother too, poor woman. She was at Saturday's tournament. She told me she saw him there.'

'How could anyone fool a mother?' Cally said. 'It's not enough to look like her son. You have to walk the same way, have the same mannerisms.'

'She saw him from a distance.' Von picked up the coffee mug. 'I think she's been looking for her son for so long that she sees what she wants to see.' A look of understanding crossed her face. 'And Toby's in on the whole thing. That conversation between him and Ranald about telling him to stay out of sight but he'd still gone to the tournament. It was Jamie they were talking about.'

'He took a hell of a risk going there,' Steve said. 'Even if he was mad keen on paintballing.'

'Maybe the risk was calculated.' She took a sip of coffee. 'He went there as Phil, not Jamie, remember.'

'Aye, right enough. So how do you think they got hold of Phil's passport?'

'I'm betting Lexie and Ranald promised him a wonderful trip abroad and got him to fetch it from his Mum's. It's obvious what they wanted it for.'

'Jamie could leave the country as Phil any time he wanted.'

'Then why did he stay around?'

Cally was gazing at the computer monitor, a finger in her mouth. 'Tying up loose ends, which I'm unlikely to unknot. I think he's been moving money around. He's been using his sister's computer to access a server at Bayne Pharmaceuticals.'

'We raided Belgrave Crescent in the wee hours of yesterday morning,' Steve said. 'We took the PC from the basement. Lexie was none too pleased.' He rubbed his chin. 'But we didn't find Jamie. Or Phil's passport, come to that. Only this, from the desk drawer.' He detached the plastic bag that was clipped to the folder sleeve.

'Strange,' Von said, half to herself. 'If the passport's gone, then it's likely he's left the country. But why not take the left-luggage locker key with him?'

Cally glanced at the bag, then turned back to the screen. 'It's not a left-luggage locker key. It's a key to a gym locker.'

'You can tell that from the shape?' Von said in surprise.

'It's identical to the ones at my gym. Gyms must use the

same make.' She took the bag and examined the key through the plastic. 'It's a master key.'

'A gym, Steve?'

'The only gym in the frame belongs to Bruce Lassiter's partner, Gavvo Skelton.'

'So what are you waiting for, lover boy? Go and pick him up.'

'She's nice,' Von said when they were in the corridor. 'Just helping with enquiries?' she added, lifting an eyebrow.

He ignored the insinuation. His brain was hurting. The women had grasped what was going on well before he had, Cally especially. His belief in himself as a detective had taken a knock. 'We need to pull in Lexie and Ranald before they flit the country too,' he said.

'Wait, Steve. There's something I didn't want to say in front of the girl.' She seemed to be struggling with something. 'Toby Hilliard followed me to the tattoo studio.'

'Toby Hilliard?'

'He's mixed up in this somehow. He was standing outside, watching me through the window. He must have known I'd tumbled to their plan.'

'Jesus, Von, what happened?'

'The tattoo artist let me out the back. But he came after me. He came into Greyfriars Kirkyard.' She was breathing heavily and he pulled her against him. 'He had a gun,' she gasped.

'God Almighty! That was you? We had a call from a resident who said she heard gunfire. By the time we got there, the place was deserted.'

'I managed to get away. I took a cab and made it drive half way around Edinburgh. I'm sure I lost him.' She grabbed at his lapel. 'But he knows where I live. He's always known. I took Georgie and the baby to a nearby B&B.' She released him. 'They're safe, provided they don't go back to the flat.'

'Oh, Von,' he murmured, shaking his head. 'Why didn't you come to me? Why?' Remorse flooded through him. While Hilliard had been terrorising Von in Greyfriars Kirkyard, he'd been exercising his sexual muscles with Cally. 'We've been looking for Hilliard everywhere. If he uses his phone, we'll know.' He looked hard at her. 'And you're staying right here at the station. No ifs or buts.'

'I can't. Georgie and the baby . . . '

'We'll bring them here.'

'That's not necessary. They're safe where they are.'

She never had been able to see the danger to herself. Her thoughts were always for others. 'It's you he's after, Von. It's you who needs to take care.'

'I will if you will.' She waved the remark away. 'Okay, Steve, I'll bring Georgie here. Now get going. You've a pile of stuff to see to. You need to get dental records, Lexie's DNA if Jamie's not on the national database, and Dewey Croker is up to something with her, so – '

He placed a hand against her mouth. 'Once a detective, always a detective, eh?'

She smiled, and he felt her lips stretch under his fingers. 'There's one thing I have to do, Steve, and I can't put it off.'

He said nothing, enjoying the sensation of being physically close to her.

'I have to see Mrs Pattullo and tell her that her son is dead.'

'Wouldn't it be best to wait until after we've got the DNA results?'

She hesitated. 'Okay, but promise me your boys won't go tramping in and taking samples before I've had a chance to speak to her.'

'I promise.'

'Right, then, I'll go and fetch Georgie and the baby.'

'I'll send a constable with you.'

'You've no men to spare if this place is anything like the Met.'

He didn't know how she'd react but he placed his hands against her hips and pulled her towards him. She let him kiss her, responding at first, and then she pushed him gently away.

'Got to go, Steve.'

He watched her hurry down the corridor. A movement behind him made him turn. Cally was standing at the door watching him, the light fading from her eyes.

Chapter 29

'What do you mean, they're not here?' Von slammed her hand against the wall, making the woman in the doorway jump. 'You let them go? When?'

The landlady pulled the cellophane off a packet of Benson and Hedges. 'Listen, hen, the lass and the baby left shortly after you did. Said they were going home. And I don't like your tone,' she added. She seemed to consider what else to say. 'This is a free country. My guests can come and go as they please.'

Von's anger evaporated, replaced with an icy fear which spread from her chest to her gut. She'd left the B&B at nine. It was now eleven. Jesus, they'd been gone for two hours.

'They went without paying,' the woman said, her reptile eyes on Von. 'The lass showed me her empty wallet. Said you'd be footing the bill. Mouthy with it too, she was.' She lit a cigarette and sucked greedily. 'Gave me your address,' she added, pointing with the fag and making it clear that Von had better not think about not settling up.

Von fumbled with her bag and went through the mechanical process of paying. Her hands trembled so much that she dropped her purse and her credit cards. Her mind was a jumble of half-formed thoughts. She felt like vomiting.

She drove like a maniac to Gardner's Crescent. Why was there so much traffic today? And why was it so slow? She ran up the stairs and collapsed breathless against the door. It swung open. She almost fell into the hall.

'Georgie!' she yelled. 'Georgie!'

She rushed into the living room, and then into the bedrooms. *Oh God, oh God, let them be here.* The flat was empty. Perhaps they hadn't arrived yet. Didn't the landlady say that Georgie had no money? So she couldn't have caught a cab. But it wouldn't have taken her two hours to walk the few blocks from the B&B. No, she'd been back here, the suitcase on the floor and the empty buggy told her that. So why had she gone out again? She had no money. Von slumped onto the sofa. The blood rushed to her head. Jesus, why hadn't she stayed with them? She hadn't needed to see Steve, she could have phoned him.

The empty buggy stared back at her, an unspoken accusation.

The buggy.

If Georgie had gone out, she wouldn't have carried the baby. She never left the buggy behind, never.

The implication hit her in the face. Her stomach lurched and she just had time to put her head between her knees before she spewed up her half-digested breakfast.

Her mobile rang. She ran to the hall and upended her bag, trying desperately to find it.

She stared at the display.

Toby.

'Toby?' she shouted.

'Oh, Mum, Mum,' came the voice, halfway between a sob and a wail. 'He's got me and the baby. He said he's going to kill us if you don't come.'

Her legs gave way and she found herself on the floor. It was several seconds before she could speak. 'Where are you, Georgie?' she heard herself say. Her teeth were chattering.

'I don't know. He made me drive his car somewhere.' There was a clunking sound, as though someone had snatched the phone away, and then a thud followed by a shriek that nearly stopped her heart.

'Georgie,' she shouted. 'Georgie!'

The girl was snivelling. 'He hit me, Mum. You've got to come. You've got to help us.'

She closed her eyes, trying to keep the panic in check. 'Tell me where you are, love.'

'He said to come to the gun club. Round the back. Oh, Mum, he's got a mask on. I'm so frightened.'

'It's all right,' she said, trying to make her voice soothing. 'You're going to be all right. I'm on my way. Just hang on.'

'He said if you phone the police or tell anyone, he'll know. And he'll kill us. Me and the baby.' The girl was hysterical. 'He said he won't hesitate. He's got a gun.'

The gun. Jesus. 'I won't phone the police. I promise. Tell him that, Georgie. Make sure you tell him.'

Before the girl could reply, the connection went dead.

She stared at the phone. Then she fell sideways onto the carpet. There was an acid taste in her mouth and her eyes were swimming. As she gazed at the wall, fear slowly drained away. She knew what she had to do. Toby wanted her, not Georgie and the baby. He'd said so. And hadn't Georgie said he was wearing a mask? If she hadn't seen his face, she couldn't identify him. He would know that. He would let them go. He would let them go . . .

She crawled to the bathroom and rinsed her mouth, her movements slow and deliberate. Her jeans were wet and her shoes slick with vomit.

In the bedroom, she tugged off her clothes. Just her luck that everything was in the wash. Her embroidered bell-bottoms were scrunched into a ball under the chair. She changed quickly, and pulled on clean trainers. As she stood up, she felt something hard in the pocket of the jeans. It was the flick knife she'd taken off the youth outside the Carphone Warehouse. She turned it over in her hands before putting it back. Then, after locking the flat, she walked purposefully down the stairs and out to the car.

'Get the warrants from the Fiscal and pull in Lexie Dyer and Ranald McCrea.' Steve was at the incident board, giving instructions to his officers. 'Put out an alert for Jamie Dyer, masquerading as Phil Pattullo. Get Phil's passport information out to airports, ports and stations. I want Dyer found. And get someone to the mortuary to bring back a sample of DNA and dental photos from the corpse registered as Jamie Dyer. You'll need to ring round the surgeries and find Phil Pattullo's dentist, assuming he was registered with one, and then pull his records for comparison. And I want Lexie Dyer's DNA.'

'Shouldn't we get Mrs Pattullo's too, guv?' one of the constables said. 'Then we'll nail the body as Phil's.'

He remembered the promise he'd made to Von. 'Until we know for sure who's lying in the freezer, I don't want anyone even hinting to her that her son's dead. Understand?'

'Got it.'

He held out the bag with the master key. 'And see if this fits the lockers in Gavvo Skelton's gym.'

The constable scratched his stomach. 'The boxing gym? Why? Was Jamie Dyer a member?' He hesitated, apparently unwilling to say anything that would spark off his boss' anger. 'I don't understand, guv, I thought Dyer was a paintballer.'

A paintballer.

Steve sank into the chair. 'Hand me that file,' he snarled.

He read through the text of his conversation with Ranald McCrea. And there it was, the man's testimony in black and white: *If someone loses a key, and it does happen from time to time, we have to take the hinges off.* But surely all lockers come with a master key. Aye, Ranald had been lying.

And then he saw how it could have happened. Phil was taken to the club by his new friends and changed with the men, leaving his clothes in a locker. But Jamie didn't play. He cried off at the last minute as he didn't want to raise suspicion by leaving an unaccounted-for jumpsuit behind. And he had something he had to do. After the others had gone out, he used the master key to open Phil's locker, and substituted his clothes for Phil's. But they'd not thought it through: they'd forgotten Phil would need trainers. He had to play in his own shoes. Steve remembered the scuffed down-at-heel leathers on the corpse's feet, not the kind that wealthy Jamie Dyer would wear. And what had Jamie done with Phil's clothes? Worn them when he was stopping at Lexie's. Von had seen him roaming around Edinburgh in them. Aye, with Phil's clothes, and the two men so alike, anyone seeing Jamie would jump to the obvious conclusion.

And they'd all been in on it: Jamie, Ranald, and Lexie. Over a week before the murder, the three of them had made the booking on the paintballing club's database. That would have been around the time they got Phil his cherry tattoo. A week of wining and dining him, knowing they were going to kill him. Steve felt his jaw clench. The murdering wee bastards.

He handed the bag to the constable. 'Forget the boxing club, son. Take this to The Paradise World of Paintballing.'

The man nodded and left.

Bruce Lassiter was still the loose end. Steve thought through his conversations with Bridget. They were so sure that Bruce and Jamie were working this shiny scam together, yet Cally had found no evidence Bruce was involved. Nor was there any evidence the corpse autopsied as Bruce Lassiter wasn't Bruce Lassiter. It was the obvious thing to do to link the two men through their work. But perhaps they were wrong. It was what detectives had to guard against: wanting, even subconsciously distorting, the facts to fit their theories. But if Bruce was innocent, why had he been killed at the same time and in the same way as Jamie? Ach, there was no point running it around again. Ranald and Lexie would tell him soon enough.

He heard the sound of running feet. An officer burst through the door.

'There's been a development, sir. A woman at Bayne Tower has just put in a 999 call.'

Steve snatched up the phone. 'Fergus? Get your rear end over here.'

Von was nearing the Calder Rifle and Pistol Club. She'd rehearsed what she would do once Toby released Georgie and the baby. But there was only so far she could go with that. She'd have to wait and see if a chance of escape presented itself and that depended on what he'd planned for her. Would he kill her there, in the gun club? That would eventually lead the police to him. No, he'd take her somewhere else, and she'd bet what little money she had left that it would be the woodland paintballing course on the other side of the road. The detective in her wondered why he'd not suggested it in the first place. Not something she'd bother to ask. Her mind would be on survival and nothing else.

Toby's black Jaguar was sitting in the car park. Careless of him to leave it there. Although the building was closed, someone arriving on spec would surely recognise the instructor's car. Perhaps he wasn't thinking straight. That could work for her.

The place seemed deserted. She parked the Ford with the nose pointing towards the exit, leaving the keys in the ignition and the doors unlocked. If she had to make a quick getaway, the last thing she needed was to have to fumble about.

She made her way to the back of the building. A wind was rising, stirring the tussocks of parched grass. Ahead was the long firing range with its human-shaped targets, and tables for the lady shooters. Beyond were the low hills, criss-crossed with dusty paths. It was midday and the sun had reached its peak.

Her short shadow bobbed in front of her as she walked towards the range.

As she passed one of the targets, she heard the familiar click of a revolver's hammer being pulled back.

She stopped and turned slowly.

A large figure in a balaclava was pointing a gun at her. He held it with both hands, the way professionals do. A little way behind, a white-faced Georgie cowered on the ground in silent terror. She was clutching the baby who, seeing Von, thrust tiny arms towards her.

'Right, you've got me,' Von said slowly, her eyes on the masked man. 'Now let them go.'

The figure said nothing, giving her time to register that his balaclava was the type which showed only the eyes, and that he was wearing jeans and a grey hooded gun-club sweatshirt.

'For God's sake,' she shouted. 'They don't know who you are. You've nothing to fear from them. I'm here now. That's what you wanted.' The words froze in her mouth.

He spoke then. He was using a voice distorter. The pitch was low and the words buzzed heavily. 'Get up,' he said to Georgie. Her snivelling turned into a wail. When she didn't move, he reached down and hauled her roughly to her feet. He kept his eyes on Von.

Georgie half-stood, half-leant, against him. He pushed her away. She stumbled but kept her balance.

'You can take a cab, Georgie,' Von said in a rush. She'd thought this part through in the car. If Toby was undecided, then perhaps if she took charge he'd let her daughter go. She held out the credit cards she'd taken from her purse earlier; she didn't want him getting jittery because she was footering about in her bag. 'If you walk down the main road, love, you'll soon find a cab. Ask the driver to take you to an ATM.'

Toby glanced at Georgie. 'Do as she says,' he growled.

The girl was rooted to the spot. As he made to grip her arm, she let out a scream that would curdle blood. He slapped her hard across the face.

Von gave a convulsive gasp but stopped herself from rushing to her daughter. Toby seemed less in control than she'd have expected from a former soldier. Who knows what he'd do if she moved suddenly?

The slap brought the girl to her senses. She ran to her mother and snatched at the cards. The baby was bawling uncontrollably. Von started to put her arms round her daughter but Georgie pushed her off.

'Go that way,' he said, gesturing to a clump of bushes. 'There's a path to the road.'

With a doubtful glance in his direction, Georgie left, hesitantly at first, and then running, the crying baby bouncing on her hip.

When they were out of sight, he waved the gun in the direction of the hills. 'Walk.'

Von was having trouble breathing. 'You're going to shoot me over there?' What was he thinking? The sound would carry. Why didn't he frogmarch her to the car and make her drive to some deserted coastline? And wouldn't questions be asked if a body were found at the gun club? He was the manager, for God's sake.

'I'm not going to shoot you,' came the reply. 'Now move.'

She walked towards the hills, aware that her chance of escape was slipping away with every step. But had Toby been telling the truth when he said he wasn't going to shoot her? He surely couldn't let her live now.

They reached the hills and followed a path up and over the crest. There was woodland beyond the rise. The same kind of woodland she'd seen at The Paradise World of Paintballing.

She stopped, unsure of where to go. Something hard pressed

into her back. 'Keep going, Von. I'll tell you when to turn.'

She followed his instructions, and they moved deeper into the wood, the only sound the crunching of acorn husks. Sunlight trickled through the trees. She tried to memorise the direction they were taking but everywhere looked the same; she'd never find the route back. She wondered if Georgie had flagged down a passing driver and help was on its way. They were near the road; she could hear cars hurtling down the A71.

'Stop here,' he snarled.

She waited in a sweat of fear. They'd stopped by a large oak. He pushed her under the branches so that she was facing the trunk. Jesus, was it going to end like this with a bullet in the back of her neck? Oh Georgie . . .

There was a sudden whooshing noise and, despite her terror, she turned round.

Toby was standing beside an open trapdoor. He gestured for her to approach. She stared into the hole.

An iron ladder descended into the cold churning blackness.

She lifted her head and gazed into the expressionless eyes.

'Yes, Von,' he said quietly. 'We're going into the tunnels.'

The lift doors opened and Steve and Fergus hurried out onto the top floor of Bayne Tower.

A tall woman with sky-blue eyes, rimmed red with crying, was standing in the corridor in a posture of defeat. Seeing the men, her expression changed to one of relief. 'Police?' she said. 'Thank God.'

'Has anyone been in there since you found him?' Steve said.

She shook her head. 'I've been here the whole time, waiting for you.'

'Alone?'

'I sent everyone away.'

He saw what it had cost her to remain at her post, listening out for the lift doors to open. 'We'll need to talk to you but we don't have to do it now,' he said gently.

She drew herself up, obviously determined to stay and help. 'I'm perfectly capable of answering questions.' She played with her hands, and then gestured to the desk. 'I'll be here in case you need me.'

He took in her tailored suit, the shiny high heels. Not a hair on her platinum-blonde head was out of place. The perfect secretary. Only her eyes gave away her inner turmoil.

They slipped into their gowns and overshoes, and pulled on gloves. He opened the door and stepped inside.

The wall on the right glittered as he moved, startling him. It was a mosaic. Aye, expensive, all that gold, the man was minted and no mistake. Something had swung out of the wall on his left, revealing a safe. He hardly gave the contents a second glance. He wanted a good look at the layout of the room before the photographer and the SOCOs arrived. In front of him were a low table and some sofas. A larger table had been overturned, taking down a few chairs with it.

A well-built man with dark-grey hair sat at his desk, his back to the window. His head had dropped onto his chin, causing the pearl-pink tie to bunch up. A casual observer would have assumed he was taking a power nap if it weren't for what was behind him. Smeared onto the window, several inches above the head, fragments of tissue and bone were visible as dark blotches in the glaze of blood.

Steve approached slowly, watching where he put his feet. He examined the body, trying not to retch as the heavy smell reached his nostrils. Blood had streamed from the exit wound and puddled at the base of the man's head, soaking into the light-blue shirt and congealing in the space between the collar and neck.

'Sir.' Fergus was pointing upwards. 'Come and see this.'

A piece of the ceiling was missing. Fragments of white plaster lay scattered on the carpet. Steve looked at the window, at the corpse, and then at the ceiling. 'He's been shot from the front. Through the mouth,' he added, seeing tooth fragments on the man's tie. 'Low angle, so the shooter was kneeling. The bullet exited the skull, ricocheted off the window, and hit the ceiling.' He skirted the desk and rapped his knuckles against the glass. 'Bullet-proof.'

The secretary had come into the room and was hovering beside the safe, as if afraid that the detectives would, in a final sacrilegious act, rob her dead employer. 'He was afraid of attacks from helicopters,' she said. 'It's why he always installed that type of glass in his offices.'

Steve gestured to the open safe, wondering if robbery had been behind the murder of Dewey Croker. 'Can you tell if anything's missing?'

'Why would anything be missing? Mr Croker opened the safe himself.'

He exchanged a glance with Fergus. 'When was this?' he said to the woman.

'I've no idea but it was closed when I left him this morning. And no-one's been in or out since.'

'No-one's been – ? Perhaps you could tell us what happened today.'

'I brought in a document for Mr Croker to read and sign. You can see it there, on the desk. Then a call came in from Stannard HealthSolutions. I buzzed Mr Croker and he asked me to put it through. A few minutes later Miss Dyer came up, and – '

'Miss Dyer?' His eyes bored into hers. 'Lexie Dyer?'

'She was in a tearing hurry. Wanted to be let into the office. I couldn't do it, of course. No-one is allowed in without Mr Croker's express permission and he was on the phone to Stannard. I knew it was an important conversation because of the merger. So I barred her way.' She looked at them with frightened eyes. 'That was when we heard the shot.'

'You mean he shot himself?'

'Of course he shot himself, you stupid man! There was nobody else in here!'

He stared at Croker's body. The arms were hanging limply, the hands brushing the silk of his navy suit. He searched the floor around the desk. No gun, no cartridge casings. If the man had shot himself with his Ruger, where was it?

He looked at the secretary. 'Did you know that Mr Croker kept a gun in this office?'

'Well, I . . .'

'Where did he hide it?'

She looked at the safe. 'But it's not there. Miss Dyer took it.' She leant heavily against the wall. 'We ran in when we heard the bang. My God, it was awful. She screamed at me for not letting her in – I thought she was going to strangle me – then she snatched the gun from Mr Croker's hand and took the little packet of bullets from the safe. She was sobbing and yelling blue murder. She ran out and I didn't try to stop her.'

'Why do you think he killed himself?' Fergus said.

The woman closed the safe, and they saw that the door was a flat-screen TV. 'I think the call from Stannard would have been about this,' she said sadly.

The men stared at the TV. The breaking news which leapt out at them from the screen was that Stannard HealthSolutions had pulled out of the merger with Bayne Pharmaceuticals. No-one as yet knew why.

Steve touched the corner of the screen and the display changed to a page of global share prices. The red figure indicating Bayne Pharmaceuticals' dropping share price continued to plunge, gathering momentum until it stood at just above zero.

'My God,' Fergus whispered. 'Bayne's have been wiped out.'

Steve looked at the company CEO, cooling on his throne-like chair. In another century, the man would have jumped.

Steve and Fergus were outside the Tower, watching the senior SOCO set up a perimeter and marshal her team. It was noon by the time they'd arrived, and Steve was none too happy that he'd had to kick his heels for an hour. The female photographer with the thick dark hair whom he'd last seen at the paintballing club hardly gave him a second glance.

'One thing needs urgent attention,' he said to the SOCO. 'There's a bullet in the ceiling. Can we get it to Ballistics in double-quick time?'

'You thinking it's the same calibre that did the paintballers, sir?'

'I don't know. They were killed with expanding ammo. There was an exit wound with this one. Can expanding exit the body if fired at close range?'

The girl's doubtful expression told him that she was as knowledgeable as he. 'Miss Prince will be able to tell us.' She smiled grimly. 'Pity we don't have the weapon.'

Aye, they didn't have the weapon but he knew where it was. The problem was that he didn't know where Lexie was. Or what she intended to do with it. Stannard had pulled out, causing Dewey to top himself, and she was acting as though there were a person she could blame for that. So, was she going after Stannard's CEO?

'Sir, over here.' Fergus had the radio to his ear and was gesticulating furiously.

Something about the expression on the sergeant's face made Steve's skin prickle. 'What it is?' he shouted.

'Toby Hilliard's used his mobile. It was earlier today, although we've only just been notified.'

'Hilliard? Where is he? Come on, son. Oh, for God's sake,

give me that.' He snatched the radio and held it to his ear. 'He's at the gun club. We've got him. Well, don't just stand there, start the engine.'

Ten minutes later, they were at the Calder Rifle and Pistol Club.

'That's Hilliard's car sir,' Fergus said, indicating the Jaguar.

'Aye, so what's he doing here? The gun club's closed.' He surveyed the terrain systematically. His heart lurched with shock as he saw the Ford. 'My God,' he gasped. 'Von.'

He closed his eyes. Why hadn't they got the bulletin the minute Hilliard used his phone? Whatever the man had planned for her he'd have done by now. It was all over. He leant against the car. The pit of his stomach seemed to have fallen out.

Fergus handed him a bottle of water. 'Drink this, sir,' he murmured discreetly.

Steve gulped greedily. Sweat was making his shirt stick to his chest. He was too late. Aye, he was always too late.

Chapter 30

Von clutched at the rungs and lowered herself slowly down the steps. She sensed Toby's bulk above her, each heavy footstep rocking the ladder. When she was nearing the bottom, he pulled the trapdoor shut and she was plunged into darkness. She felt a momentary panic as he brushed past her. And then the lights came on with a click.

A wide tunnel, high enough for a man to stand up in, disappeared into the distance. A line of naked bulbs was strung along the ceiling, their light dim, but more than enough to see by. A damp chill seemed to seep out of the walls.

She noticed the side tunnels. But would they lead to dead ends? She took a few steps forward, suppressing the urge to run. If he fired, he couldn't miss, not here. 'Is this where you're going to murder me, Toby?' she said quietly.

'You're probably wondering where you are.' The cold air made his voice seem close but she knew that he was still at the foot of the steps. 'These tunnels were started decades ago to provide shelter in the event of a nuclear war, but they were never finished. Someone decided Fife was a better location and they built a bunker there.' He paused, and she felt him move towards her. 'They connect the gun club with The Paradise World of Paintballing. We're going in that direction.'

'And is that the gun that shot Phil Pattullo?' she said, facing him.

'No, this is my grandfather's service revolver, a Webley Mark

IV. He never gave it back after he was demobbed.'

'The police are on their way. They've been monitoring the calls from your mobile.'

'Really?' He gestured for her to start walking. 'Don't think the good guys are coming to save you, Von. These tunnels are impossible to find even if you know of their existence. And almost no-one does.'

'Phil knew,' she said, wanting to keep him talking. She glanced from side to side but all she saw were dark walls.

'Yes, we brought him here for his first paintballing game. The cognoscenti use these tunnels for the odd high-octane match. There was no harm in letting him see our secret place.'

'Because you knew you'd be killing him.'

He spoke softly, as though to himself. 'I needed to be sure he was dead. I had to go out there and turn him over.'

'And Bruce Lassiter?'

There was a sharp intake of breath. Through the voice distorter, it sounded like an animal's whine. 'Keep going,' he said sharply. 'Take the tunnel on the left.'

She moved further underground, her mind in turmoil. Minutes later, the air, which had been damp and smelling of earth, grew foetid. There was a scurrying squeaking noise. She stopped and peered ahead.

The tunnel was boiling with rats. They were crawling over something in the shape of a person.

She felt the cry rise in her throat. At the sound, the rats scattered, scampering away in random directions. Her heart bumped against her ribs as she approached the body.

The figure was lying on his back, his arms outstretched as though crucified. Bile filled her mouth and she gagged loudly. His face had been eaten away, the eye sockets gaping, the pink bone glistening through what little blackened flesh was left. The paintballing suit had been almost completely chewed through.

The rats returned and climbed onto the body to continue picking over the remains of the carcass. She forced herself to look again at the ravaged face. The yellow scarf round the victim's forehead was grimy and bloodstained, but it was by the dog-tags that she recognised him.

She sprang back and stared up at her abductor. 'Who are you?' she said in a voice choking with fear.

He pulled off the balaclava and voice distorter. 'You didn't expect it to be me, did you, Von?' he said, wiping a thread of saliva from his chin. 'I've been enjoying leading you on, and anticipating the surprise. There's nothing quite like delayed gratification.'

She stared in mute horror. He'd used Toby's mobile and brought Georgie to the gun club in Toby's car. The police would be searching for Toby and they wouldn't think to look for her anywhere but at his club. They'd never find that trapdoor in the woods, not in a million years.

Ranald nodded at the corpse. 'I shot him during Saturday's tournament. There are several entrances to these tunnels and it was easy to dump his body in here without being seen.' He looked squarely at her. 'You've been something of a thorn in our side, Von. I realised you were going to be trouble when I saw you at Lexie's reception. All that hoopla, pretending to be a caterer just to find out what we were up to. You really need a better disguise. I saw you at the gun-club car park and again that night you broke into Lexie's. Did you find anything useful?' When she said nothing, he added, 'No, I didn't think so.'

'Why did you kill Toby?'

'He was the only weak link in our perfect plan. You see, he'd convinced himself you'd worked out what was going on. He collared me after the final match. Said he was going straight to the police. I guessed he'd try to cut a deal to save his skin. I had no choice.' He brushed the hair off his brow. 'Anyway,

Toby was a murderer,' he added, as though this made killing him acceptable. 'He shot Phil and Bruce.'

'Toby?'

'It's amazing what people will do for money,' he said with irony. 'Jamie promised him enough to buy that gun club several times over, enough to retire on if he wanted to.' He gazed at her thoughtfully. 'I reckoned we'd be home free. With him disappeared, the police might think he was the killer. And you'd drop your missing-persons investigation for lack of information. But what he'd said began to niggle and I decided I'd better see what you were up to. When I followed you to the tattoo parlour – '

'That was you?' she said in a small voice.

'I guessed you weren't going there to get a tat. When I saw you talking to the tattoo artist, I knew it was just a matter of time before you'd figure out who had got Phil that design, and then you'd figure out why.' He waved the Webley. 'I've taken to carrying this around. It was unbelievably stupid of me to fire at you in the dark like that. I was in a bit of a panic at that point.'

'The police know everything, Ranald.'

'I doubt that. Okay, we knew they'd turn the spotlight on us because we were all there paintballing. We expected them to search my place and Lexie's. But they found nothing to link us to the murders. And they'll find nothing on Lexie's PC.'

She stared at him in the semi-darkness. If she could keep him talking . . .

'Do you think your life will just go on and you'll be going back to Bayne's tomorrow?' she said.

'Oh, Bayne's is no more.' He must have registered her incomprehension. 'It was a great place to work. I'd hoped for a long and prosperous career. But then Dewey Croker came along and slimed all over it. Do you know what he did? Shall I tell you?'

She registered the anger in his voice. If she could fuel it, it might knock him off guard. 'Mr Croker seemed a genuinely nice person when I met him,' she said.

'Nice?' Even in the gloom she could see his colour rise. 'With him, everything's a pissing match. I warned him ages ago that the Lazinex series was unsafe and Bayne's were pushing the product out before proper testing. It's totally different from the medications currently prescribed for rheumatoid arthritis. It's the first drug that not only slows down the progression of the disease but actually reverses it. I told him about the side effects and that Lazinex needed more work but, oh no, he had to have it start making money. It was a badge of honour with him, trying to get Bayne's into the top league. I know for a fact that he bribed people to alter the test results, and got a ghost writer claiming he was an academic to publish in the medical journals.'

'So what are the side effects?'

'The main one is prolonged clinical depression. But another is early dementia.'

And then she knew. 'Your Dad was prescribed Lazinex, wasn't he?'

'There's no cure,' he said in a strangled voice. 'My father was a marvellous man, a great benefactor. I can't speak highly enough of him. How do you summarise a life dedicated to the service of others?'

'How did it happen?'

'He was living in Stamford Bridge at the time. He didn't tell me he'd changed his medication till it was too late. If I'd known – ' He rallied. 'Croker had to pay. I did something today that will hurt him, no question.'

He lowered the gun but his eyes were on her face. If she could distract him, she'd have a chance. A well-placed kick in the groin and she could grab the weapon off him.

He pushed the hair out of his eyes. 'Yesterday afternoon, I contacted Stannard and hinted there might be something wrong with one of Bayne's products. I told them who I was and that I knew what I was talking about. I knew they'd want to check me out in case it was a crank call. They put their merger talks on hold. But I also got in touch anonymously with the press, saying I'd heard there was trouble with the merger talks. They went to print with it and Bayne's share price started to fall.' He smiled coldly. 'And then I delivered the coup de grâce. First thing this morning, one of Stannard's top scientists contacted me. I told her I was the researcher who'd worked on Lazinex. I emailed her the real test results, the ones Dewey was keen to suppress. And I said I intended to publish them to the world and, once people knew that the premature release of Lazinex had caused those side effects, Bayne's would be inundated with lawsuits.'

'So Stannard pulled out?'

'Instantly and entirely. I mean, wouldn't you? I've been checking the news on my mobile. Bayne's are history.' His smile broadened. 'A sort of corporate double tap, Von. By hinting there was something wrong with Lazinex, and then sending my data to Stannard, I've brought Bayne's down.'

'But not Dewey Croker. He strikes me as a phoenix. He'll rise from Bayne's ashes.'

'If he thinks he can come back from this, he's whistling Dixie.' He laughed mirthlessly. 'He was going to get an obscene bonus for his part in the merger, and I know for a fact that he's converted all his stock options in Bayne's to shares. But it's not just the money with Dewey. He was going to be the superman that took Bayne's into the Big Pharma league. He's finished. No-one will employ him now. I can't wait to read about his decline and fall tomorrow,' he added with relish. 'It's better than killing him. His obituary would have made a poor substitute.'

He raised a hand to wipe the sweat from his eyes, and she saw her chance. She made a move towards him but he sprang back, jerking up the Webley and holding it with both hands.

'Tut, tut,' he said, pointing it at her chest. 'And you were doing so nicely, too.' He gestured at Toby's body. 'Sit down over there.' He reached into his pocket and pulled out a loop of notched plastic. 'Put this round your wrists and tighten it with your teeth,' he said, throwing it at her feet.

She hesitated. With her hands tied, her last chance of overpowering him would disappear.

'Don't make me say it twice, Von.'

She sank to the ground. Leaning against the wall, she put the string round her wrists and pulled at it with her teeth.

'Tighter.'

'Why don't you just shoot me and be done with it?'

'Because I'm not sure how safe these tunnels are.' He reached down and yanked the plastic, making her yelp with pain. 'A shot could bring the ceiling down on our heads.' He took out another loop and tied her ankles.

So that was his intention. Jesus, he was going to leave her there for the rats; trussed up, she had no hope of wriggling away. A few rodents in search of fresh meat were already showing an interest, nibbling at her feet, crawling over her legs. Her terror deepened. She jerked her body, trying to kick with both legs. The rats scuttled away. But they didn't go far. They swarmed in little circles, moving ever closer. Another jerk and they backed away. But she knew she couldn't keep this up. And they would come to know it too.

'You can't leave me here,' she said, her voice rising in panic. 'Dear God, not like this. You're not a bad man, Ranald. I saw how you were with your father.'

'Don't expect any pity from me. What happened to my father has left me cold.' He looked on as she struggled, his eyes devoid of expression. 'Goodbye, Von,' he said in a matter-of-fact way.

He stepped over Toby's body, kicking at the rodents milling

about his feet, and walked steadily down the tunnel. She tried to call after him but her throat closed in on the words.

She felt a sudden searing pain. A rat had bitten into the fleshy part of her thumb. In pure panic, she rolled over from side to side, but all she achieved was to make herself dizzy. Weak with fear, she lay shuddering convulsively as the sleek animals swarmed over her body. Lacerating pain shot through her leg and she screamed in agony. A rat had chewed through the embroidery at the bottom of her jeans. She thrashed around, kicking her legs and sobbing uncontrollably. She could taste her terror now.

She rolled away from Toby's body and tried to sit up. The rats had followed her and were crawling over her legs in a seething mass of black fur and pink tails. But although her brain was fogged with fear, it was still working. Ignoring the biting animals, she thrust her fingers into the pocket of her jeans and tugged out the flick knife. She pulled at the blade with her teeth and, with shaking hands, sawed furiously, cutting through the plastic binding her ankles.

Somehow, she managed to struggle onto her knees and get herself to her feet. The rats clung to her jeans but fell away as she shook her legs. She stumbled down the tunnel, the frenzied squeaking growing fainter as she distanced herself from Toby's corpse.

She leant against the wall, breathing heavily. Blood had seeped into her jeans and, now that the adrenaline was leaving her body, pain flared in her legs. Holding the blade in her mouth, she twisted her hands so that the palms were together. Then, clutching the handle between her fingers, she moved the knife back and forth until the plastic round her wrists fell away. Her hands throbbed with returning circulation.

She looked around in desperation. How far into the tunnels was she? And was she going in the same direction as Ranald?

The thought of running into him as she rounded a corner made her heart lurch with terror. If the worst came to the worst, she'd make him shoot her. It was better than being eaten alive.

She hurried on, pausing to look round the corners. It struck her that when Ranald reached the surface he'd switch off the lights. Her legs buckled as she imagined herself in the dark with the rats. But it could be worse. All she had to do was keep a hand on the wall and eventually she'd find a ladder. Minutes later, the tunnel veered to the left and she saw empty paintball cylinders. What had Ranald said? The tunnels connect with the paintballing club. So where would they lead out? Surely not into the clubhouse. No, it would be somewhere in the wood. Hadn't she nearly fallen into a tunnel when she'd been there with Toby?

That was when she heard it.

Footsteps. The sound of running. And it was growing louder.

She stared into the tunnel. A dark shape was heading in her direction. She froze, numb with fear. Was Ranald returning? But why? Jesus, if he found her . . .

She was looking around frantically for somewhere to hide when a shot rang out, so close that it nearly deafened her. There was a scream. The shape dropped to the ground and writhed around for a few seconds until, finally, it lay still. The smell of gunpowder reached her. The air seemed to vibrate, and clumps of soil fell off the wall.

She took a tentative step forward. Like a ghost, a small pale figure appeared. It grew larger until it filled the tunnel. Lexie Dyer stopped, her arms at her sides, the dim light glinting off the blue steel of the gun. Her hair was tangled and her cream trouser suit was grimy and smudged. She ignored the sprawling figure of Ranald McCrea and peered ahead, as though trying to focus her eyes. Seeing Von, a look of wonder appeared on her face.

The women stared at each other. Then Lexie raised the pistol.

Before she could pull the trigger, there was a sudden roaring. The ground shook and the ceiling fell in. A rush of dank air knocked Von backwards.

She struggled to her feet, coughing and retching, blinded by the dust. When the air cleared, she looked around in a daze.

Lexie had disappeared. Where she'd been standing, there was a mountain of earth.

Chapter 31

'I'm all right, Steve, really I am, so stop fussing. And concentrate on what you're doing or you'll kill us both.'

They were in the Ford and Steve was driving. Every so often, he took his eyes off the road and stared at her.

She was relieved that he'd come on the scene so quickly after getting her phone call, arriving to help her dig out Lexie's body. But then, he'd not had far to go – he and his men had been at the gun club, searching for her. He'd wanted to take her directly to the hospital but she'd made him drive her to Gardner's Crescent. She had to check on Georgie and the baby. The girl hadn't contacted the police, nor was she answering her phone. She'd been shit-scared, of that there was no doubt, but if she'd decided to punish her mother with the silent treatment, this was not the time.

'I do think you need to get to A and E, Von. I don't like those,' he added, nodding at her bloodstained legs.

'I've never liked these either,' she said mischievously. 'Embroidered bell-bottoms went out with the Ark.'

'For God's sake, you were nearly killed. And all you can do is joke.'

She saw the anguish on his face. 'I can afford to joke, Steve. I've got you to worry about me. Anyway, I never dwell on the what-might-have-been. That way madness lies.'

'We should have taken my car,' he muttered. 'It's faster than this heap of junk.'

'I think it's Fergus who's faster, not your car.'

She threw him a sideways glance. He was smiling.

They reached Gardner's Crescent. She limped up the stairs, wincing with pain. Her legs were on fire. And God knows what diseases you can catch from rat bites. Once she was sure that Georgie and the baby were safe, she'd get out the Dettol.

The front door was unlocked. She pushed it open hesitantly, feeling a sudden uneasiness. Steve pulled her back and stepped inside.

The flat had been ransacked.

She squeezed past him and rushed through the rooms. It was when she found the letter on the kitchen table that she understood what had happened.

'Georgie's gone,' she murmured. 'Back to London.'

'Why did she mess the place up like this?' he said, running a hand over his neck.

'She was looking for something.' Von reached into the back of the cupboard where the cleaning things were kept. 'She's taken the passbook for the savings account. I thought it would be safe there. She never does any cleaning.'

He nodded sympathetically, and she saw from his face that he appreciated for the first time what her life had become. She looked away, not wanting to see the pity in his eyes. 'I gave her my credit cards. She'll have withdrawn up to the overdraft limit.'

'We'll find her, Von. She can't have gone far.'

'I wouldn't waste your time,' she said thickly. She held out the letter.

He took the sheet. As he read, the expression on his face changed from curiosity, to concern, then to anger.

'You see what she says about me?' Von shouted in a voice ragged with grief. She snatched back the sheet and read: 'Dear Mum, by the time you get this, I'll be on my way to London with Kylie. Don't come after us. You won't find us. I'll make sure of that. We're better off without you. And safer too. You never really wanted either of us, did you, Mum? Your job always had to come first. Well, now you won't have us under your feet so you can devote all your time to your precious career. Your daughter, Georgie.' The words 'your daughter' had been crossed out twice.

She looked up to see Steve frowning. 'She's right, isn't she, Steve? One of my outstanding talents has always been to mess up her life. I'm not capable of looking after her and the baby.' She leant against the kitchen table, her daughter's words tearing at her heart. 'I'm wondering if there's anything else I can screw up or should I stop now? No, I think I'll continue. Why break the habit of a lifetime?' Her throat ached with the effort of not crying. Oh, what was the point? She let her tears run freely, sobbing like a child.

He wrapped his arms round her, and she rested her head against his chest. When she was done, she wiped her eyes with her hands, smearing soil over her face.

He held out a handkerchief. 'Here, take it. I've never known a woman who has one of these when she needs it.'

'Where would I be without you, Steve?' she murmured.

'Aye, right enough, where would you be?' He lifted her chin, and she gazed into his warm brown eyes. 'You don't know a good thing when you see it, Von.'

Steve gazed at the woman sitting opposite. It was a bit pot and kettle, as he'd not changed out of his muddy clothes, but she was a mess and no mistake. Her clothes and face were filthy and there was soil in her hair. Perhaps the fact that she'd just been arrested for murder accounted for her apparent lack of interest in her appearance.

'We know about Jamie and the scam with the mislabelled chemicals,' he said. 'And we also know that you know.' When there was no reaction, he added, 'You won't help your case by not talking to us.'

Lexie kept her eyes on the glass of water in her hand. She sat hunched over, her natural exuberance evaporated. 'Very well, Inspector,' she said listlessly. 'Ask your questions.'

'How did Jamie get involved with the Triads? You don't just knock on their door asking for a job.'

'He was approached by one of Snake Eyes' men.'

'When was this?'

'Ages ago. I can't remember exactly.'

'One year? Two years?'

'Longer than that.' She hesitated. 'Snake Eyes chose Jamie because he managed the imports. His signature was on all the papers.'

Aye, right enough, if anyone could mislabel chemicals and make them disappear, it would be the import manager. 'So why did he fake his own death, Miss Dyer?'

'To save himself.' She lifted her head. 'He'd decided to stop selling Snake Eyes the chemicals, you see.'

'You're saying he had a crisis of conscience?'

'I suppose so.'

'Or maybe he wanted to retire because he'd made enough money.'

She shook her head. 'He told me he was sick of what he'd done. All those young lives he'd ruined. He wanted to stop. He made it clear to Snake Eyes that he'd have to get his Ecstasy chemicals from someone else. Well, of course Snake Eyes threatened to kill him. Not just kill him, but do horrible things to him first.' She shuddered. 'When Jamie told me what he'd said, I was nearly sick. Snake Eyes had his men tail him everywhere. I saw them outside his house. Jamie was terrified. And I knew I had to help him. He was my brother and, despite what he'd done, I loved him.'

'So you murdered an innocent man.' When she said nothing, he added, 'Why didn't Jamie just leave his clothes on the beach and do a runner?'

'It would have been too obvious. Haven't there been loads of faked deaths done that way? Anyway, Jamie can't swim. He never goes near beaches.' She played with the glass. 'He did think of disappearing but he knew that Snake Eyes would always be looking for him. The Triads never forget. We've seen enough telly to know that. And there was another reason.' Her eyes drifted to a spot behind his shoulder. 'If Jamie simply left the country, Snake Eyes would turn his attention on me. Much better have Jamie die and leave behind a body. It would be in all the papers. Snake Eyes couldn't fail to see it.'

'So, what, Snake Eyes would think Jamie had been dealing simultaneously with another gang?'

'Yes, and he'd double-crossed them, and they'd got to him first.'

It was tidy, he had to give her that. 'Whose idea was the swap, Miss Dyer?'

'Jamie's.' The lines on her forehead deepened. 'But I can't deny my part in it. You see, Phil used to come to the fountain in Princes Street Gardens. He wasn't a regular, though. His Mum fed him most of the time. I met her once or twice.' She smiled sadly. 'Lovely lady.'

'And you told Jamie about Phil?'

'I let slip I'd seen someone who looked just like him, but with long hair. Jamie came to see for himself. He said the fact that Phil was homeless was perfect, the police wouldn't go looking for him. Ranald and I were appalled. We tried to talk him out of it.' She pushed a strand of muddy hair off her face. 'I refused to have anything to do with it.'

'And Ranald?'

'Ranald too.'

He sat back, studying her. 'So what made you change your mind?'

'Jamie was desperate. He begged me to help him.' She spread her hands. 'What was I supposed to do? He was my brother. My twin. I couldn't abandon him, could I? It was a rotten situation.' She picked at the dirt under her nails. 'Ranald was easier to persuade. Jamie promised him enough money that he could leave Bayne's and look after his father.'

'But Jamie offered you money, too,' he said, not bothering to keep the disgust from his voice.

She looked startled. 'Why would he? My salary at Bayne's is more than I need. No, Jamie didn't pay me a penny.'

'Aye, right.' He stared her out. 'So tell me how you did it, Miss Dyer.'

She seemed reluctant to continue. 'We took Phil clubbing a couple of times, then, after a few drinks, we persuaded him to get a haircut. We took him back to mine, and Jamie did it with one of those electrical clippers. The following evening, we got him the tattoo. He seemed keen on the idea. Said he'd always wanted one.' A look of pain crossed her face. 'I can't believe I went along with it now.'

'And the selling of the chemicals to Snake Eyes? Was Bruce in on it?'

She gave her head a dismissive shake. 'It was Jamie, and only Jamie, who got mixed up with Snake Eyes. Bruce turned up to play and none of us knew. It was all a dreadful mistake.'

A mistake? He stared at the ceiling. They'd been chasing their tails trying to find the link between the dead men. 'So how did Toby get involved?' he said, rubbing his face.

'He wanted to buy Dewey out of the gun club but he didn't have the cash. Jamie sounded him out carefully, and he finally said he'd take the contract.'

'You mean he agreed to kill Phil Pattullo for money?'

She nodded. 'The paintballing club was his idea. The woodland course was ideal. He knew about the tunnels, that they ran under the road to his gun club. He could get back there before anyone realised he was missing.' She grew thoughtful. 'We took Phil to the tunnels once or twice for a practice run. He loved being underground. Said something about there not being any angels there.'

'Didn't you and Ranald realise you'd come under suspicion? A murder while you were all out paintballing?'

'Initially, yes, but Jamie worked in Glasgow so he thought you'd go looking for the killer there. He knew you'd probably uncover what he'd been doing, and you'd assume the murderer was Snake Eyes, but by then he'd be long gone.'

'So what happened on the day Phil and Bruce were killed?'

She took a deep breath, as though preparing herself for something unpleasant. 'Jamie had had his Maserati valet-cleaned, and he let Phil drive it around so that his prints were all over it. He wore gloves all the time after that. He suspected you'd take Phil's prints and compare them with those in the car. It was also why he had his house professionally cleaned. Twice, I think. He had his clothes laundered and everything. He was convinced that you'd take his DNA from the house.'

'We didn't, as a matter of fact. A formal identification by the next of kin is considered sufficient. Carry on with your account, Miss Dyer.'

'On the day Toby was going to do it, Phil drove Jamie's Maserati to the club. Ranald was already there.'

'Jamie didn't come with Phil?'

'Jamie came with me. He told Phil that something urgent had come up at the last minute, and he'd get himself there. I dropped him off on the main road. He walked through the woods to somewhere near the club, and waited. Phil, Ranald, and I changed into our paintballing togs. Ranald and I went out first, and then Phil. Toby was hiding in the woods. He knew the order we'd be going out in, and let Ranald and me go past. We told him that the two of us would be wearing our yellow tournament scarves, but Phil didn't have one, and that's how he'd know it was him. The face guards don't actually cover the top of the head, but we needed Toby to be absolutely sure which of us was Phil. When we heard the shots, we went back to the main building. I showered and drove to Bayne's. Ranald went out to check that Phil was dead before calling the police.'

'And Jamie?'

'After we started the knockabout, he came into the building. Ranald had given him the master key to the lockers. He put on Phil's clothes and left his own in Phil's locker. He'd bought all new stuff, shower gel and everything.'

'We found the master key in your flat. Why did Jamie leave it there?'

'Maybe he intended to give it back to Ranald, but forgot.' Her lips twisted. 'More likely he wasn't thinking straight. By then, none of us was.'

He gazed at her steadily. 'So Bruce was just in the wrong place at the wrong time.'

'I simply couldn't believe it when you told me.' Her emotion seemed genuine. 'Phil must have got lost on the course, and Toby saw Bruce first. Bruce wasn't wearing a yellow scarf. Why would he? We only wear them for tournaments. When Toby saw a second man coming along, he realised he may have shot the wrong one so he killed him too. He tracked down Ranald later in the day and told him what had happened. He was angry. Really, really angry. Why were there two people on the course and not the one? We didn't have an answer.'

'And Jamie hid out at yours while he prepared to leave the country.'

'We knew you'd be searching the houses, mine and Ranald's,

so he spent a night in Princes Street Gardens. He thought it would be a real jape to see how it felt being homeless. Stupid, stupid, boy,' she murmured, shaking her head. 'Then he came to mine. I had an awful shock a couple of days after he moved in. He simply disappeared. I became quite frantic and rang his Glasgow place. Turned out I'd just missed him. He'd gone there to fetch the CD with the Panama bank details.'

It was the day Steve had gone to look around Jamie's. Aye, he remembered the phone ringing and the caller hanging up. She'd been smart enough to use a pay-as-you-go.

'He took a huge risk going back to Glasgow, Inspector. He could have been spotted.'

And not just by the police. The news of his death might not yet have reached Snake Eyes. His men could still have been hanging around Jamie's house. 'Okay, Miss Dyer, let's turn now to Ranald McCrea. Why did you kill him?'

She played with her hands. 'Dewey and I were in love.' She stressed the word, as if it were important for Steve to know this. 'He was intending to divorce his wife and marry me. Obviously, he had to hold back till the merger went through. I was quite happy to wait.' She lifted her head, almost as a challenge. 'Because I knew he loved me.'

'But he loved money more.'

Her eyes narrowed. 'Do you want to hear the rest or don't you?' she spat.

'I'm sorry.'

After a pause, she said, 'I saw the share price falling this morning. I couldn't believe it. I rang Ranald to see if he knew what was happening. He told me everything. Lazinex, his Dad, calling Stannard. I ran up to Dewey's office to warn him, but I got there too late.' A tear rolled down her cheek, making a clear trail through the grime. 'I took the Ruger from his hand and drove to Ranald's house. While I was on the road, he rang and told me where he was, and that Toby had cracked and was going to the police, and he'd had to silence him. He said the lady investigator had found out about Phil's tattoo, and he was going to have to kill her too. I turned the car round. I knew how to get into the tunnels from the paintballing side.' She was silent for a moment. 'You know the rest.'

'Didn't Ranald realise how you felt about Dewey?'

'Dewey wanted me to tell no-one. I thought it was just because of the merger,' she said, her voice drifting, 'but I wonder now whether he'd ever intended to leave his wife.' Her eyes filmed over.

'Where is Toby's handgun, Miss Dyer? The one that fires .45 ACP cartridges.'

'I've no idea,' she said, wiping her nose. 'Toby handled all that. We didn't want to know. That's the unvarnished truth.'

'And I don't suppose you know where Jamie is?'

She stared at him in wonder. 'I thought you had him in custody.' A look of joy appeared on her face. 'If you haven't arrested him then he's made it. He's free. And he's safe from Snake Eyes. That bastard would almost certainly have got to him in prison.'

'Where would he go, Miss Dyer?'

'With the money he's got now, he could be anywhere. There's enough to get him to the moon and back.' A smile flickered on her lips. 'I'm betting your Fraud Squad hasn't found it.'

He pushed a pad across. 'I need the name of the Panama bank.'

She stared at the pad as though it might speak to her. 'I'd like to help you with that but I don't know those details. Why would I? Those were Jamie's accounts. And Ranald's and Toby's. They were the only people who knew the account numbers, and what the passwords were and everything.'

He looked into her eyes. Was she lying? It defied common sense that Jamie hadn't also set her up with a fortune. Aye, and she probably thought she'd be free in a couple of years' time to spend it. He couldn't help feeling that the real Lexie Dyer wasn't someone who'd found herself trapped in a nightmare situation, and simply felt she had no choice but to collude in the murder of an innocent man. Had she and Jamie put their minds to it, they could have found another way out of their dilemma. He recalled her performance at the mortuary, the tears, the near collapse into the arms of the Family Liaison Officer. No, she was a calculating murderess. And a jury would come to the same conclusion.

She was watching him. 'I bet you've got Interpol and everyone looking, Inspector. Well, you won't find him. You'll never find him. Using Phil's passport to get away was only the first step. He's got umpteen others. That week he was at mine, he had several made.' She smiled happily. 'He's alive. Somewhere, he's alive. And he's free.'

'Which is more than can be said for you, Miss Dyer.'

'You mean I'm under arrest?' She seemed to consider this. Her face grew slack. 'I suspect my career's over too, isn't it?'

He stared, unbelieving. 'You've murdered a man and were complicit in the murder of another, and you're worried about your career?' He glanced at the window, knowing that Von and Cally were watching unseen behind it. 'You're going down, Miss Dyer. For a very long time.'

She took a sip of water, and pressed the cool glass to her cheek. She gazed at him in bewilderment, and then her expression slowly changed as the meaning of his words became clear. Sobs racked her body and she took loud gulps of air which turned into hiccups.

He watched with satisfaction as tears coursed down her cheeks. Aye, the look of misery on her face almost made her human.

Chapter 32
Wednesday, June 27th

Von watched as the worried-looking man with the springy hair threw the final shovelful of earth onto the grave. Unlike some funerals that she'd attended, the heavens hadn't opened and wept for the departed. But as Phil's coffin was being lowered into the ground, his mother had let out a howl that rivalled the keening of the wind.

Looking at the grass wilting between the gravestones, Von wondered if it ever rained in Dean Cemetery. The hot bright afternoon suggested that the blistering summer was set to continue and, had she not been supporting Mrs Pattullo, she'd have loosened the buttons of her black jacket.

On the woman's other side, Mhairi, contemplating the closed grave, stood in the clothes that Von had bought her. She'd ignored Von's suggestion that they go to John Lewis, insisting instead on a rootle about in the charity shops. She was wearing borrowed pink lipstick, and had tamed her frizzy hair by stuffing it under a wide black headscarf.

Mrs Pattullo was in the navy blazer that Von had last seen her wear at the paintballing tournament. As she rocked silently back and forth, her hopes vanished like dust before the wind, the sun glinted on and off the jacket's shiny buttons. At a signal from Mhairi, Von stood back and let the women pass. She'd arranged for Mhairi to take Mrs Pattullo for tea somewhere, although she herself couldn't face it. The day before, she'd called in at the Balmoral and returned Phil's shoes (there being no trace of the clothes Jamie had taken from him), the blurred photograph of Phil, and his paintings of the angels. His mother had clutched the effects to her chest, her face distorted with grief, the chef's hat slipping off her bobbed hair. She rallied briefly, struggling to catch her breath, and then collapsed, convulsed with sobbing.

Von watched the women walk slowly down the gravel path. They passed the familiar Victorian headstone without giving it a second glance:

There was a door to which I found no key.
There was a veil past which I could not see.

A movement to her right reminded her that Steve said he'd stop by. 'Any news?' she said, wiping her eyes.

'Of Jamie?' He shook his head. 'We were too late. He's vanished.'

'Par for the course, isn't it, the bad guy getting away.'

'We'll find him, Von.'

She doubted it. In her experience as a detective, the bad guy often got away with it. 'And that last shipment from China? Did you nab Snake Eyes?'

'We followed the chemicals from the dock all the way to Bayne's. Nothing doing. He was tipped off.'

'How did that happen?'

'Ach, must be a leak somewhere. Maybe the Fraud Squad. Maybe the Drugs Squad. Who knows how many coppers Snake Eyes has in his pocket?'

'At least those shipments have stopped.'

'For now. But Snake Eyes will be up and running again. I'd bet my police pension on it.' He looked into the distance. 'The only loose end is the murder weapon. The bullets we extracted from Croker's ceiling and Ranald McCrea's body didn't match those that killed Phil and Bruce.' He smiled thinly. 'Sounds strange, saying it. Phil and Bruce. After we've been saying Jamie and Bruce for so long.'

'We didn't expect it to be the Ruger once we knew that Toby was the killer.'

'Aye, right enough. So where's the weapon? Where would Toby have put it?'

'Where's the best place to hide something, Steve? In plain sight, surely.'

'We searched his house. And everything there is in plain sight.'

She looked at him for a long moment. Then she shook her head, laughing softly. 'It's in plainer sight than that. In the gun-club reception, there's a display cabinet full of World War II firearms. I saw a Thompson sub-machine gun there.'

'You think he used that?'

'It fires .45 ACPs, but he'd have taken something smaller. There's a pistol, a Colt M1911, hidden behind the bigger pieces.' When his expression told her that he wasn't following, she added, 'The famous Colt 45 designed by John Browning. It fires ACPs too.'

'Hold on, they're all deactivated. We saw the deactivation certificates.'

'Did you check the proof marks? Did you even look at the pieces?'

He rubbed his head, saying nothing.

'It's the obvious choice, Steve. The guns used by club members can't be taken out without someone knowing. But the cabinet is such a common fixture that no-one gives it a second glance. It would have been easy for Toby to remove the Colt after hours and replace it the same way. I should have known there was something special about that piece when he said Dewey loved taking it out and showing it to people. Of course the man wouldn't have had it deactivated. I'm betting the magazine still has the ammo in it.'

'How many bullets in an M1911 magazine?'

'It holds seven, more than enough for the job.'

'Will we find Toby's prints on it?'

'He handled the gun when he showed it around. But Dewey's prints will be all over it, too. And who knows who else's? It's an ideal weapon to kill with.' She pushed the hair away from her face. 'I hear you're going back to Glasgow.'

He nodded.

'With Miss Cockrill?' she said, smiling.

'She went last week.'

'You going to see her again?'

He looked at his feet.

'Not a complete no, then.'

'Ach, we're not an item, Von. Her tastes are too skew-whiff for the likes of me.' When she said nothing, he added, 'So what about you? I suppose you're away down south to look for Georgie.'

She saw the regret in his eyes. 'I've no idea where she is. I expect she'll come back when she runs out of money.' She paused. 'I had an unexpected visitor yesterday. Norrie. Georgie's boyfriend.'

'Looking for her?'

'He was returning her dresses. He'd stolen them to sell, but found he couldn't go through with it. He wanted to see her and apologise.'

'Restores your faith in human nature, doesn't it?'

'Too late for Georgie, though. I'll hold onto the dresses until I next see her. Assuming I ever do.'

The silence lengthened.

'You got time for a quick wee bevvie before I catch the train?' he said, shifting his weight.

'I need to get back to the office. My boss has a new case for me. Sorry.'

He ran his foot through the chippings, piling them into bunches. 'So I'll be seeing you,' he said softly.

She took his hand and squeezed it. 'In all the old familiar places.'

After he'd gone, she wandered through the cemetery. She had a little time before her meeting, so she didn't hurry. The air was heavy and perfumed, and she found herself wondering why leaves were falling on a summer's day. A pair of stone angels stood high on a plinth. They were gazing into each other's eyes like lovers, their feathered wings outspread as though ready to take flight.

She walked slowly towards the gates, her feet slipping slightly on the gravel, a hand raised against the sun.

Epilogue

Steve was seated at his desk waiting for Bridget to come in for the briefing, the last before they packed up for Christmas. He had been placed on call, something that happened often to single men. Not that he minded. Aye, a bit of action was always better than falling asleep halfway through the Queen's Christmas Message.

He picked up The Herald. It wasn't a newspaper he read from choice, but a colleague had brought it in.

He skimmed the first few pages, his mind only half on what he was reading. Stannard HealthSolutions was still in the news. The merger between it and another well-known pharma company hadn't helped either organisation. Bayne Tower was still standing empty.

He was folding the newspaper when his eye fell on the article at the bottom of the front page. More specifically, it was the name that leapt out at him. There were just a few lines:

Alexandra Dyer, serving life imprisonment for crimes including murder and conspiracy to murder, was found dead yesterday, hanging in her prison cell in Cornton Vale. Home Office psychiatrists are astonished at this turn of events as they did not assess Dyer as being at risk to herself. She had settled into prison life well and had campaigned vigorously for the introduction of educational programs in what is still Scotland's only women's prison. The Governor told our reporter that, although Dyer was adapting well, she was still showing the same lack of remorse that she'd displayed in court. The trial, which ended only a month ago, was marked by loud outbursts from Gavin Skelton, the partner of Bruce Lassiter, one of the murdered paintballers. No-one knows how Dyer came to have a length of washing-line in her possession but police are not treating the death as suspicious. Gavin Skelton was unavailable for comment yesterday.

The young man with the cherry tattoo on his arm was lying on the beach, his lithe tanned body stretched out on a lounger. He had a cocktail in one hand and a murder-mystery novel in the other. Although the sun lay heavy overhead, every so often he'd give a slight shiver as though a sea breeze had touched him unexpectedly. Or maybe it was the knowledge that his riches – more money than he could spend in several lifetimes – could only be enjoyed clandestinely, and he would never again be able to live under his own identity.

It had been a difficult transition, shrugging off his previous existence. He'd been someone else for just under a year and it took a little getting used to, hearing a name called that wasn't his own and recounting (usually over drinks) the details of a fabricated life-history that he told to others (mainly women). Strangely, the hedonistic lifestyle he'd embraced hadn't brought him happiness, and he was considering moving on to another watering hole. It would be a shame to give up the local wildlife, the long-haired girls with brown eyes and full lips, but women were women, and there were plenty more pebbles on the white sands of the private beaches he now owned.

He had another reason for wanting to move on. For some weeks, he'd had the feeling he was being watched. It was nothing he could put his finger on, which was part of the problem. At first, he thought it had been that Englishman, the one with the bad skin who kept calling him 'mate'. The man looked like an ex-soldier and had the confident swagger of Special Forces. He'd shown a great interest in him, asking all sorts of questions about his life, and trying to trip him up when he answered. It was when the man's eyes had rested on the cherry tattoo that he realised he should have resisted the sentimental urge to keep it. He shivered again. In another life, and if he'd been another person altogether, he'd have hired someone to make the man disappear. But he was no longer that person. And the Englishman had disappeared anyway.

He finished his margarita and beckoned to the waiter hovering discreetly by the wooden lodges. The sand shimmered in the heat, the warm air making the edge of the sea dance. He removed his Ray-Bans and wiped his face. God, the sun felt good on his skin. But, lying here day after day, he was in danger of becoming a slob. It was time for his daily dip. He was glad he'd finally learnt to swim, although he was still afraid of the water and would never be a strong swimmer.

He signalled to the approaching waiter to leave his drink beside the lounger and walked into the sea, wading slowly out to his chest. He glanced back, expecting to see the waiter standing to attention by the lodges, but the man had disappeared. A figure was walking towards him. The brilliant sunlight made him appear clothed in white, washing out his features and bleaching his hair. He wasn't in a hurry, he just strolled purposefully. It was when the figure reached the water's edge that he recognised the pockmarked Englishman. He felt a sudden inexplicable fear. He turned and, with growing panic, struck out away from the beach.

He didn't see the hands that grasped his ankles and pulled him down, although he felt the rabbit punch to his neck. Terror surged through him as his mouth and airways filled with water. He clawed frantically at the hands holding him under, gasping for breath and sucking water into his lungs, every sound magnified. His killer's face shimmered and dissolved and then grew dim, finally fading into darkness. A feeling of peace stole over him. His thrashings ceased, his arms fell gently to his sides, and he rose to the surface, staring sightlessly into the opal sky.

I would like to thank the following people for reading the manuscript, and suggesting ways in which the novel could be improved: Andrea Bremner, Jenny Brown, Jonathan Cameron, Liz Cole-Hamilton, Dorothy Graham, Moira Jardine, Anne McCreanor, Val Smith, Krystyna Szawelski, and Annette Zimmermann. A special thanks to Dorothy Graham for roaming around Dean Cemetery with me.

I would also like to thank Strathclyde Police for their help with matters of police procedure. Any procedural inaccuracies in the text are mine and not theirs.

I owe a huge debt of gratitude to Allan Guthrie for his editorial help and advice. Heartfelt thanks also go to my agent, Jenny Brown, for all the support she has given me, and to Adrian Searle and everyone at Freight Books for taking on the publishing of this novel.